RUDY GOBERT

HELLEF BAY   **VINCE SERRANO**

TITAN
NOVA

TITAN COMICS
Editorial Assistant Calum Collins
Group Editor Jake Devine
Editor Phoebe Hedges
Senior Creative Editor David Manley-Leach
Art Director Oz Browne
Production Controllers Caterina Falqui & Kelly Fenlon
Production Manager Jackie Flook
Sales & Circulation Manager Steve Tothill
Marketing Coordinator Lauren Noding
Publicity & Sales Coordinator Alexandra Iciek
Publicity Manager Will O'Mullane
Digital & Marketing Manager Jo Teather
Head Of Rights Jenny Boyce
Acquisitions Editor Duncan Baizley
Publishing Director Ricky Claydon & John Dziewiatkowski
Group Operations Director Alex Ruthen
Executive Vice President Andrew Sumner
Publishers Vivian Cheung & Nick Landau

Published by Titan Comics,
a division of Titan Publishing Group, Ltd,
144 Southwark Street, London SE1 0UP, UK.
Titan Comics is a registered trademark of Titan Publishing Group Ltd.
First published in France by Michel Lafon
© Éditions Michel Lafon, 2021, BASH !

10 9 8 7 6 5 4 3 2 1
First edition: February 2023
Printed in Spain
ISBN: 9781787739888
A CIP catalogue record for this title is available from the British Library.

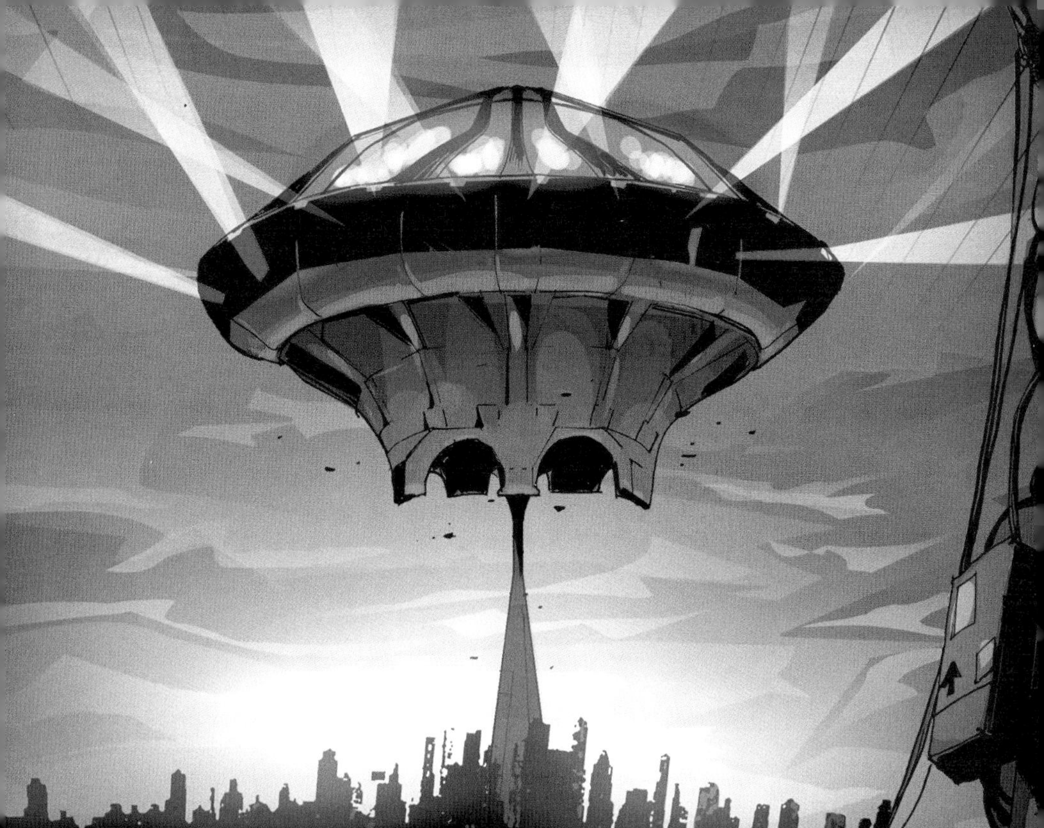

RUDY GOBERT

BASH!

STORY: **RUDY GOBERT** & **HELLEF BAY**

ART: **VINCE SERRANO**

COLORS: **FEZZO**

TRANSLATION: **CHRISTOPHER POPE**

LETTERING: **LAUREN BOWES**

TITAN NOVA

CONTENTS

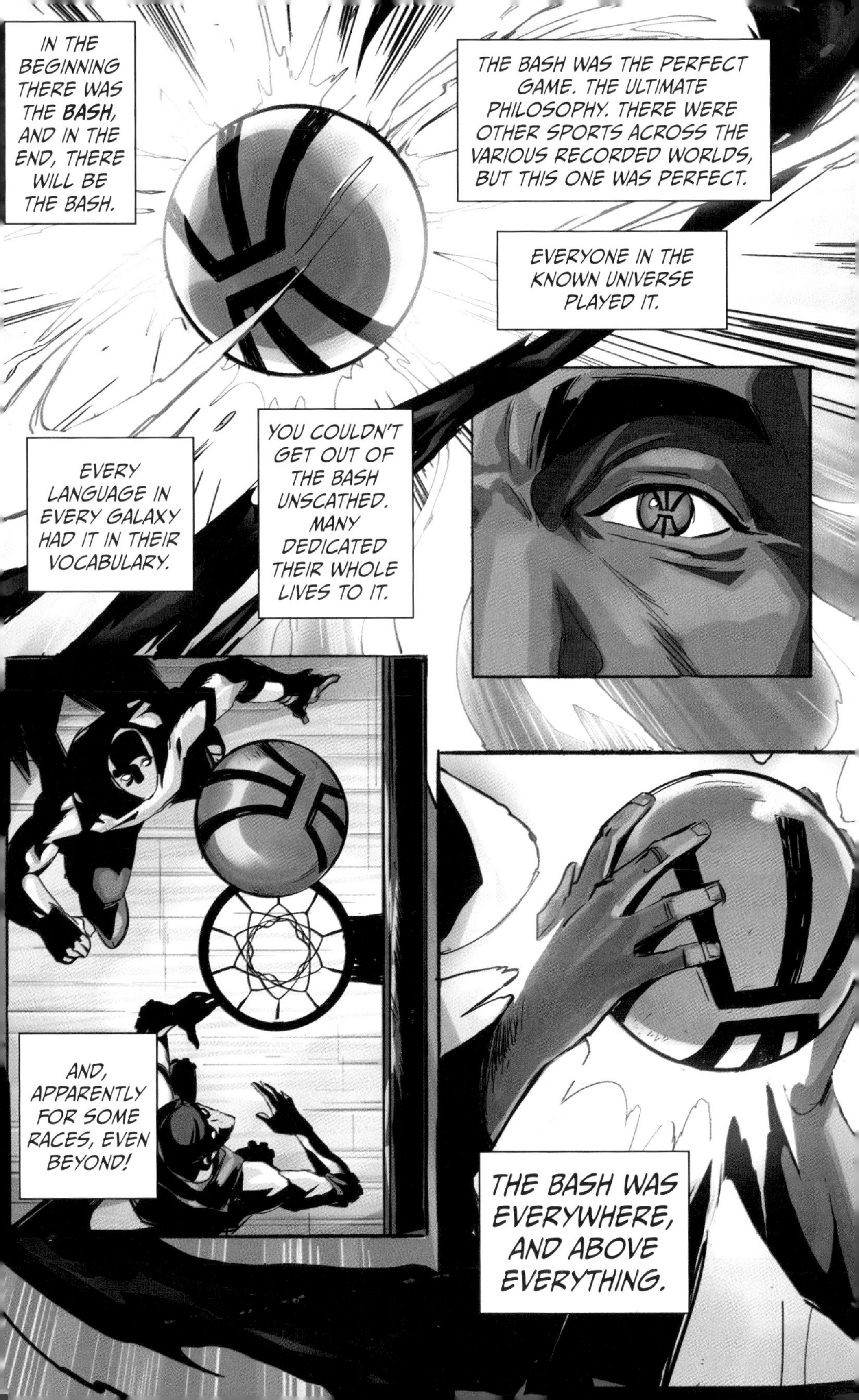
IN THE BEGINNING THERE WAS THE **BASH**, AND IN THE END, THERE WILL BE THE BASH.
THE BASH WAS THE PERFECT GAME. THE ULTIMATE PHILOSOPHY. THERE WERE OTHER SPORTS ACROSS THE VARIOUS RECORDED WORLDS, BUT THIS ONE WAS PERFECT.
EVERYONE IN THE KNOWN UNIVERSE PLAYED IT.
EVERY LANGUAGE IN EVERY GALAXY HAD IT IN THEIR VOCABULARY.
YOU COULDN'T GET OUT OF THE BASH UNSCATHED. MANY DEDICATED THEIR WHOLE LIVES TO IT.
AND, APPARENTLY FOR SOME RACES, EVEN BEYOND!
THE BASH WAS EVERYWHERE, AND ABOVE EVERYTHING.

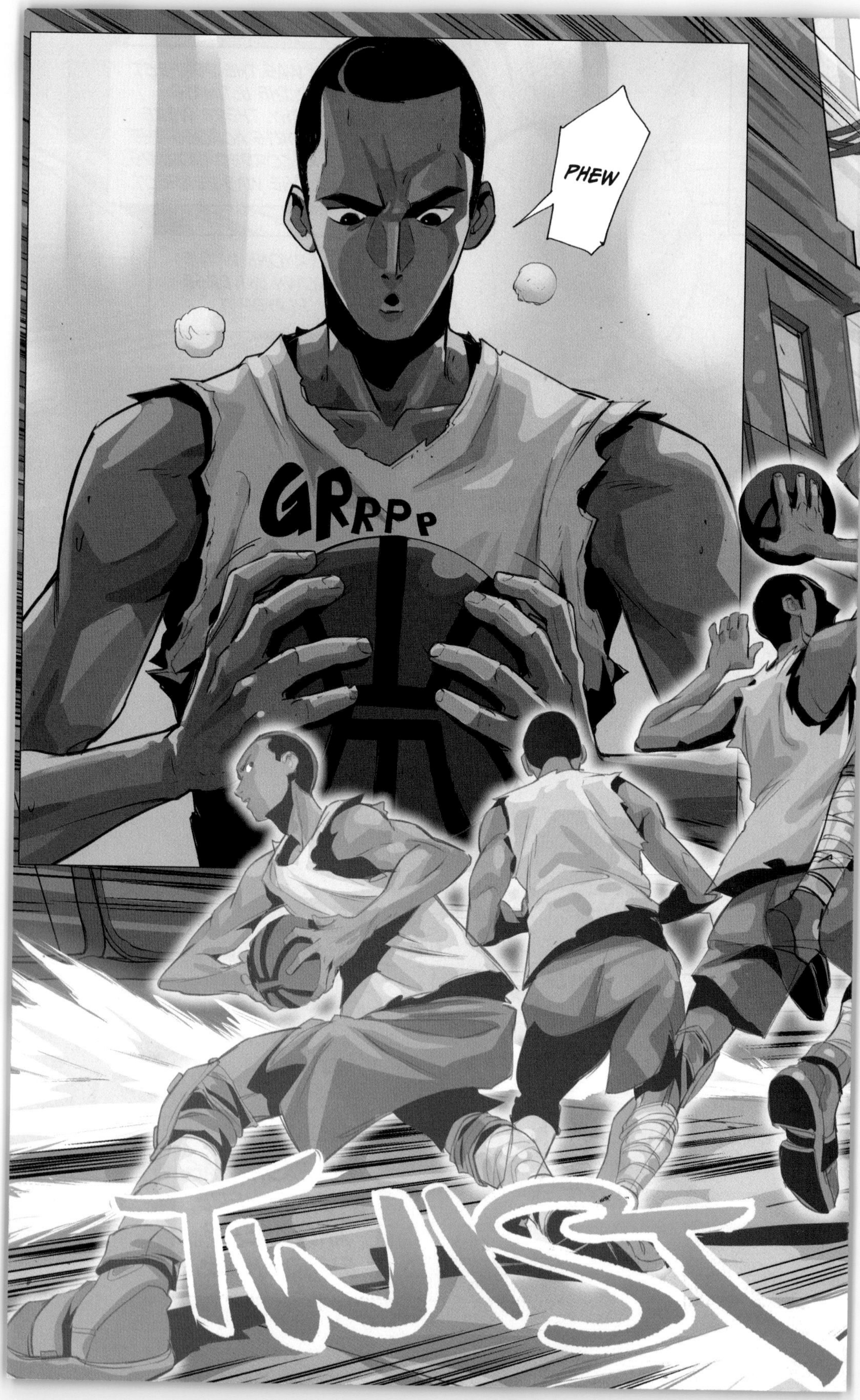
PHEW
GRRPP
TWIST

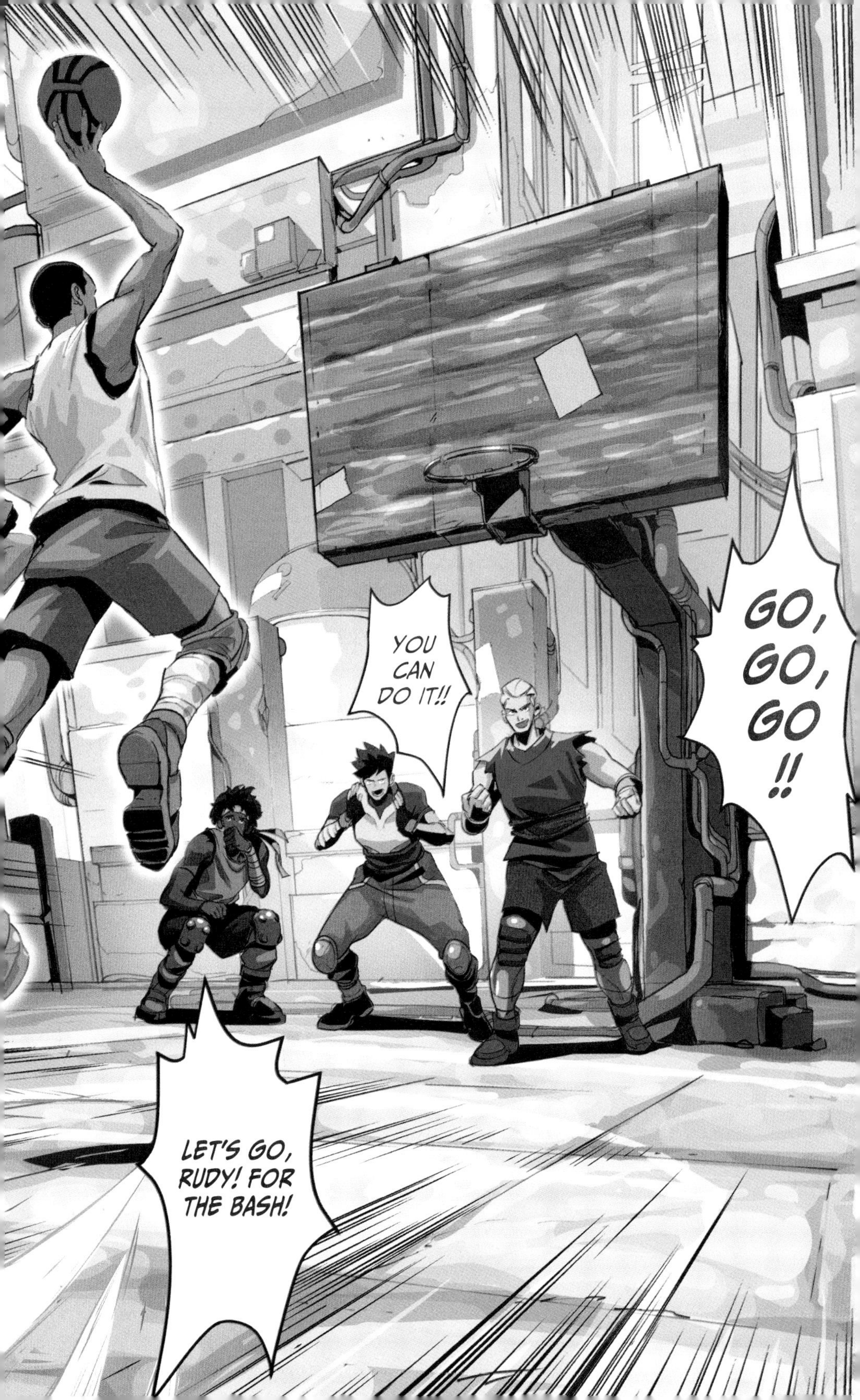
GO, GO, GO, GO!!
YOU CAN DO IT!!
LET'S GO, RUDY! FOR THE BASH!

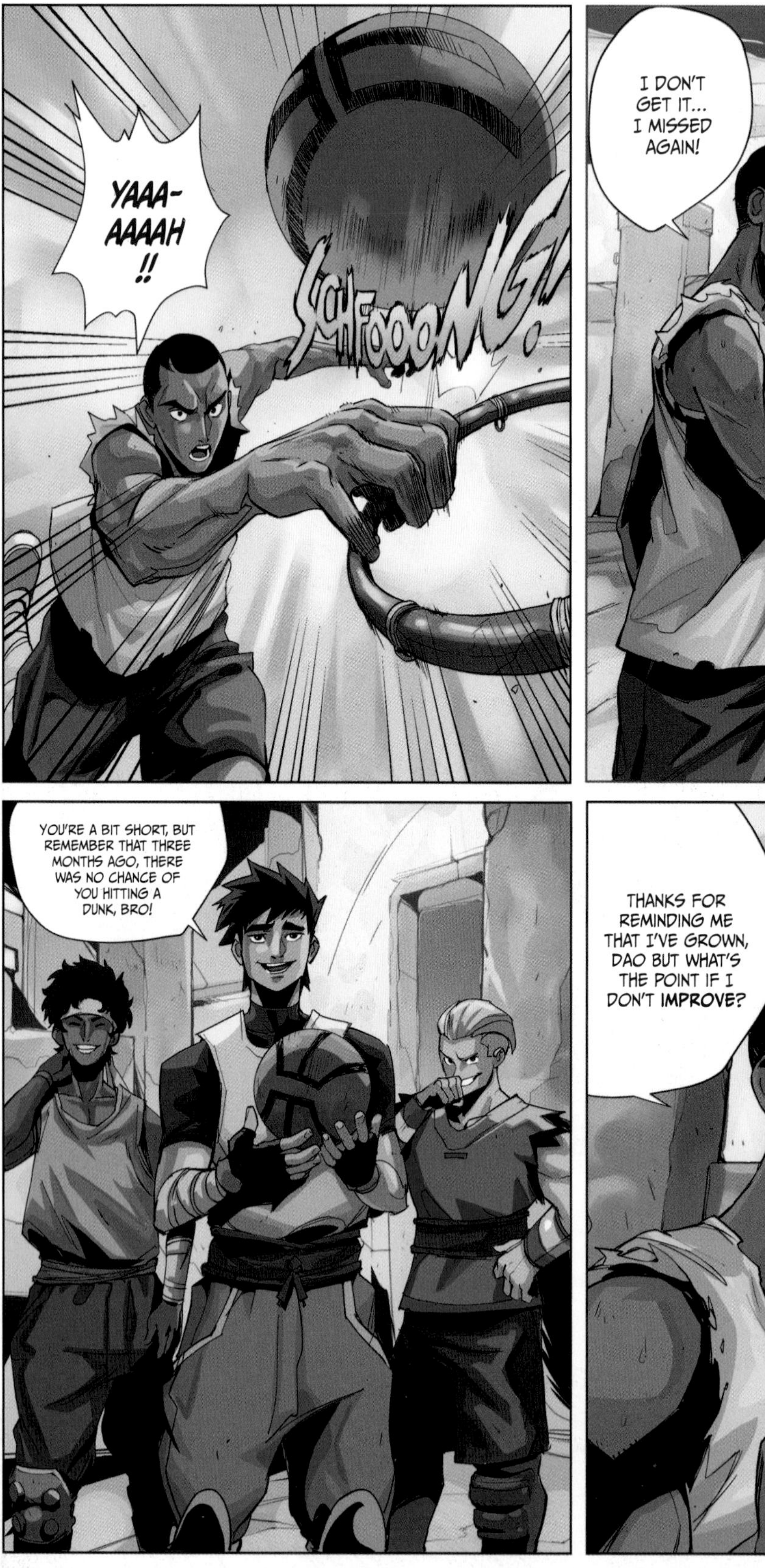
YAAA-AAAAH !!
SCHFOOONG!
I DON'T GET IT... I MISSED AGAIN!
YOU'RE A BIT SHORT, BUT REMEMBER THAT THREE MONTHS AGO, THERE WAS NO CHANCE OF YOU HITTING A DUNK, BRO!
THANKS FOR REMINDING ME THAT I'VE GROWN, DAO BUT WHAT'S THE POINT IF I DON'T **IMPROVE**?

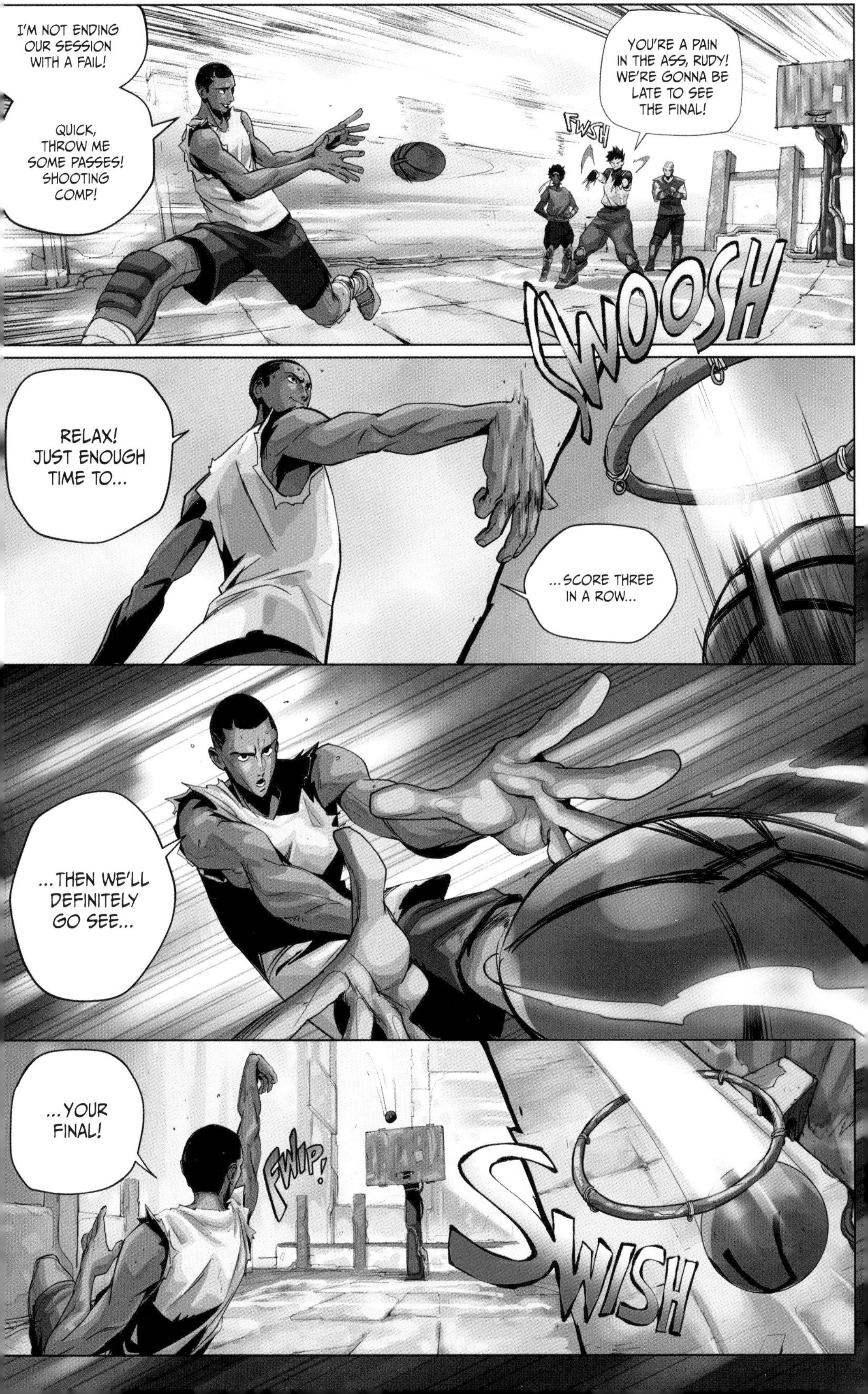
I'M NOT ENDING OUR SESSION WITH A FAIL!
QUICK, THROW ME SOME PASSES! SHOOTING COMP!
YOU'RE A PAIN IN THE ASS, RUDY! WE'RE GONNA BE LATE TO SEE THE FINAL!
FWSH
WOOSH
RELAX! JUST ENOUGH TIME TO...
...SCORE THREE IN A ROW...
...THEN WE'LL DEFINITELY GO SEE...
...YOUR FINAL!
FWIP!
SWISH

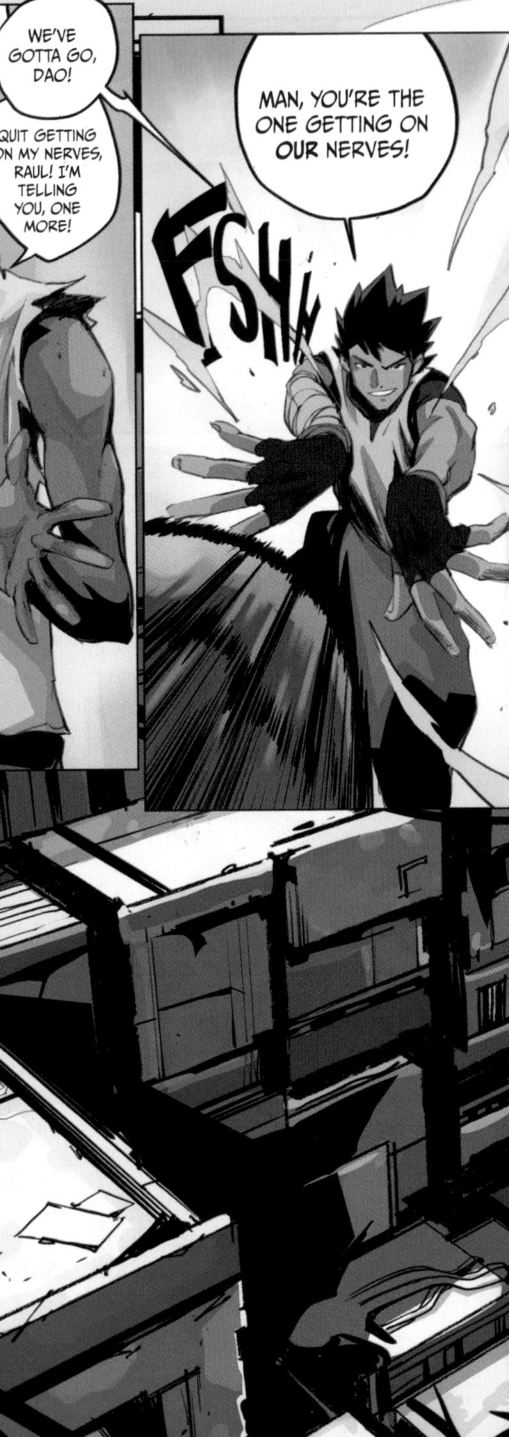

WE'VE GOTTA GO, DAO!
QUIT GETTING ON MY NERVES, RAUL! I'M TELLING YOU, ONE MORE!
MAN, YOU'RE THE ONE GETTING ON OUR NERVES!
FSHH

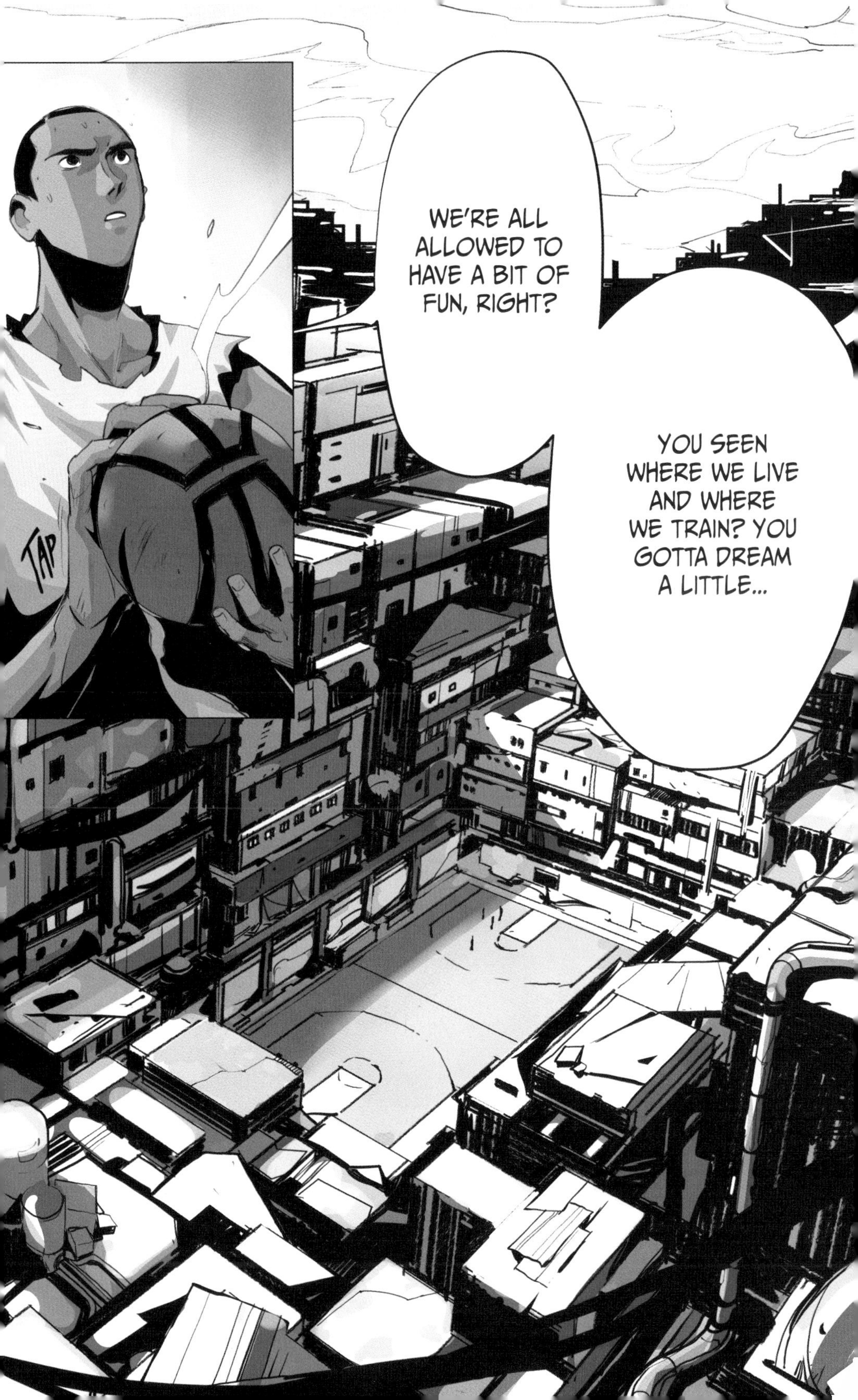
WE'RE ALL ALLOWED TO HAVE A BIT OF FUN, RIGHT?
YOU SEEN WHERE WE LIVE AND WHERE WE TRAIN? YOU GOTTA DREAM A LITTLE...
TAP

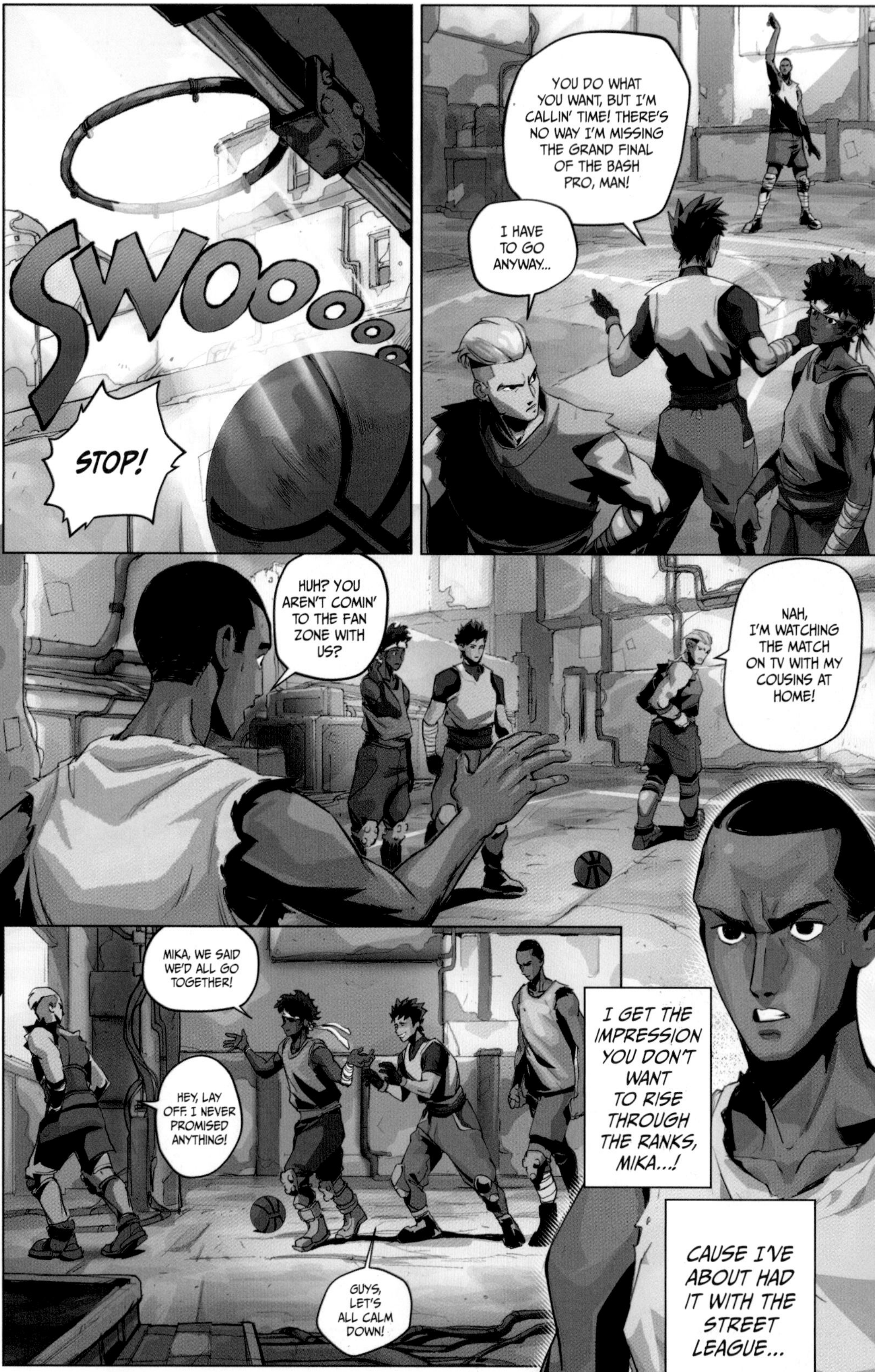
SWOOOOO
STOP!
YOU DO WHAT YOU WANT, BUT I'M CALLIN' TIME! THERE'S NO WAY I'M MISSING THE GRAND FINAL OF THE BASH PRO, MAN!
I HAVE TO GO ANYWAY...
HUH? YOU AREN'T COMIN' TO THE FAN ZONE WITH US?
NAH, I'M WATCHING THE MATCH ON TV WITH MY COUSINS AT HOME!
MIKA, WE SAID WE'D ALL GO TOGETHER!
HEY, LAY OFF. I NEVER PROMISED ANYTHING!
GUYS, LET'S ALL CALM DOWN!
I GET THE IMPRESSION YOU DON'T WANT TO RISE THROUGH THE RANKS, MIKA...!
CAUSE I'VE ABOUT HAD IT WITH THE STREET LEAGUE...

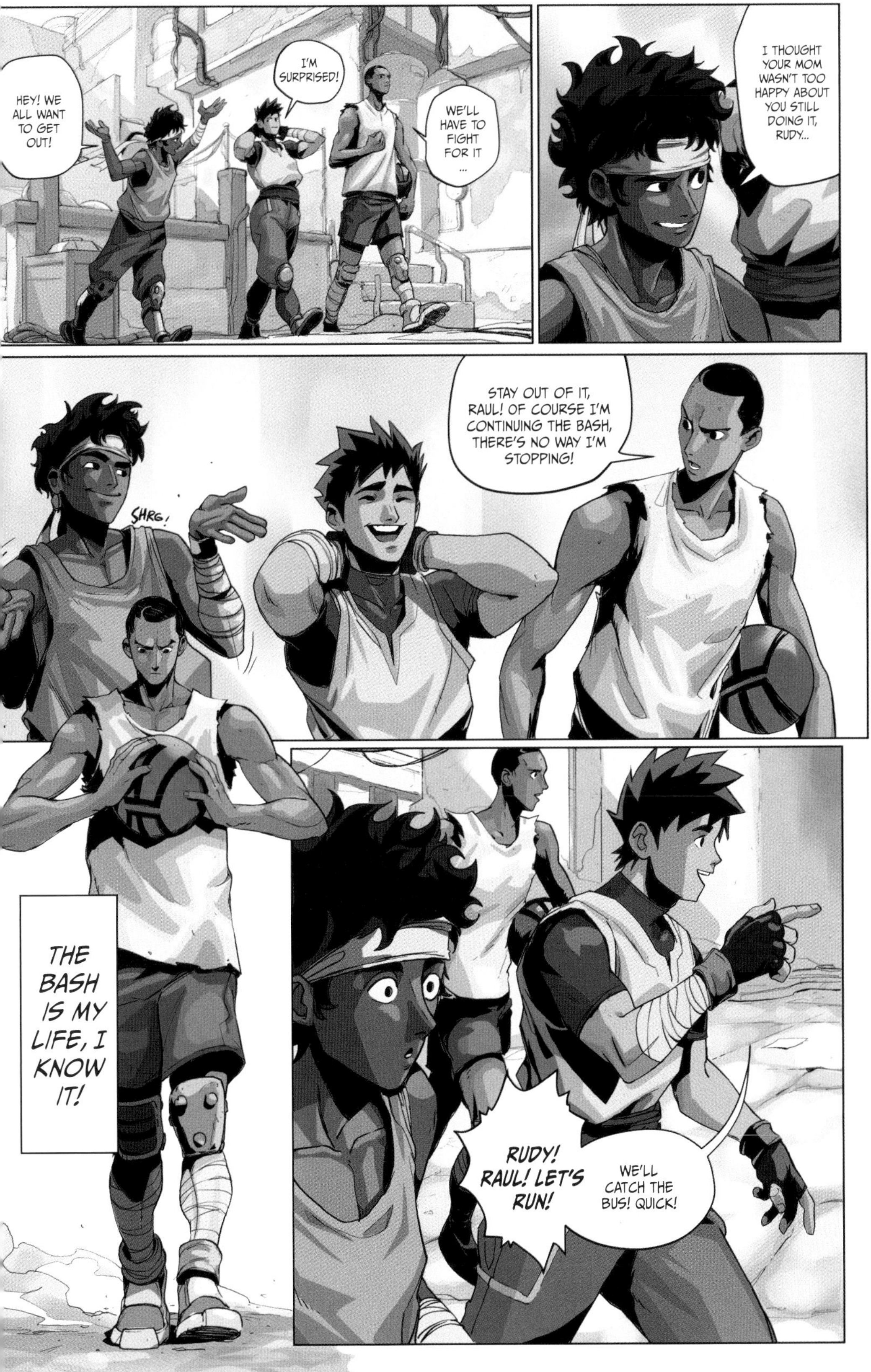
HEY! WE ALL WANT TO GET OUT!
I'M SURPRISED!
WE'LL HAVE TO FIGHT FOR IT ...
I THOUGHT YOUR MOM WASN'T TOO HAPPY ABOUT YOU STILL DOING IT, RUDY...
STAY OUT OF IT, RAUL! OF COURSE I'M CONTINUING THE BASH, THERE'S NO WAY I'M STOPPING!
SHRG!
THE BASH IS MY LIFE, I KNOW IT!
RUDY! RAUL! LET'S RUN!
WE'LL CATCH THE BUS! QUICK!

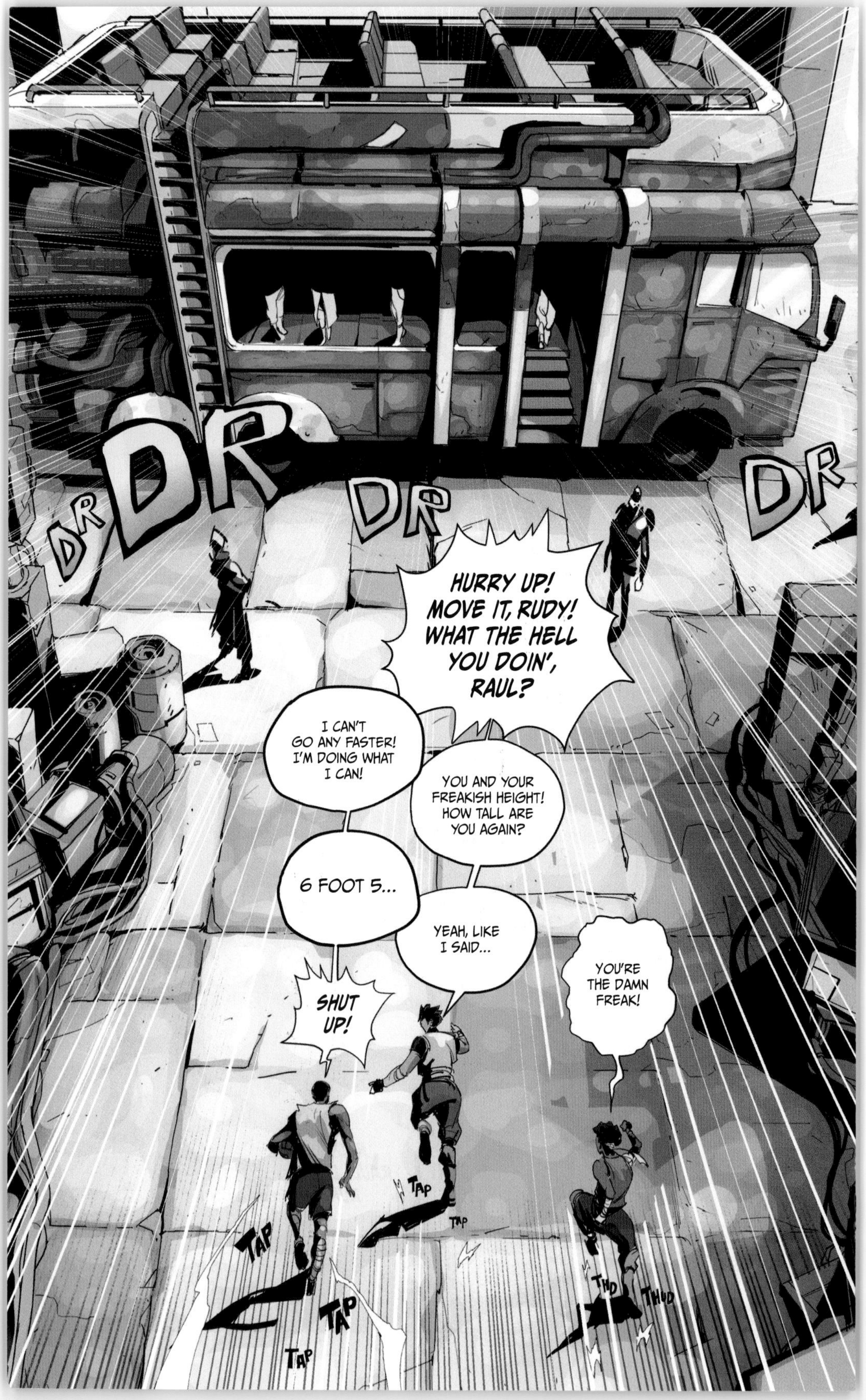
DR DR
DR
DR
HURRY UP! MOVE IT, RUDY! WHAT THE HELL YOU DOIN', RAUL?
I CAN'T GO ANY FASTER! I'M DOING WHAT I CAN!
YOU AND YOUR FREAKISH HEIGHT! HOW TALL ARE YOU AGAIN?
6 FOOT 5...
YEAH, LIKE I SAID...
YOU'RE THE DAMN FREAK!
SHUT UP!
TAP
TAP
TAP
TAP
TAP
THUD
THUD

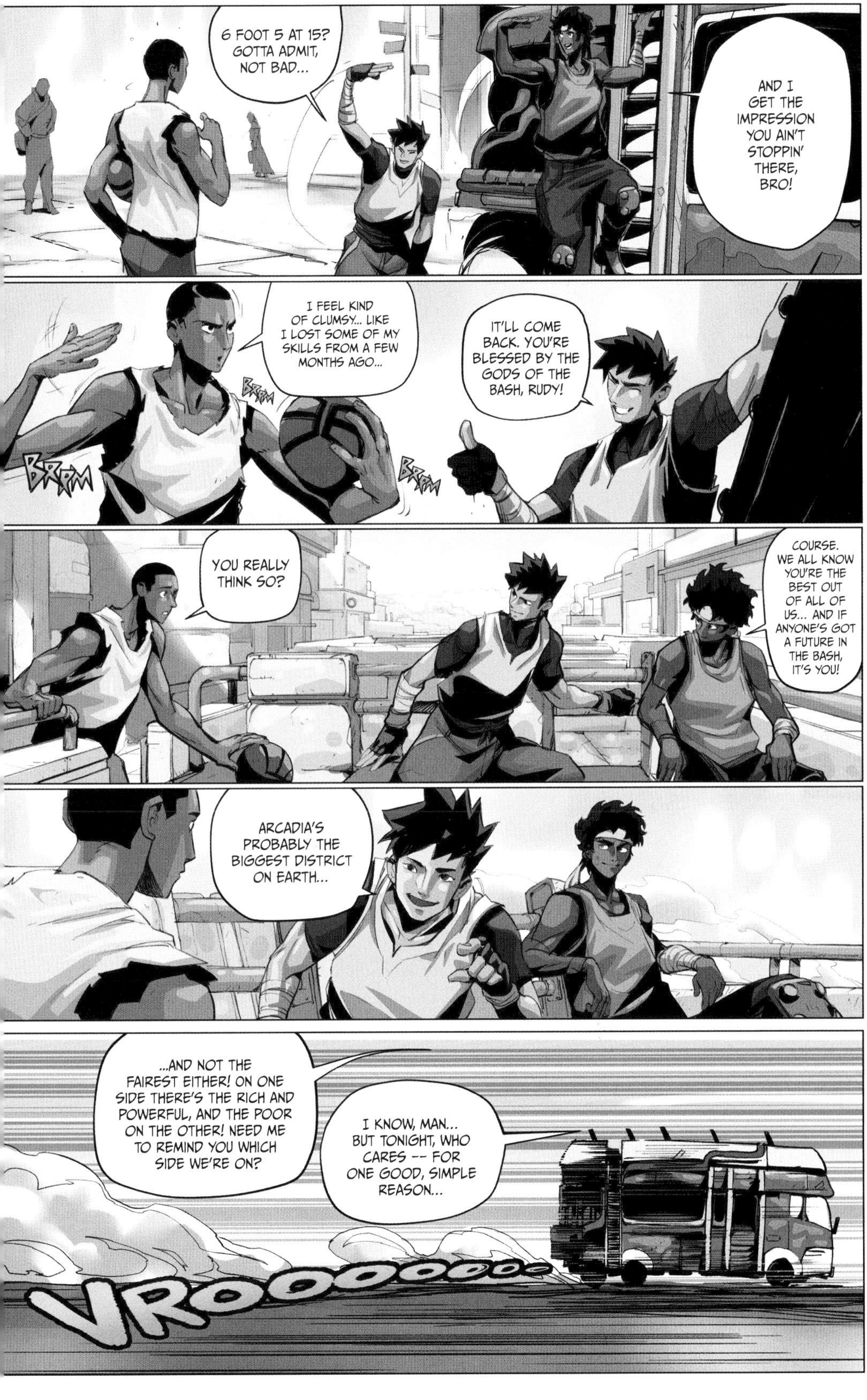
6 FOOT 5 AT 15? GOTTA ADMIT, NOT BAD...
AND I GET THE IMPRESSION YOU AIN'T STOPPIN' THERE, BRO!
I FEEL KIND OF CLUMSY... LIKE I LOST SOME OF MY SKILLS FROM A FEW MONTHS AGO...
BRPM
BRPM
BRPM
IT'LL COME BACK. YOU'RE BLESSED BY THE GODS OF THE BASH, RUDY!
YOU REALLY THINK SO?
COURSE. WE ALL KNOW YOU'RE THE BEST OUT OF ALL OF US... AND IF ANYONE'S GOT A FUTURE IN THE BASH, IT'S YOU!
ARCADIA'S PROBABLY THE BIGGEST DISTRICT ON EARTH...
...AND NOT THE FAIREST EITHER! ON ONE SIDE THERE'S THE RICH AND POWERFUL, AND THE POOR ON THE OTHER! NEED ME TO REMIND YOU WHICH SIDE WE'RE ON?
I KNOW, MAN... BUT TONIGHT, WHO CARES -- FOR ONE GOOD, SIMPLE REASON...
VROOOOOOOO

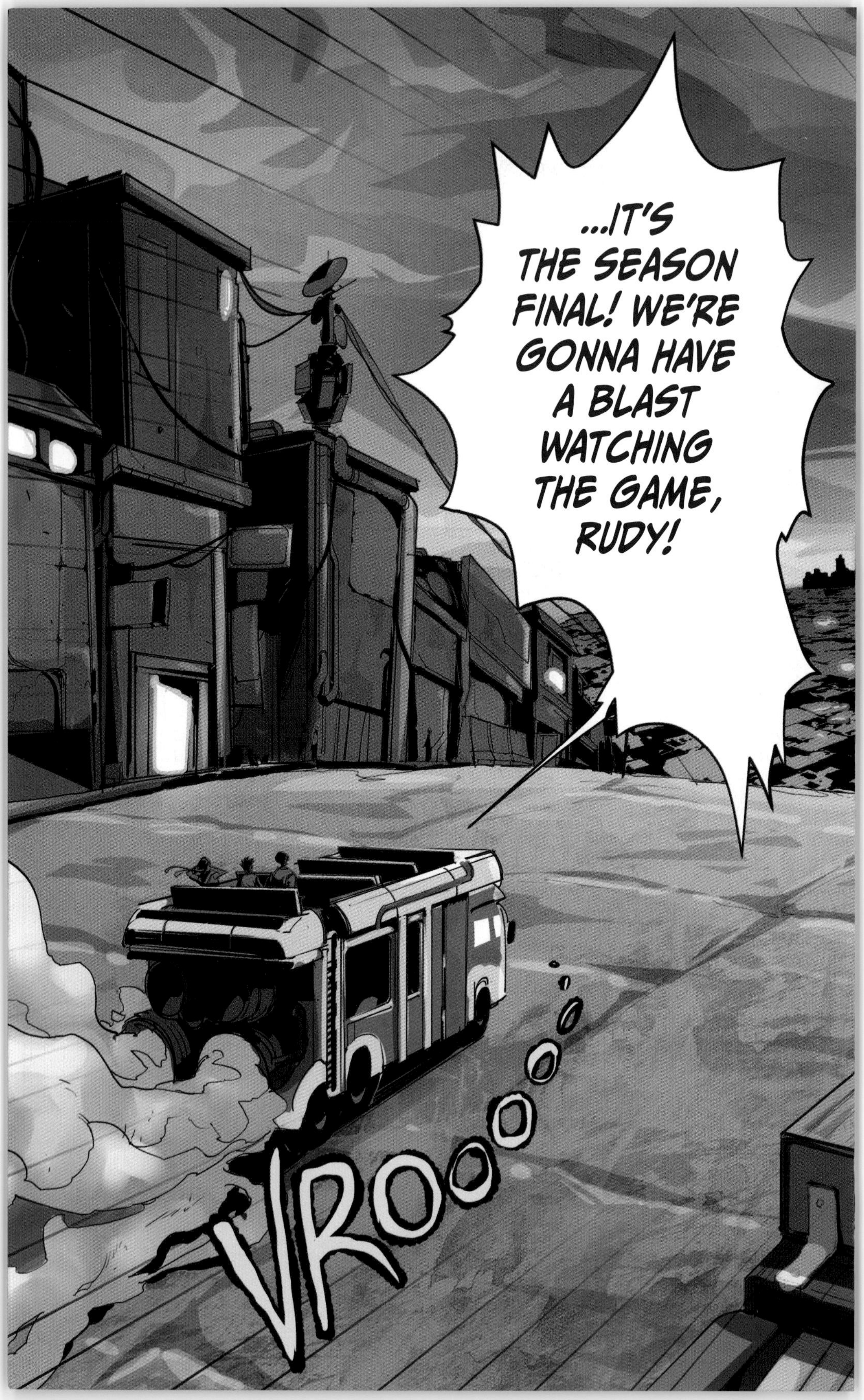
...IT'S THE SEASON FINAL! WE'RE GONNA HAVE A BLAST WATCHING THE GAME, RUDY!
VROOooo

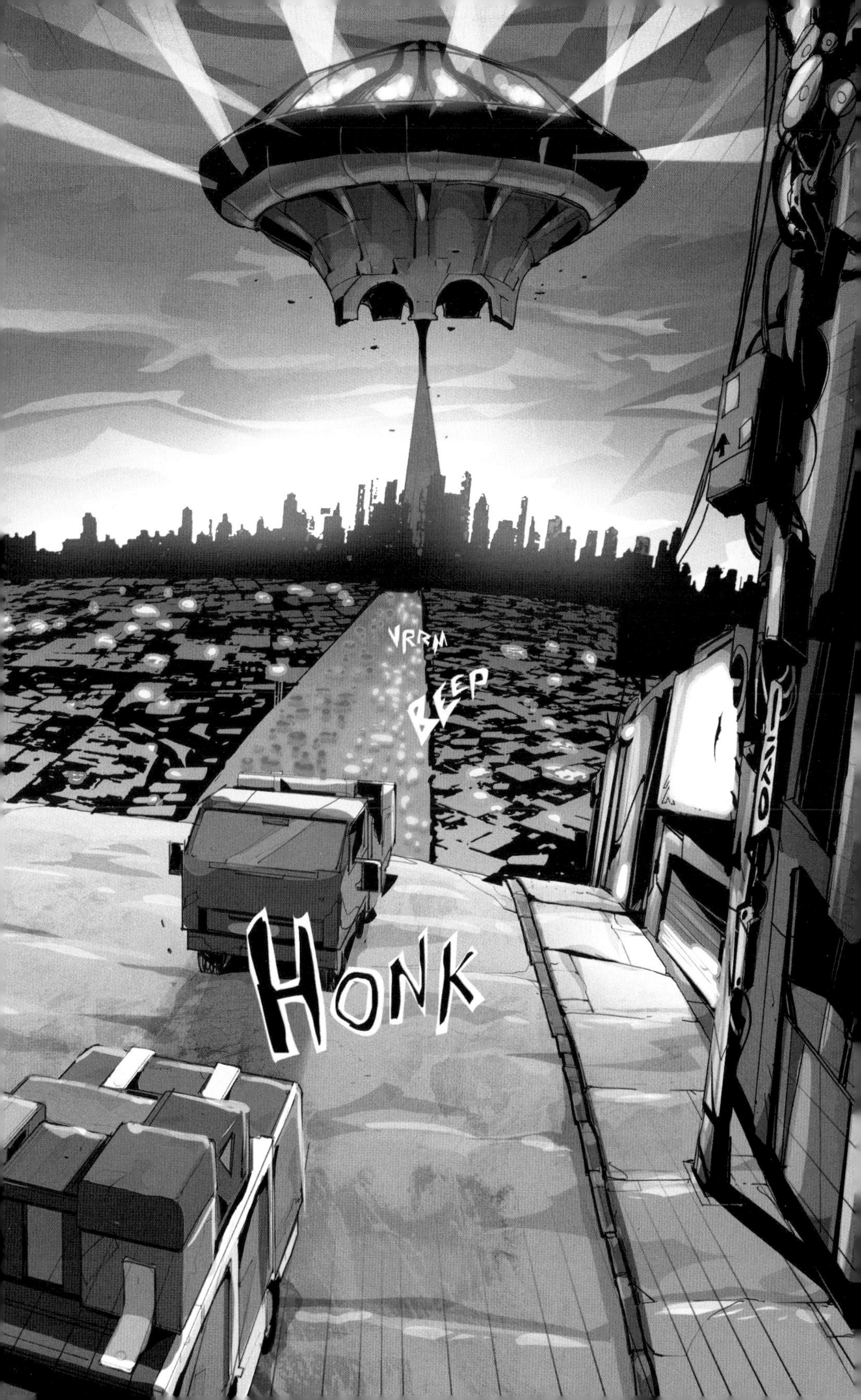
VRRM
BEEP
HONK

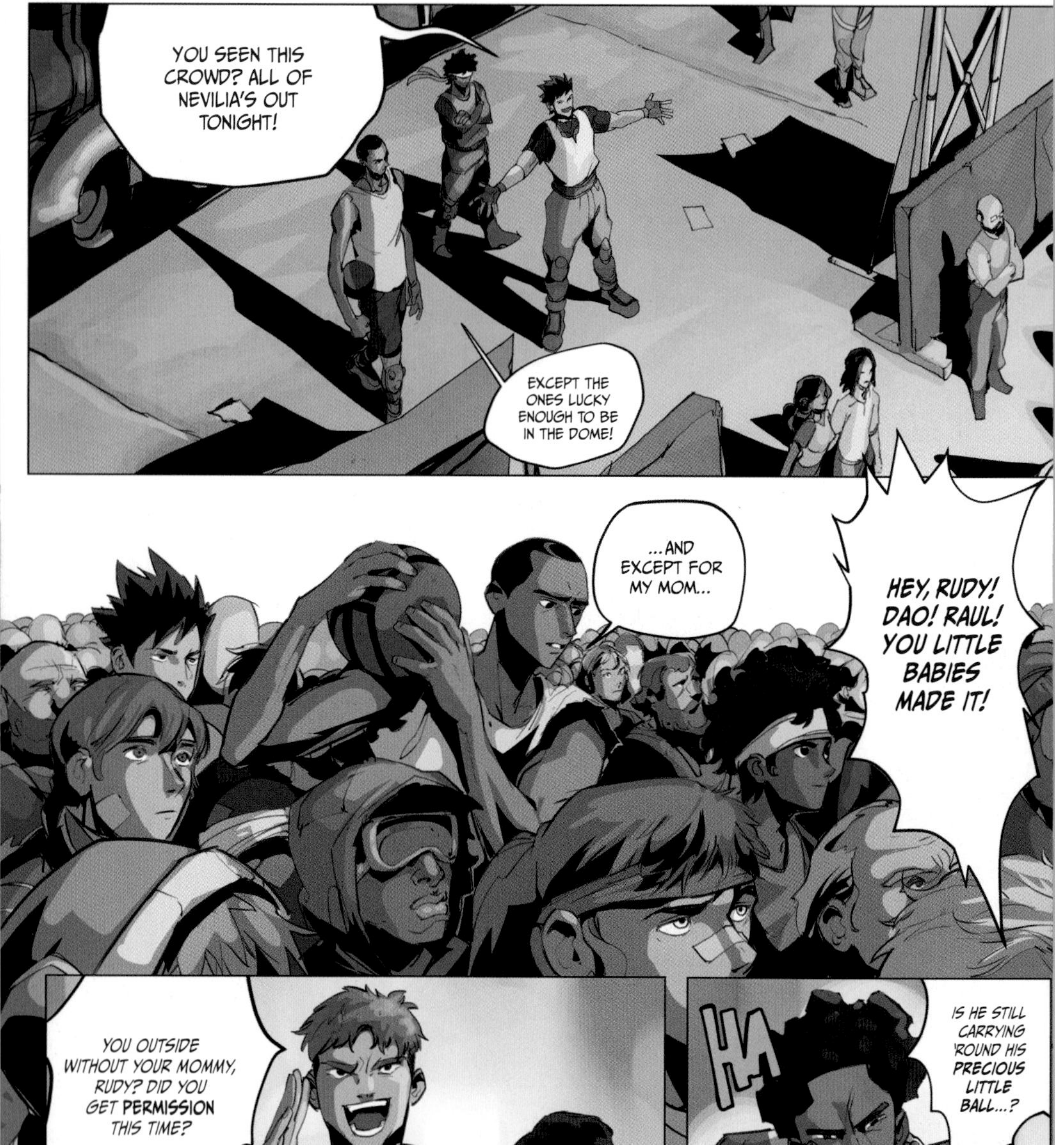
YOU SEEN THIS CROWD? ALL OF NEVILIA'S OUT TONIGHT!
EXCEPT THE ONES LUCKY ENOUGH TO BE IN THE DOME!
...AND EXCEPT FOR MY MOM...
HEY, RUDY! DAO! RAUL! YOU LITTLE BABIES MADE IT!
YOU OUTSIDE WITHOUT YOUR MOMMY, RUDY? DID YOU GET PERMISSION THIS TIME?
HA
IS HE STILL CARRYING 'ROUND HIS PRECIOUS LITTLE BALL...?

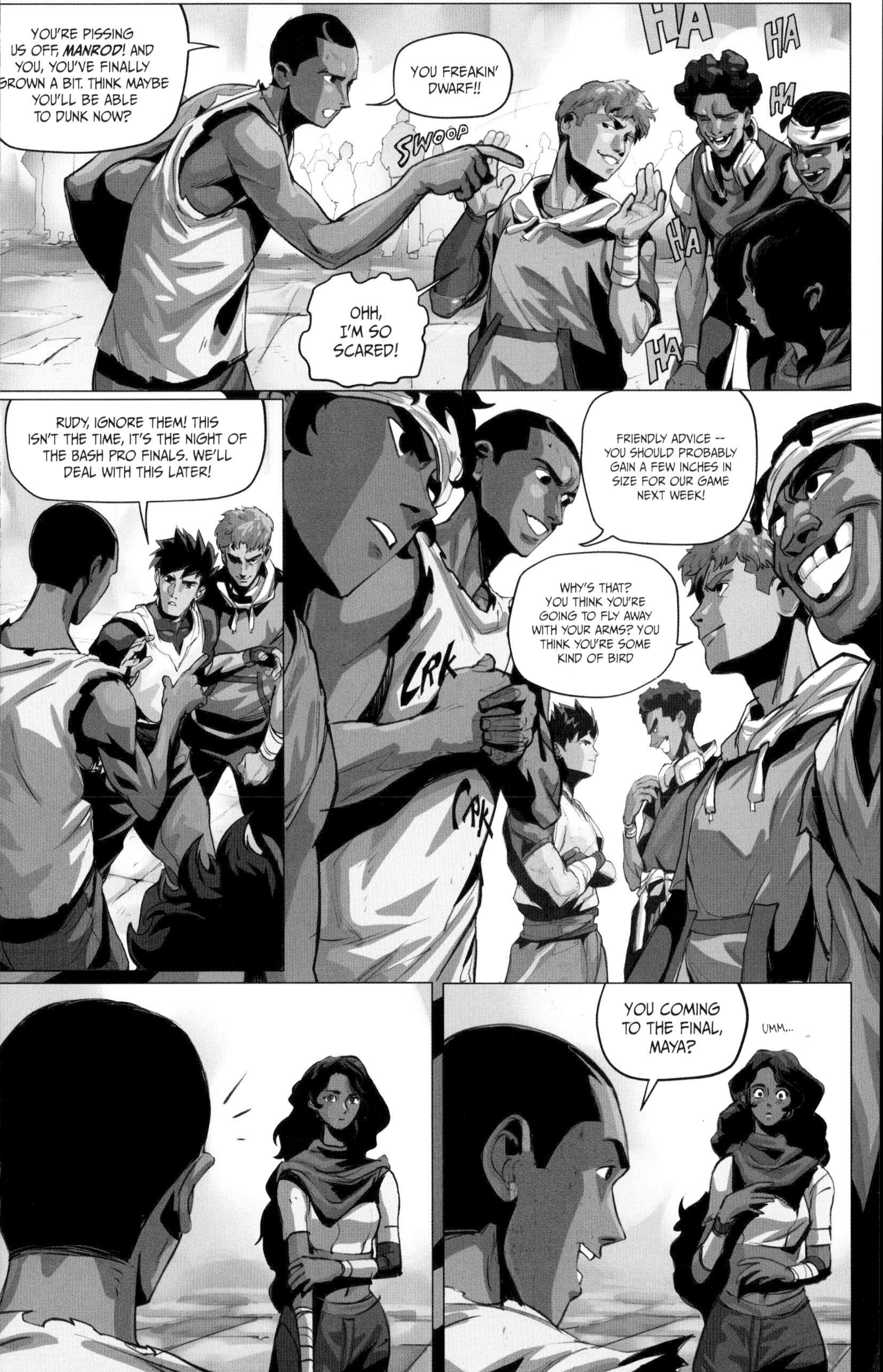

YOU'RE PISSING US OFF, ***MANROD!*** AND YOU, YOU'VE FINALLY GROWN A BIT. THINK MAYBE YOU'LL BE ABLE TO DUNK NOW?
YOU FREAKIN' DWARF!!
SWOOP
HA
HA
HA
HA
HA
OHH, I'M SO SCARED!
RUDY, IGNORE THEM! THIS ISN'T THE TIME, IT'S THE NIGHT OF THE BASH PRO FINALS. WE'LL DEAL WITH THIS LATER!
FRIENDLY ADVICE -- YOU SHOULD PROBABLY GAIN A FEW INCHES IN SIZE FOR OUR GAME NEXT WEEK!
CRK
WHY'S THAT? YOU THINK YOU'RE GOING TO FLY AWAY WITH YOUR ARMS? YOU THINK YOU'RE SOME KIND OF BIRD
CRK
YOU COMING TO THE FINAL, MAYA?
UMM...

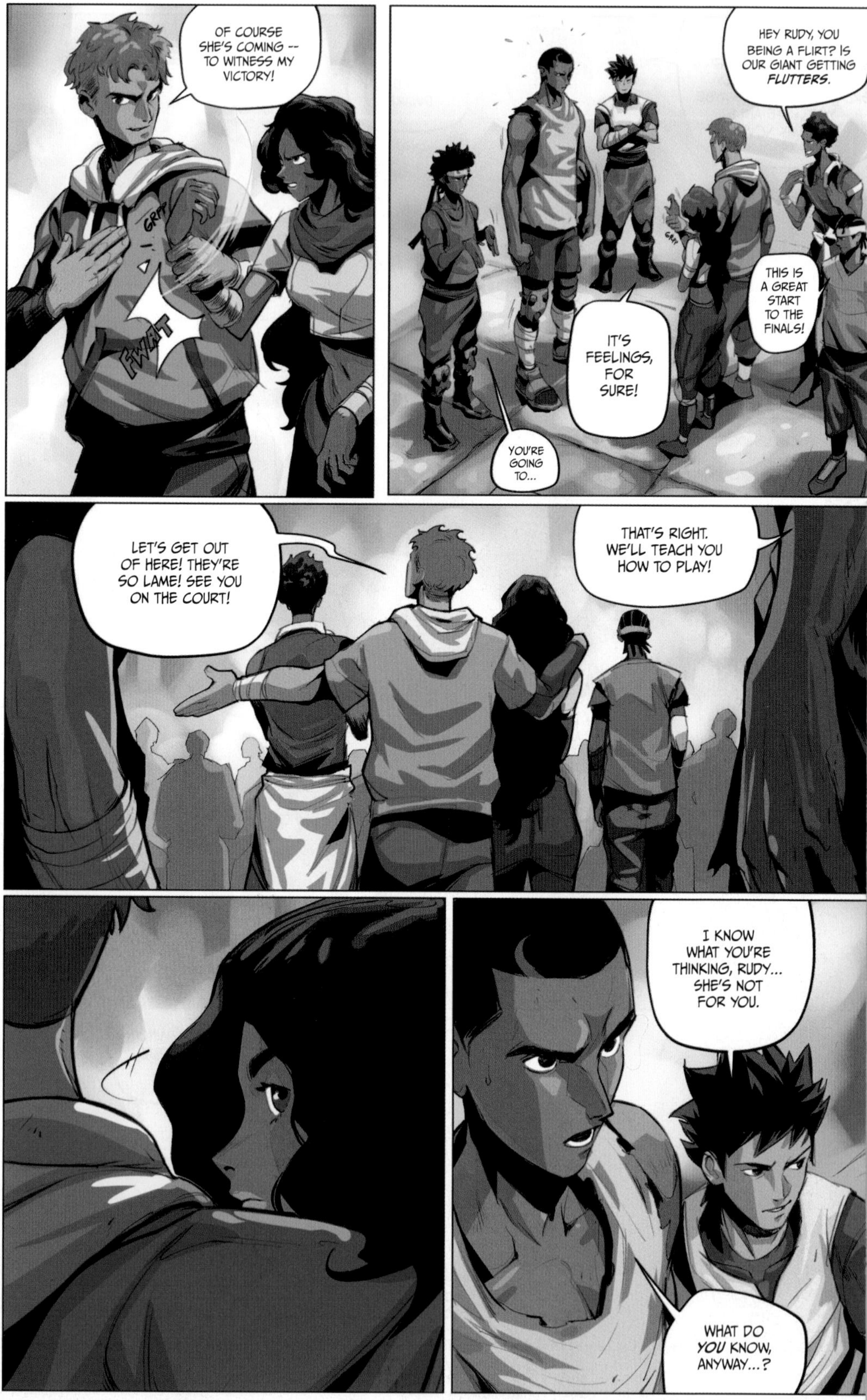
OF COURSE SHE'S COMING -- TO WITNESS MY VICTORY!
GRPP
FWAT
HEY RUDY, YOU BEING A FLIRT? IS OUR GIANT GETTING *FLUTTERS*.
THIS IS A GREAT START TO THE FINALS!
IT'S FEELINGS, FOR SURE!
YOU'RE GOING TO...
LET'S GET OUT OF HERE! THEY'RE SO LAME! SEE YOU ON THE COURT!
THAT'S RIGHT. WE'LL TEACH YOU HOW TO PLAY!
I KNOW WHAT YOU'RE THINKING, RUDY... SHE'S NOT FOR YOU.
WHAT DO *YOU* KNOW, ANYWAY...?

DA-DUM
LADIES AND GENTLEMEN, WELCOME TO THE 317TH BASH PRO FINAL! THE BIGGEST MATCH OF THE SEASON AND THE MOST WATCHED EVENT IN THE WORLD!

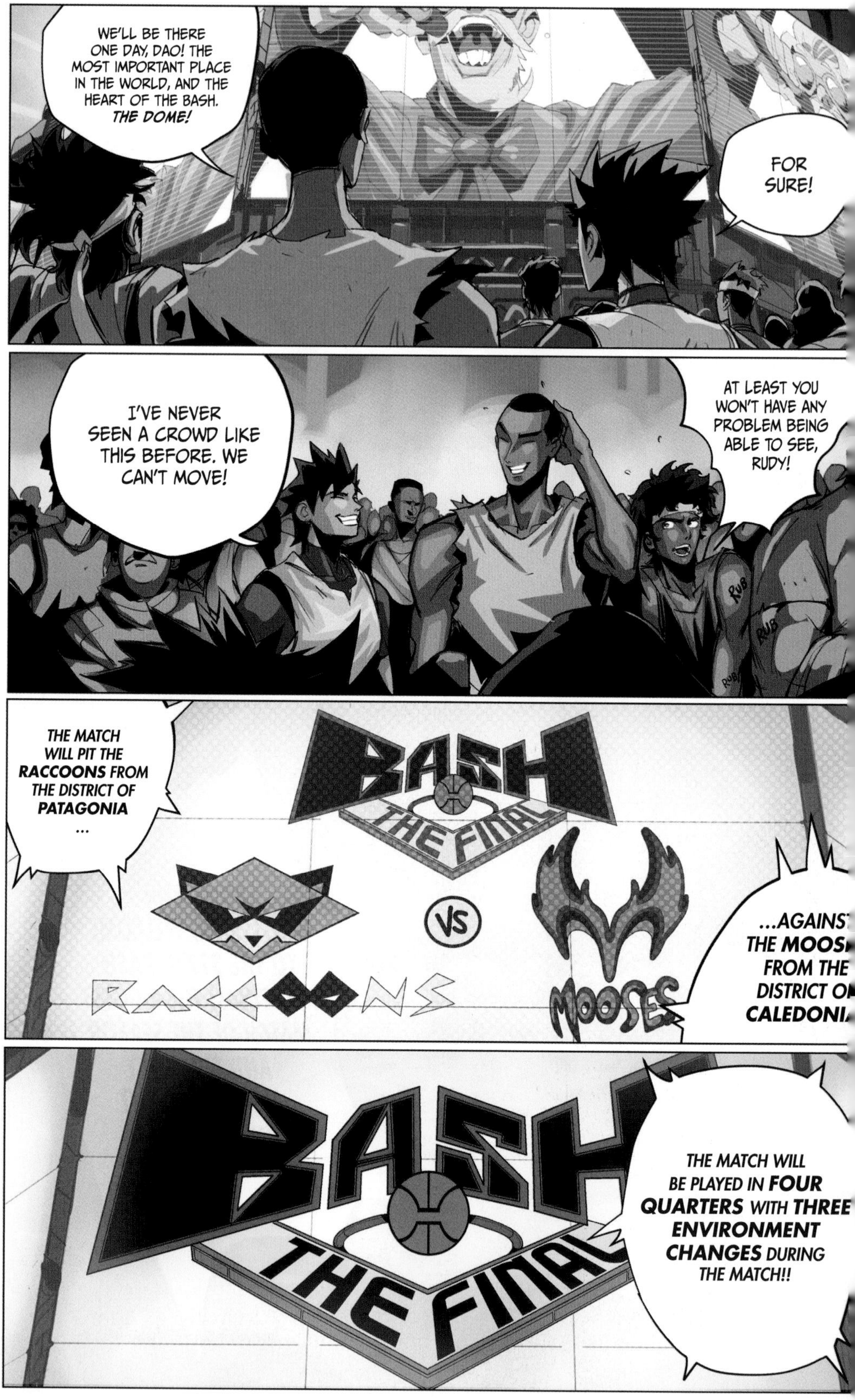

WE'LL BE THERE ONE DAY, DAO! THE MOST IMPORTANT PLACE IN THE WORLD, AND THE HEART OF THE BASH. THE DOME!
FOR SURE!
I'VE NEVER SEEN A CROWD LIKE THIS BEFORE. WE CAN'T MOVE!
AT LEAST YOU WON'T HAVE ANY PROBLEM BEING ABLE TO SEE, RUDY!
RUB
RUB
RUB
THE MATCH WILL PIT THE RACCOONS FROM THE DISTRICT OF PATAGONIA ...
BASH THE FINAL
VS
RACCOONS
MOOSES
...AGAINST THE MOOSES FROM THE DISTRICT OF CALEDONIA
BASH THE FINAL
THE MATCH WILL BE PLAYED IN FOUR QUARTERS WITH THREE ENVIRONMENT CHANGES DURING THE MATCH!!

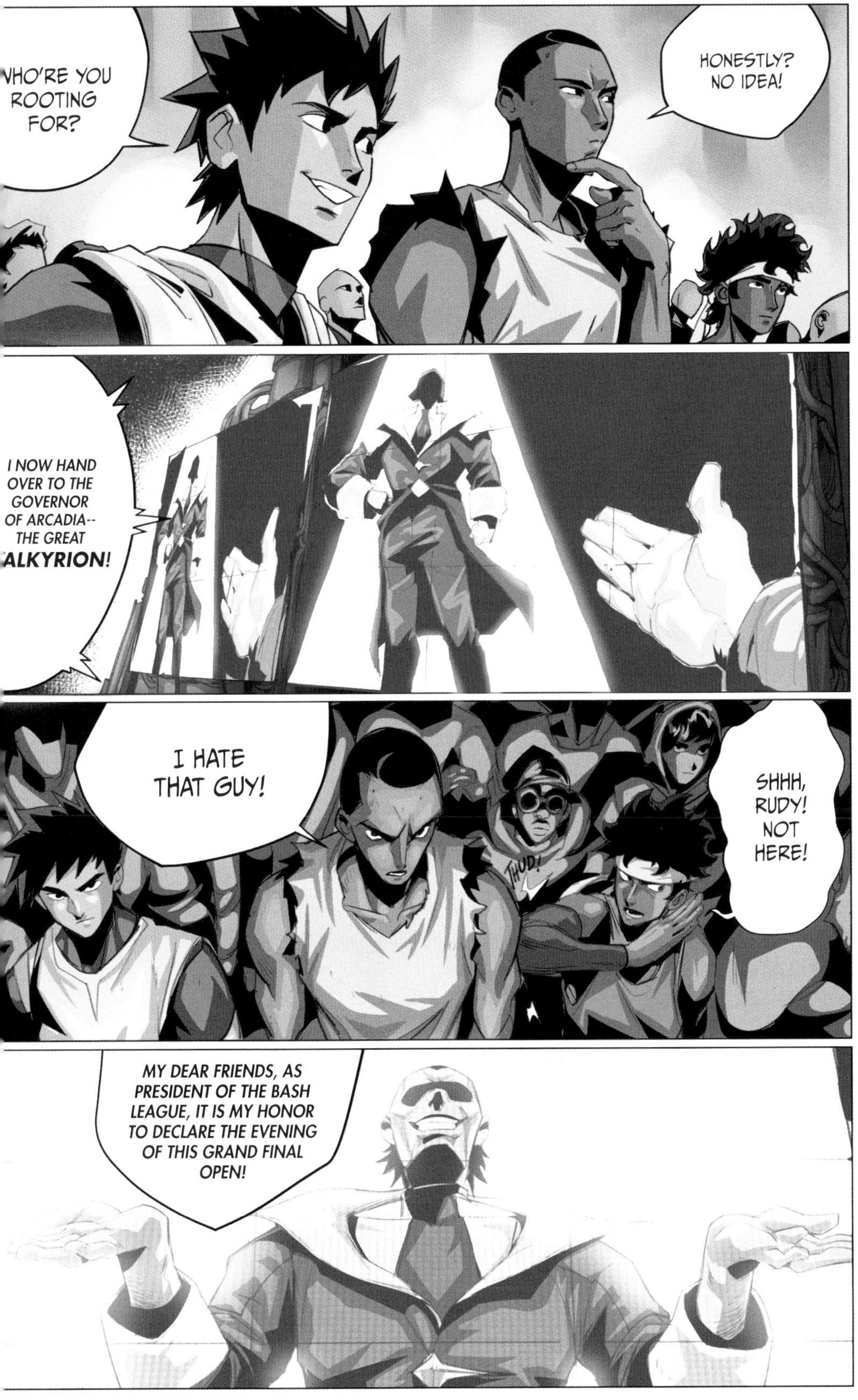
WHO'RE YOU ROOTING FOR?
HONESTLY? NO IDEA!
I NOW HAND OVER TO THE GOVERNOR OF ARCADIA-- THE GREAT VALKYRION!
I HATE THAT GUY!
THUD!
SHHH, RUDY! NOT HERE!
MY DEAR FRIENDS, AS PRESIDENT OF THE BASH LEAGUE, IT IS MY HONOR TO DECLARE THE EVENING OF THIS GRAND FINAL OPEN!

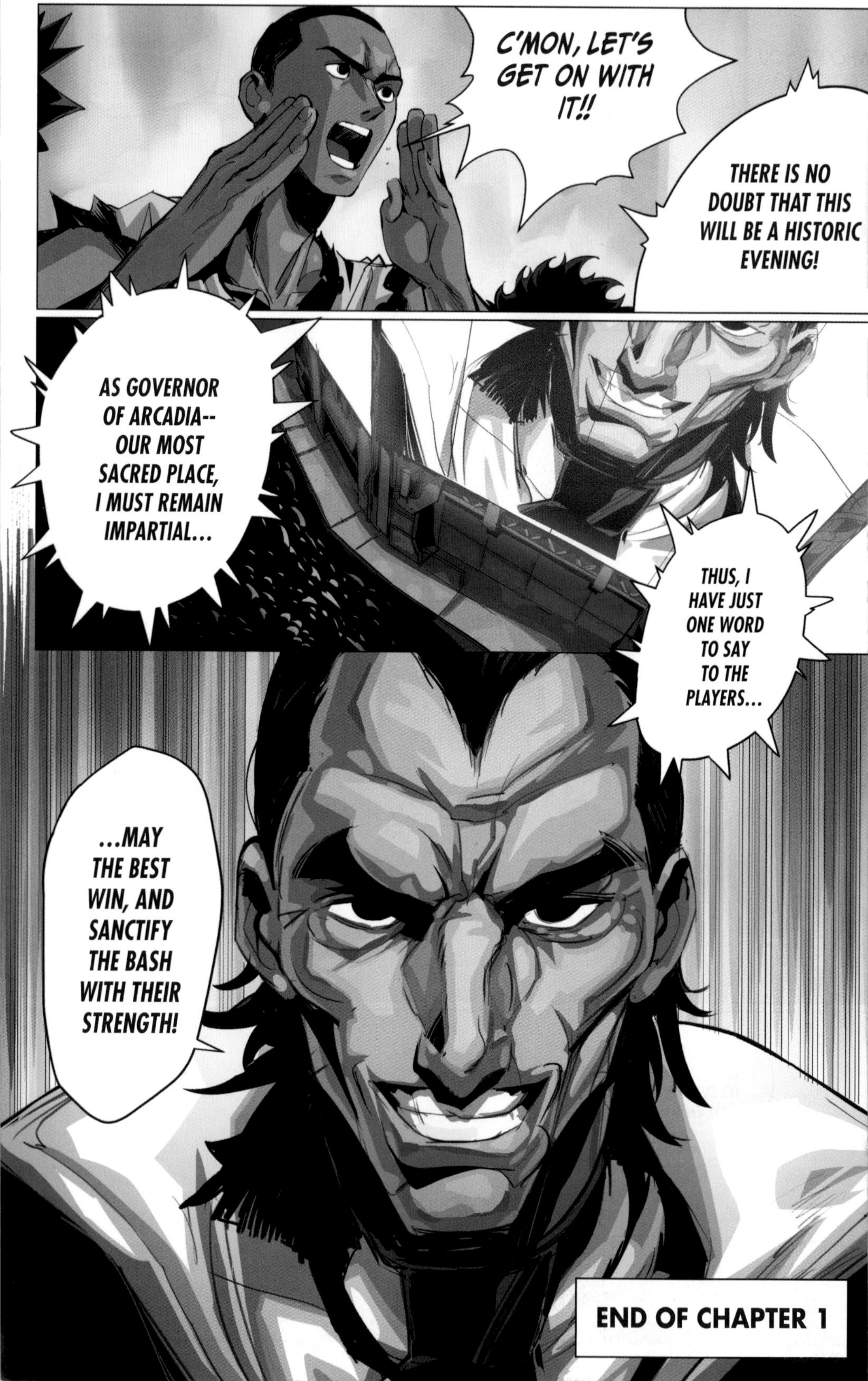
C'MON, LET'S GET ON WITH IT!!
THERE IS NO DOUBT THAT THIS WILL BE A HISTORIC EVENING!
AS GOVERNOR OF ARCADIA-- OUR MOST SACRED PLACE, I MUST REMAIN IMPARTIAL...
THUS, I HAVE JUST ONE WORD TO SAY TO THE PLAYERS...
...MAY THE BEST WIN, AND SANCTIFY THE BASH WITH THEIR STRENGTH!
END OF CHAPTER 1

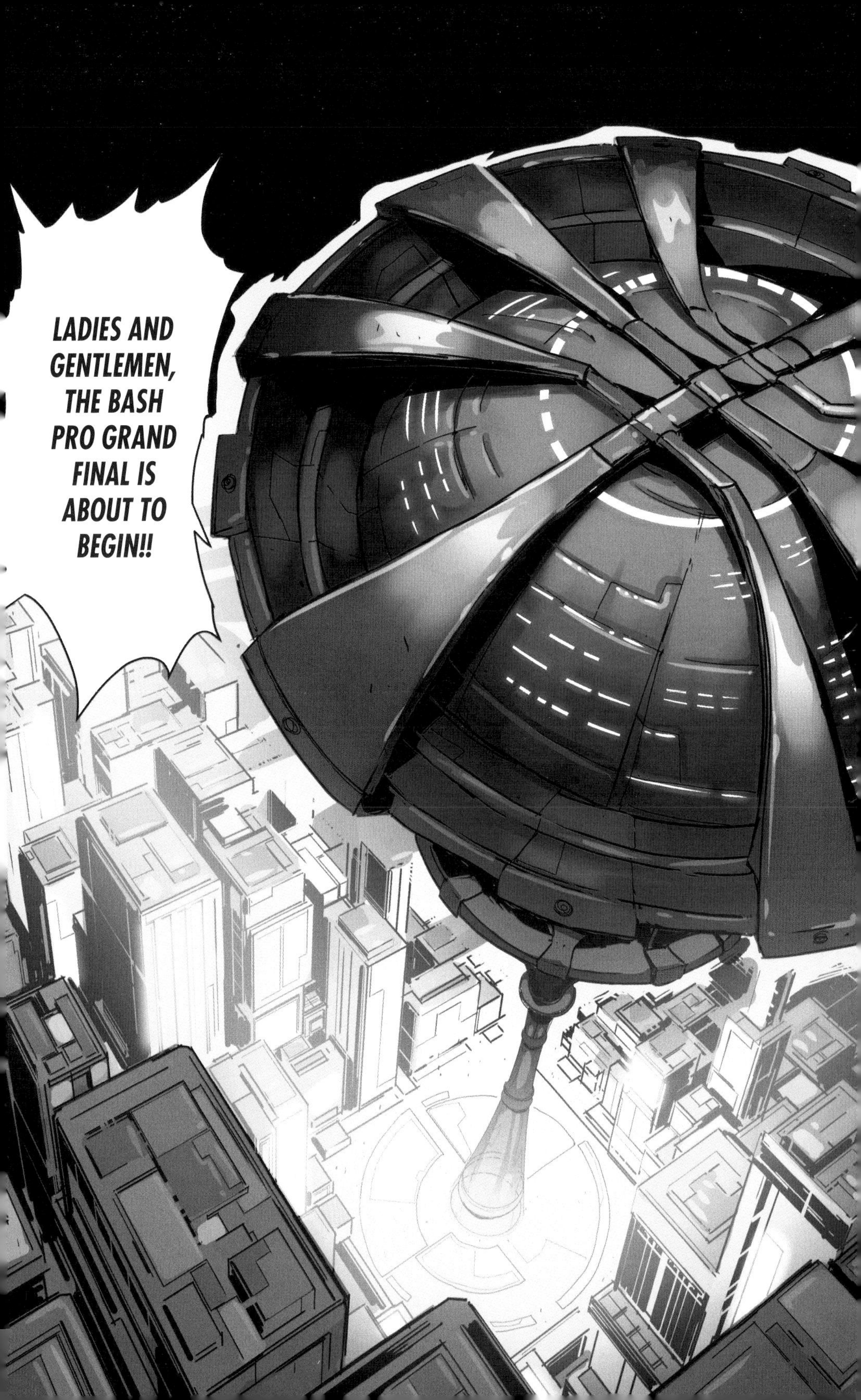
LADIES AND GENTLEMEN, THE BASH PRO GRAND FINAL IS ABOUT TO BEGIN!!

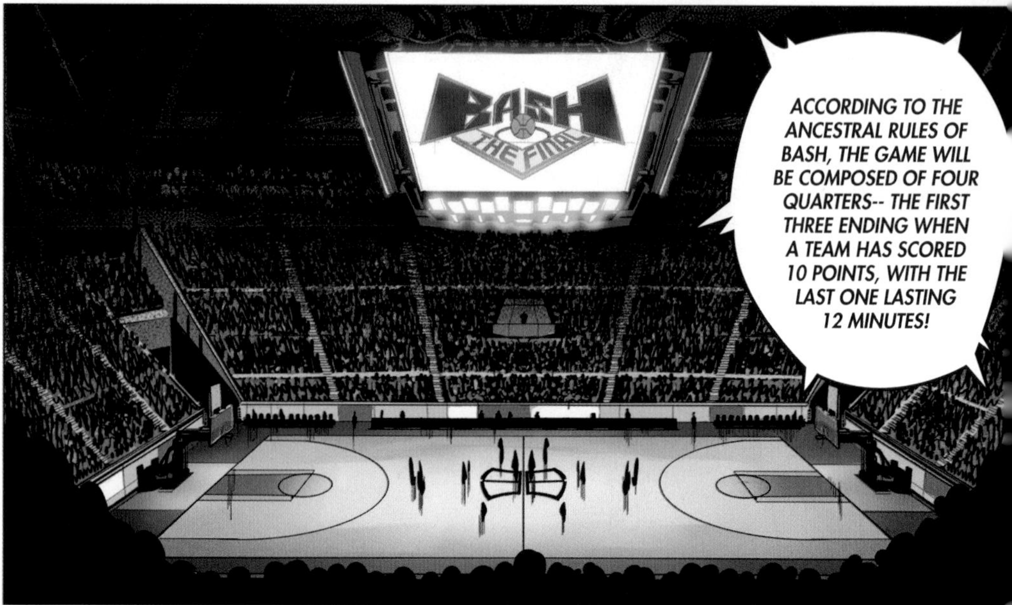
BASH
THE FINAL
ACCORDING TO THE ANCESTRAL RULES OF BASH, THE GAME WILL BE COMPOSED OF FOUR QUARTERS-- THE FIRST THREE ENDING WHEN A TEAM HAS SCORED 10 POINTS, WITH THE LAST ONE LASTING 12 MINUTES!
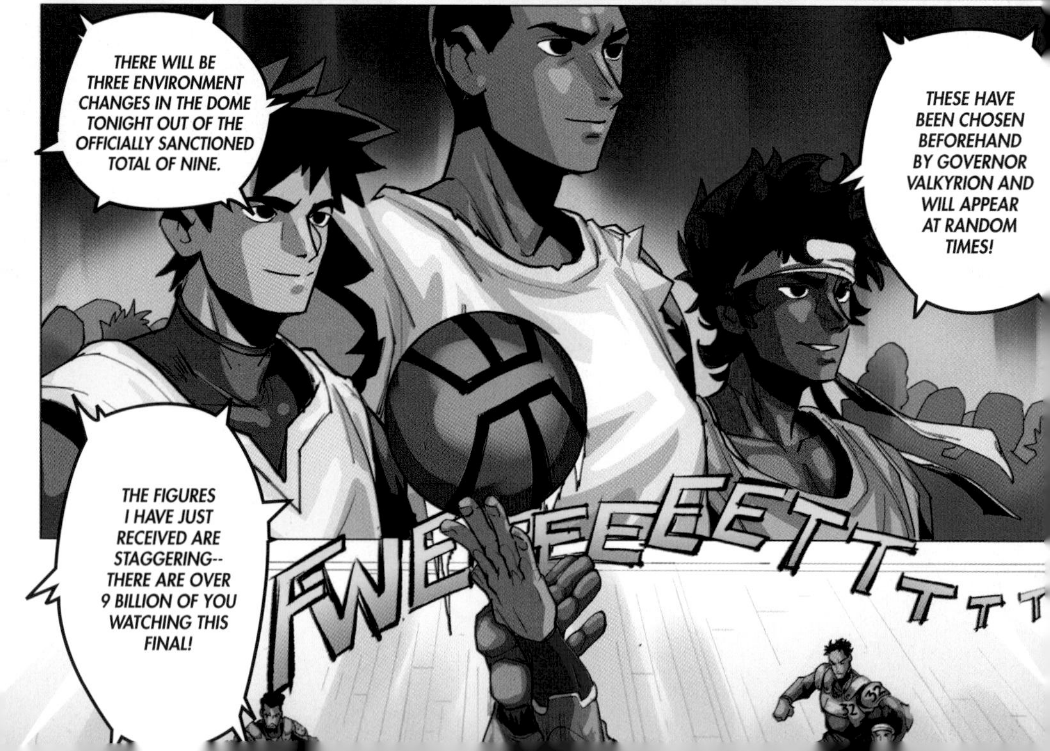
THERE WILL BE THREE ENVIRONMENT CHANGES IN THE DOME TONIGHT OUT OF THE OFFICIALLY SANCTIONED TOTAL OF NINE.
THESE HAVE BEEN CHOSEN BEFOREHAND BY GOVERNOR VALKYRION AND WILL APPEAR AT RANDOM TIMES!
THE FIGURES I HAVE JUST RECEIVED ARE STAGGERING-- THERE ARE OVER 9 BILLION OF YOU WATCHING THIS FINAL!
FWEEEEEETTTTT

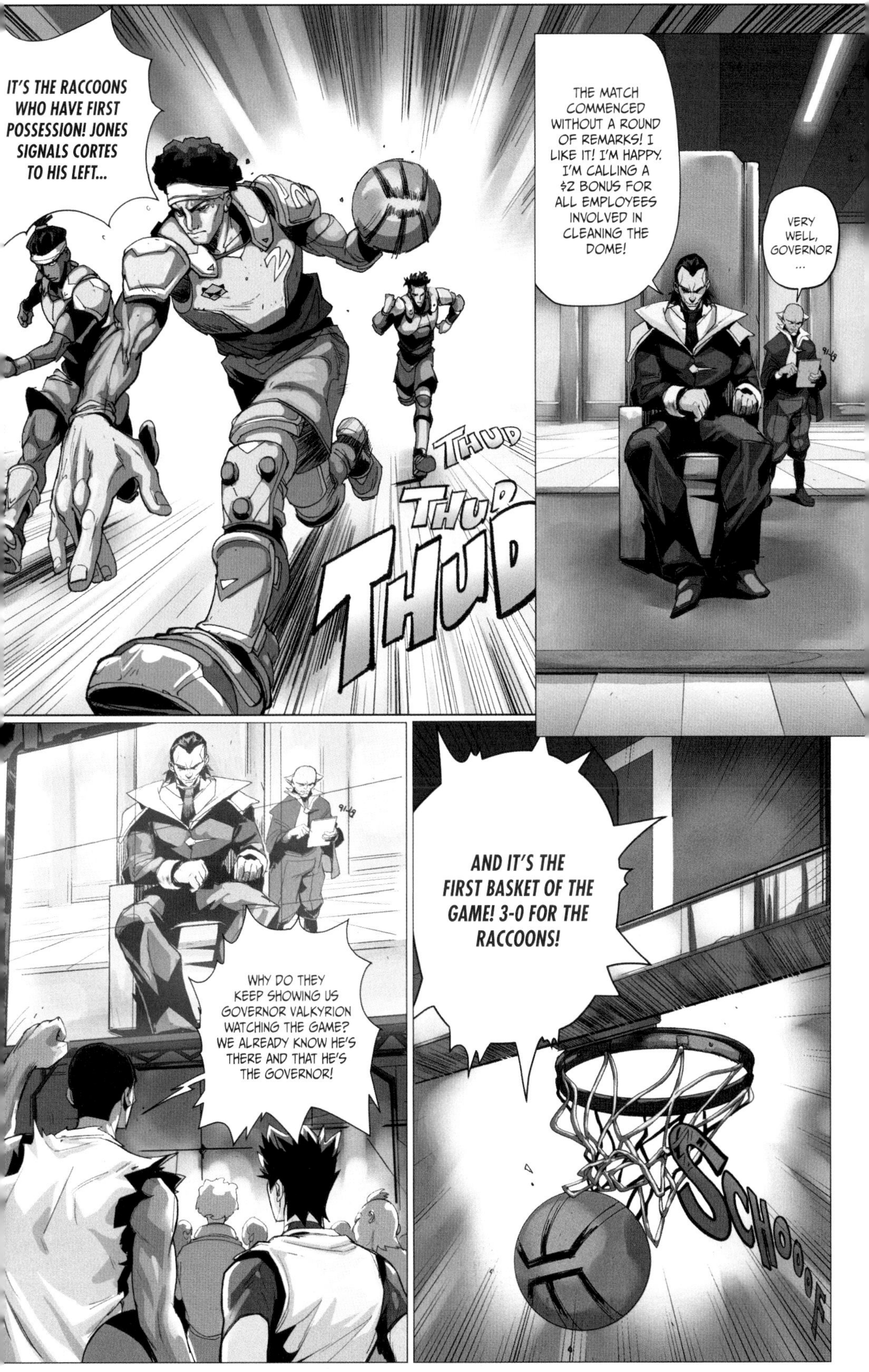
IT'S THE RACCOONS WHO HAVE FIRST POSSESSION! JONES SIGNALS CORTES TO HIS LEFT...
THUD
THUD
THUD
THE MATCH COMMENCED WITHOUT A ROUND OF REMARKS! I LIKE IT! I'M HAPPY. I'M CALLING A $2 BONUS FOR ALL EMPLOYEES INVOLVED IN CLEANING THE DOME!
VERY WELL, GOVERNOR ...
WHY DO THEY KEEP SHOWING US GOVERNOR VALKYRION WATCHING THE GAME? WE ALREADY KNOW HE'S THERE AND THAT HE'S THE GOVERNOR!
AND IT'S THE FIRST BASKET OF THE GAME! 3-0 FOR THE RACCOONS!
SCHOOOF

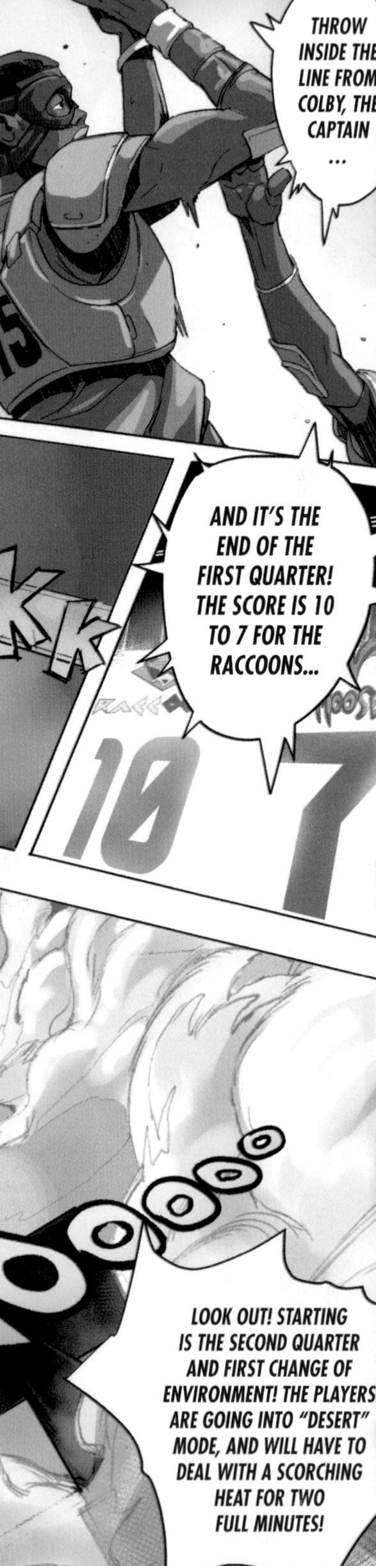
THROW INSIDE THE LINE FROM COLBY, THE CAPTAIN ...
AND IT'S THE END OF THE FIRST QUARTER! THE SCORE IS 10 TO 7 FOR THE RACCOONS...
10
7
LOOK OUT! STARTING IS THE SECOND QUARTER AND FIRST CHANGE OF ENVIRONMENT! THE PLAYERS ARE GOING INTO "DESERT" MODE, AND WILL HAVE TO DEAL WITH A SCORCHING HEAT FOR TWO FULL MINUTES!

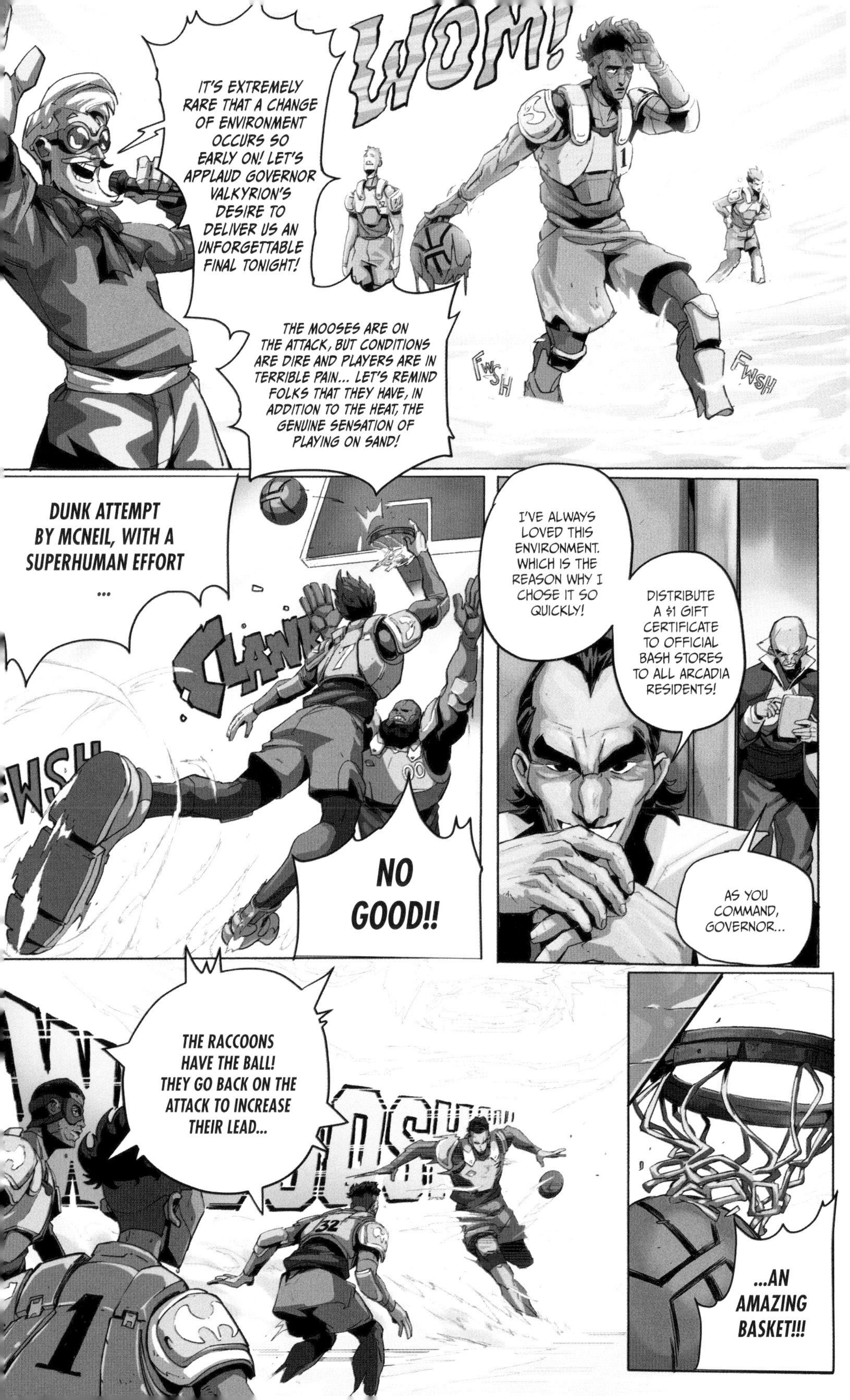
WOM!
IT'S EXTREMELY RARE THAT A CHANGE OF ENVIRONMENT OCCURS SO EARLY ON! LET'S APPLAUD GOVERNOR VALKYRION'S DESIRE TO DELIVER US AN UNFORGETTABLE FINAL TONIGHT!
THE MOOSES ARE ON THE ATTACK, BUT CONDITIONS ARE DIRE AND PLAYERS ARE IN TERRIBLE PAIN... LET'S REMIND FOLKS THAT THEY HAVE, IN ADDITION TO THE HEAT, THE GENUINE SENSATION OF PLAYING ON SAND!
FWSH
FWSH
DUNK ATTEMPT BY MCNEIL, WITH A SUPERHUMAN EFFORT ...
NO GOOD!!
I'VE ALWAYS LOVED THIS ENVIRONMENT. WHICH IS THE REASON WHY I CHOSE IT SO QUICKLY!
DISTRIBUTE A $1 GIFT CERTIFICATE TO OFFICIAL BASH STORES TO ALL ARCADIA RESIDENTS!
AS YOU COMMAND, GOVERNOR...
THE RACCOONS HAVE THE BALL! THEY GO BACK ON THE ATTACK TO INCREASE THEIR LEAD...
...AN AMAZING BASKET!!!

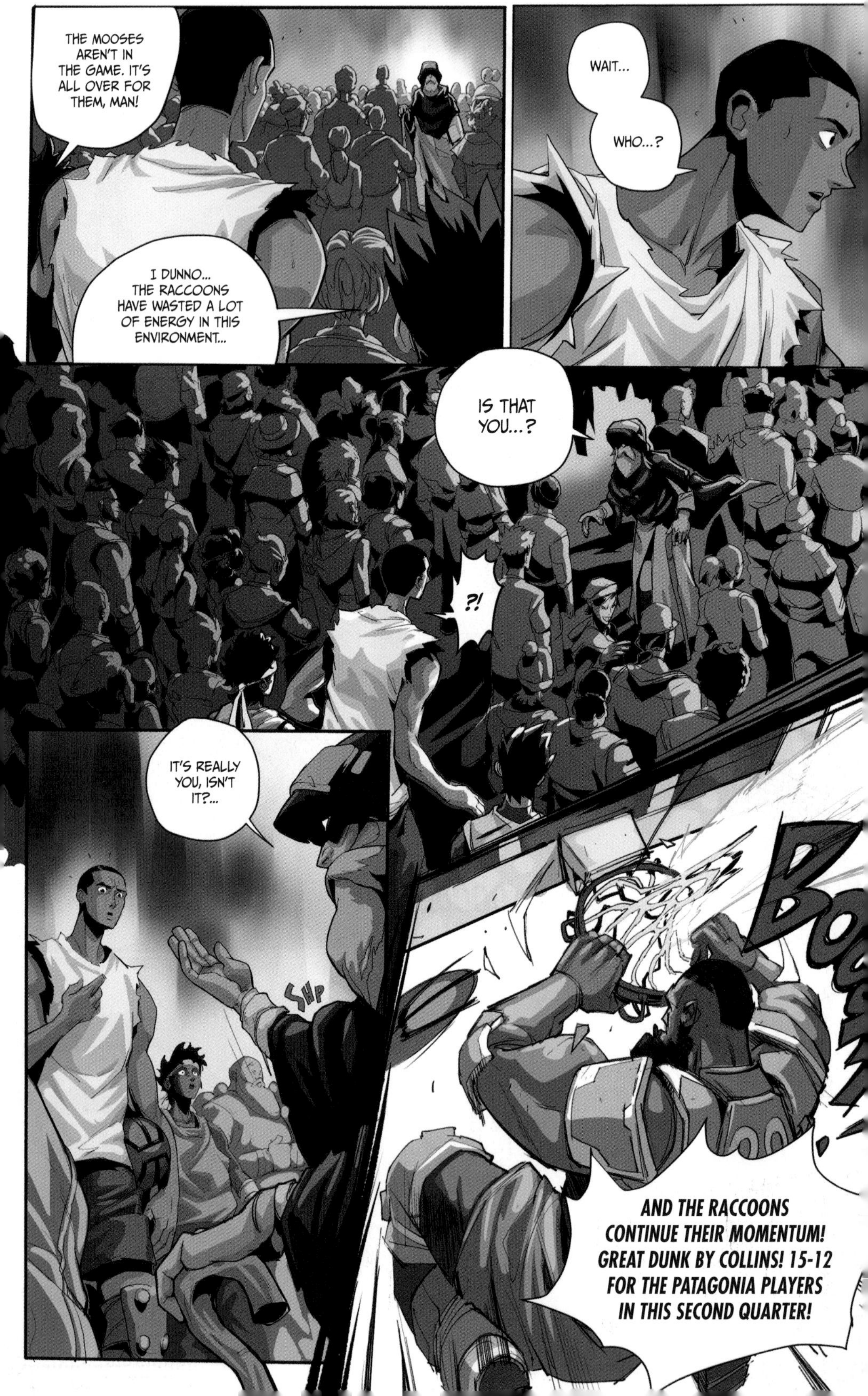
THE MOOSES AREN'T IN THE GAME. IT'S ALL OVER FOR THEM, MAN!
I DUNNO... THE RACCOONS HAVE WASTED A LOT OF ENERGY IN THIS ENVIRONMENT...
WAIT...
WHO...?
IS THAT YOU...?
?!
IT'S REALLY YOU, ISN'T IT?...
SHP
BOOM
AND THE RACCOONS CONTINUE THEIR MOMENTUM! GREAT DUNK BY COLLINS! 15-12 FOR THE PATAGONIA PLAYERS IN THIS SECOND QUARTER!

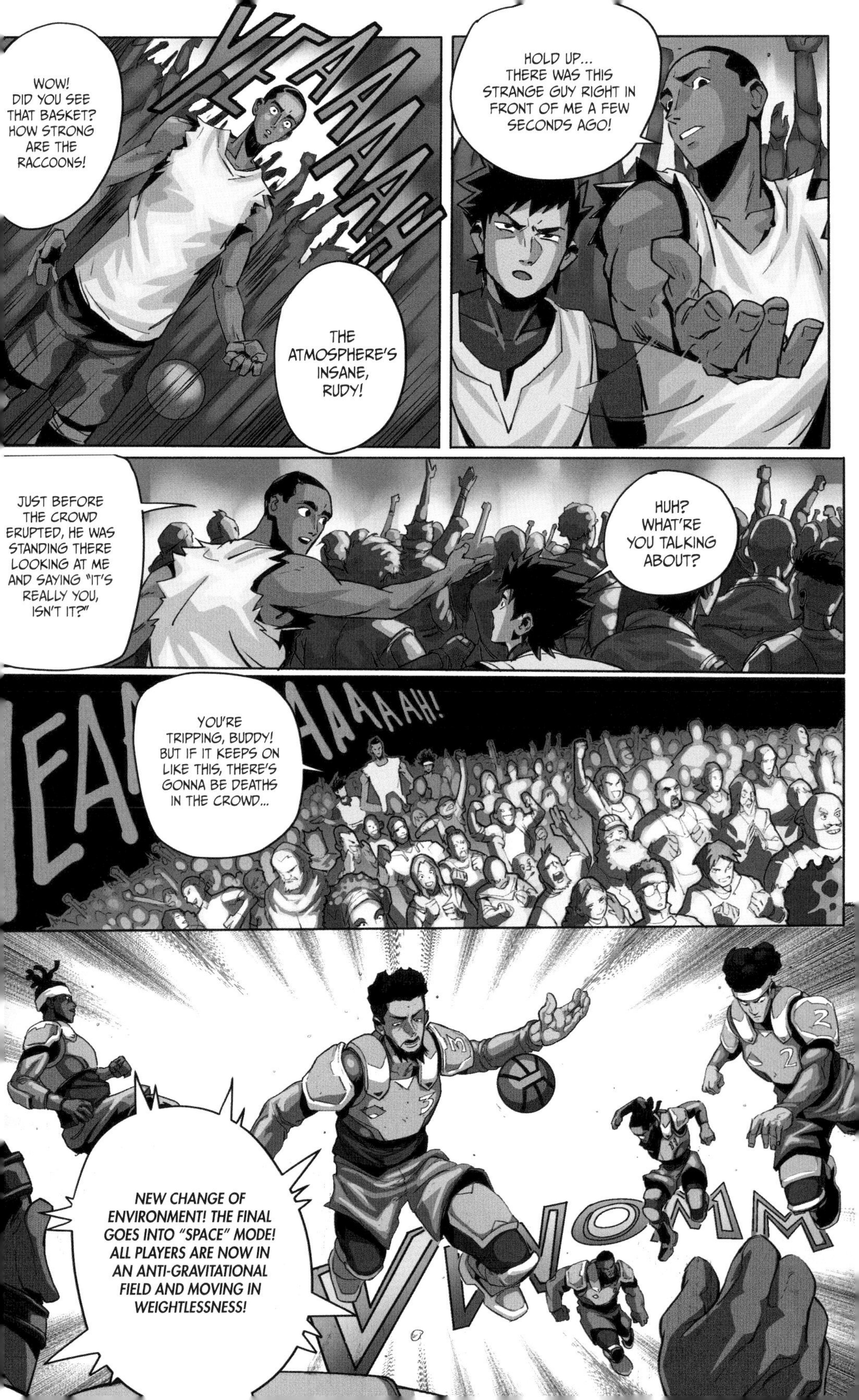
YEAAAAAAH!
WOW! DID YOU SEE THAT BASKET? HOW STRONG ARE THE RACCOONS!
THE ATMOSPHERE'S INSANE, RUDY!
HOLD UP... THERE WAS THIS STRANGE GUY RIGHT IN FRONT OF ME A FEW SECONDS AGO!
JUST BEFORE THE CROWD ERUPTED, HE WAS STANDING THERE LOOKING AT ME AND SAYING "IT'S REALLY YOU, ISN'T IT?"
HUH? WHAT'RE YOU TALKING ABOUT?
YOU'RE TRIPPING, BUDDY! BUT IF IT KEEPS ON LIKE THIS, THERE'S GONNA BE DEATHS IN THE CROWD...
AAAAAH!
NEW CHANGE OF ENVIRONMENT! THE FINAL GOES INTO "SPACE" MODE! ALL PLAYERS ARE NOW IN AN ANTI-GRAVITATIONAL FIELD AND MOVING IN WEIGHTLESSNESS!
VWOMM

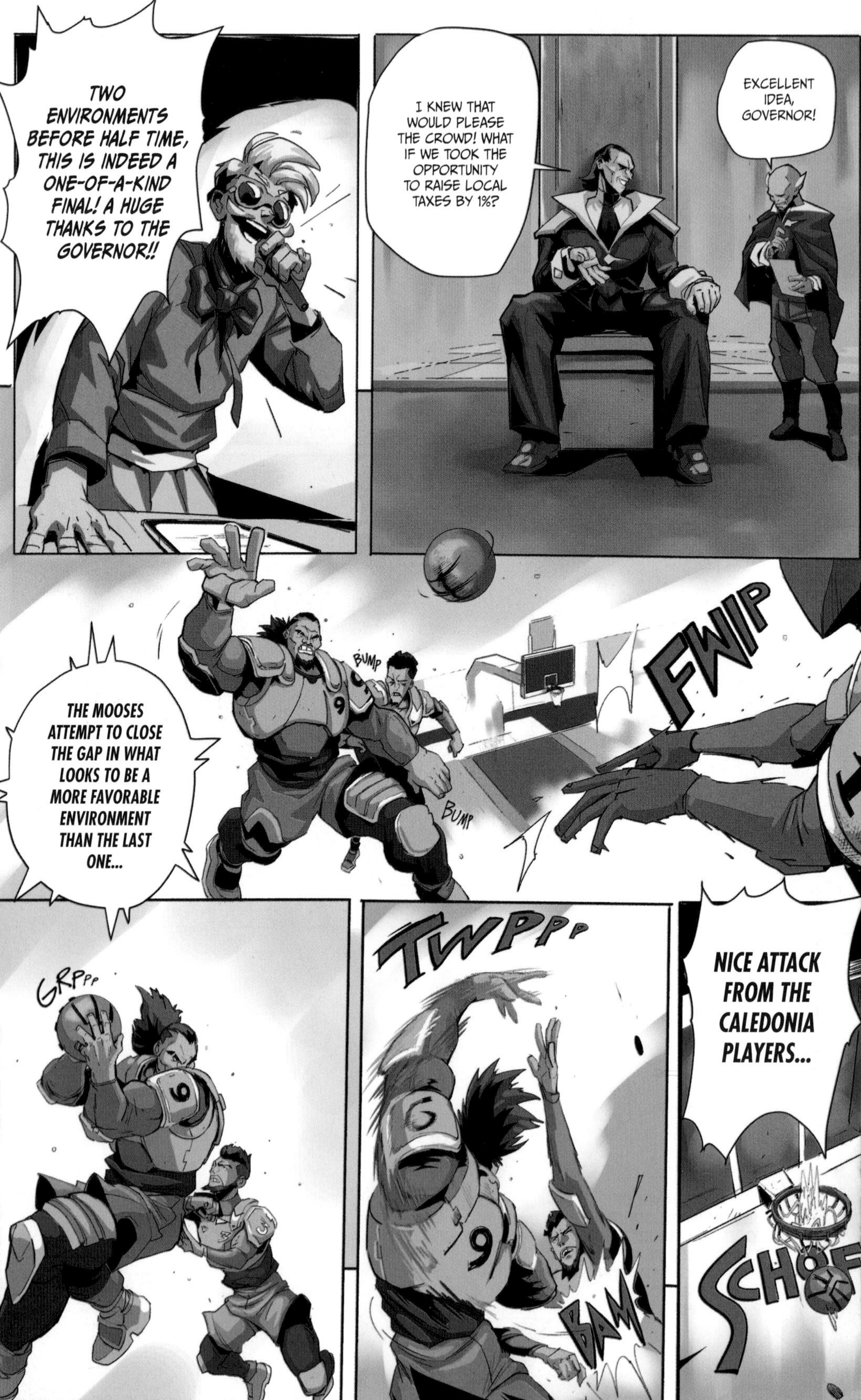
TWO ENVIRONMENTS BEFORE HALF TIME, THIS IS INDEED A ONE-OF-A-KIND FINAL! A HUGE THANKS TO THE GOVERNOR!!
I KNEW THAT WOULD PLEASE THE CROWD! WHAT IF WE TOOK THE OPPORTUNITY TO RAISE LOCAL TAXES BY 1%?
EXCELLENT IDEA, GOVERNOR!
THE MOOSES ATTEMPT TO CLOSE THE GAP IN WHAT LOOKS TO BE A MORE FAVORABLE ENVIRONMENT THAN THE LAST ONE...
BUMP
BUMP
FWIP
GRPPP
TWPPP
BAM
NICE ATTACK FROM THE CALEDONIA PLAYERS...
SCHOF

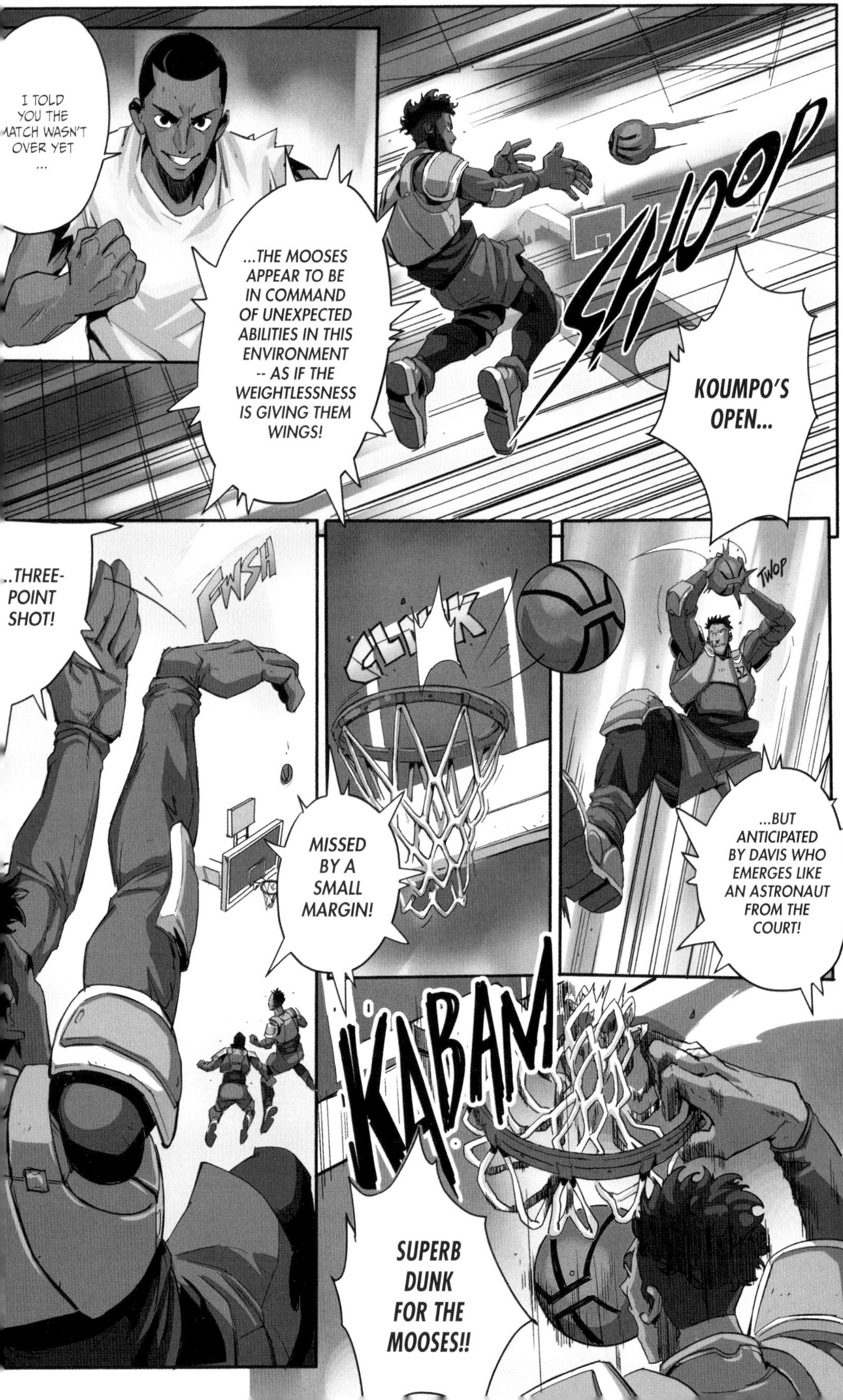
I TOLD YOU THE MATCH WASN'T OVER YET ...
...THE MOOSES APPEAR TO BE IN COMMAND OF UNEXPECTED ABILITIES IN THIS ENVIRONMENT -- AS IF THE WEIGHTLESSNESS IS GIVING THEM WINGS!
SHOOP
KOUMPO'S OPEN...
..THREE-POINT SHOT!
FWSH
MISSED BY A SMALL MARGIN!
TWOP
...BUT ANTICIPATED BY DAVIS WHO EMERGES LIKE AN ASTRONAUT FROM THE COURT!
KABAM
SUPERB DUNK FOR THE MOOSES!!

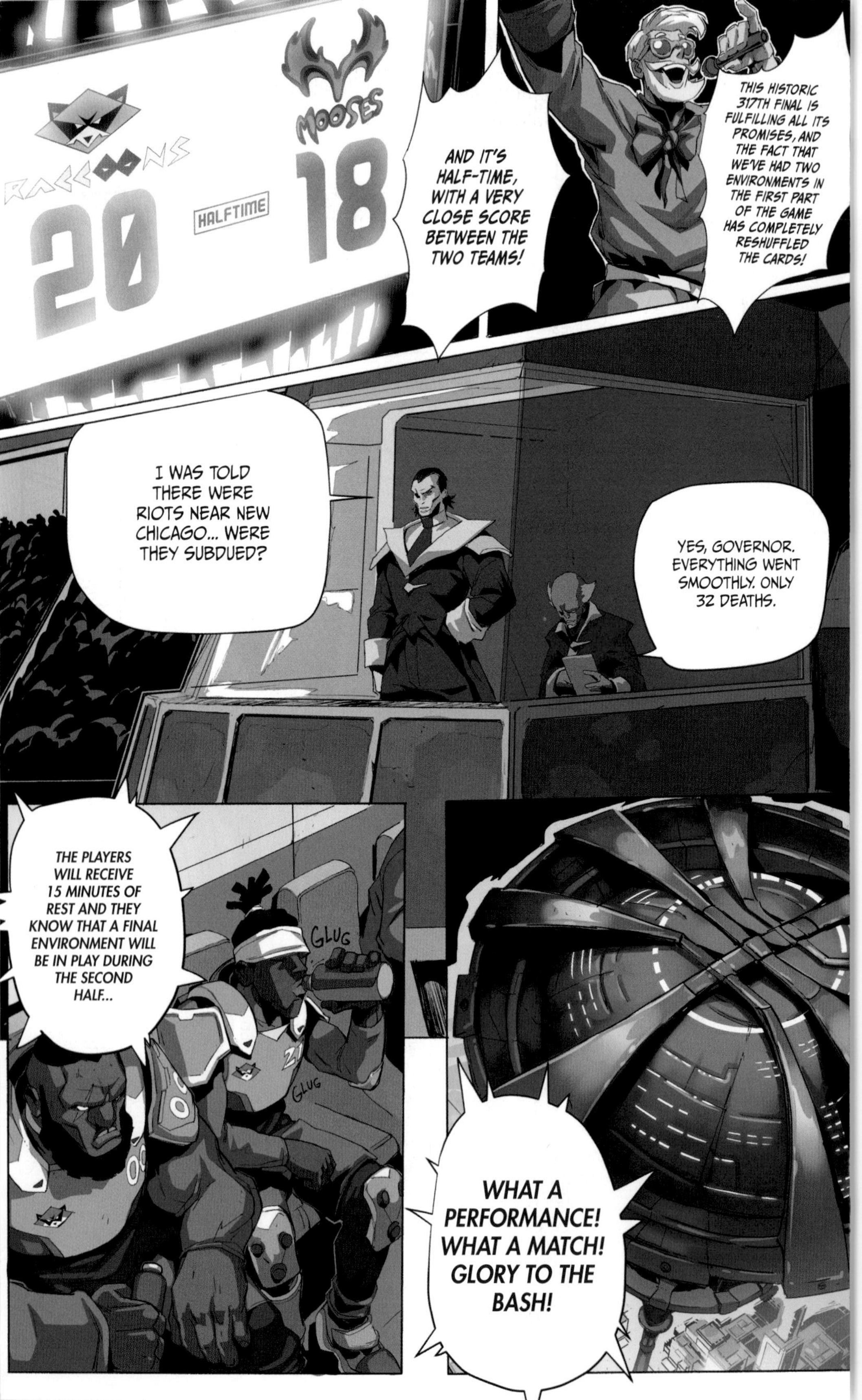
RACCOONS
MOOSES
20
HALFTIME
18
AND IT'S HALF-TIME, WITH A VERY CLOSE SCORE BETWEEN THE TWO TEAMS!
THIS HISTORIC 317TH FINAL IS FULFILLING ALL ITS PROMISES, AND THE FACT THAT WE'VE HAD TWO ENVIRONMENTS IN THE FIRST PART OF THE GAME HAS COMPLETELY RESHUFFLED THE CARDS!
I WAS TOLD THERE WERE RIOTS NEAR NEW CHICAGO... WERE THEY SUBDUED?
YES, GOVERNOR. EVERYTHING WENT SMOOTHLY. ONLY 32 DEATHS.
THE PLAYERS WILL RECEIVE 15 MINUTES OF REST AND THEY KNOW THAT A FINAL ENVIRONMENT WILL BE IN PLAY DURING THE SECOND HALF...
GLUG
GLUG
WHAT A PERFORMANCE! WHAT A MATCH! GLORY TO THE BASH!

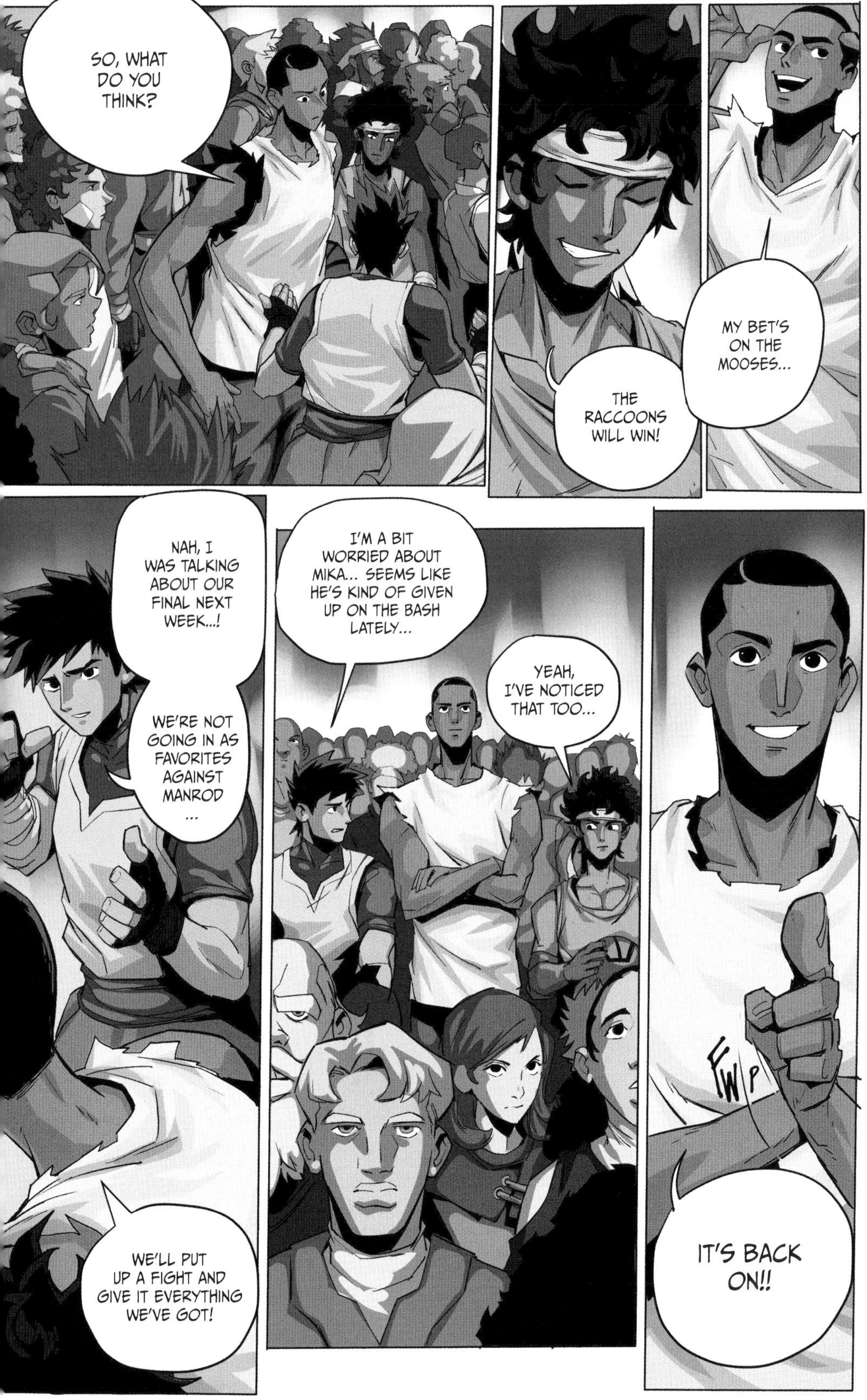
SO, WHAT DO YOU THINK?
MY BET'S ON THE MOOSES...
THE RACCOONS WILL WIN!
NAH, I WAS TALKING ABOUT OUR FINAL NEXT WEEK...!
WE'RE NOT GOING IN AS FAVORITES AGAINST MANROD ...
WE'LL PUT UP A FIGHT AND GIVE IT EVERYTHING WE'VE GOT!
I'M A BIT WORRIED ABOUT MIKA... SEEMS LIKE HE'S KIND OF GIVEN UP ON THE BASH LATELY...
YEAH, I'VE NOTICED THAT TOO...
FWP
IT'S BACK ON!!

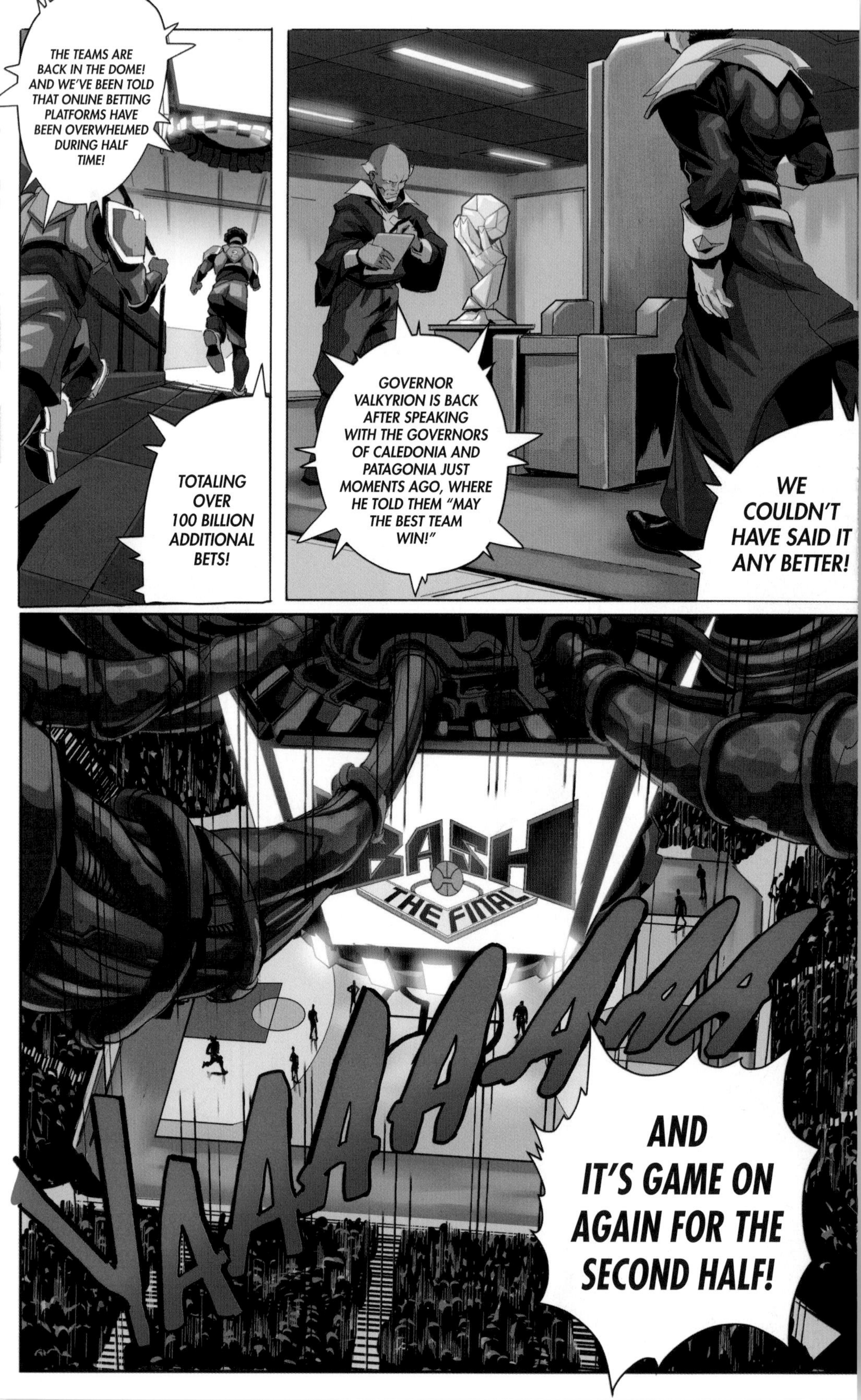
THE TEAMS ARE BACK IN THE DOME! AND WE'VE BEEN TOLD THAT ONLINE BETTING PLATFORMS HAVE BEEN OVERWHELMED DURING HALF TIME!
TOTALING OVER 100 BILLION ADDITIONAL BETS!
GOVERNOR VALKYRION IS BACK AFTER SPEAKING WITH THE GOVERNORS OF CALEDONIA AND PATAGONIA JUST MOMENTS AGO, WHERE HE TOLD THEM "MAY THE BEST TEAM WIN!"
WE COULDN'T HAVE SAID IT ANY BETTER!
BASH
THE FINAL
YAAAAAAAAA
AND IT'S GAME ON AGAIN FOR THE SECOND HALF!

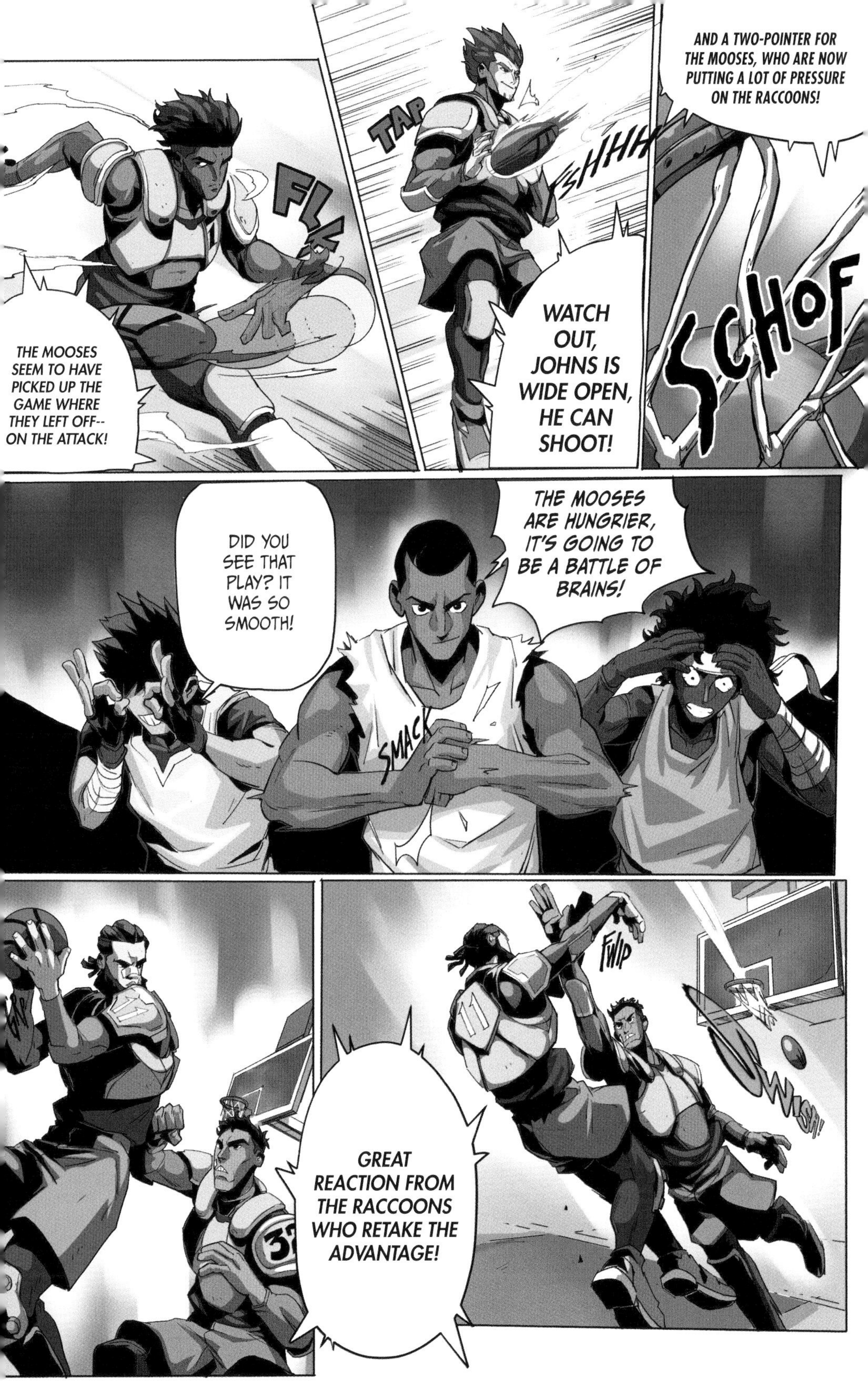
THE MOOSES SEEM TO HAVE PICKED UP THE GAME WHERE THEY LEFT OFF-- ON THE ATTACK!
FLIK
TAP
FSHHH
WATCH OUT, JOHNS IS WIDE OPEN, HE CAN SHOOT!
AND A TWO-POINTER FOR THE MOOSES, WHO ARE NOW PUTTING A LOT OF PRESSURE ON THE RACCOONS!
SCHOF
DID YOU SEE THAT PLAY? IT WAS SO SMOOTH!
THE MOOSES ARE HUNGRIER, IT'S GOING TO BE A BATTLE OF BRAINS!
SMACK
GREAT REACTION FROM THE RACCOONS WHO RETAKE THE ADVANTAGE!
FWIP
SWISH!

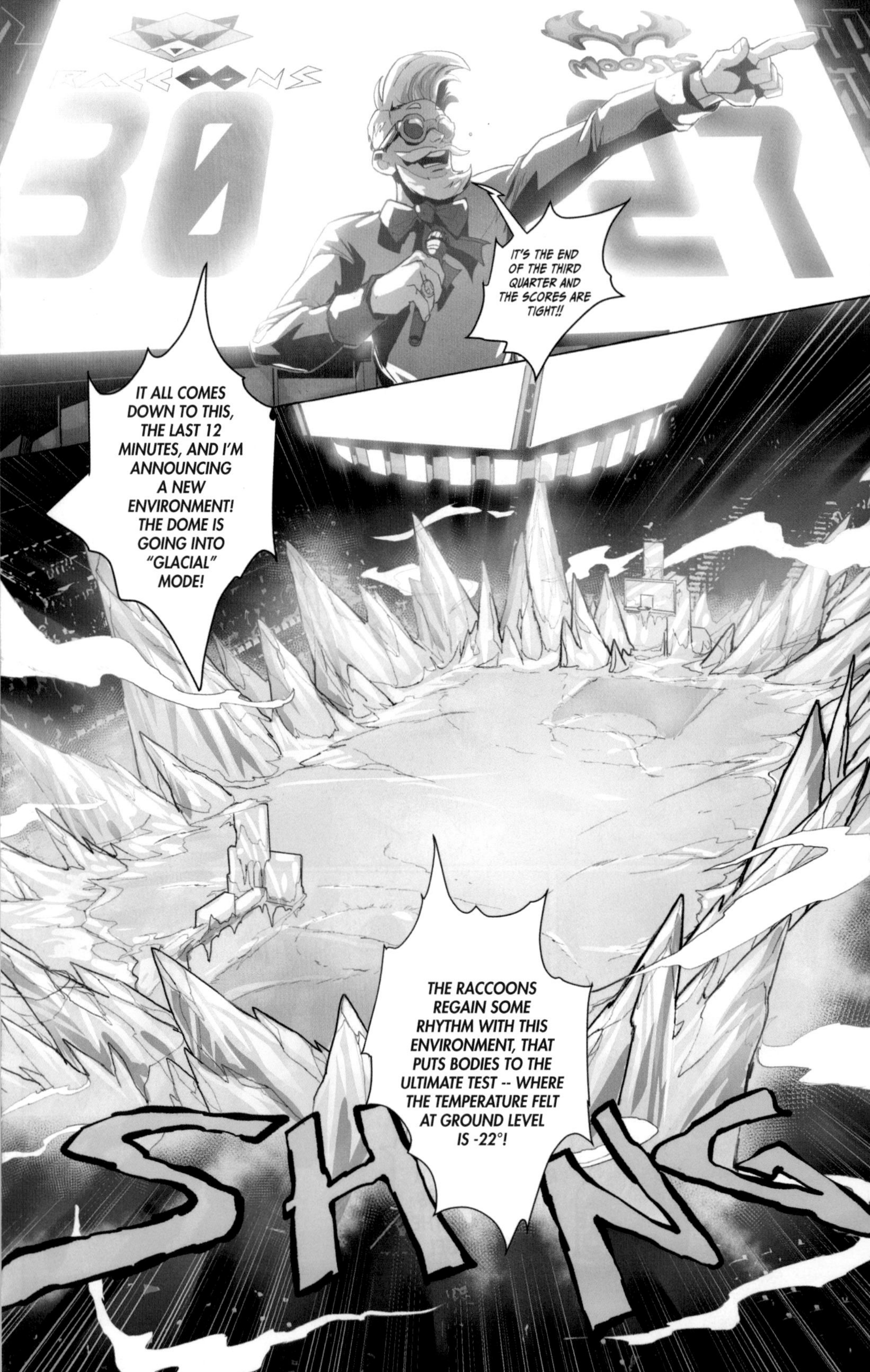
RACCOONS
30
MOOSES
27
IT'S THE END OF THE THIRD QUARTER AND THE SCORES ARE TIGHT!!
IT ALL COMES DOWN TO THIS, THE LAST 12 MINUTES, AND I'M ANNOUNCING A NEW ENVIRONMENT! THE DOME IS GOING INTO "GLACIAL" MODE!
THE RACCOONS REGAIN SOME RHYTHM WITH THIS ENVIRONMENT, THAT PUTS BODIES TO THE ULTIMATE TEST -- WHERE THE TEMPERATURE FELT AT GROUND LEVEL IS -22°!
SHING

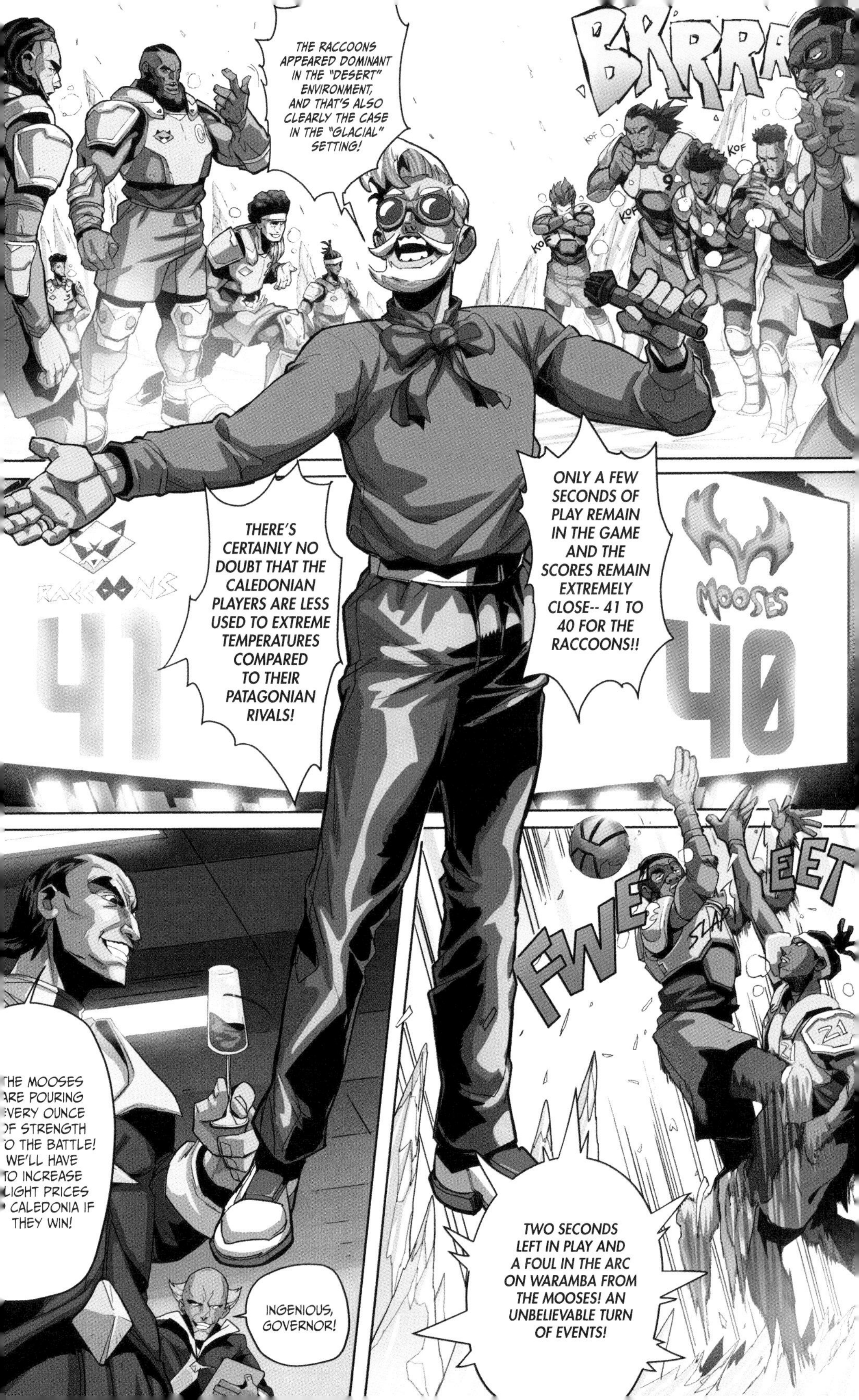
BKRRR
THE RACCOONS APPEARED DOMINANT IN THE "DESERT" ENVIRONMENT, AND THAT'S ALSO CLEARLY THE CASE IN THE "GLACIAL" SETTING!
KOF
KOF
KOF
KOF
RACCOONS
41
THERE'S CERTAINLY NO DOUBT THAT THE CALEDONIAN PLAYERS ARE LESS USED TO EXTREME TEMPERATURES COMPARED TO THEIR PATAGONIAN RIVALS!
ONLY A FEW SECONDS OF PLAY REMAIN IN THE GAME AND THE SCORES REMAIN EXTREMELY CLOSE-- 41 TO 40 FOR THE RACCOONS!!
MOOSES
40
THE MOOSES ARE POURING EVERY OUNCE OF STRENGTH TO THE BATTLE! WE'LL HAVE TO INCREASE LIGHT PRICES CALEDONIA IF THEY WIN!
INGENIOUS, GOVERNOR!
FWEEET
SLAP
TWO SECONDS LEFT IN PLAY AND A FOUL IN THE ARC ON WARAMBA FROM THE MOOSES! AN UNBELIEVABLE TURN OF EVENTS!

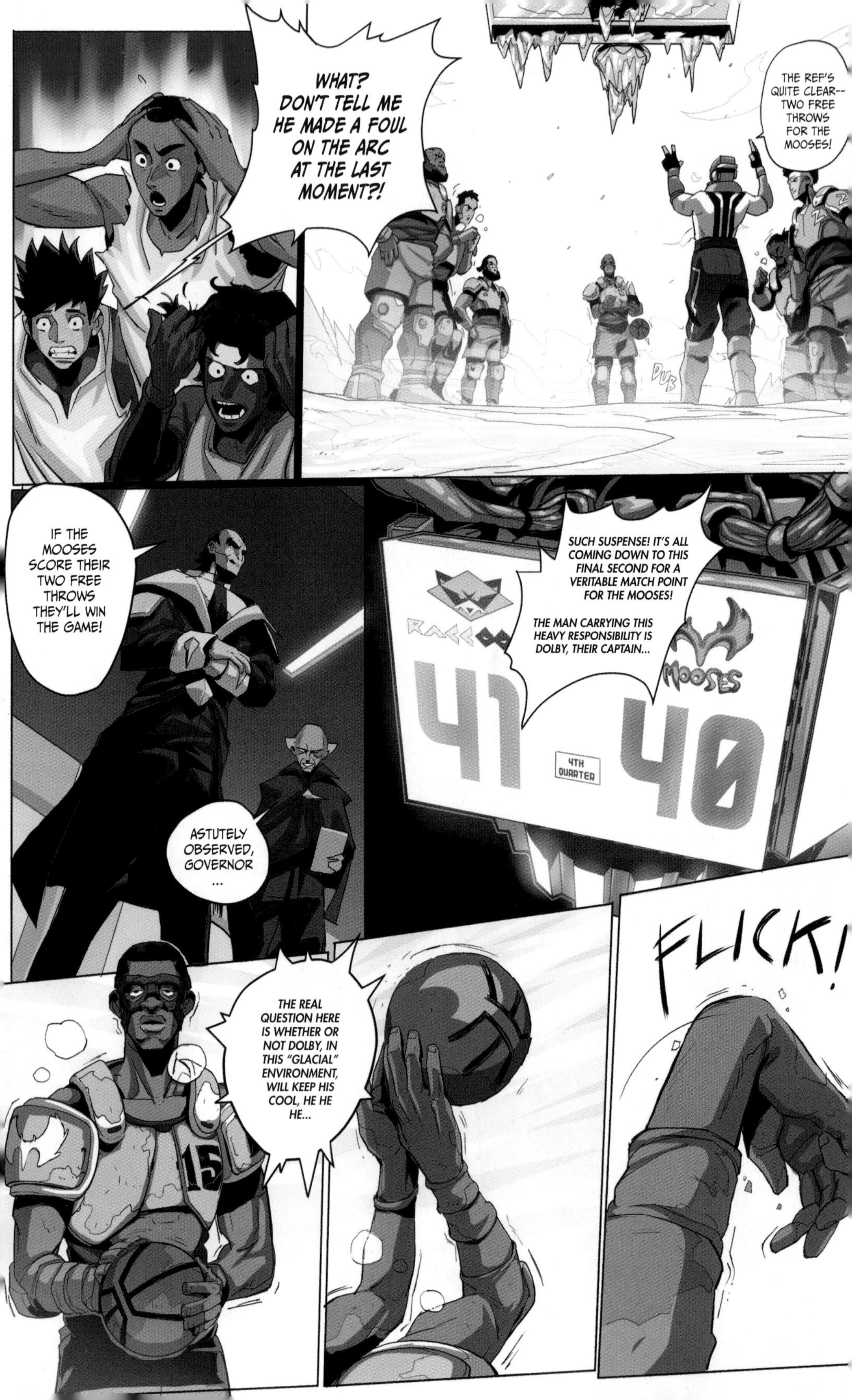
WHAT? DON'T TELL ME HE MADE A FOUL ON THE ARC AT THE LAST MOMENT?!
THE REF'S QUITE CLEAR-- TWO FREE THROWS FOR THE MOOSES!
DUB
IF THE MOOSES SCORE THEIR TWO FREE THROWS THEY'LL WIN THE GAME!
ASTUTELY OBSERVED, GOVERNOR ...
SUCH SUSPENSE! IT'S ALL COMING DOWN TO THIS FINAL SECOND FOR A VERITABLE MATCH POINT FOR THE MOOSES!
THE MAN CARRYING THIS HEAVY RESPONSIBILITY IS DOLBY, THEIR CAPTAIN...
MOOSES
41
4TH QUARTER
40
THE REAL QUESTION HERE IS WHETHER OR NOT DOLBY, IN THIS "GLACIAL" ENVIRONMENT, WILL KEEP HIS COOL, HE HE HE...
15
FLICK!

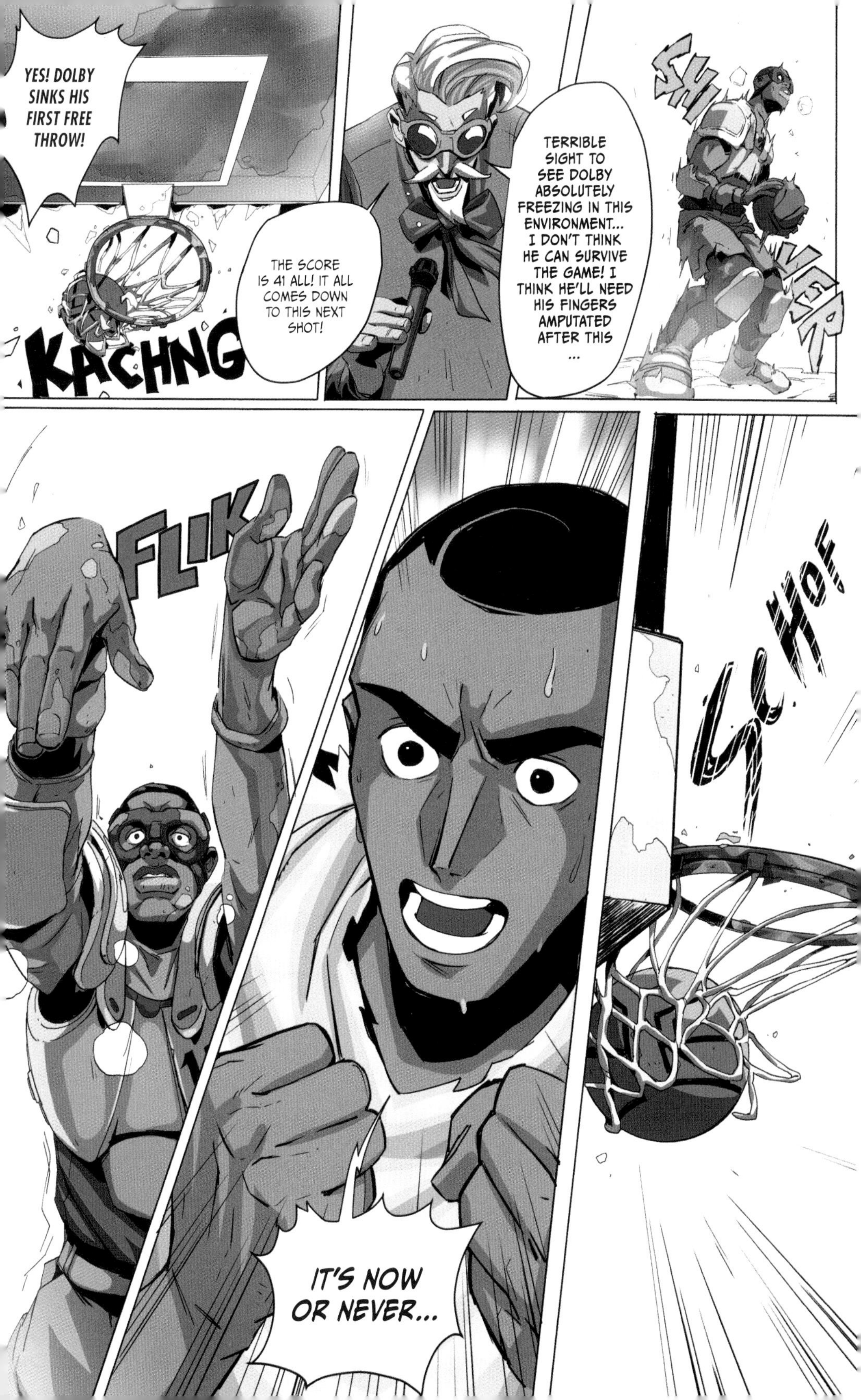
YES! DOLBY SINKS HIS FIRST FREE THROW!
KACHNG
THE SCORE IS 41 ALL! IT ALL COMES DOWN TO THIS NEXT SHOT!
TERRIBLE SIGHT TO SEE DOLBY ABSOLUTELY FREEZING IN THIS ENVIRONMENT... I DON'T THINK HE CAN SURVIVE THE GAME! I THINK HE'LL NEED HIS FINGERS AMPUTATED AFTER THIS ...
SHIVVER
FLIK
SCHOF!
IT'S NOW OR NEVER...

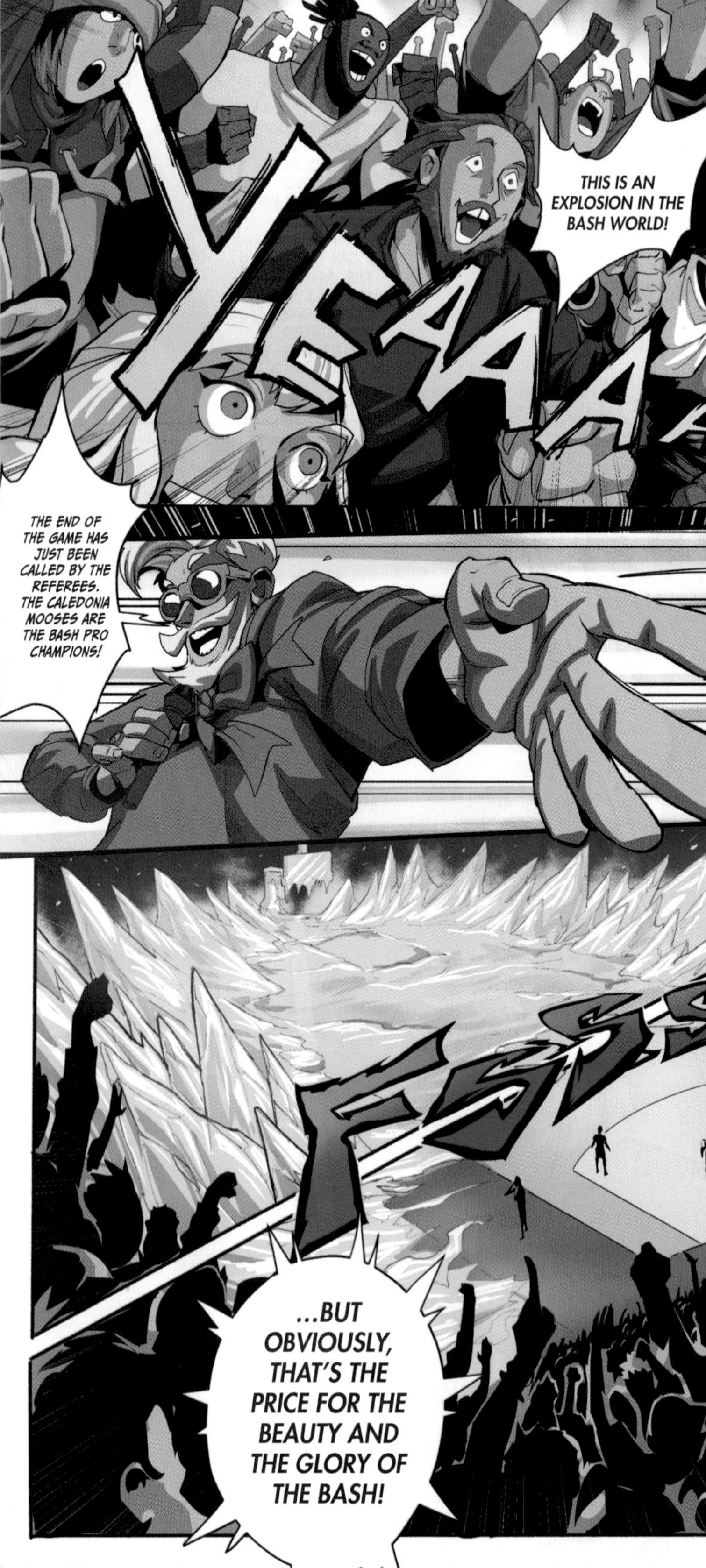
YEAAAA
THIS IS AN EXPLOSION IN THE BASH WORLD!
THE END OF THE GAME HAS JUST BEEN CALLED BY THE REFEREES. THE CALEDONIA MOOSES ARE THE BASH PRO CHAMPIONS!
FSSS
...BUT OBVIOUSLY, THAT'S THE PRICE FOR THE BEAUTY AND THE GLORY OF THE BASH!

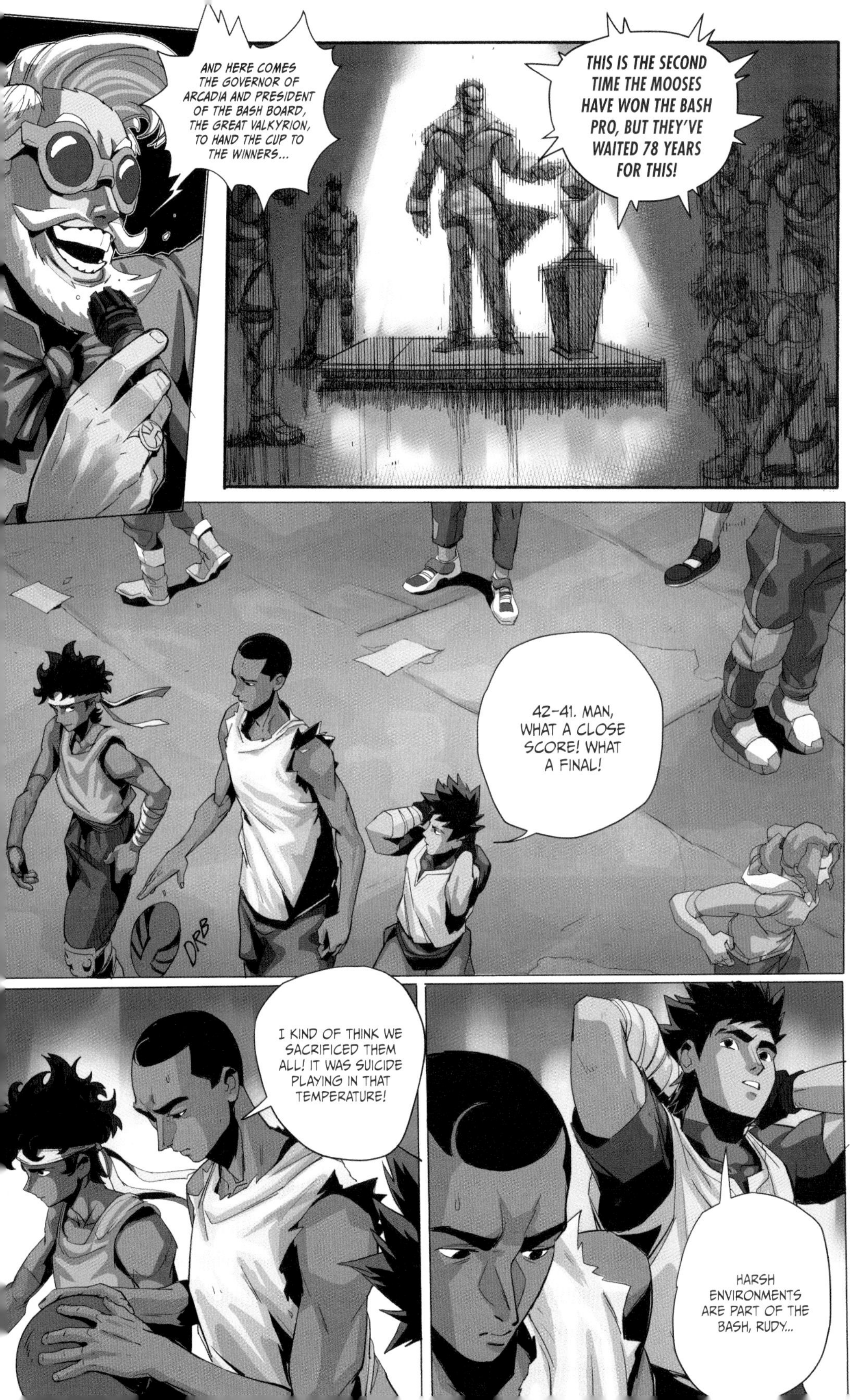
AND HERE COMES THE GOVERNOR OF ARCADIA AND PRESIDENT OF THE BASH BOARD, THE GREAT VALKYRION, TO HAND THE CUP TO THE WINNERS...
THIS IS THE SECOND TIME THE MOOSES HAVE WON THE BASH PRO, BUT THEY'VE WAITED 78 YEARS FOR THIS!
DRB
42-41. MAN, WHAT A CLOSE SCORE! WHAT A FINAL!
I KIND OF THINK WE SACRIFICED THEM ALL! IT WAS SUICIDE PLAYING IN THAT TEMPERATURE!
HARSH ENVIRONMENTS ARE PART OF THE BASH, RUDY...

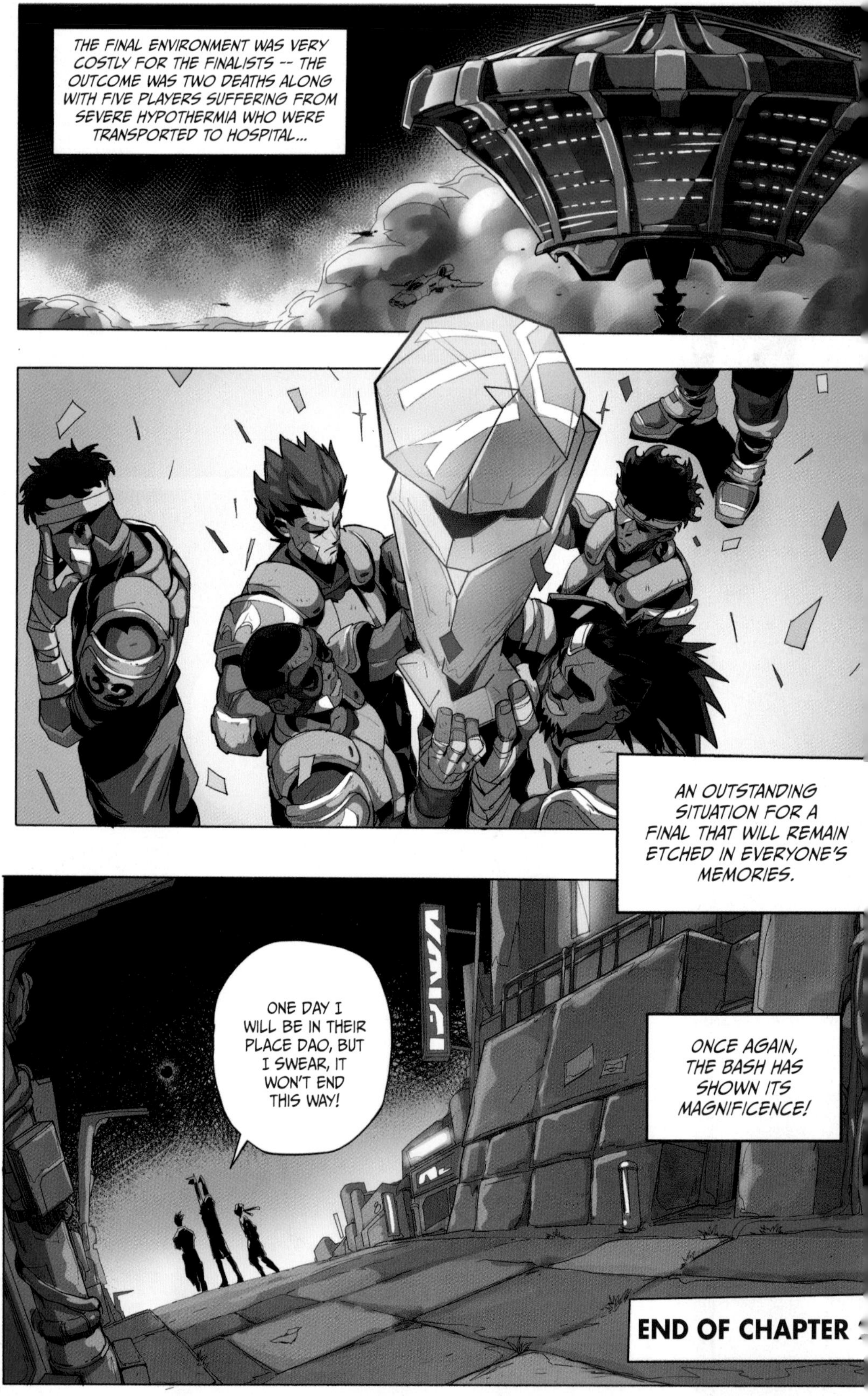
THE FINAL ENVIRONMENT WAS VERY COSTLY FOR THE FINALISTS -- THE OUTCOME WAS TWO DEATHS ALONG WITH FIVE PLAYERS SUFFERING FROM SEVERE HYPOTHERMIA WHO WERE TRANSPORTED TO HOSPITAL...
32
AN OUTSTANDING SITUATION FOR A FINAL THAT WILL REMAIN ETCHED IN EVERYONE'S MEMORIES.
ONE DAY I WILL BE IN THEIR PLACE DAO, BUT I SWEAR, IT WON'T END THIS WAY!
ONCE AGAIN, THE BASH HAS SHOWN ITS MAGNIFICENCE!
END OF CHAPTER

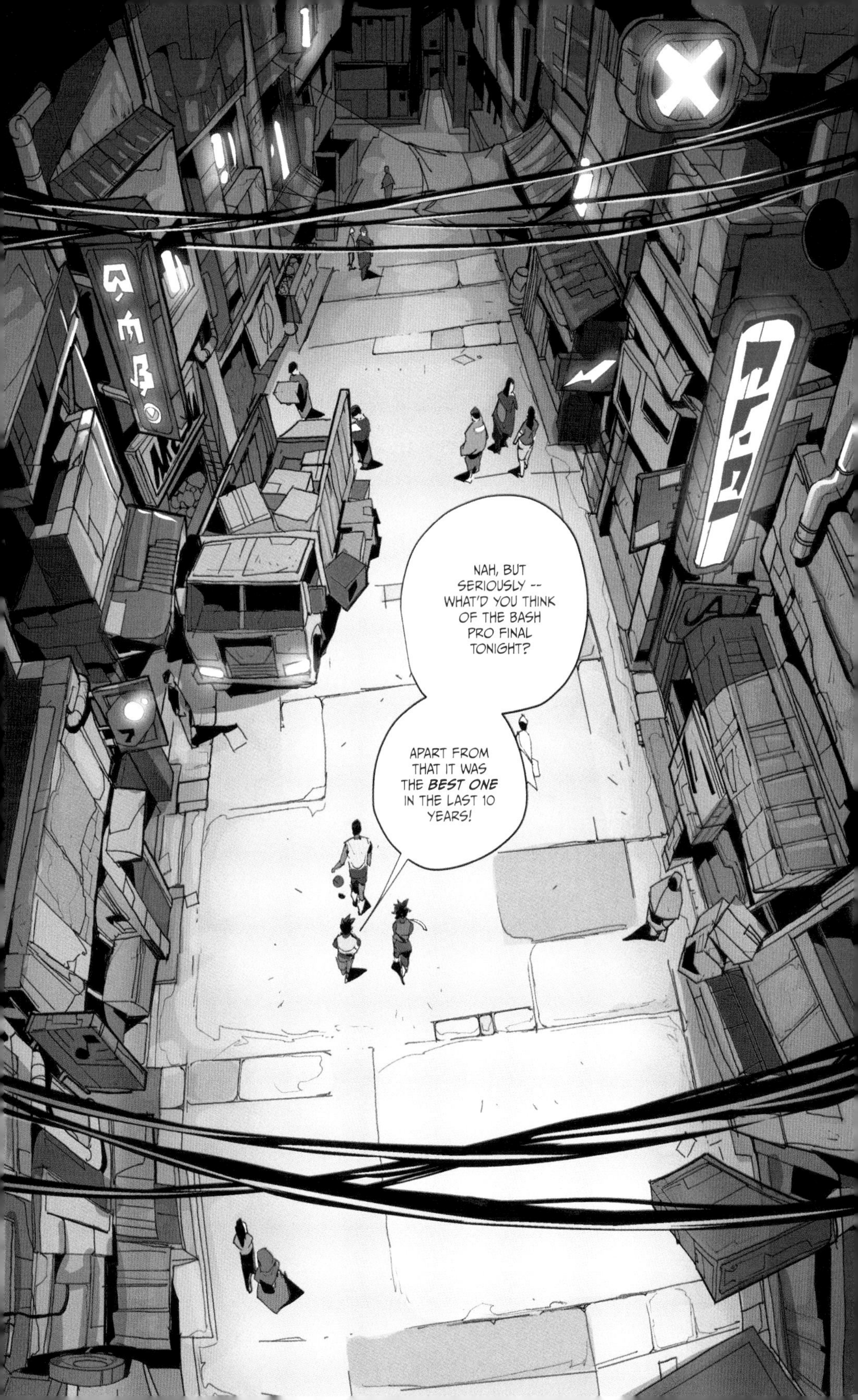
NAH, BUT SERIOUSLY -- WHAT'D YOU THINK OF THE BASH PRO FINAL TONIGHT?
APART FROM THAT IT WAS THE ***BEST ONE*** IN THE LAST 10 YEARS!

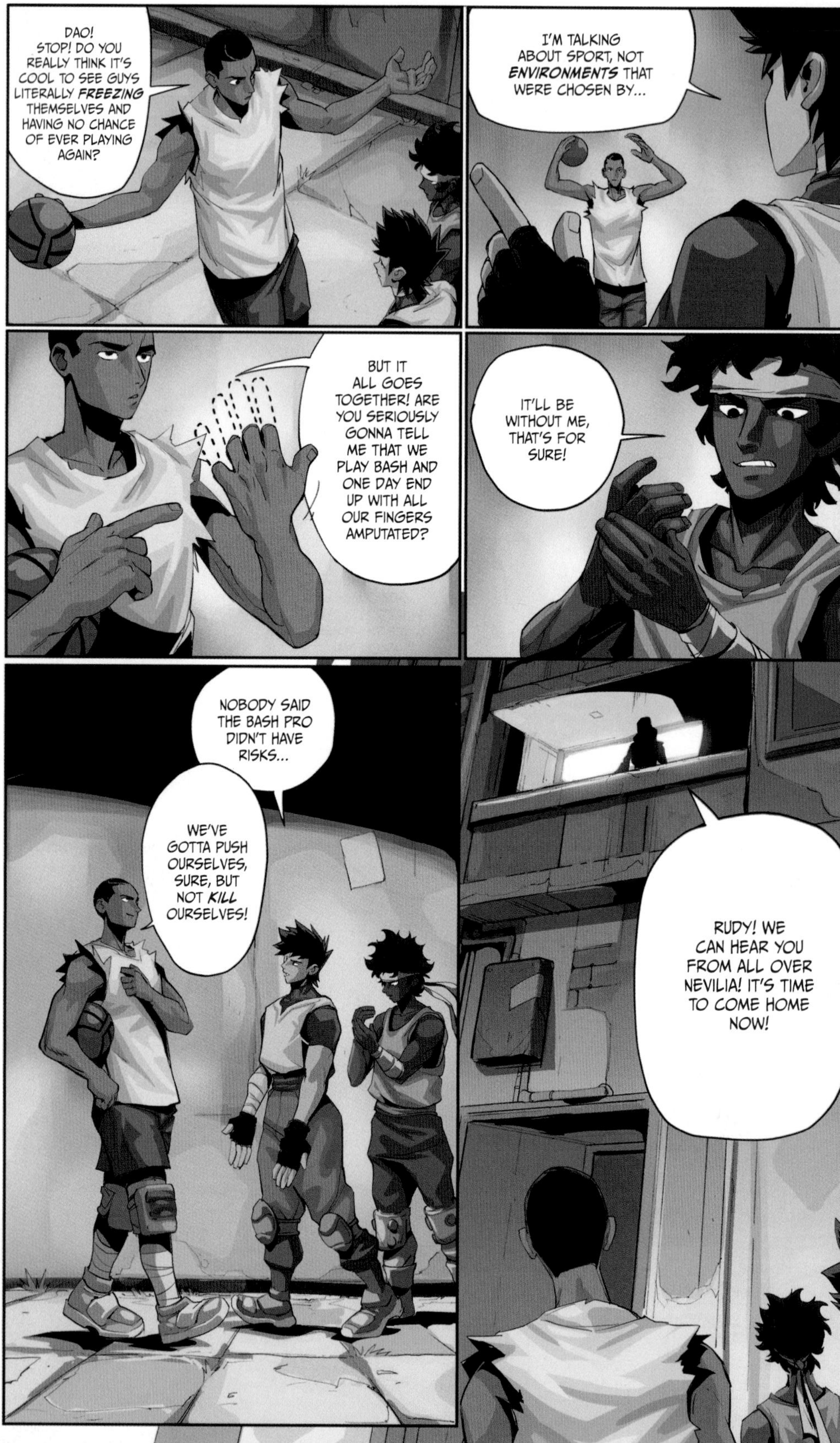
DAO! STOP! DO YOU REALLY THINK IT'S COOL TO SEE GUYS LITERALLY *FREEZING* THEMSELVES AND HAVING NO CHANCE OF EVER PLAYING AGAIN?
I'M TALKING ABOUT SPORT, NOT *ENVIRONMENTS* THAT WERE CHOSEN BY...
BUT IT ALL GOES TOGETHER! ARE YOU SERIOUSLY GONNA TELL ME THAT WE PLAY BASH AND ONE DAY END UP WITH ALL OUR FINGERS AMPUTATED?
IT'LL BE WITHOUT ME, THAT'S FOR SURE!
NOBODY SAID THE BASH PRO DIDN'T HAVE RISKS...
WE'VE GOTTA PUSH OURSELVES, SURE, BUT NOT *KILL* OURSELVES!
RUDY! WE CAN HEAR YOU FROM ALL OVER NEVILIA! IT'S TIME TO COME HOME NOW!

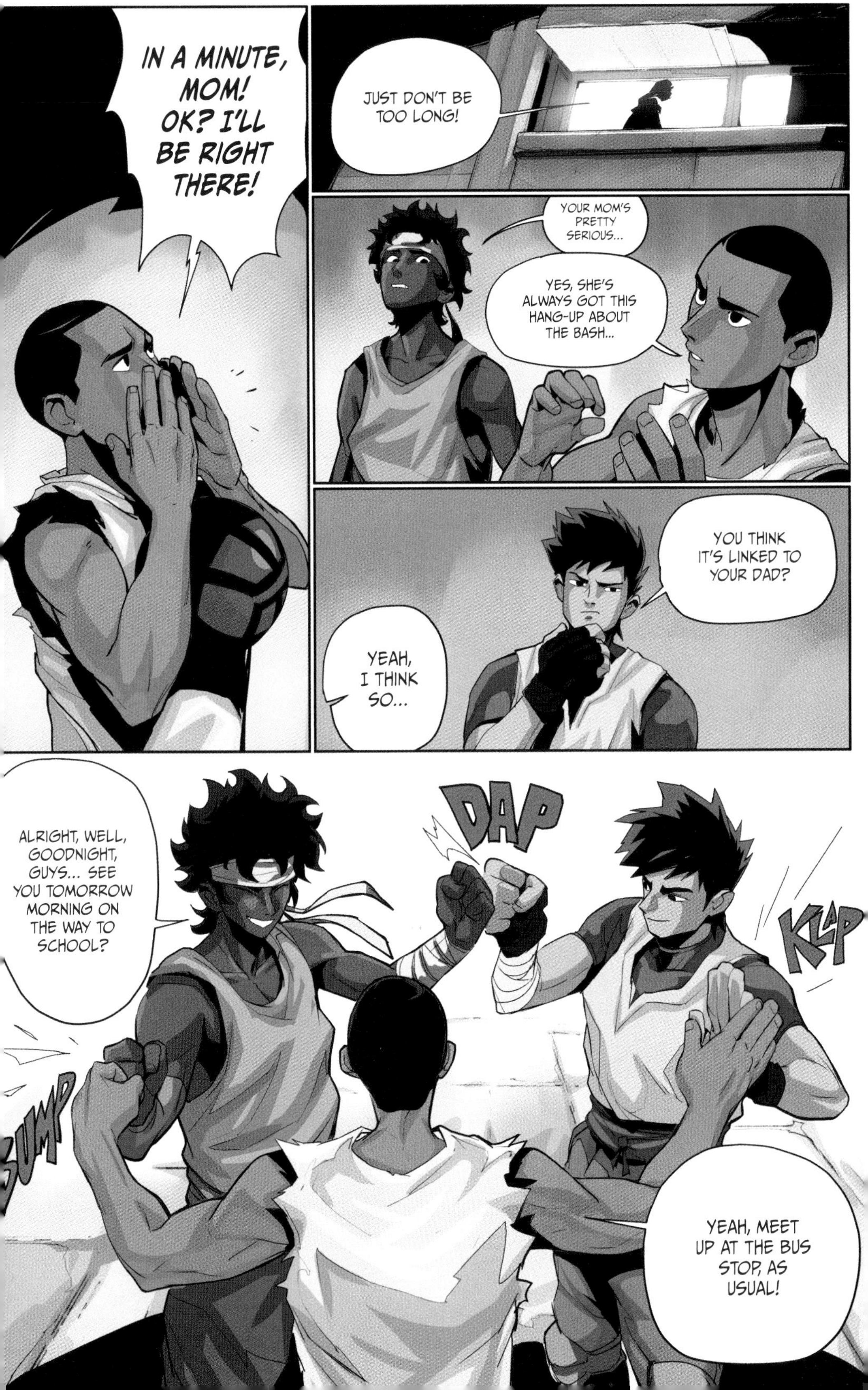
IN A MINUTE, MOM! OK? I'LL BE RIGHT THERE!
JUST DON'T BE TOO LONG!
YOUR MOM'S PRETTY SERIOUS...
YES, SHE'S ALWAYS GOT THIS HANG-UP ABOUT THE BASH...
YOU THINK IT'S LINKED TO YOUR DAD?
YEAH, I THINK SO...
ALRIGHT, WELL, GOODNIGHT, GUYS... SEE YOU TOMORROW MORNING ON THE WAY TO SCHOOL?
DAP
KLAP
BUMP
YEAH, MEET UP AT THE BUS STOP, AS USUAL!

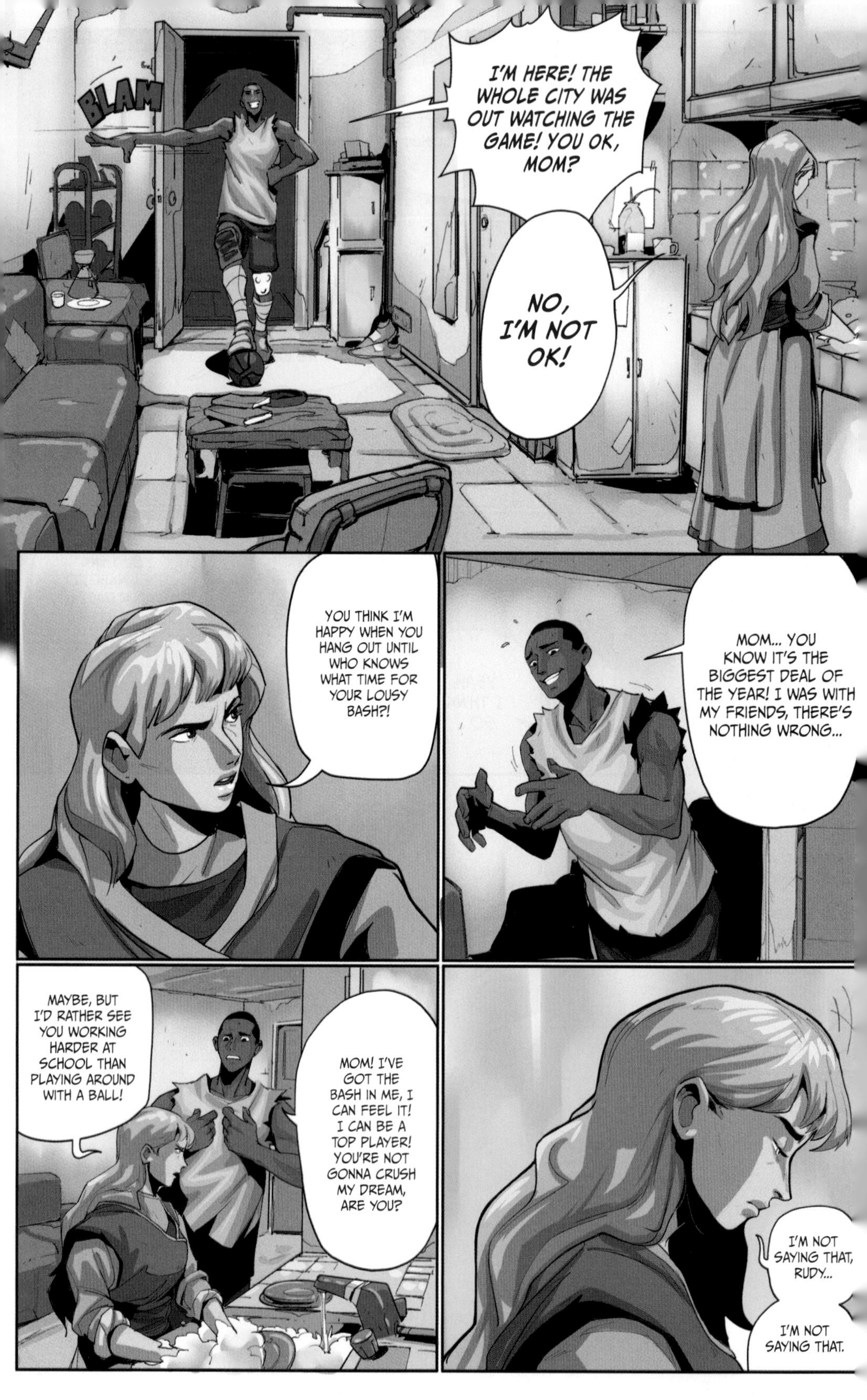
BLAM
I'M HERE! THE WHOLE CITY WAS OUT WATCHING THE GAME! YOU OK, MOM?
NO, I'M NOT OK!
YOU THINK I'M HAPPY WHEN YOU HANG OUT UNTIL WHO KNOWS WHAT TIME FOR YOUR LOUSY BASH?!
MOM... YOU KNOW IT'S THE BIGGEST DEAL OF THE YEAR! I WAS WITH MY FRIENDS, THERE'S NOTHING WRONG...
MAYBE, BUT I'D RATHER SEE YOU WORKING HARDER AT SCHOOL THAN PLAYING AROUND WITH A BALL!
MOM! I'VE GOT THE BASH IN ME, I CAN FEEL IT! I CAN BE A TOP PLAYER! YOU'RE NOT GONNA CRUSH MY DREAM, ARE YOU?
I'M NOT SAYING THAT, RUDY...
I'M NOT SAYING THAT.

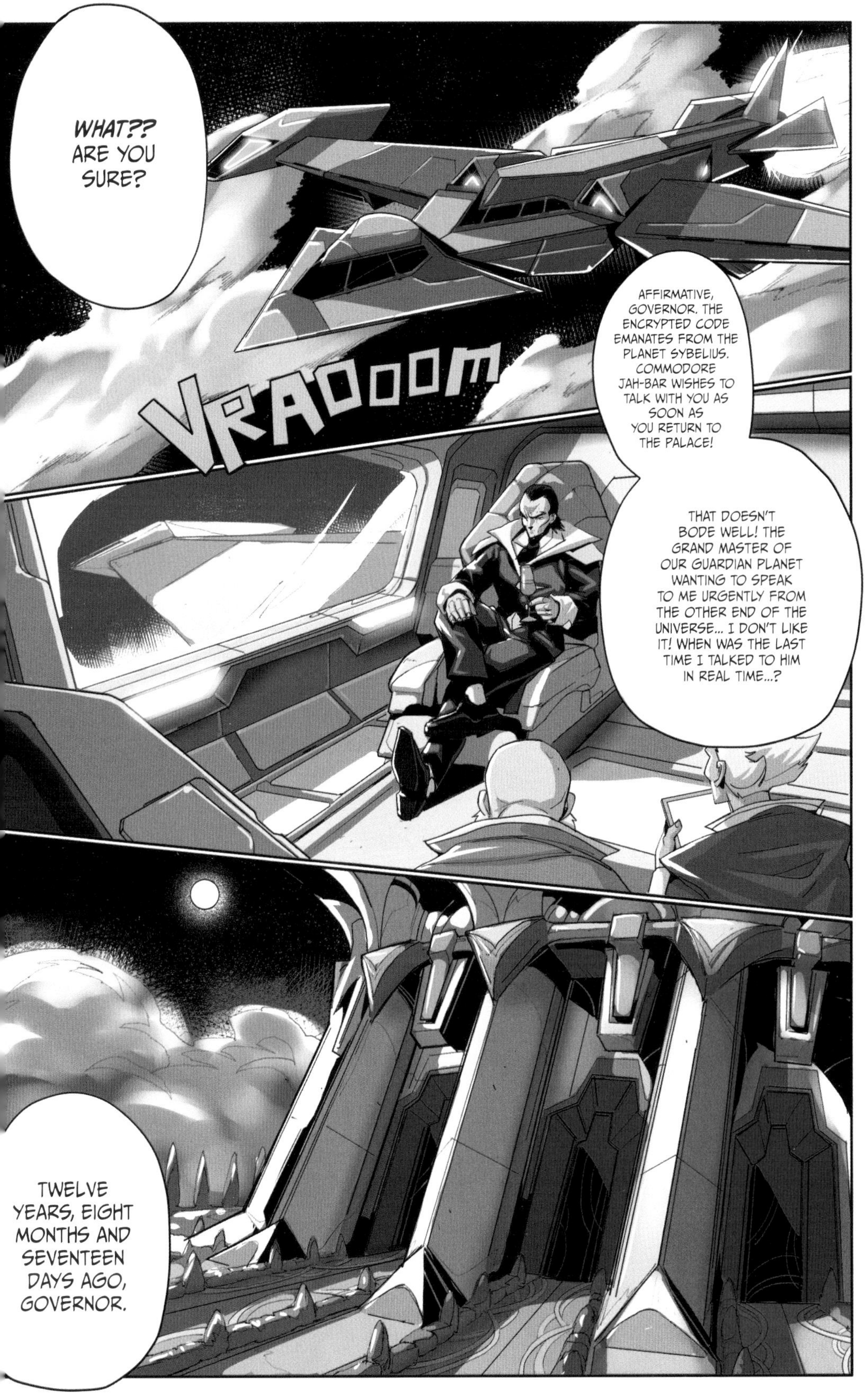
WHAT?? ARE YOU SURE?
AFFIRMATIVE, GOVERNOR. THE ENCRYPTED CODE EMANATES FROM THE PLANET SYBELIUS. COMMODORE JAH-BAR WISHES TO TALK WITH YOU AS SOON AS YOU RETURN TO THE PALACE!
VRAOOOM
THAT DOESN'T BODE WELL! THE GRAND MASTER OF OUR GUARDIAN PLANET WANTING TO SPEAK TO ME URGENTLY FROM THE OTHER END OF THE UNIVERSE... I DON'T LIKE IT! WHEN WAS THE LAST TIME I TALKED TO HIM IN REAL TIME...?
TWELVE YEARS, EIGHT MONTHS AND SEVENTEEN DAYS AGO, GOVERNOR.

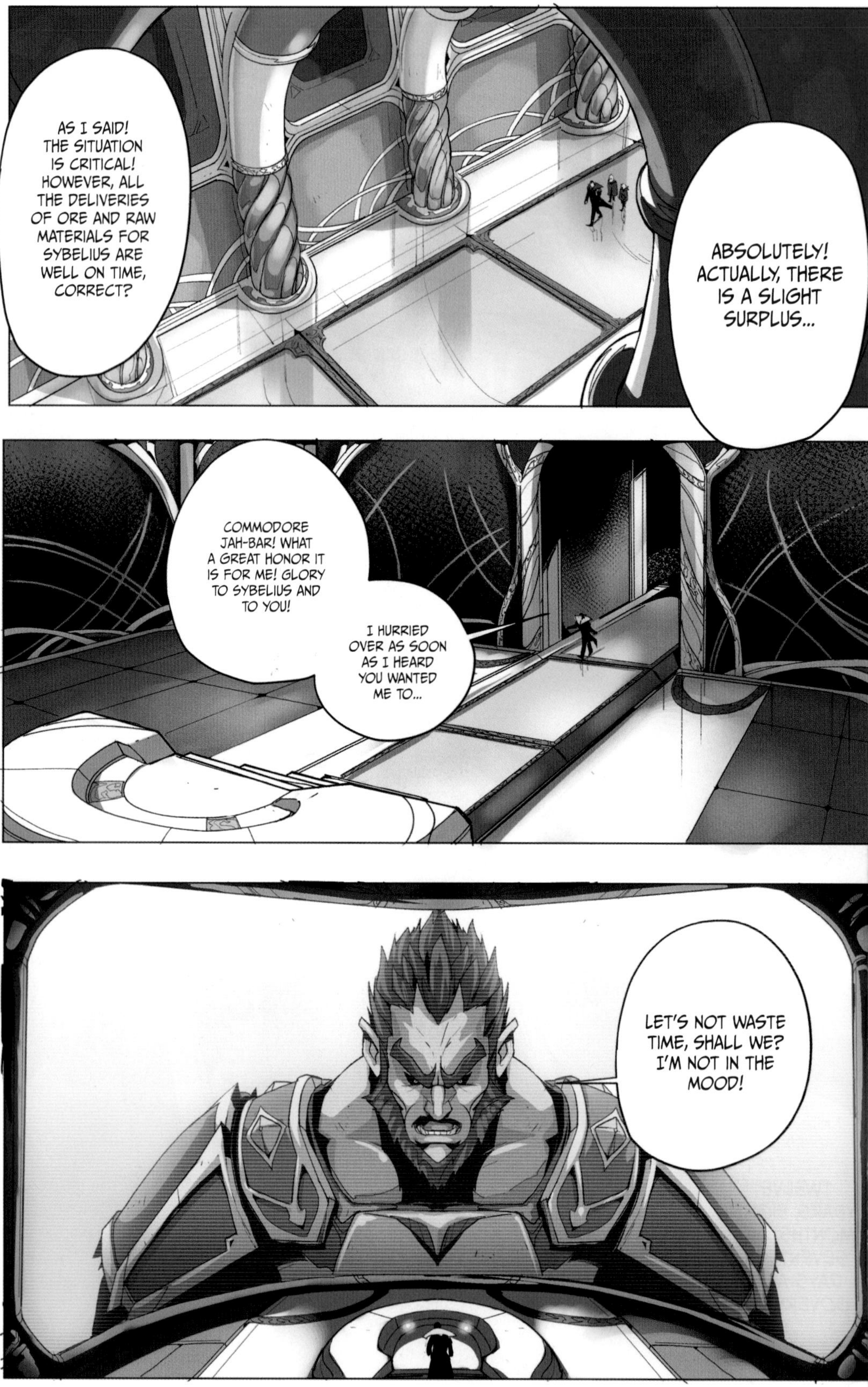
AS I SAID! THE SITUATION IS CRITICAL! HOWEVER, ALL THE DELIVERIES OF ORE AND RAW MATERIALS FOR SYBELIUS ARE WELL ON TIME, CORRECT?
ABSOLUTELY! ACTUALLY, THERE IS A SLIGHT SURPLUS...
COMMODORE JAH-BAR! WHAT A GREAT HONOR IT IS FOR ME! GLORY TO SYBELIUS AND TO YOU!
I HURRIED OVER AS SOON AS I HEARD YOU WANTED ME TO...
LET'S NOT WASTE TIME, SHALL WE? I'M NOT IN THE MOOD!

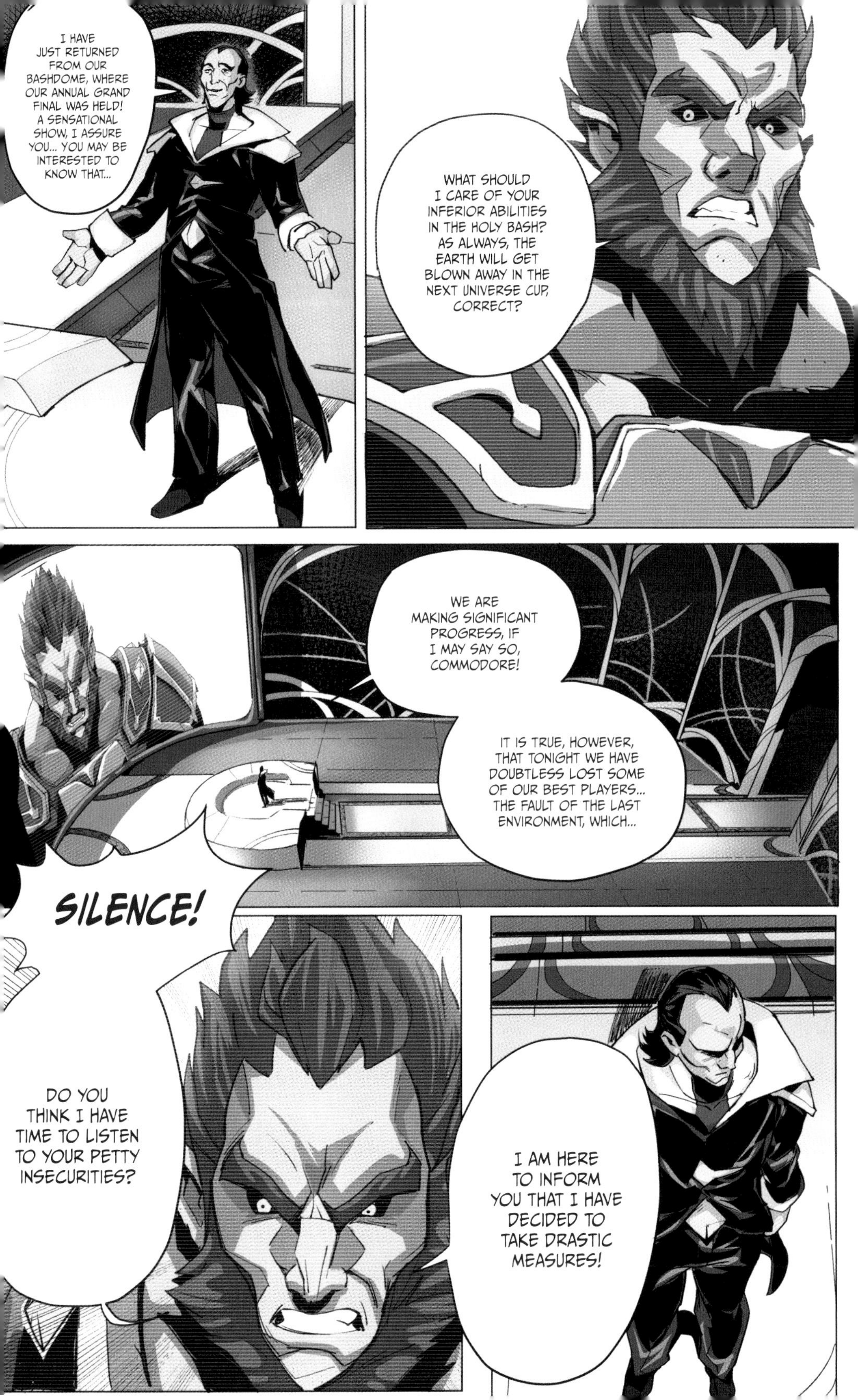
I HAVE JUST RETURNED FROM OUR BASHDOME, WHERE OUR ANNUAL GRAND FINAL WAS HELD! A SENSATIONAL SHOW, I ASSURE YOU... YOU MAY BE INTERESTED TO KNOW THAT...
WHAT SHOULD I CARE OF YOUR INFERIOR ABILITIES IN THE HOLY BASH? AS ALWAYS, THE EARTH WILL GET BLOWN AWAY IN THE NEXT UNIVERSE CUP, CORRECT?
WE ARE MAKING SIGNIFICANT PROGRESS, IF I MAY SAY SO, COMMODORE!
IT IS TRUE, HOWEVER, THAT TONIGHT WE HAVE DOUBTLESS LOST SOME OF OUR BEST PLAYERS... THE FAULT OF THE LAST ENVIRONMENT, WHICH...
SILENCE!
DO YOU THINK I HAVE TIME TO LISTEN TO YOUR PETTY INSECURITIES?
I AM HERE TO INFORM YOU THAT I HAVE DECIDED TO TAKE DRASTIC MEASURES!

I'M NOT HERE TO STOP YOU FROM GROWING UP, RUDY... BUT FRANKLY, THE BASH...
IS THAT REALLY YOUR GOAL IN LIFE?
YOU'RE AN AGRICULTURAL ENGINEER BUT YOU WORK IN A CRAPPY LAB FOR A LOUSY WAGE -- THAT ANY BETTER?
HOW DARE YOU! DO YOU KNOW WHAT IT'S LIKE TO RAISE A CHILD ALONE, IN A CITY LIKE NEVILIA? DO YOU KNOW HOW MANY SACRIFICES I'VE MADE FOR YOU?
I KNOW, MOM...
I KNOW...

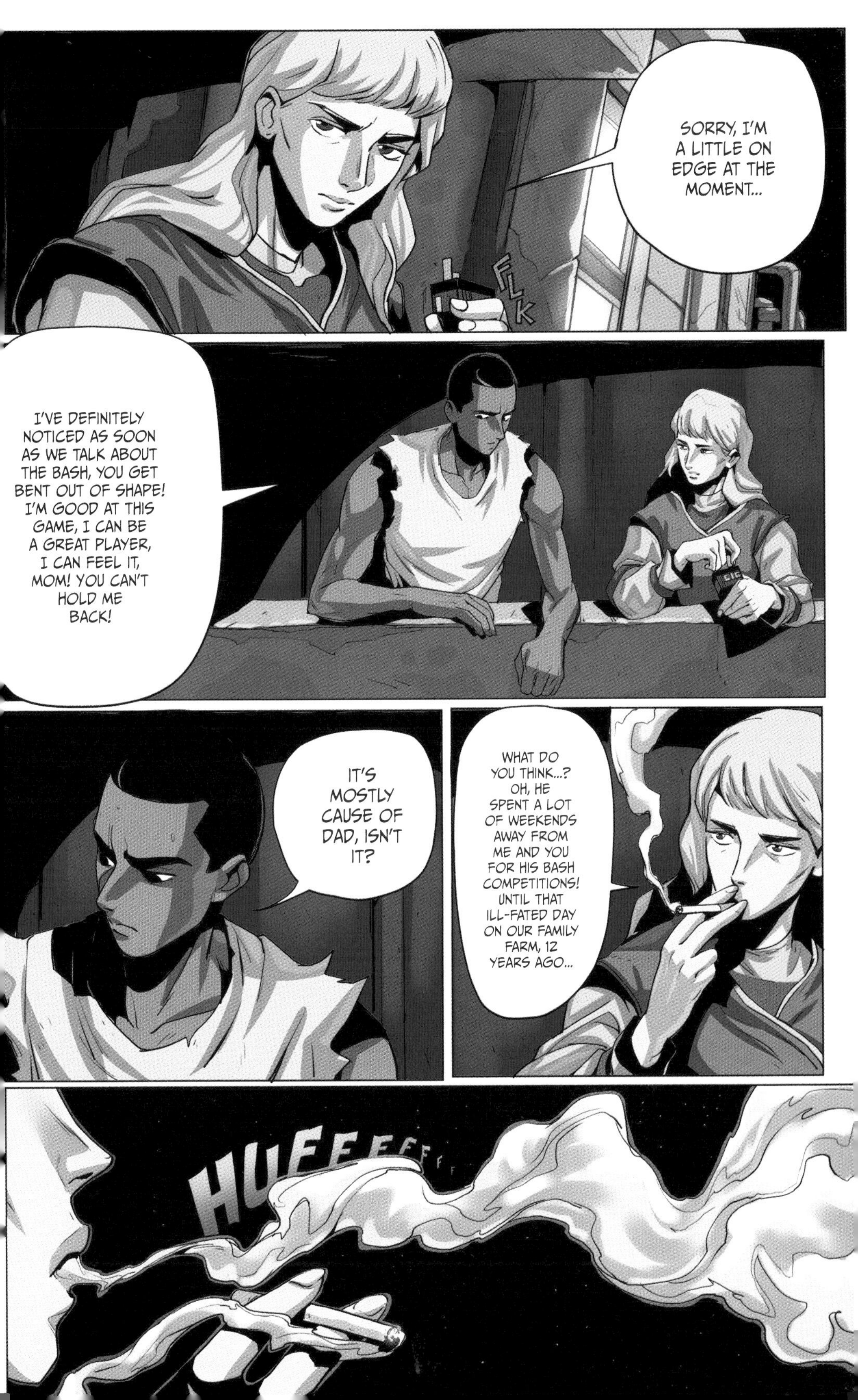
SORRY, I'M A LITTLE ON EDGE AT THE MOMENT...
FLK
I'VE DEFINITELY NOTICED AS SOON AS WE TALK ABOUT THE BASH, YOU GET BENT OUT OF SHAPE! I'M GOOD AT THIS GAME, I CAN BE A GREAT PLAYER, I CAN FEEL IT, MOM! YOU CAN'T HOLD ME BACK!
IT'S MOSTLY CAUSE OF DAD, ISN'T IT?
WHAT DO YOU THINK...? OH, HE SPENT A LOT OF WEEKENDS AWAY FROM ME AND YOU FOR HIS BASH COMPETITIONS! UNTIL THAT ILL-FATED DAY ON OUR FAMILY FARM, 12 YEARS AGO...
HUFFFFFF

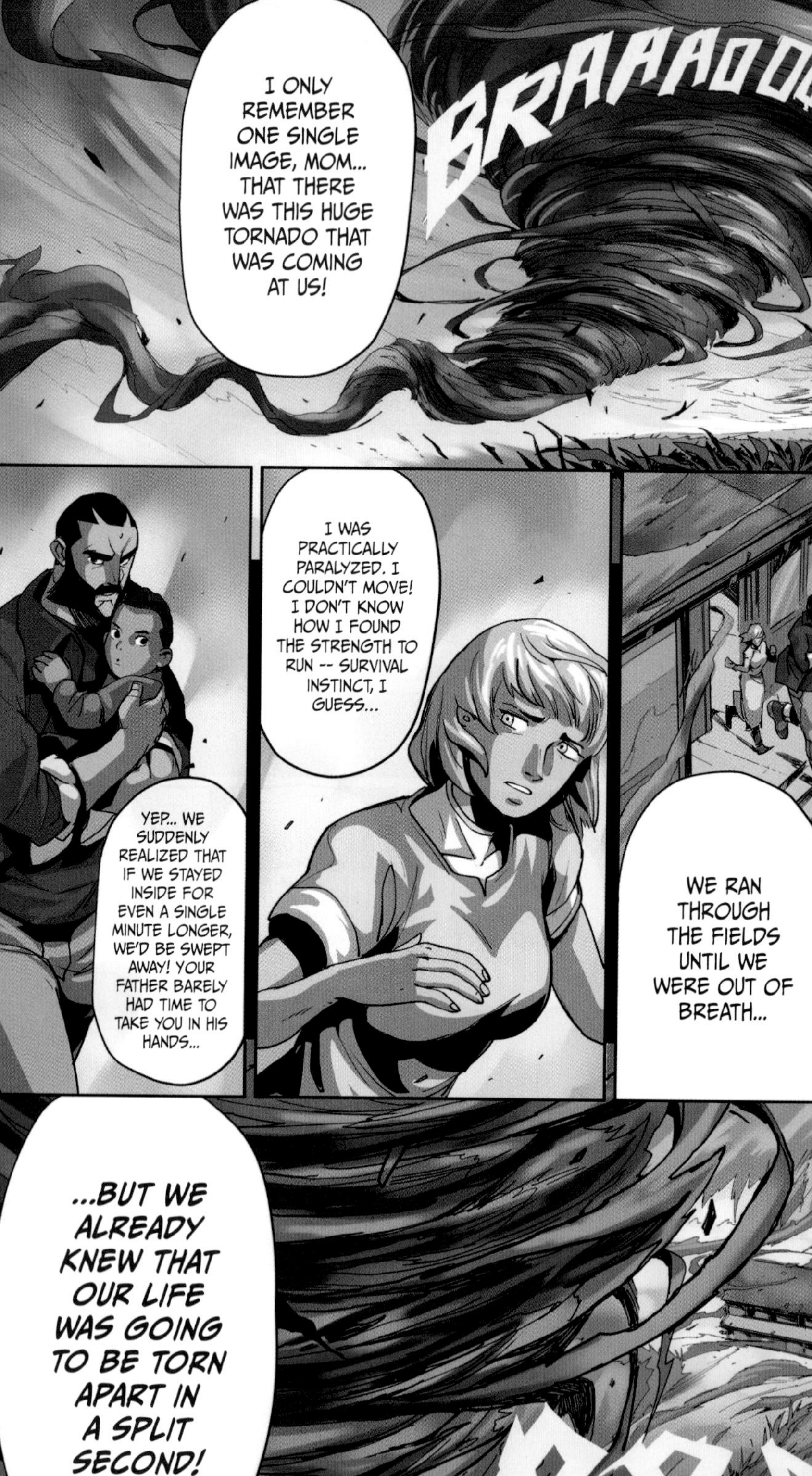

I ONLY REMEMBER ONE SINGLE IMAGE, MOM... THAT THERE WAS THIS HUGE TORNADO THAT WAS COMING AT US!
BRAAAAOO
I WAS PRACTICALLY PARALYZED. I COULDN'T MOVE! I DON'T KNOW HOW I FOUND THE STRENGTH TO RUN -- SURVIVAL INSTINCT, I GUESS...
YEP... WE SUDDENLY REALIZED THAT IF WE STAYED INSIDE FOR EVEN A SINGLE MINUTE LONGER, WE'D BE SWEPT AWAY! YOUR FATHER BARELY HAD TIME TO TAKE YOU IN HIS HANDS...
WE RAN THROUGH THE FIELDS UNTIL WE WERE OUT OF BREATH...
...BUT WE ALREADY KNEW THAT OUR LIFE WAS GOING TO BE TORN APART IN A SPLIT SECOND!

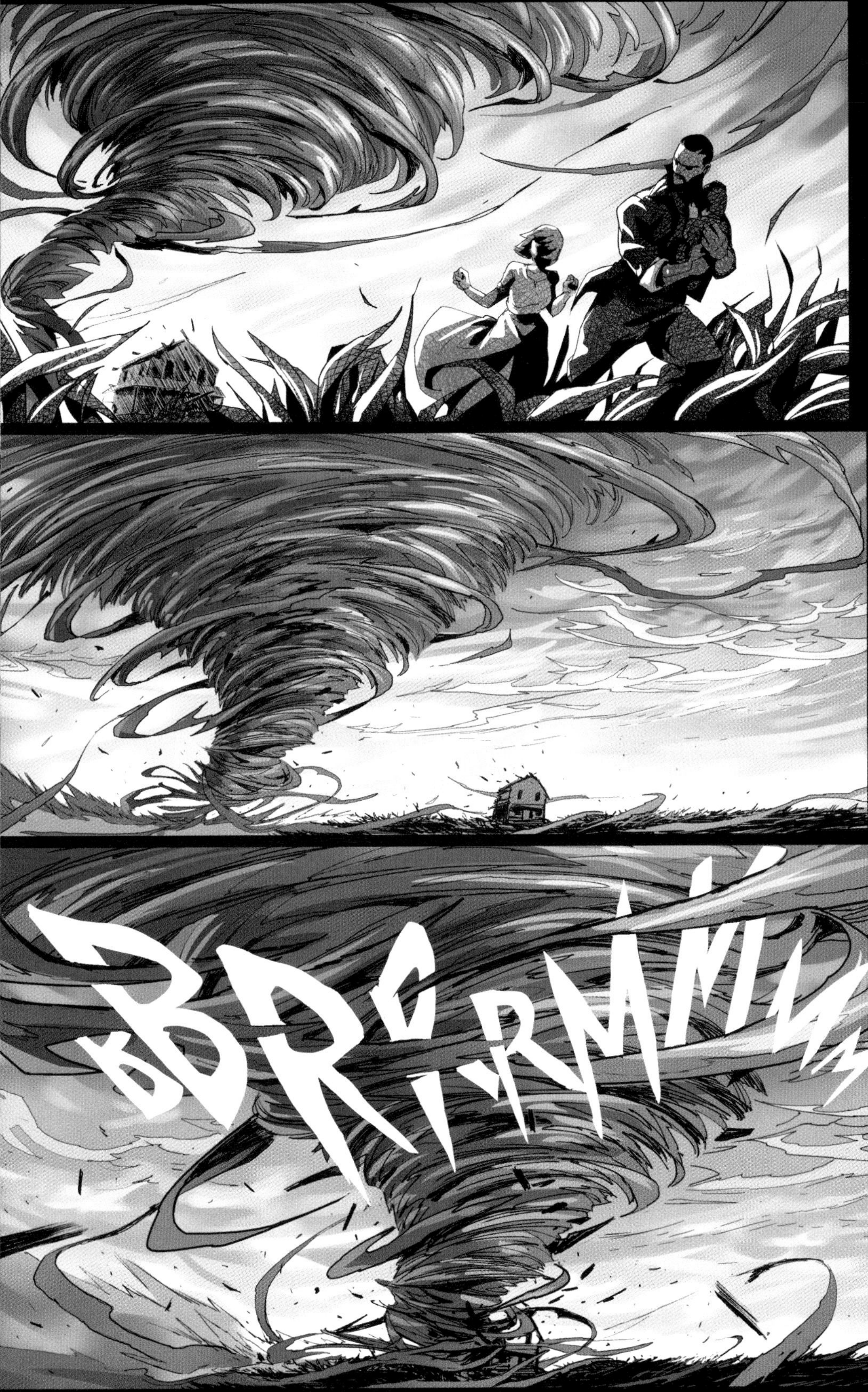
BBRRRMMMM

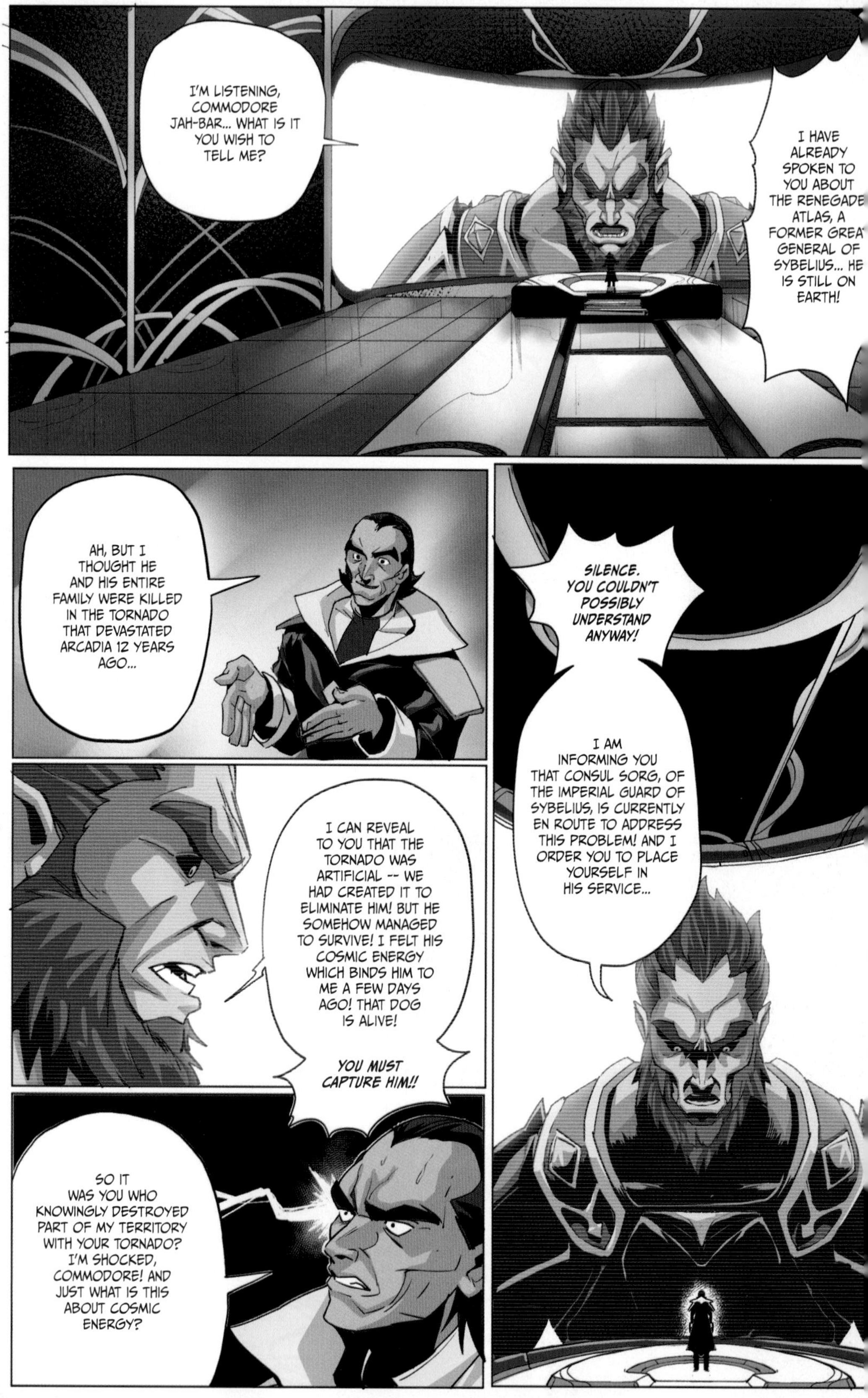
I'M LISTENING, COMMODORE JAH-BAR... WHAT IS IT YOU WISH TO TELL ME?
I HAVE ALREADY SPOKEN TO YOU ABOUT THE RENEGADE ATLAS, A FORMER GREA GENERAL OF SYBELIUS... HE IS STILL ON EARTH!
AH, BUT I THOUGHT HE AND HIS ENTIRE FAMILY WERE KILLED IN THE TORNADO THAT DEVASTATED ARCADIA 12 YEARS AGO...
I CAN REVEAL TO YOU THAT THE TORNADO WAS ARTIFICIAL -- WE HAD CREATED IT TO ELIMINATE HIM! BUT HE SOMEHOW MANAGED TO SURVIVE! I FELT HIS COSMIC ENERGY WHICH BINDS HIM TO ME A FEW DAYS AGO! THAT DOG IS ALIVE!
YOU MUST CAPTURE HIM!!
SO IT WAS YOU WHO KNOWINGLY DESTROYED PART OF MY TERRITORY WITH YOUR TORNADO? I'M SHOCKED, COMMODORE! AND JUST WHAT IS THIS ABOUT COSMIC ENERGY?
SILENCE. YOU COULDN'T POSSIBLY UNDERSTAND ANYWAY!
I AM INFORMING YOU THAT CONSUL SORG, OF THE IMPERIAL GUARD OF SYBELIUS, IS CURRENTLY EN ROUTE TO ADDRESS THIS PROBLEM! AND I ORDER YOU TO PLACE YOURSELF IN HIS SERVICE...

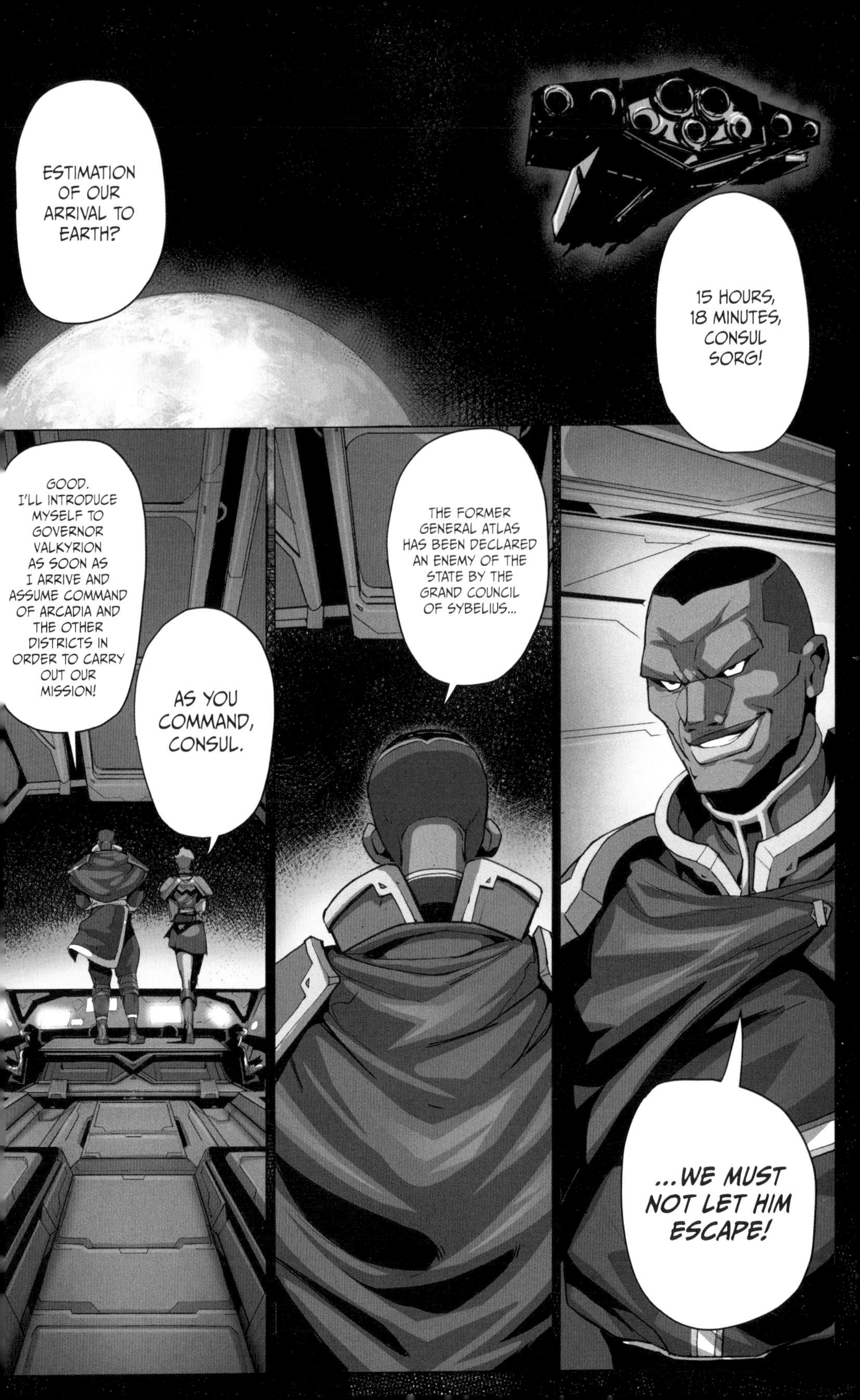
ESTIMATION OF OUR ARRIVAL TO EARTH?
15 HOURS, 18 MINUTES, CONSUL SORG!
GOOD. I'LL INTRODUCE MYSELF TO GOVERNOR VALKYRION AS SOON AS I ARRIVE AND ASSUME COMMAND OF ARCADIA AND THE OTHER DISTRICTS IN ORDER TO CARRY OUT OUR MISSION!
AS YOU COMMAND, CONSUL.
THE FORMER GENERAL ATLAS HAS BEEN DECLARED AN ENEMY OF THE STATE BY THE GRAND COUNCIL OF SYBELIUS...
...WE MUST NOT LET HIM ESCAPE!

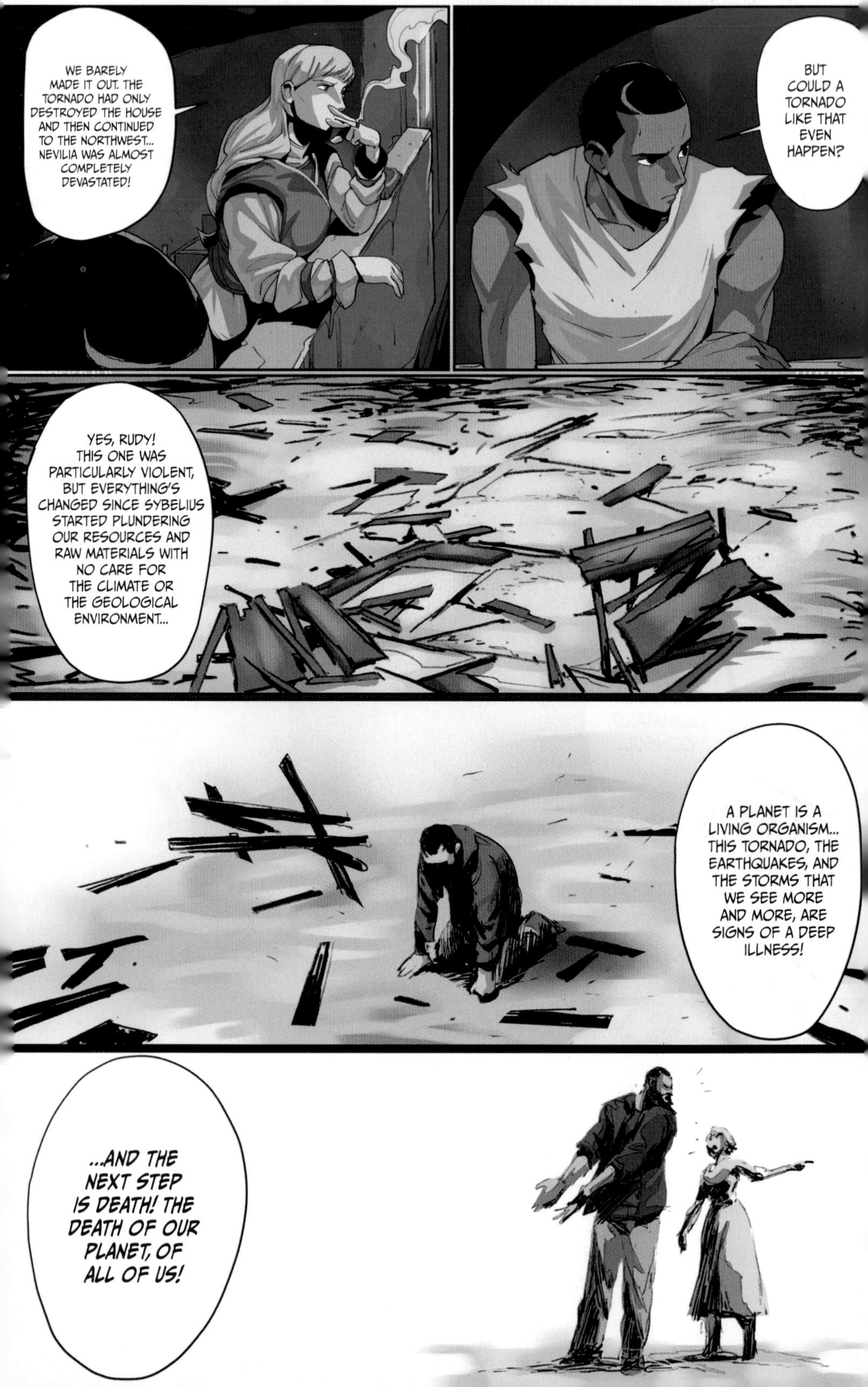
WE BARELY MADE IT OUT. THE TORNADO HAD ONLY DESTROYED THE HOUSE AND THEN CONTINUED TO THE NORTHWEST... NEVILIA WAS ALMOST COMPLETELY DEVASTATED!
BUT COULD A TORNADO LIKE THAT EVEN HAPPEN?
YES, RUDY! THIS ONE WAS PARTICULARLY VIOLENT, BUT EVERYTHING'S CHANGED SINCE SYBELIUS STARTED PLUNDERING OUR RESOURCES AND RAW MATERIALS WITH NO CARE FOR THE CLIMATE OR THE GEOLOGICAL ENVIRONMENT...
A PLANET IS A LIVING ORGANISM... THIS TORNADO, THE EARTHQUAKES, AND THE STORMS THAT WE SEE MORE AND MORE, ARE SIGNS OF A DEEP ILLNESS!
...AND THE NEXT STEP IS DEATH! THE DEATH OF OUR PLANET, OF ALL OF US!

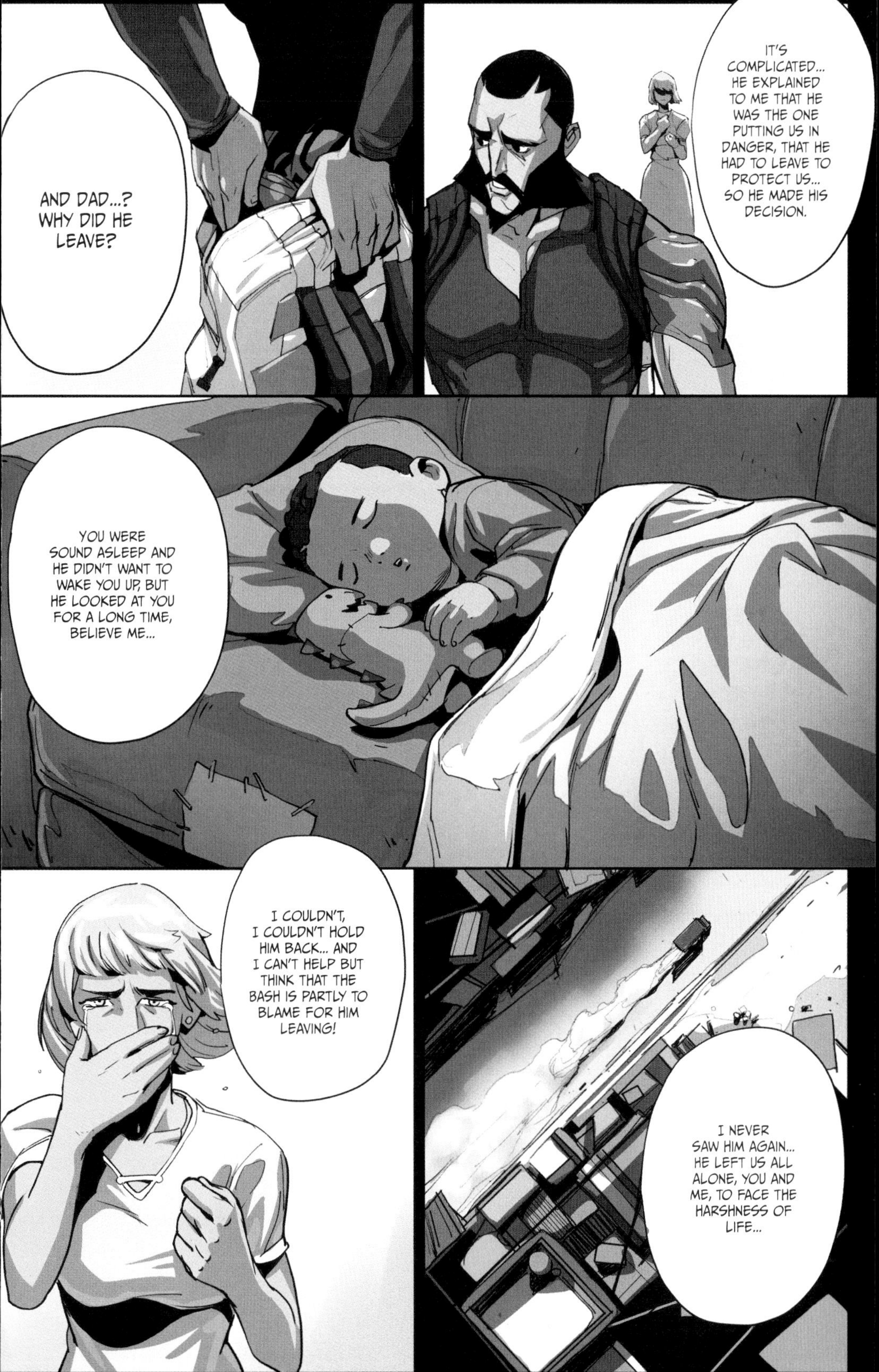
AND DAD...? WHY DID HE LEAVE?
IT'S COMPLICATED... HE EXPLAINED TO ME THAT HE WAS THE ONE PUTTING US IN DANGER, THAT HE HAD TO LEAVE TO PROTECT US... SO HE MADE HIS DECISION.
YOU WERE SOUND ASLEEP AND HE DIDN'T WANT TO WAKE YOU UP, BUT HE LOOKED AT YOU FOR A LONG TIME, BELIEVE ME...
I COULDN'T, I COULDN'T HOLD HIM BACK... AND I CAN'T HELP BUT THINK THAT THE BASH IS PARTLY TO BLAME FOR HIM LEAVING!
I NEVER SAW HIM AGAIN... HE LEFT US ALL ALONE, YOU AND ME, TO FACE THE HARSHNESS OF LIFE...

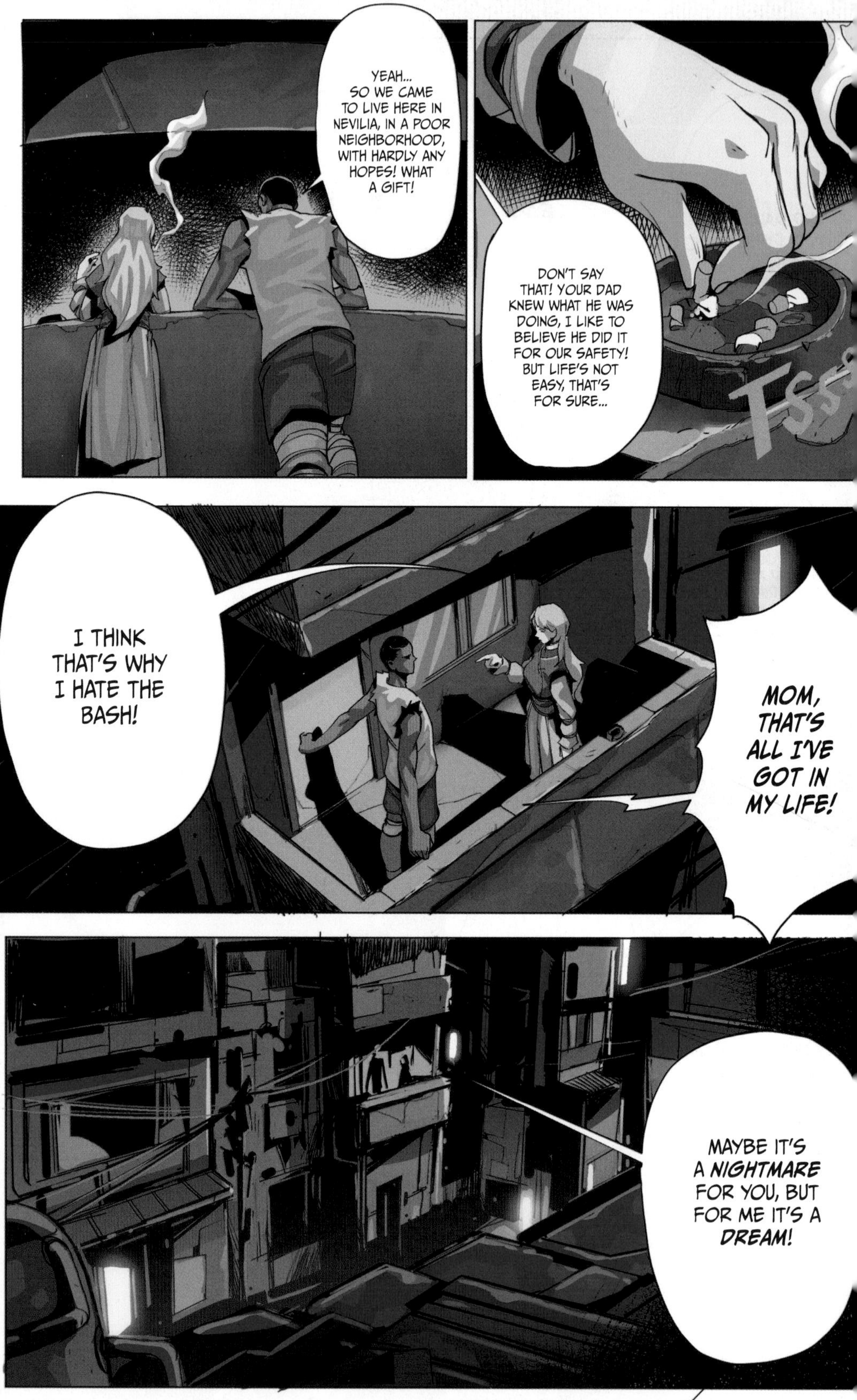
YEAH... SO WE CAME TO LIVE HERE IN NEVILIA, IN A POOR NEIGHBORHOOD, WITH HARDLY ANY HOPES! WHAT A GIFT!
DON'T SAY THAT! YOUR DAD KNEW WHAT HE WAS DOING, I LIKE TO BELIEVE HE DID IT FOR OUR SAFETY! BUT LIFE'S NOT EASY, THAT'S FOR SURE...
TSSS
I THINK THAT'S WHY I HATE THE BASH!
MOM, THAT'S ALL I'VE GOT IN MY LIFE!
MAYBE IT'S A NIGHTMARE FOR YOU, BUT FOR ME IT'S A DREAM!

AND WE'RE BACK TO THE GREATEST BASH PLAYER IN THE WORLD, THE GREAT RUDY!!
LOOK AT HIM IN ACTION, HAS ANYONE EVER SEEN ANOTHER BASH PLAYER LIKE HIM ON EARTH?
OR EVEN THE UNIVERSE?

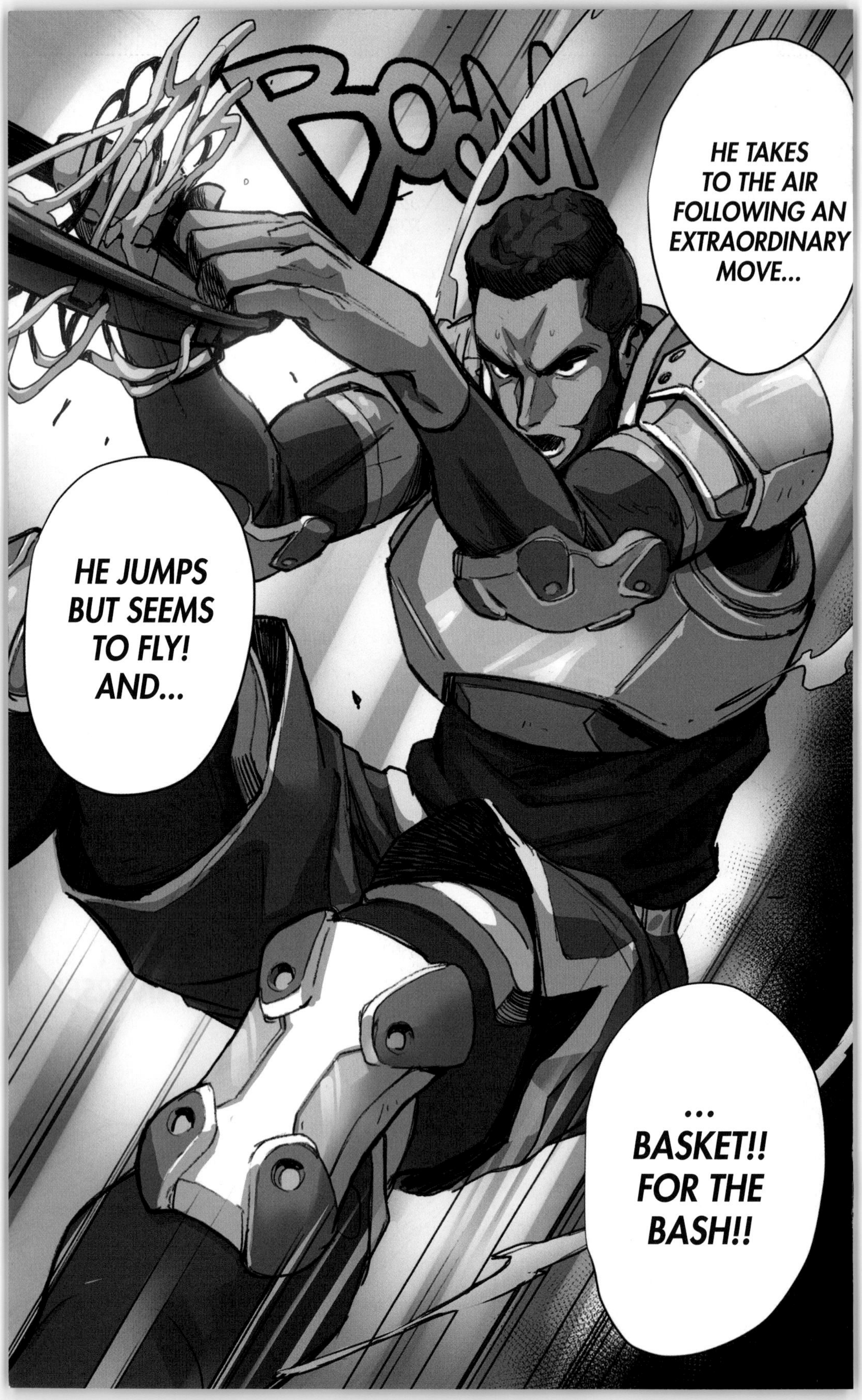
BOOM
HE TAKES TO THE AIR FOLLOWING AN EXTRAORDINARY MOVE...
HE JUMPS BUT SEEMS TO FLY! AND...
... BASKET!! FOR THE BASH!!

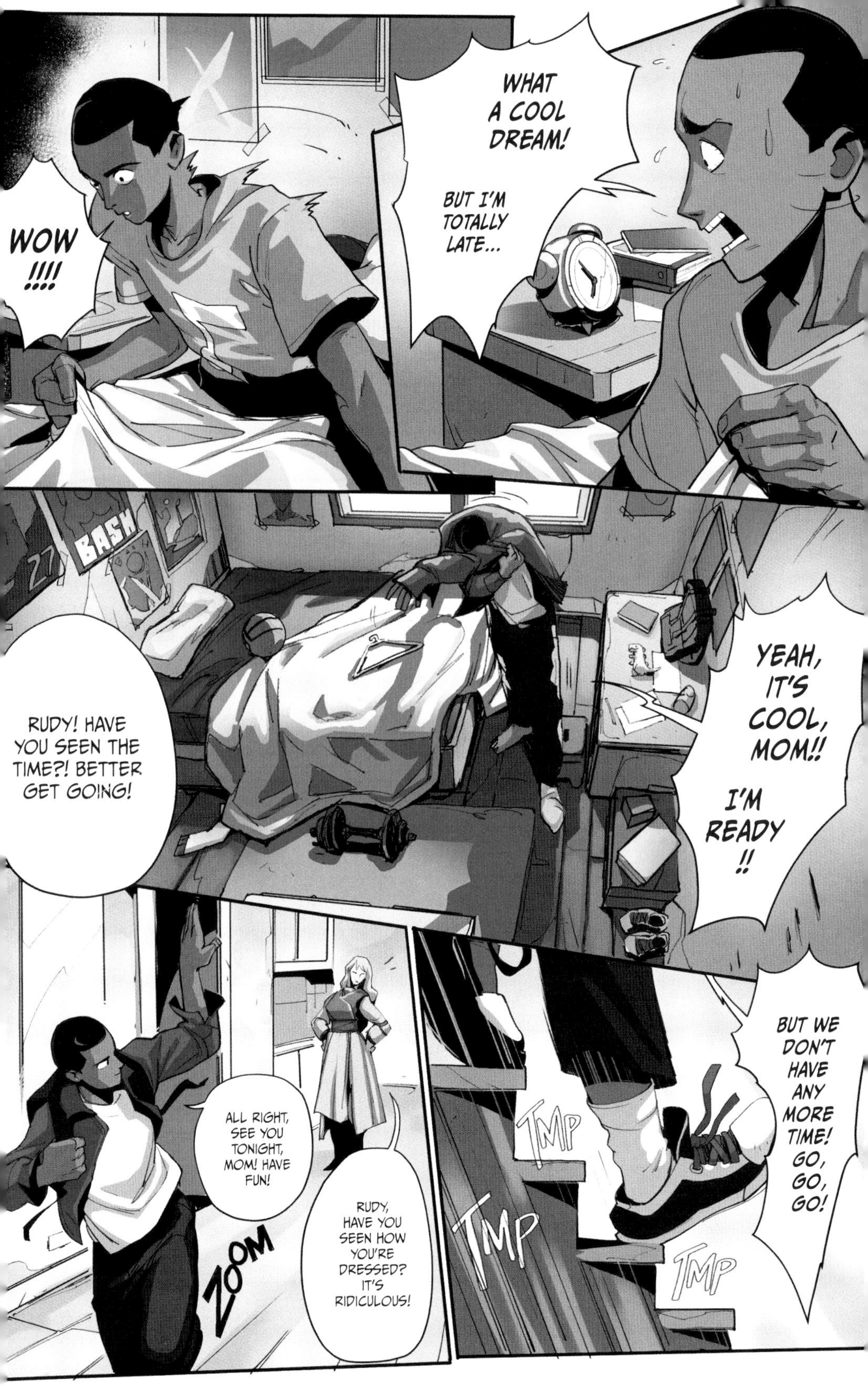
WOW !!!!
WHAT A COOL DREAM!
BUT I'M TOTALLY LATE...
RUDY! HAVE YOU SEEN THE TIME?! BETTER GET GOING!
BASH
27
YEAH, IT'S COOL, MOM!!
I'M READY !!
ALL RIGHT, SEE YOU TONIGHT, MOM! HAVE FUN!
RUDY, HAVE YOU SEEN HOW YOU'RE DRESSED? IT'S RIDICULOUS!
ZOOM
TMP
TMP
TMP
BUT WE DON'T HAVE ANY MORE TIME! GO, GO, GO!

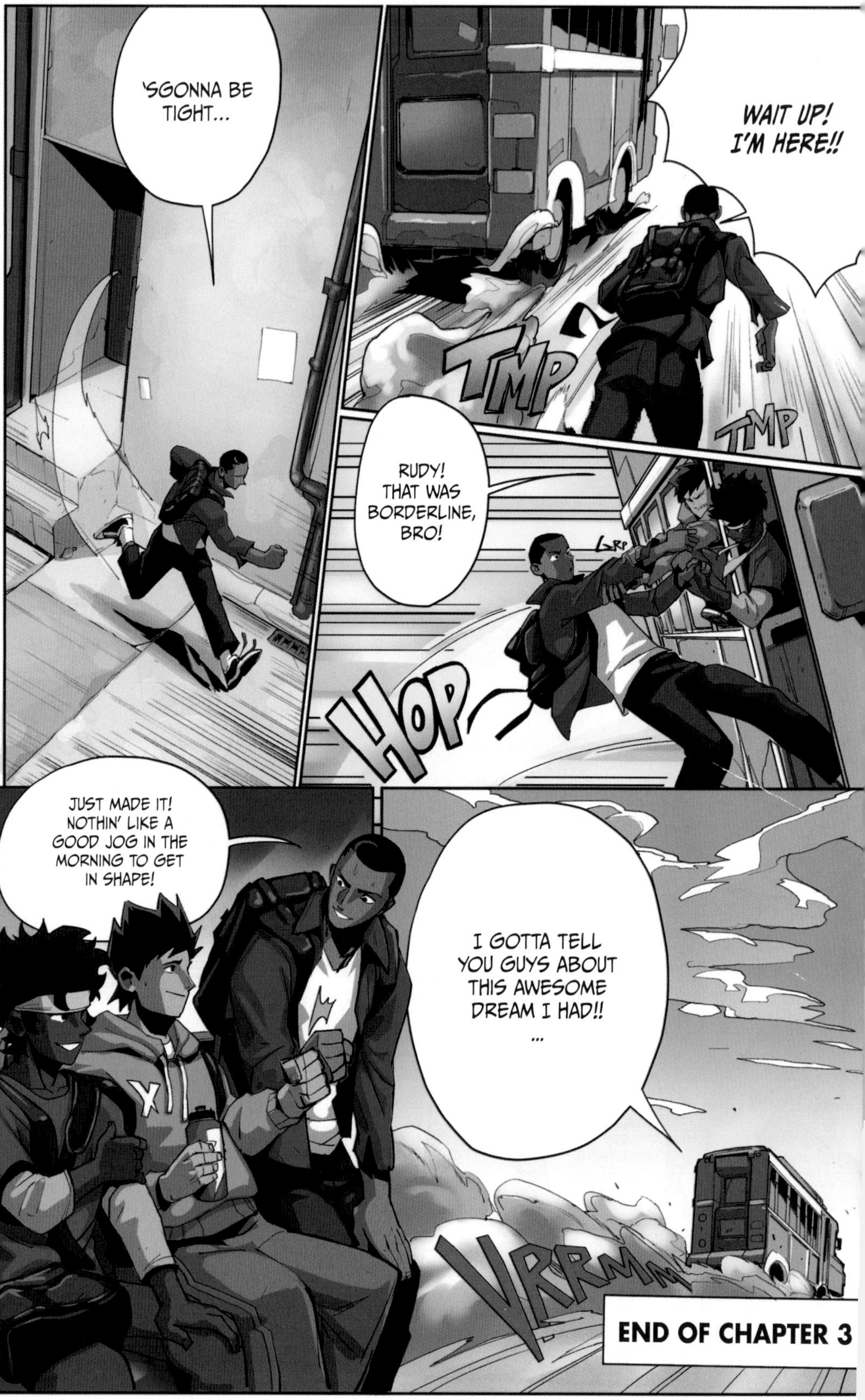
'SGONNA BE TIGHT...
WAIT UP! I'M HERE!!
TMP
TMP
RUDY! THAT WAS BORDERLINE, BRO!
GRP
HOP
JUST MADE IT! NOTHIN' LIKE A GOOD JOG IN THE MORNING TO GET IN SHAPE!
I GOTTA TELL YOU GUYS ABOUT THIS AWESOME DREAM I HAD!! ...
VRRMM
END OF CHAPTER 3

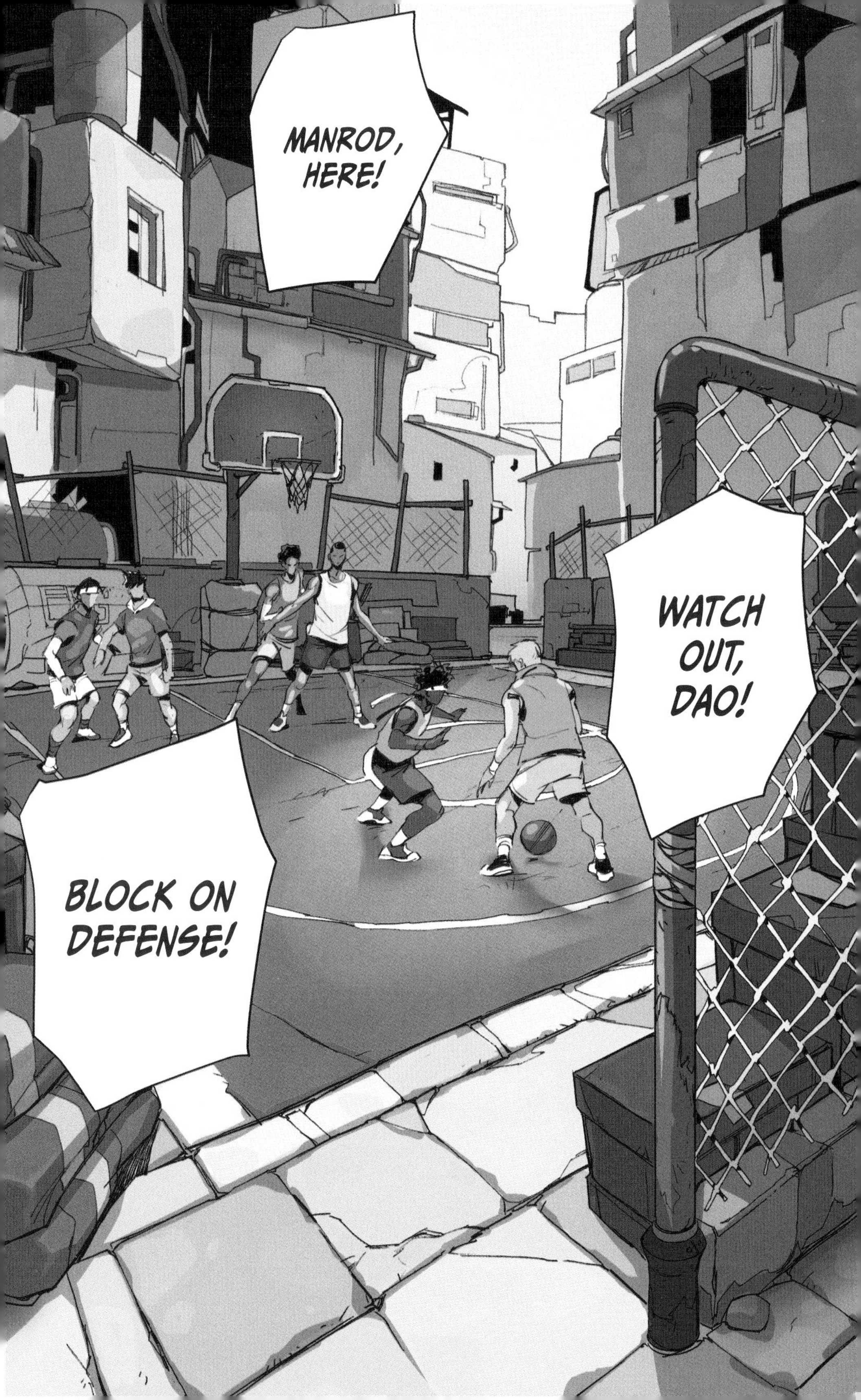
MANROD, HERE!
WATCH OUT, DAO!
BLOCK ON DEFENSE!

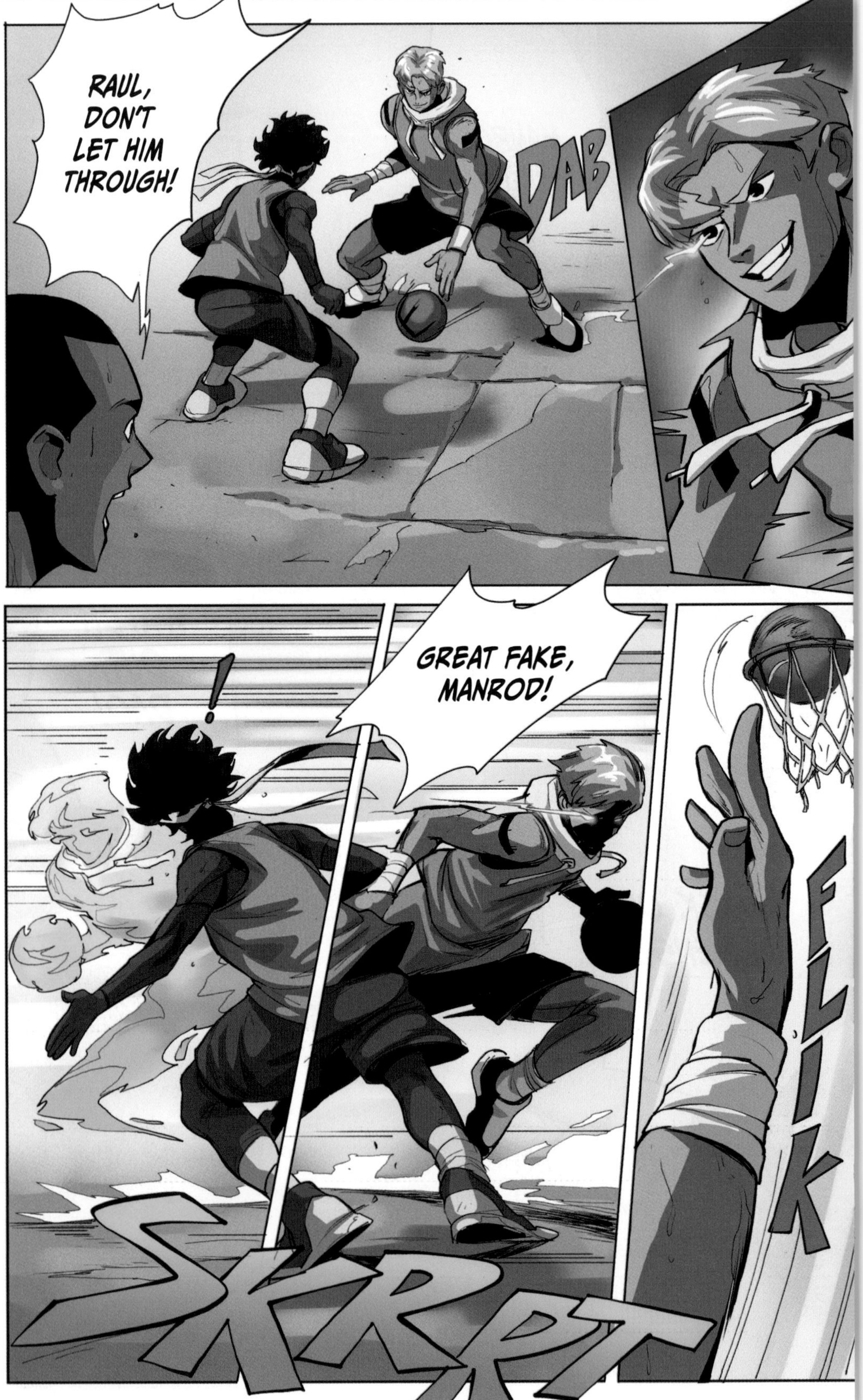
RAUL, DON'T LET HIM THROUGH!
DAB
GREAT FAKE, MANROD!
!
SKRRT
FLIK

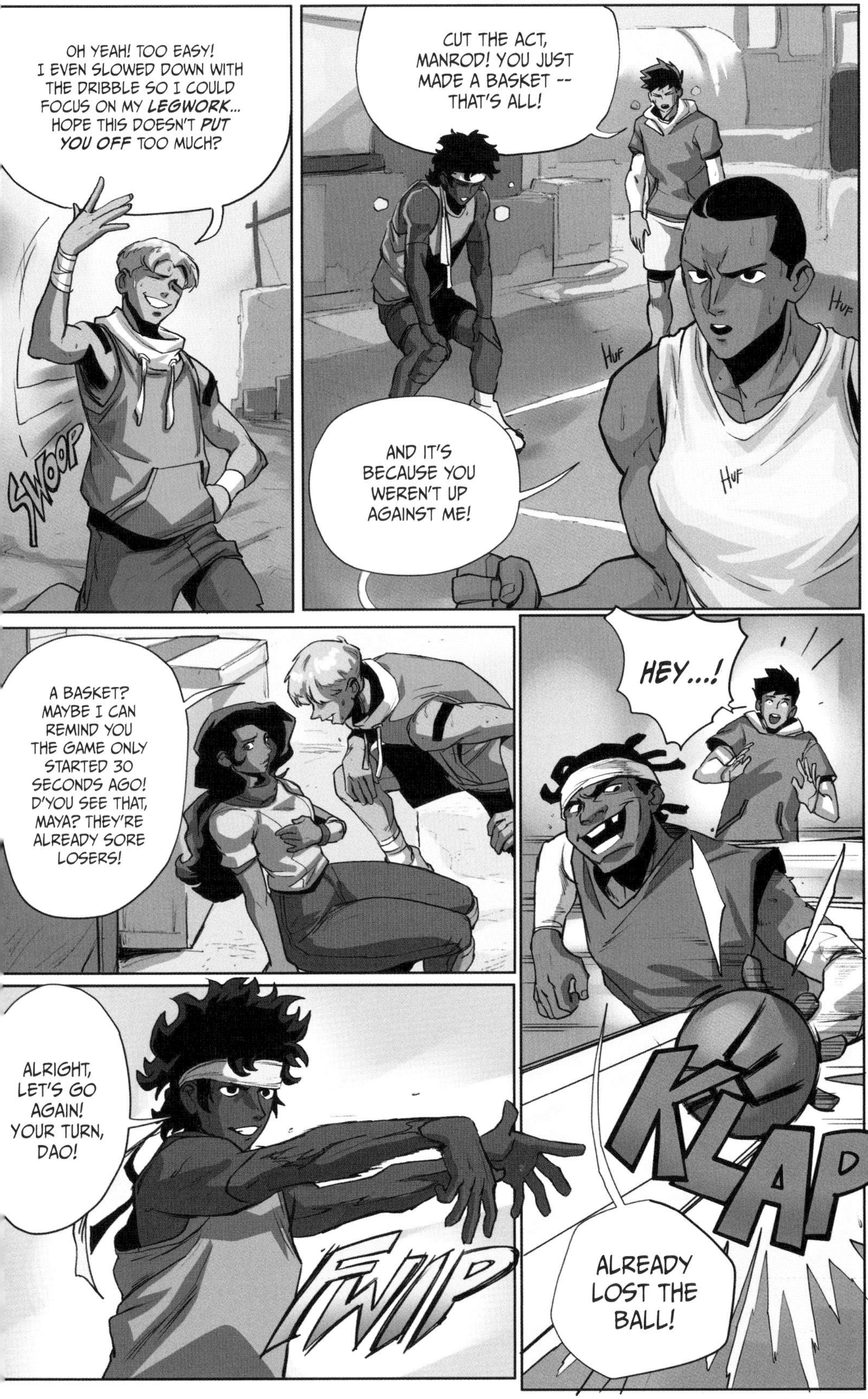
OH YEAH! TOO EASY! I EVEN SLOWED DOWN WITH THE DRIBBLE SO I COULD FOCUS ON MY LEGWORK... HOPE THIS DOESN'T PUT YOU OFF TOO MUCH?
SWOOP
CUT THE ACT, MANROD! YOU JUST MADE A BASKET -- THAT'S ALL!
HUF
HUF
HUF
AND IT'S BECAUSE YOU WEREN'T UP AGAINST ME!
A BASKET? MAYBE I CAN REMIND YOU THE GAME ONLY STARTED 30 SECONDS AGO! D'YOU SEE THAT, MAYA? THEY'RE ALREADY SORE LOSERS!
ALRIGHT, LET'S GO AGAIN! YOUR TURN, DAO!
FWIP
HEY...!
KLAP
ALREADY LOST THE BALL!

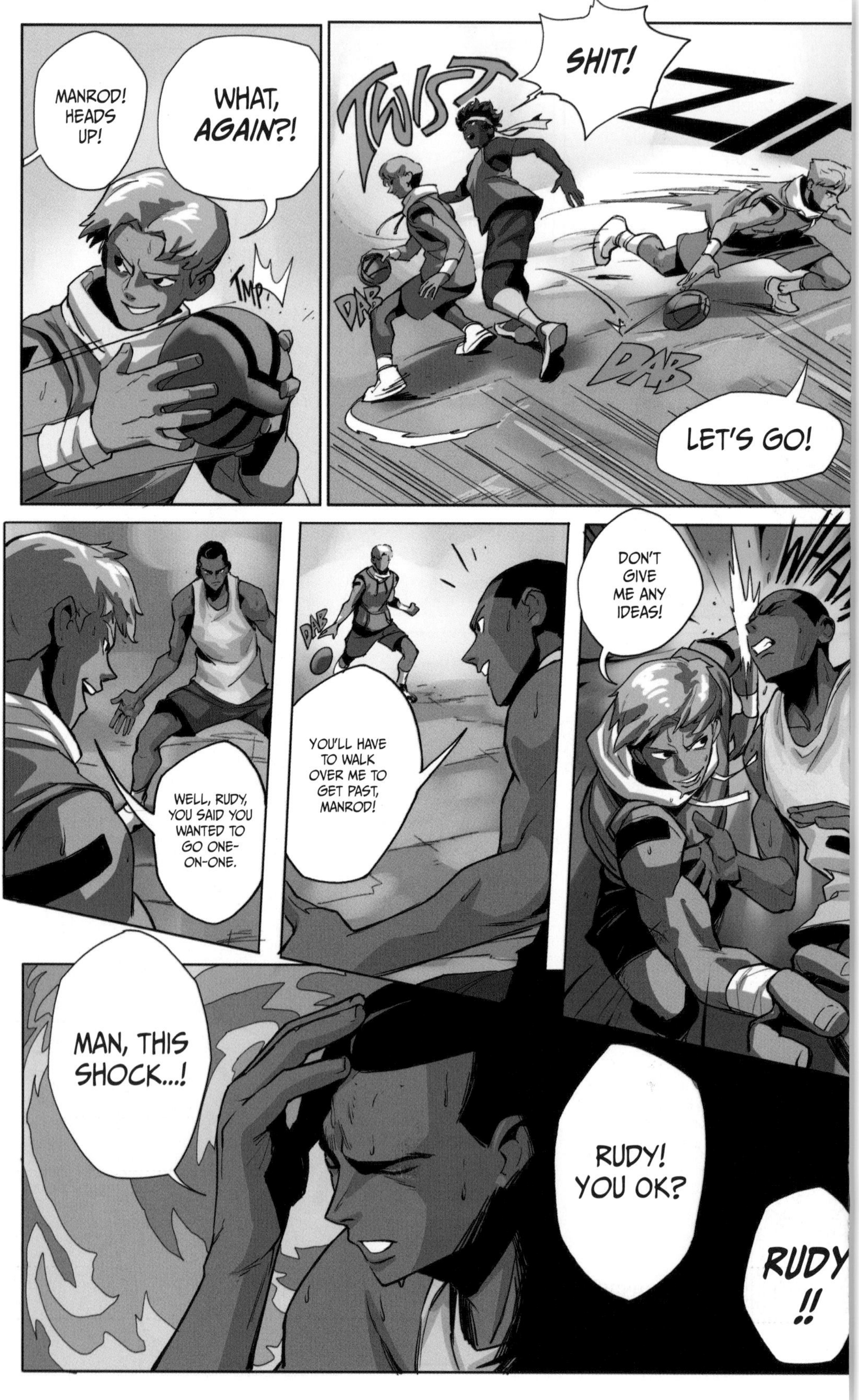
MANROD! HEADS UP!
WHAT, AGAIN?!
TMP
TWIST
SHIT!
ZIP
DAB
DAB
LET'S GO!
WELL, RUDY, YOU SAID YOU WANTED TO GO ONE-ON-ONE.
DAB
YOU'LL HAVE TO WALK OVER ME TO GET PAST, MANROD!
DON'T GIVE ME ANY IDEAS!
MAN, THIS SHOCK...!
RUDY! YOU OK?
RUDY !!

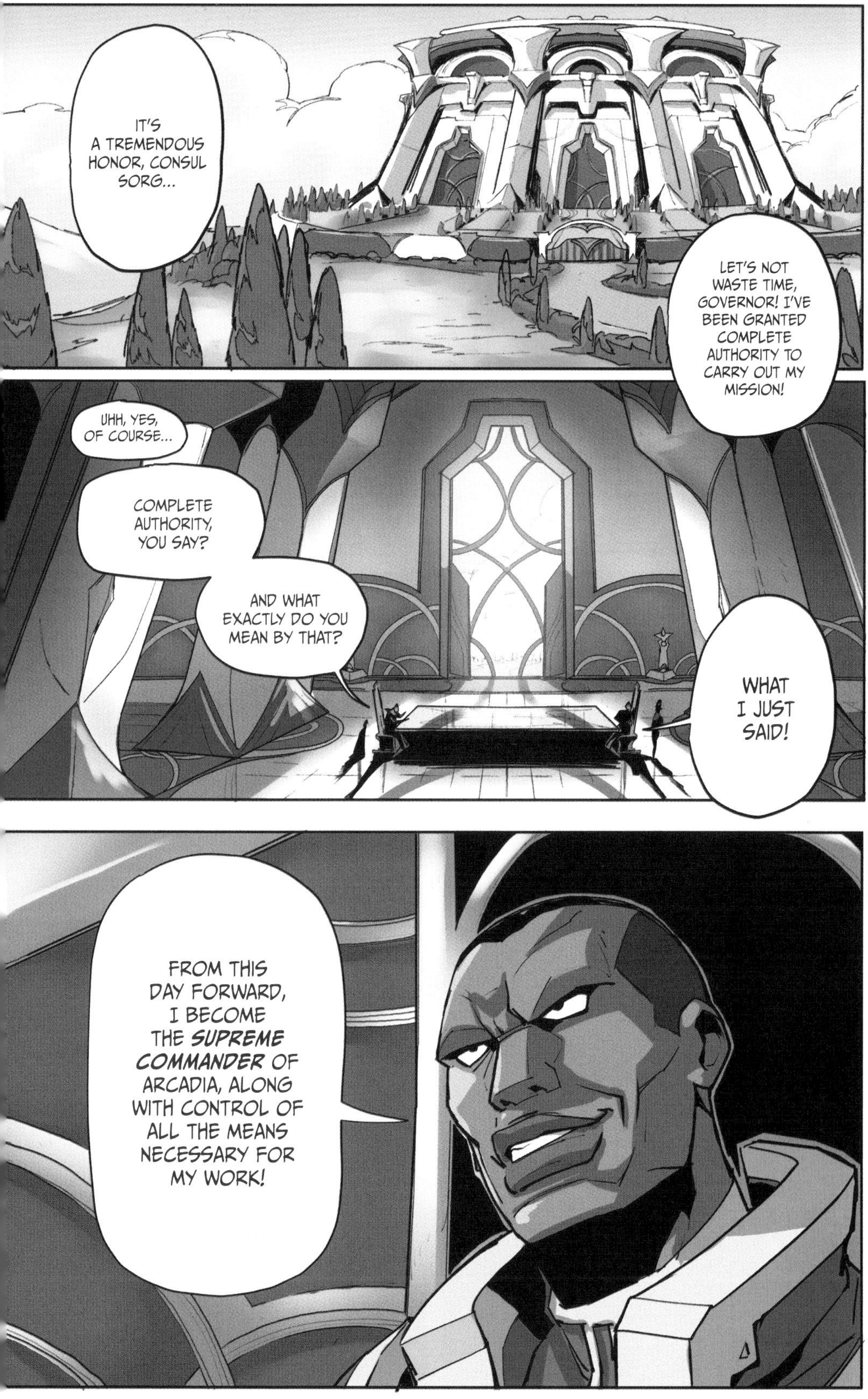

IT'S A TREMENDOUS HONOR, CONSUL SORG...
LET'S NOT WASTE TIME, GOVERNOR! I'VE BEEN GRANTED COMPLETE AUTHORITY TO CARRY OUT MY MISSION!
UHH, YES, OF COURSE...
COMPLETE AUTHORITY, YOU SAY?
AND WHAT EXACTLY DO YOU MEAN BY THAT?
WHAT I JUST SAID!
FROM THIS DAY FORWARD, I BECOME THE ***SUPREME COMMANDER*** OF ARCADIA, ALONG WITH CONTROL OF ALL THE MEANS NECESSARY FOR MY WORK!

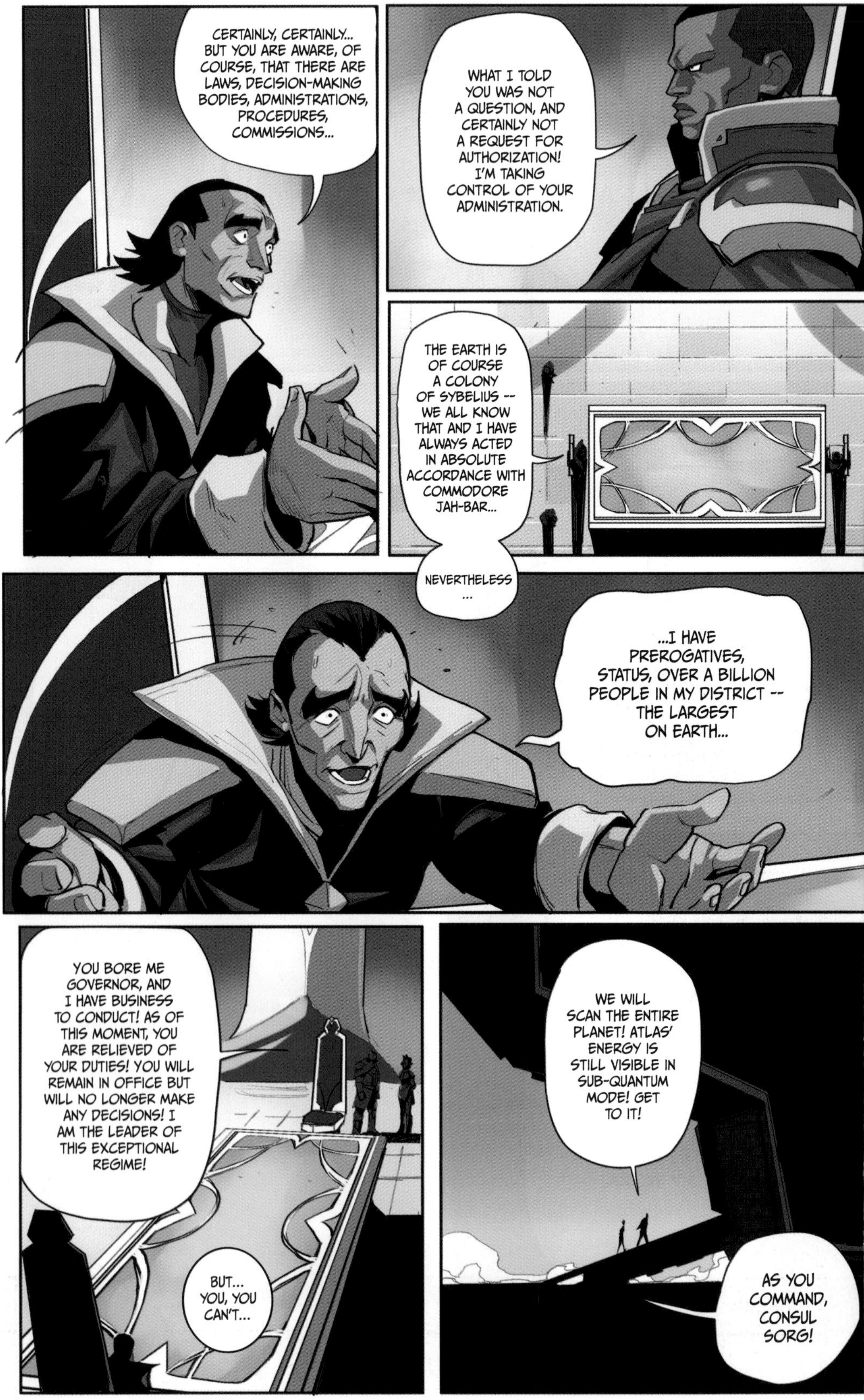
CERTAINLY, CERTAINLY... BUT YOU ARE AWARE, OF COURSE, THAT THERE ARE LAWS, DECISION-MAKING BODIES, ADMINISTRATIONS, PROCEDURES, COMMISSIONS...
WHAT I TOLD YOU WAS NOT A QUESTION, AND CERTAINLY NOT A REQUEST FOR AUTHORIZATION! I'M TAKING CONTROL OF YOUR ADMINISTRATION.
THE EARTH IS OF COURSE A COLONY OF SYBELIUS -- WE ALL KNOW THAT AND I HAVE ALWAYS ACTED IN ABSOLUTE ACCORDANCE WITH COMMODORE JAH-BAR...
NEVERTHELESS...
...I HAVE PREROGATIVES, STATUS, OVER A BILLION PEOPLE IN MY DISTRICT -- THE LARGEST ON EARTH...
YOU BORE ME GOVERNOR, AND I HAVE BUSINESS TO CONDUCT! AS OF THIS MOMENT, YOU ARE RELIEVED OF YOUR DUTIES! YOU WILL REMAIN IN OFFICE BUT WILL NO LONGER MAKE ANY DECISIONS! I AM THE LEADER OF THIS EXCEPTIONAL REGIME!
BUT... YOU, YOU CAN'T...
WE WILL SCAN THE ENTIRE PLANET! ATLAS' ENERGY IS STILL VISIBLE IN SUB-QUANTUM MODE! GET TO IT!
AS YOU COMMAND, CONSUL SORG!

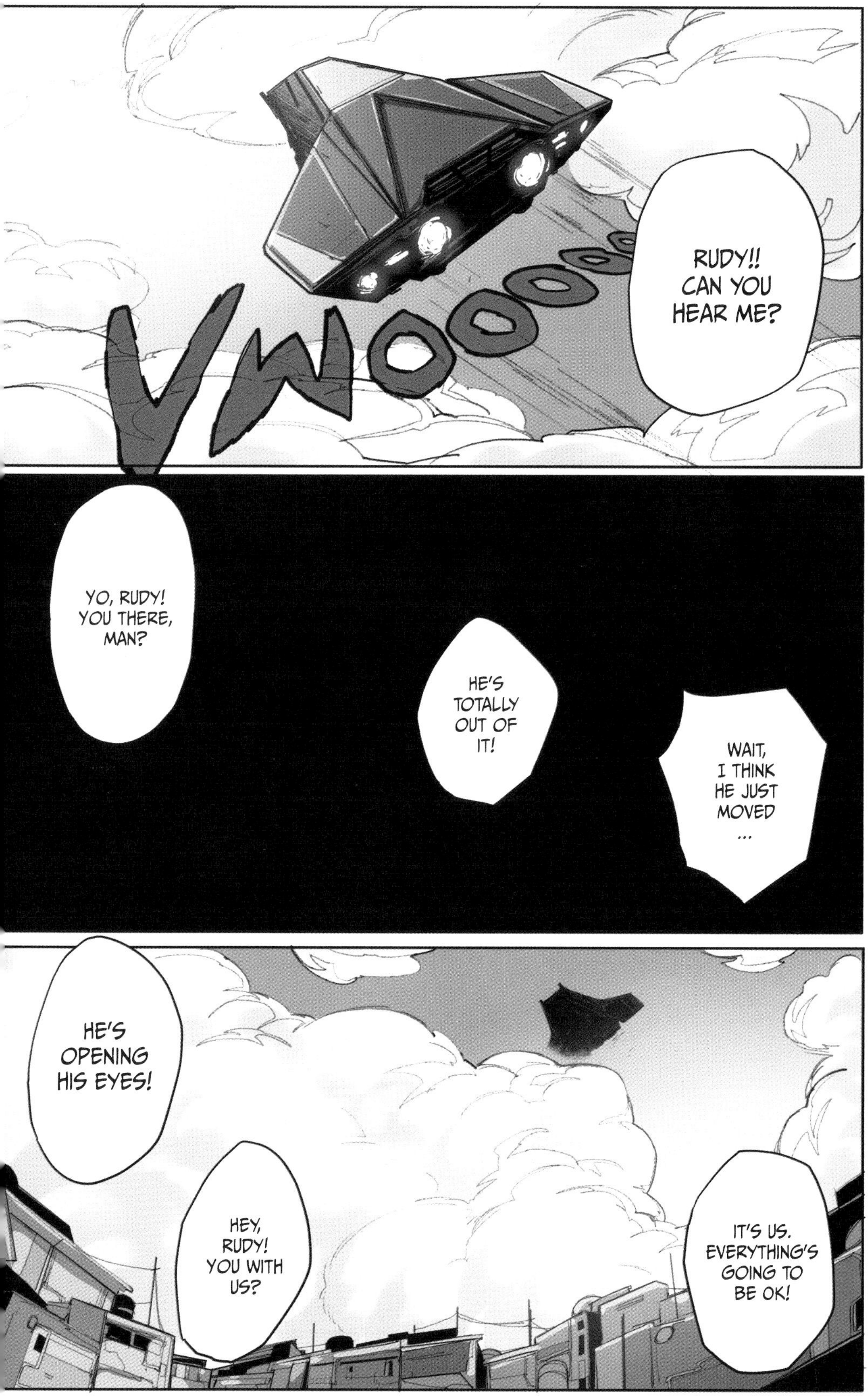
VWOOOOO
RUDY!! CAN YOU HEAR ME?
YO, RUDY! YOU THERE, MAN?
HE'S TOTALLY OUT OF IT!
WAIT, I THINK HE JUST MOVED ...
HE'S OPENING HIS EYES!
HEY, RUDY! YOU WITH US?
IT'S US. EVERYTHING'S GOING TO BE OK!

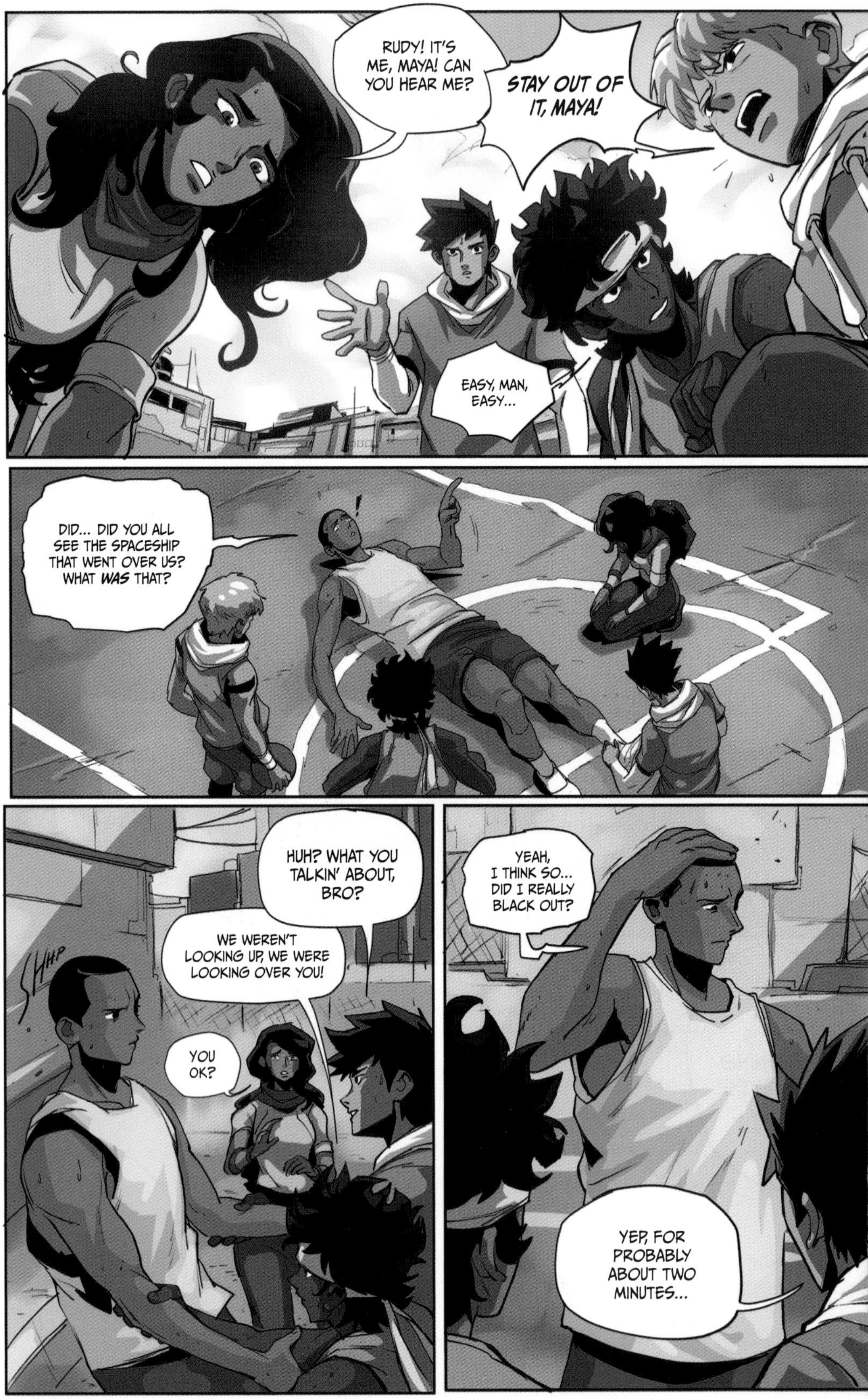
RUDY! IT'S ME, MAYA! CAN YOU HEAR ME?
STAY OUT OF IT, MAYA!
EASY, MAN, EASY...
DID... DID YOU ALL SEE THE SPACESHIP THAT WENT OVER US? WHAT WAS THAT?
SHHP
HUH? WHAT YOU TALKIN' ABOUT, BRO?
WE WEREN'T LOOKING UP, WE WERE LOOKING OVER YOU!
YOU OK?
YEAH, I THINK SO... DID I REALLY BLACK OUT?
YEP, FOR PROBABLY ABOUT TWO MINUTES...

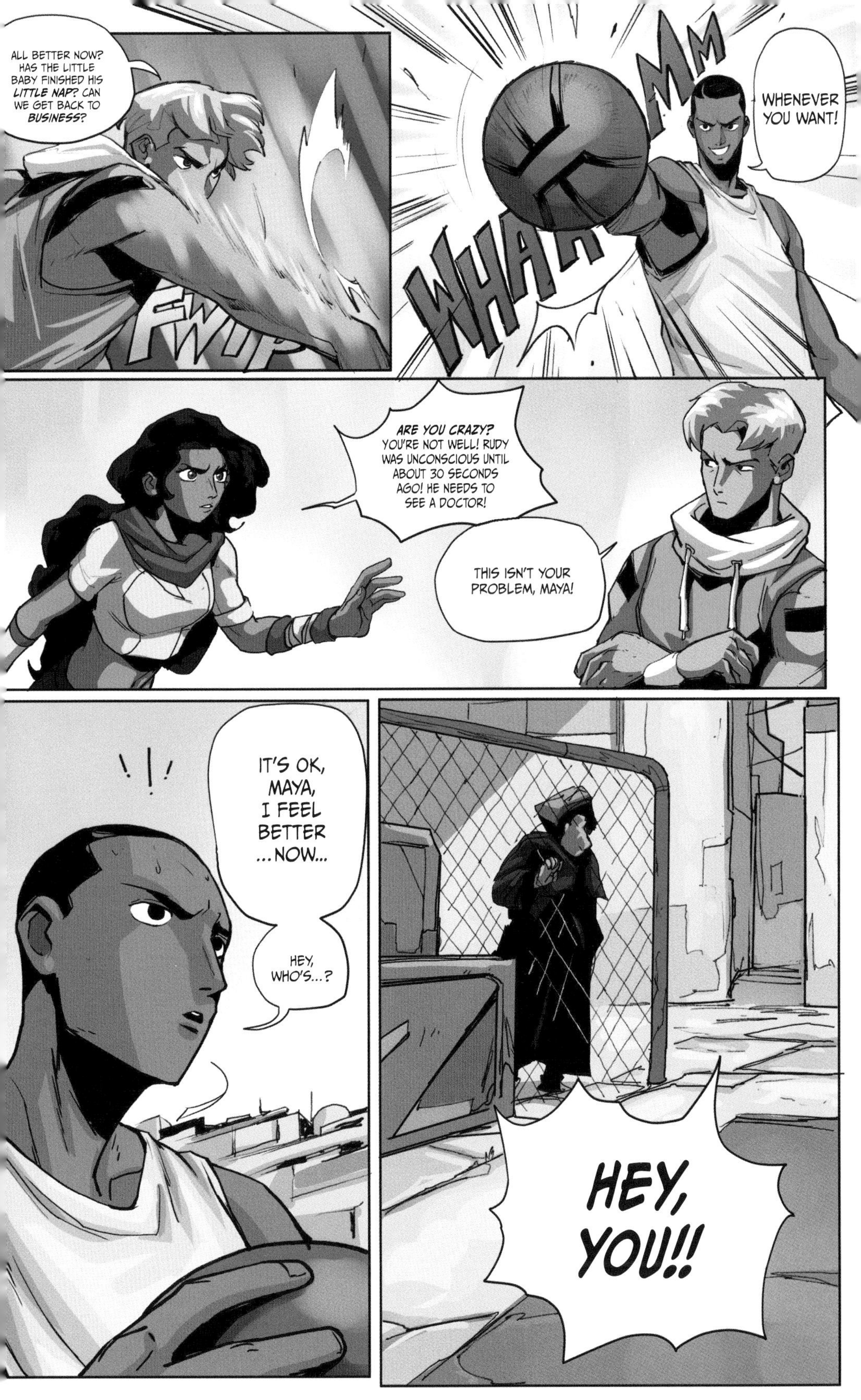
ALL BETTER NOW? HAS THE LITTLE BABY FINISHED HIS *LITTLE NAP?* CAN WE GET BACK TO *BUSINESS?*
FWUP
WHAMM
WHENEVER YOU WANT!
ARE YOU CRAZY? YOU'RE NOT WELL! RUDY WAS UNCONSCIOUS UNTIL ABOUT 30 SECONDS AGO! HE NEEDS TO SEE A DOCTOR!
THIS ISN'T YOUR PROBLEM, MAYA!
! | !
IT'S OK, MAYA, I FEEL BETTER ...NOW...
HEY, WHO'S...?
HEY, YOU!!

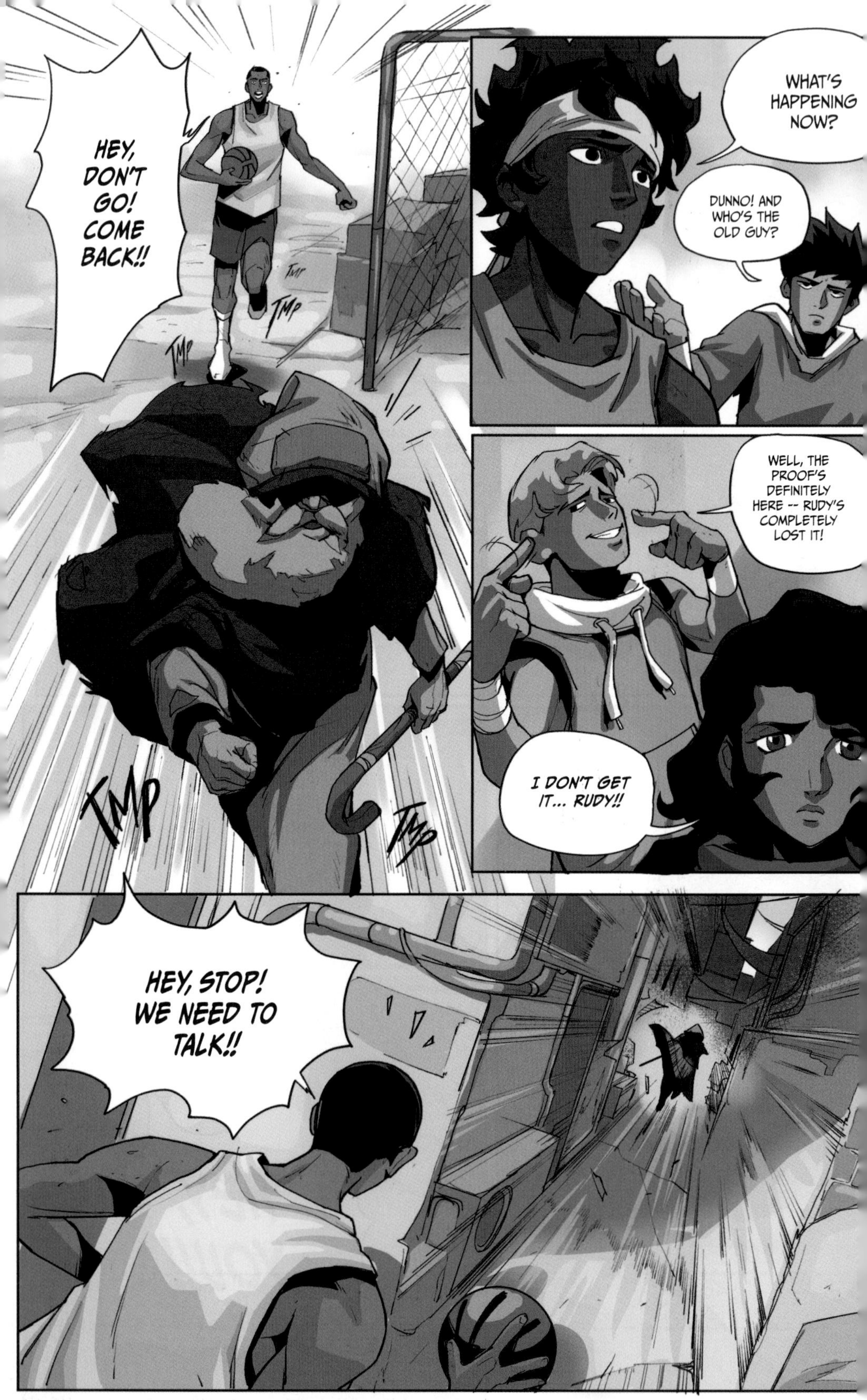
HEY, DON'T GO! COME BACK!!
WHAT'S HAPPENING NOW?
DUNNO! AND WHO'S THE OLD GUY?
WELL, THE PROOF'S DEFINITELY HERE -- RUDY'S COMPLETELY LOST IT!
I DON'T GET IT... RUDY!!
HEY, STOP! WE NEED TO TALK!!

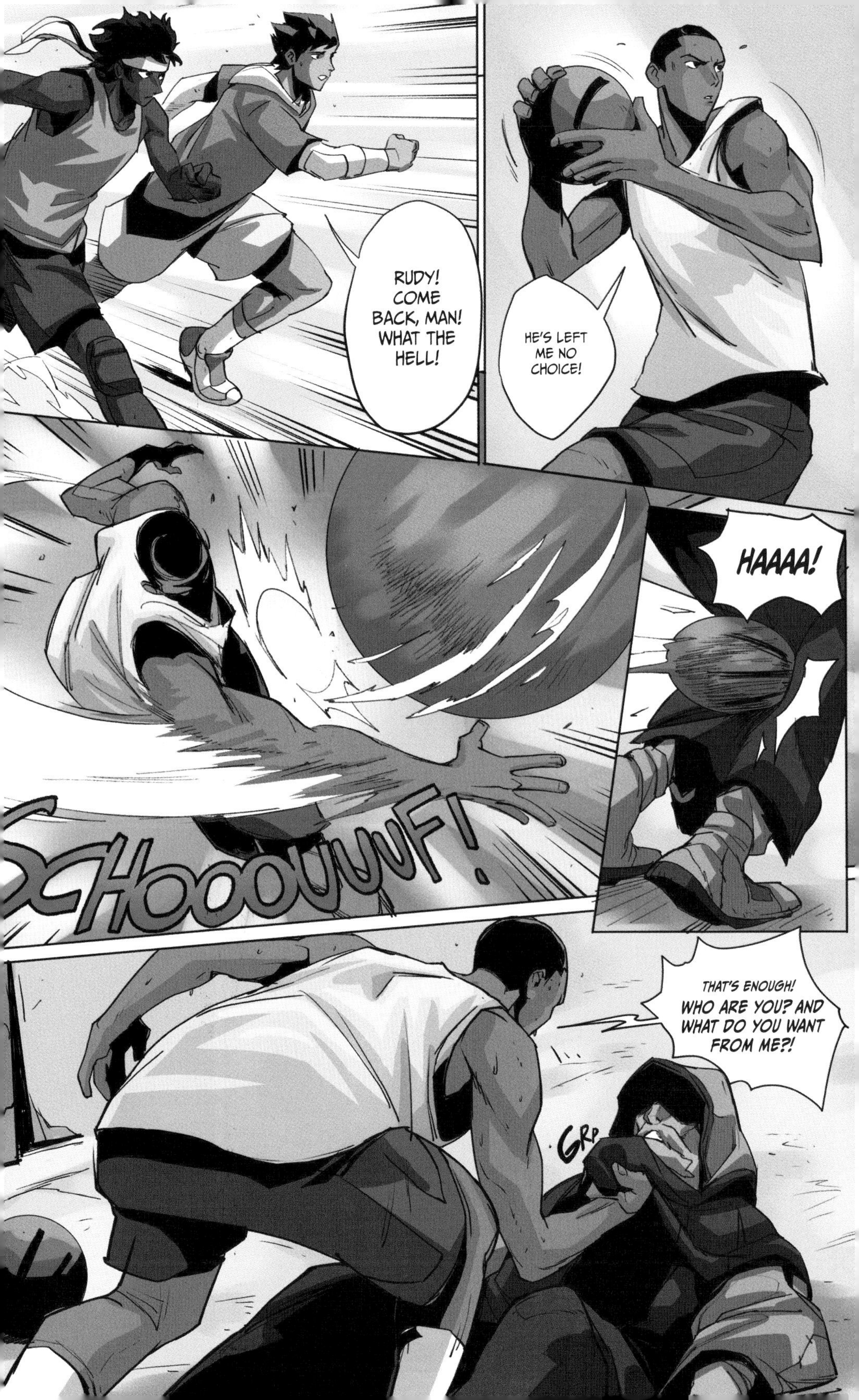
RUDY! COME BACK, MAN! WHAT THE HELL!
HE'S LEFT ME NO CHOICE!
HAAAA!
SCHOOUUUF!
THAT'S ENOUGH! WHO ARE YOU? AND WHAT DO YOU WANT FROM ME?!
GRP

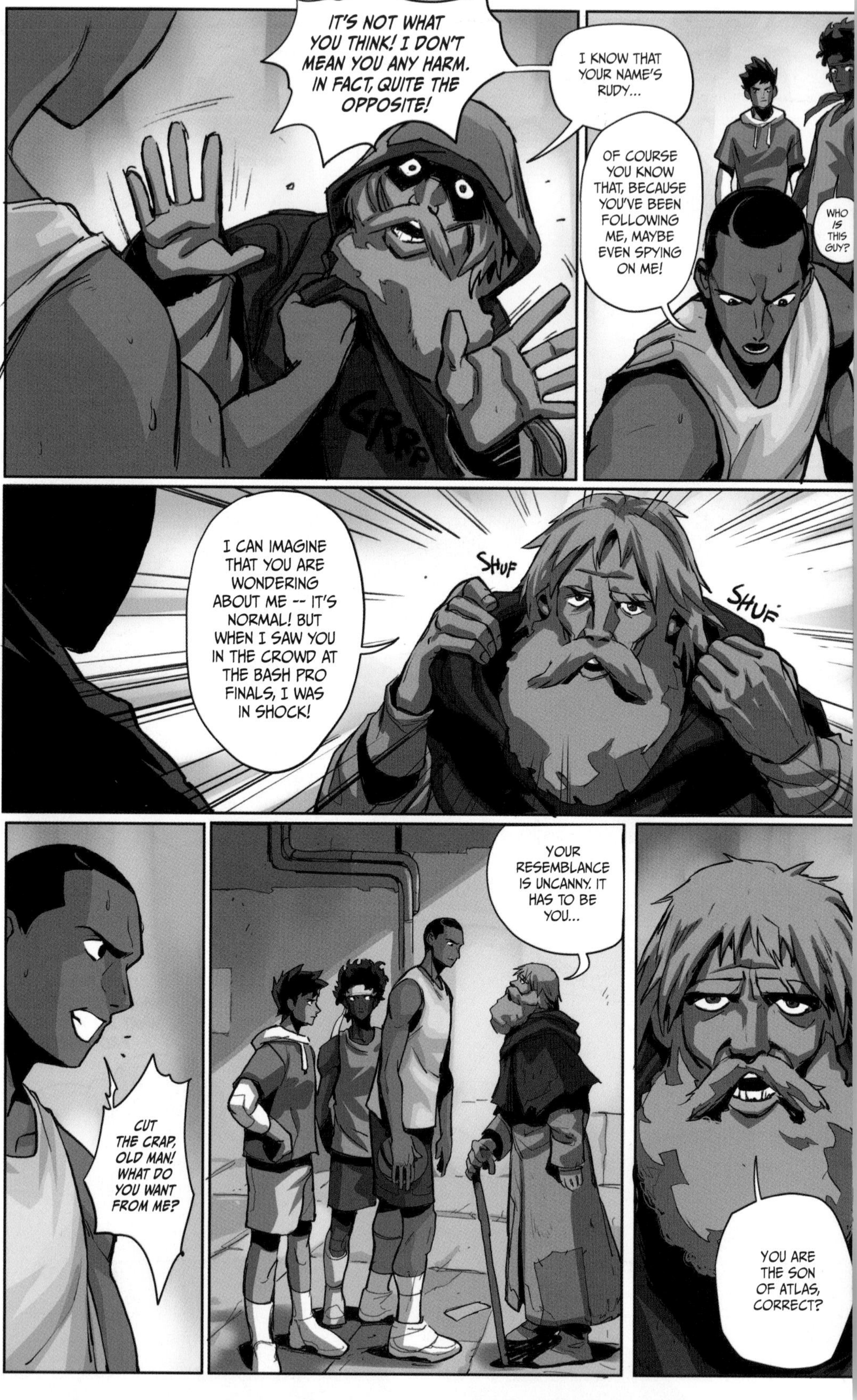
IT'S NOT WHAT YOU THINK! I DON'T MEAN YOU ANY HARM. IN FACT, QUITE THE OPPOSITE!
GRRR
I KNOW THAT YOUR NAME'S RUDY...
OF COURSE YOU KNOW THAT, BECAUSE YOU'VE BEEN FOLLOWING ME, MAYBE EVEN SPYING ON ME!
WHO IS THIS GUY?
I CAN IMAGINE THAT YOU ARE WONDERING ABOUT ME -- IT'S NORMAL! BUT WHEN I SAW YOU IN THE CROWD AT THE BASH PRO FINALS, I WAS IN SHOCK!
SHUF
SHUF
CUT THE CRAP, OLD MAN! WHAT DO YOU WANT FROM ME?
YOUR RESEMBLANCE IS UNCANNY. IT HAS TO BE YOU...
YOU ARE THE SON OF ATLAS, CORRECT?

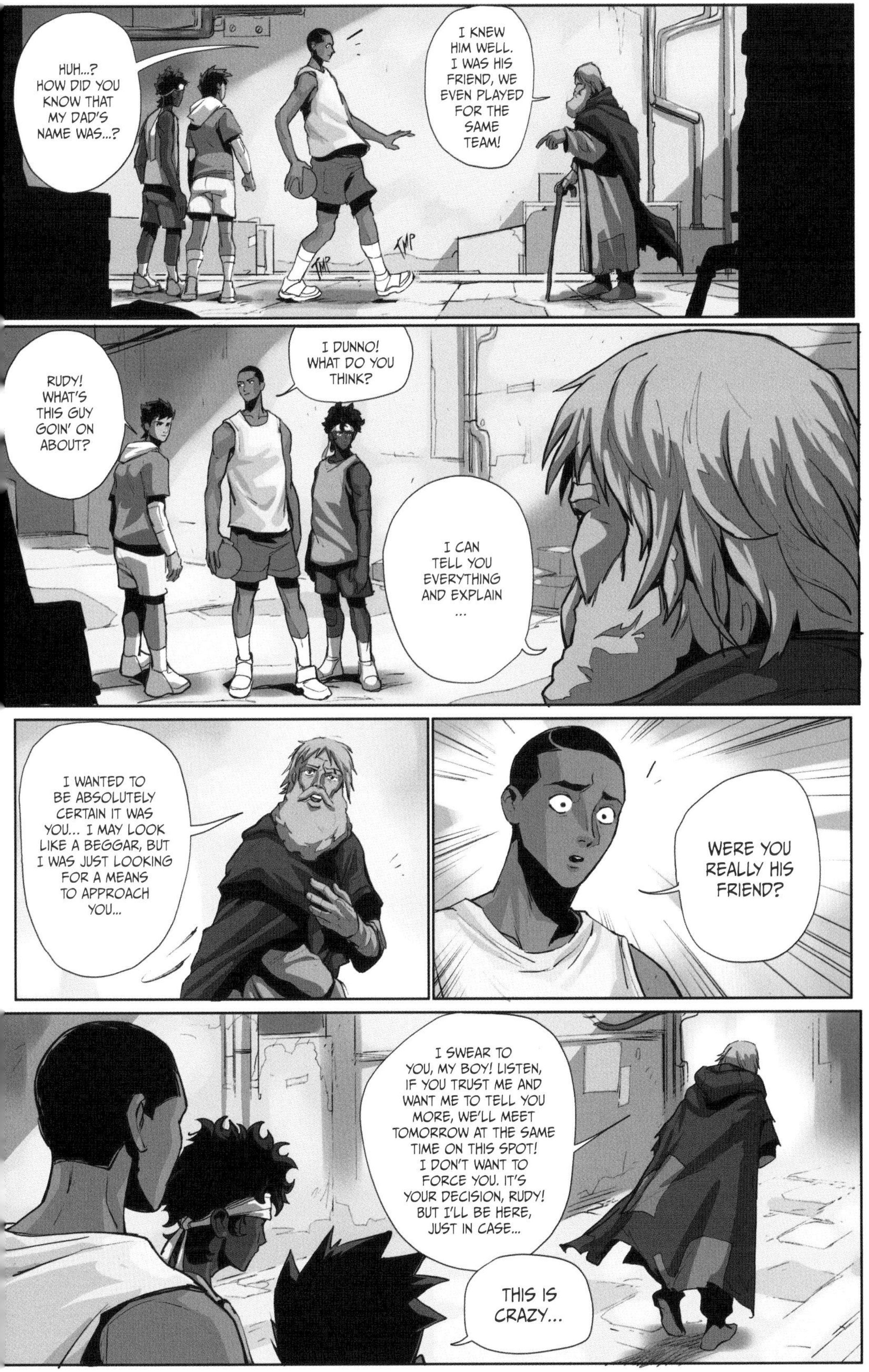
HUH...? HOW DID YOU KNOW THAT MY DAD'S NAME WAS...?
I KNEW HIM WELL. I WAS HIS FRIEND, WE EVEN PLAYED FOR THE SAME TEAM!
TMP
TMP
RUDY! WHAT'S THIS GUY GOIN' ON ABOUT?
I DUNNO! WHAT DO YOU THINK?
I CAN TELL YOU EVERYTHING AND EXPLAIN ...
I WANTED TO BE ABSOLUTELY CERTAIN IT WAS YOU... I MAY LOOK LIKE A BEGGAR, BUT I WAS JUST LOOKING FOR A MEANS TO APPROACH YOU...
WERE YOU REALLY HIS FRIEND?
I SWEAR TO YOU, MY BOY! LISTEN, IF YOU TRUST ME AND WANT ME TO TELL YOU MORE, WE'LL MEET TOMORROW AT THE SAME TIME ON THIS SPOT! I DON'T WANT TO FORCE YOU. IT'S YOUR DECISION, RUDY! BUT I'LL BE HERE, JUST IN CASE...
THIS IS CRAZY...

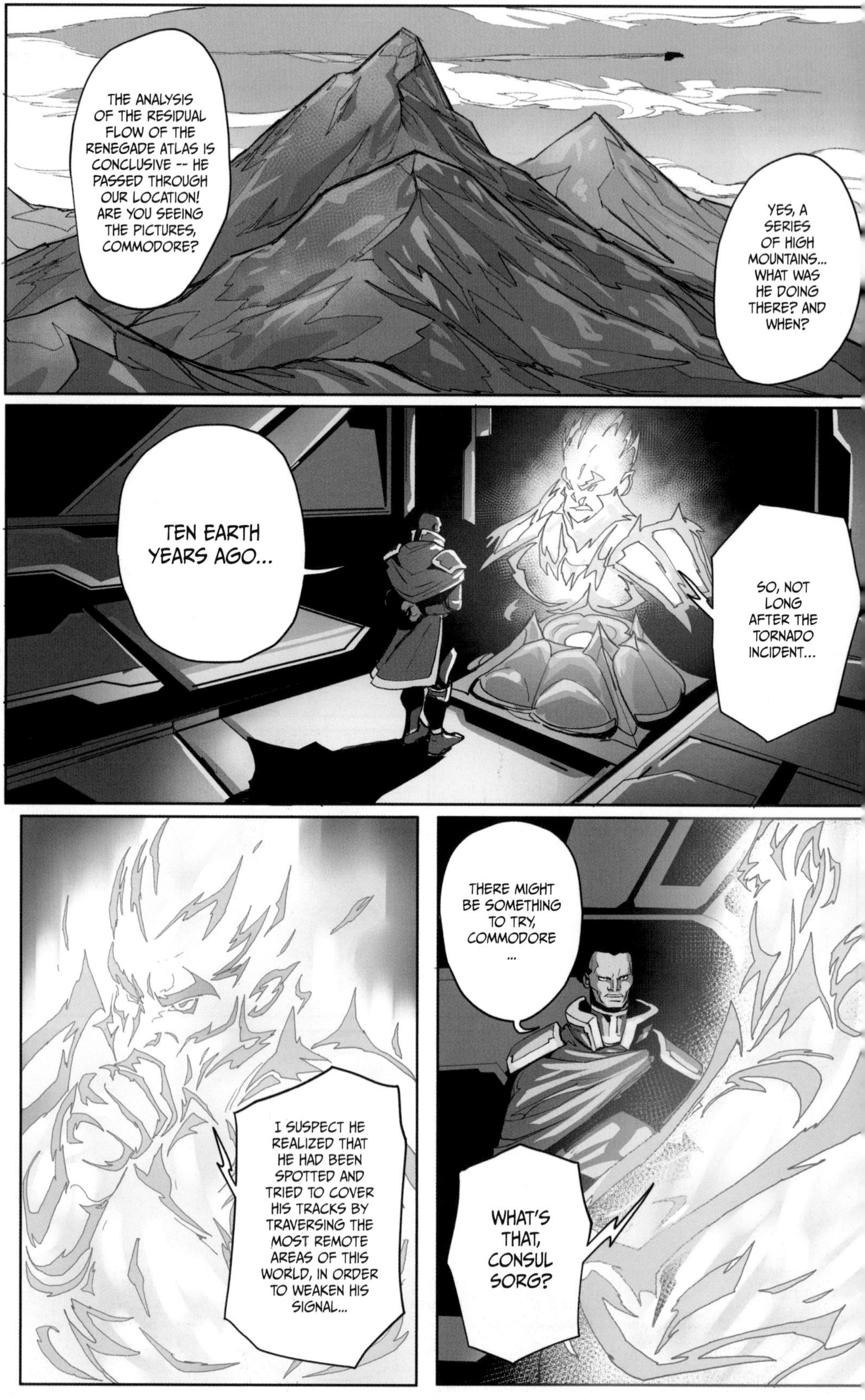
THE ANALYSIS OF THE RESIDUAL FLOW OF THE RENEGADE ATLAS IS CONCLUSIVE -- HE PASSED THROUGH OUR LOCATION! ARE YOU SEEING THE PICTURES, COMMODORE?
YES, A SERIES OF HIGH MOUNTAINS... WHAT WAS HE DOING THERE? AND WHEN?
TEN EARTH YEARS AGO...
SO, NOT LONG AFTER THE TORNADO INCIDENT...
I SUSPECT HE REALIZED THAT HE HAD BEEN SPOTTED AND TRIED TO COVER HIS TRACKS BY TRAVERSING THE MOST REMOTE AREAS OF THIS WORLD, IN ORDER TO WEAKEN HIS SIGNAL...
THERE MIGHT BE SOMETHING TO TRY, COMMODORE ...
WHAT'S THAT, CONSUL SORG?

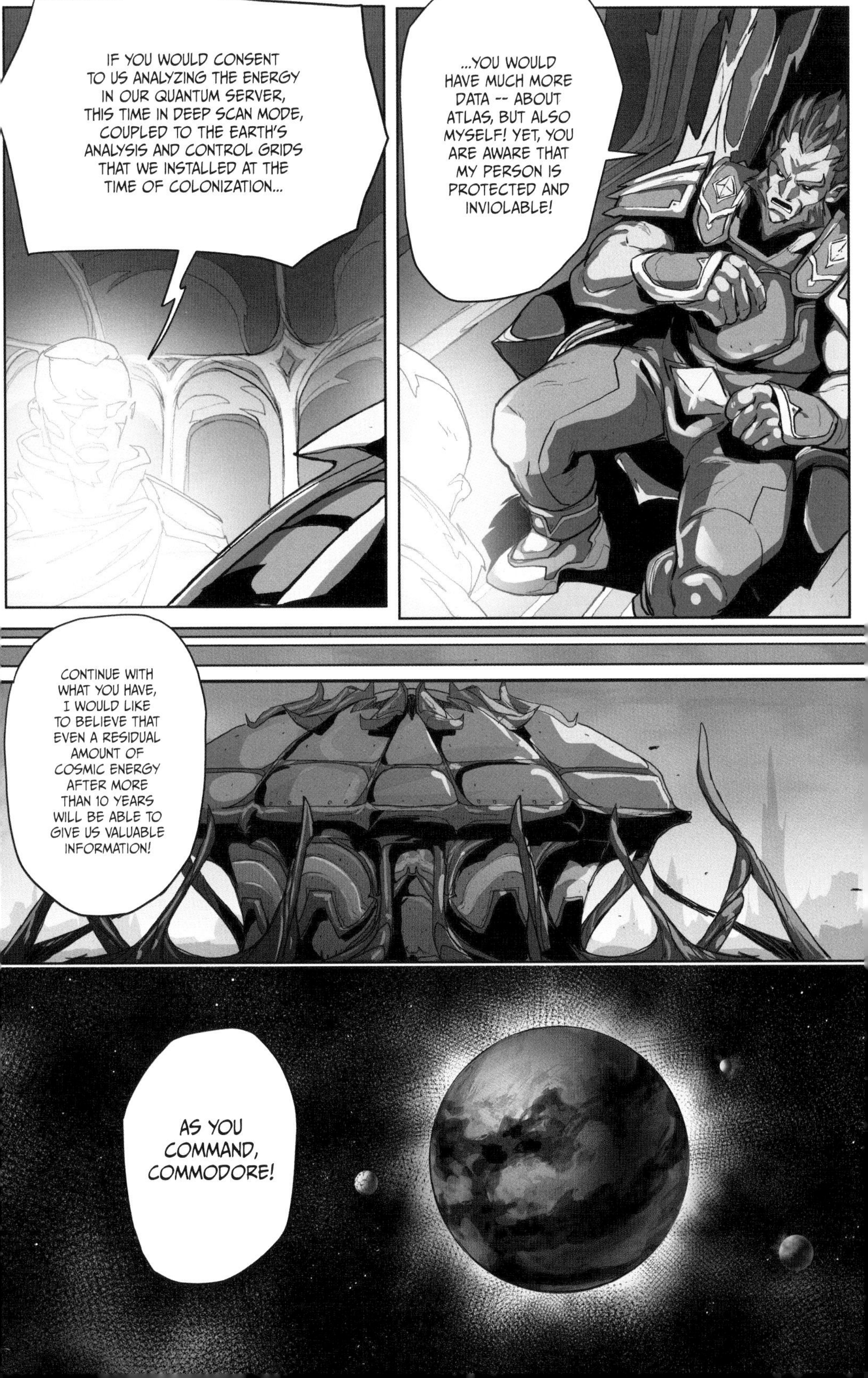
IF YOU WOULD CONSENT TO US ANALYZING THE ENERGY IN OUR QUANTUM SERVER, THIS TIME IN DEEP SCAN MODE, COUPLED TO THE EARTH'S ANALYSIS AND CONTROL GRIDS THAT WE INSTALLED AT THE TIME OF COLONIZATION...
...YOU WOULD HAVE MUCH MORE DATA -- ABOUT ATLAS, BUT ALSO MYSELF! YET, YOU ARE AWARE THAT MY PERSON IS PROTECTED AND INVIOLABLE!
CONTINUE WITH WHAT YOU HAVE, I WOULD LIKE TO BELIEVE THAT EVEN A RESIDUAL AMOUNT OF COSMIC ENERGY AFTER MORE THAN 10 YEARS WILL BE ABLE TO GIVE US VALUABLE INFORMATION!
AS YOU COMMAND, COMMODORE!

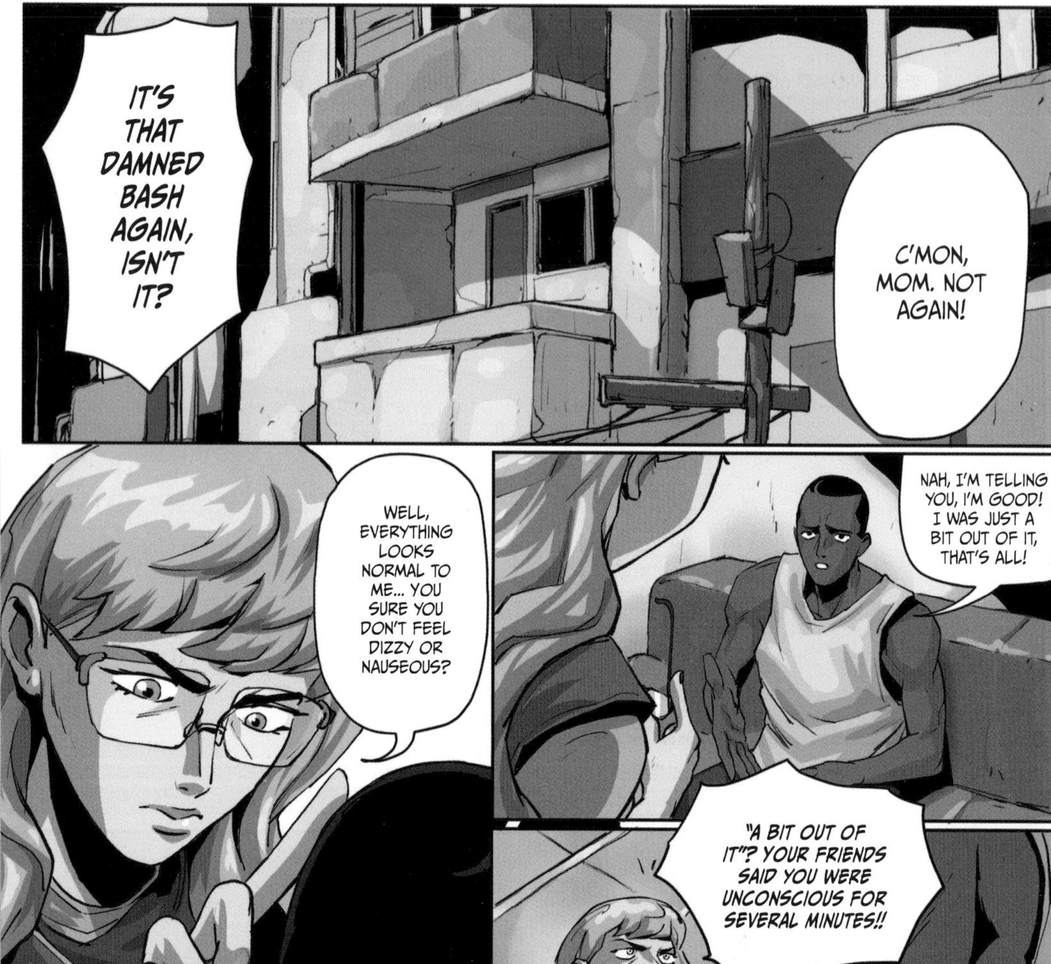
IT'S THAT DAMNED BASH AGAIN, ISN'T IT?
C'MON, MOM. NOT AGAIN!
WELL, EVERYTHING LOOKS NORMAL TO ME... YOU SURE YOU DON'T FEEL DIZZY OR NAUSEOUS?
NAH, I'M TELLING YOU, I'M GOOD! I WAS JUST A BIT OUT OF IT, THAT'S ALL!
"A BIT OUT OF IT"? YOUR FRIENDS SAID YOU WERE UNCONSCIOUS FOR SEVERAL MINUTES!!

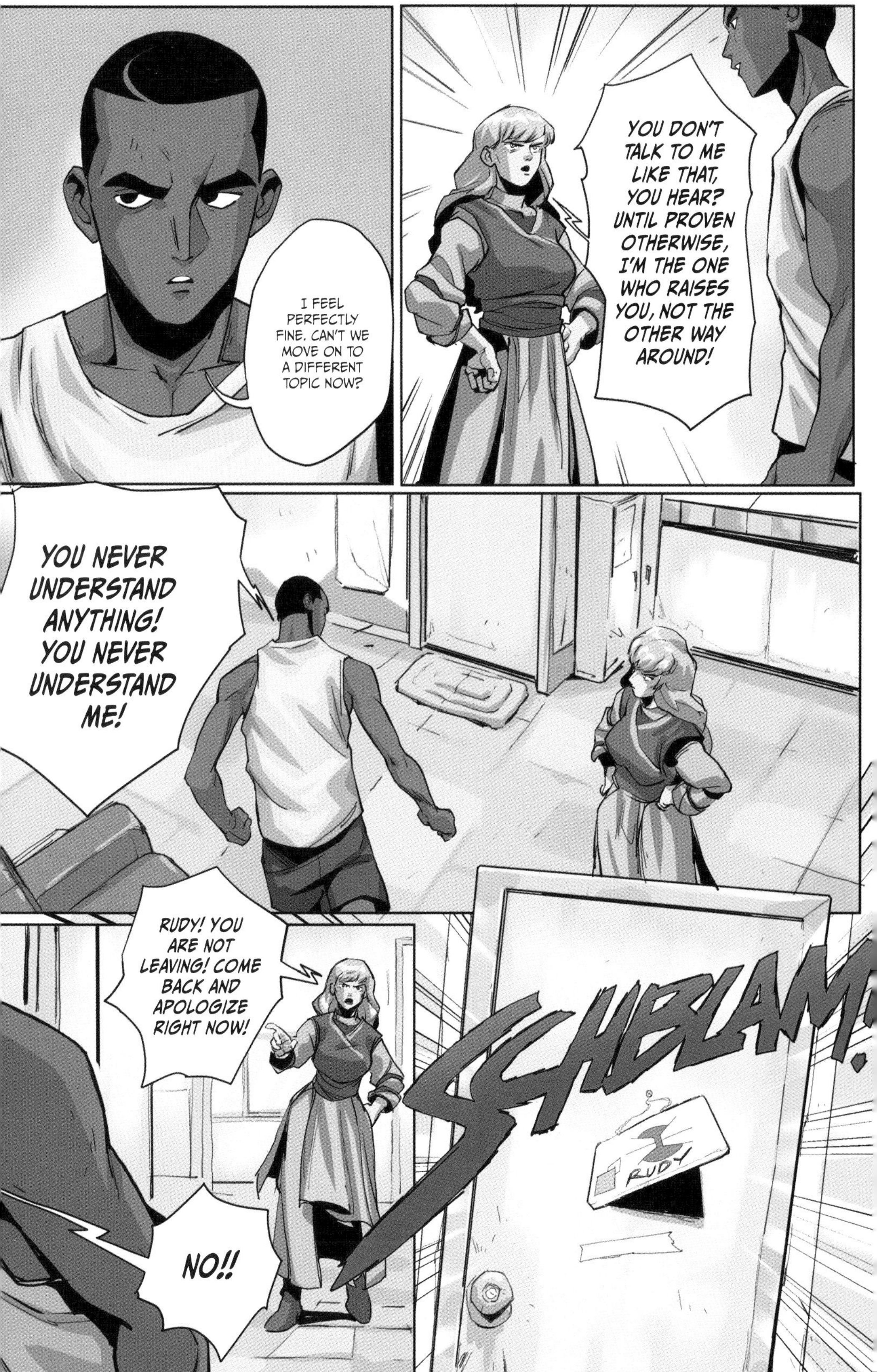
I FEEL PERFECTLY FINE. CAN'T WE MOVE ON TO A DIFFERENT TOPIC NOW?
YOU DON'T TALK TO ME LIKE THAT, YOU HEAR? UNTIL PROVEN OTHERWISE, I'M THE ONE WHO RAISES YOU, NOT THE OTHER WAY AROUND!
YOU NEVER UNDERSTAND ANYTHING! YOU NEVER UNDERSTAND ME!
RUDY! YOU ARE NOT LEAVING! COME BACK AND APOLOGIZE RIGHT NOW!
NO!!
SCHBLAM!
RUDY

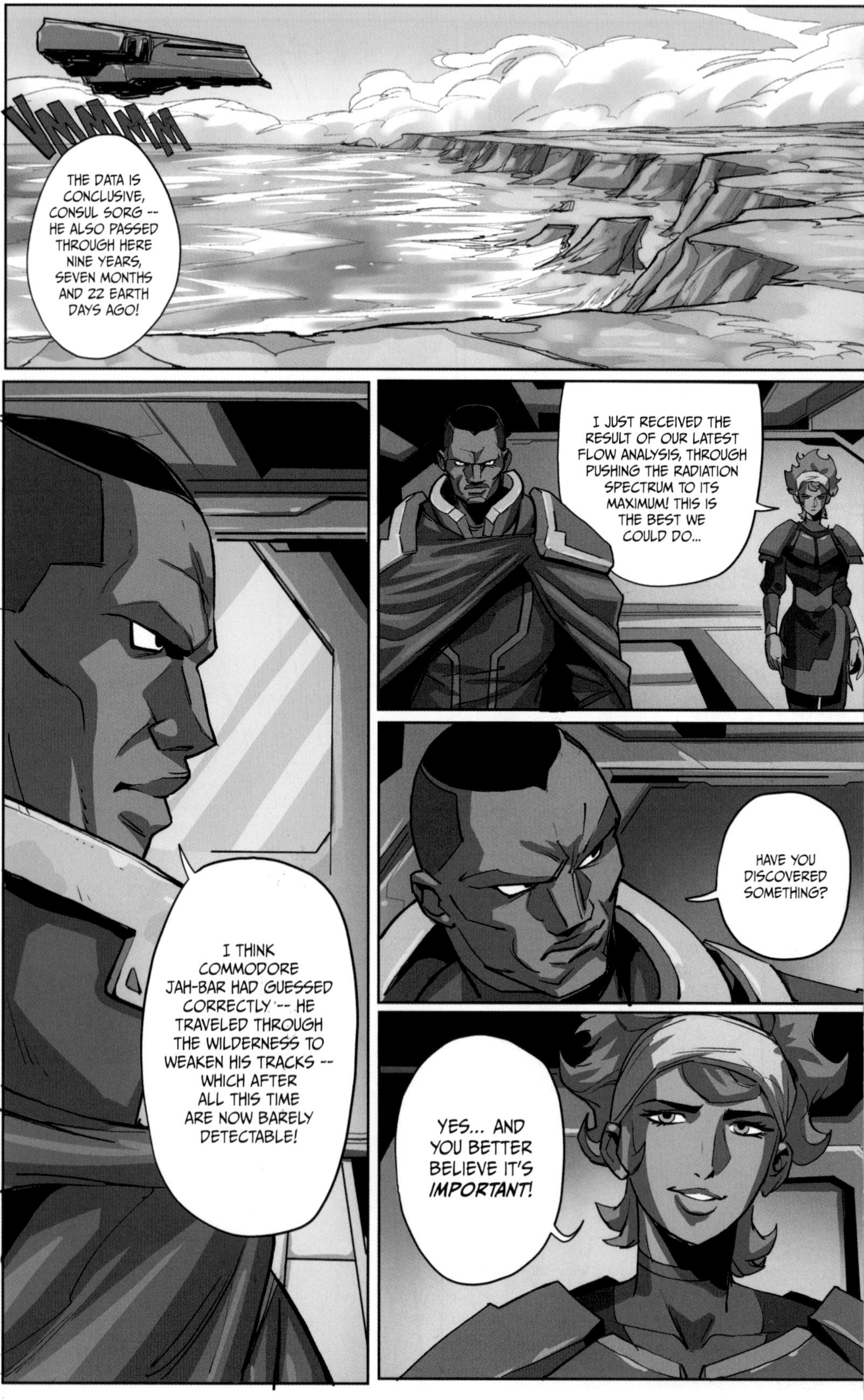
VMMMM
THE DATA IS CONCLUSIVE, CONSUL SORG -- HE ALSO PASSED THROUGH HERE NINE YEARS, SEVEN MONTHS AND 22 EARTH DAYS AGO!
I JUST RECEIVED THE RESULT OF OUR LATEST FLOW ANALYSIS, THROUGH PUSHING THE RADIATION SPECTRUM TO ITS MAXIMUM! THIS IS THE BEST WE COULD DO...
HAVE YOU DISCOVERED SOMETHING?
YES... AND YOU BETTER BELIEVE IT'S *IMPORTANT*!
I THINK COMMODORE JAH-BAR HAD GUESSED CORRECTLY -- HE TRAVELED THROUGH THE WILDERNESS TO WEAKEN HIS TRACKS -- WHICH AFTER ALL THIS TIME ARE NOW BARELY DETECTABLE!

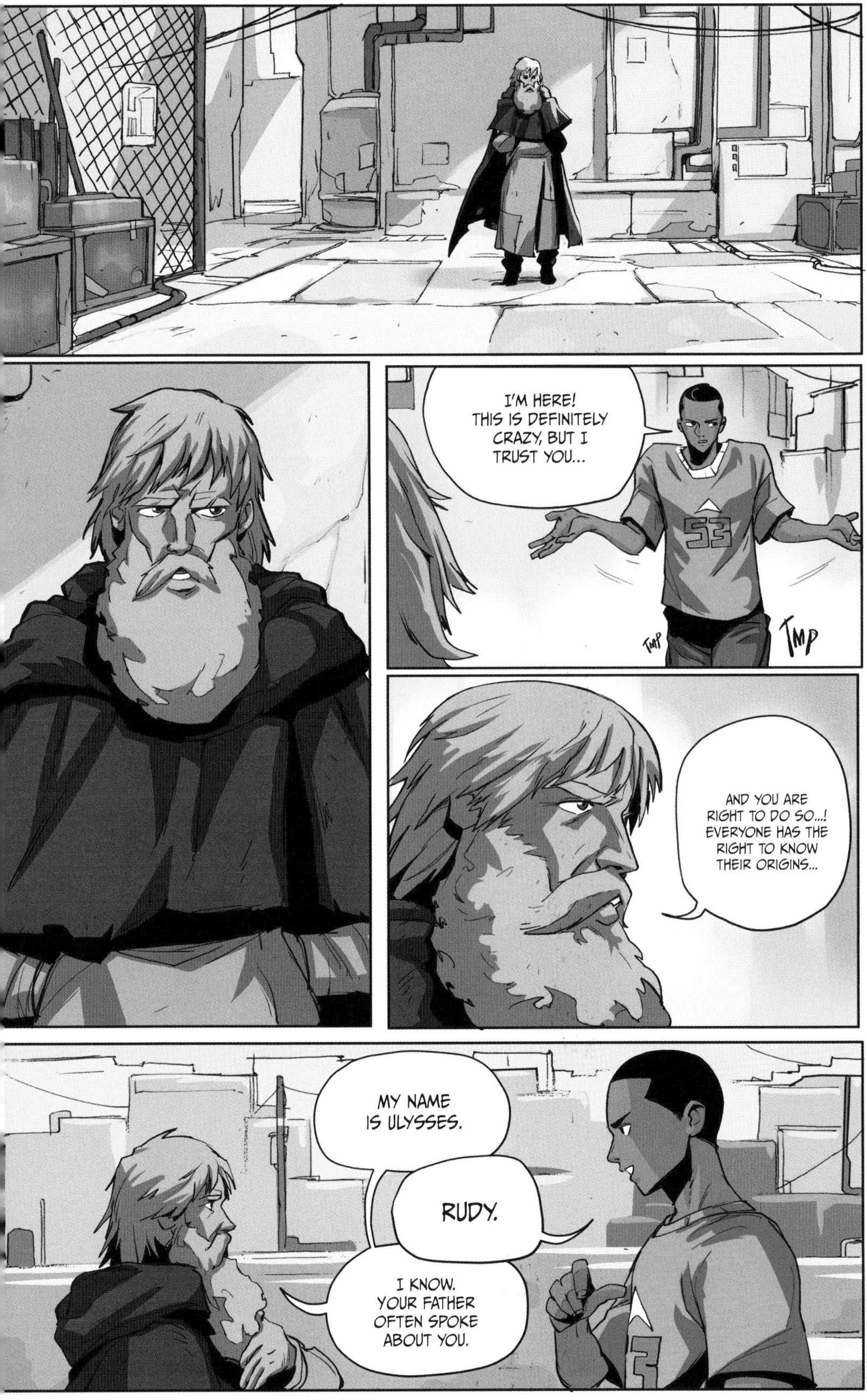
I'M HERE! THIS IS DEFINITELY CRAZY, BUT I TRUST YOU...
TMP
TMP
AND YOU ARE RIGHT TO DO SO...! EVERYONE HAS THE RIGHT TO KNOW THEIR ORIGINS...
MY NAME IS ULYSSES.
RUDY.
I KNOW. YOUR FATHER OFTEN SPOKE ABOUT YOU.

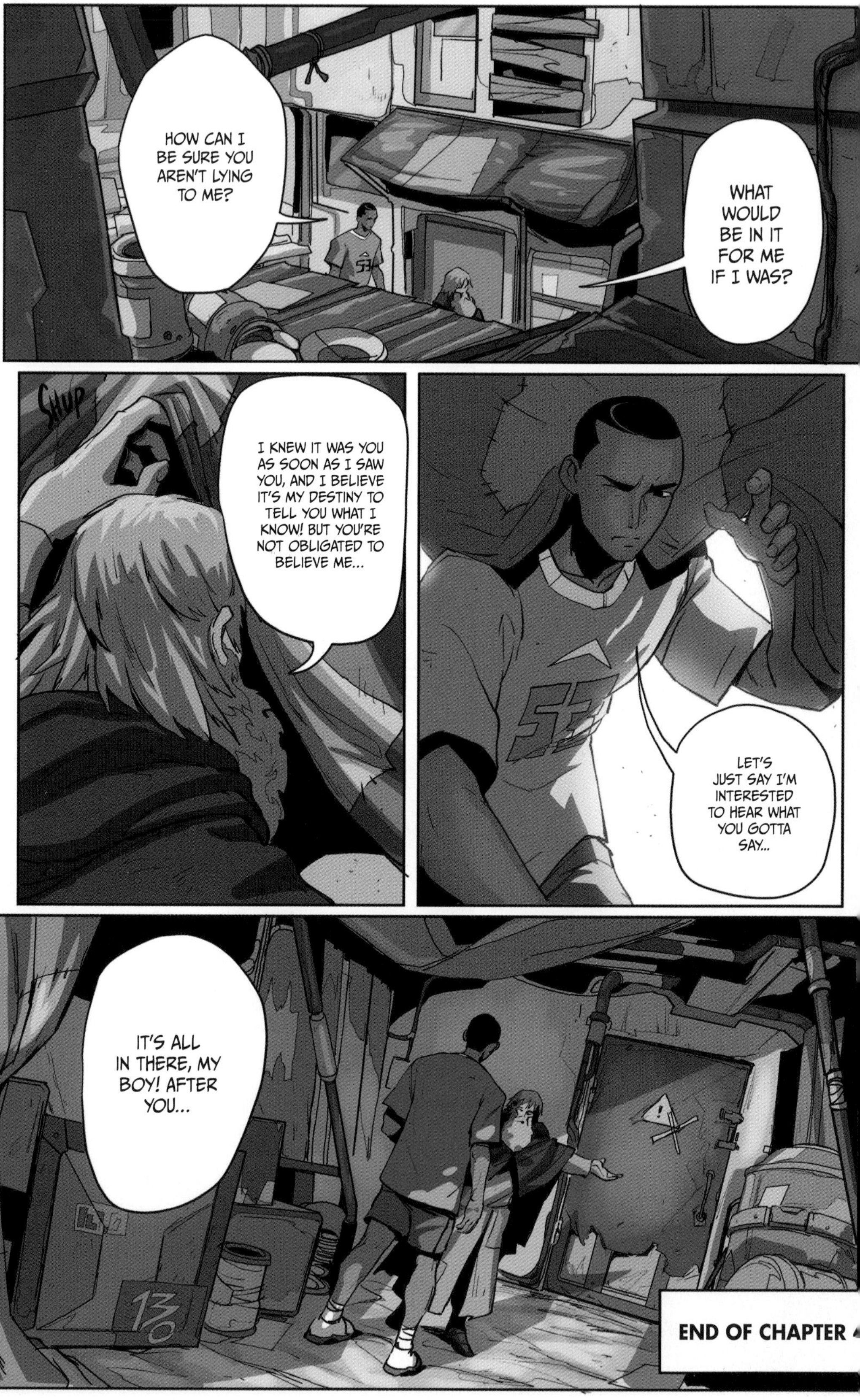
HOW CAN I BE SURE YOU AREN'T LYING TO ME?
WHAT WOULD BE IN IT FOR ME IF I WAS?
SHUP
I KNEW IT WAS YOU AS SOON AS I SAW YOU, AND I BELIEVE IT'S MY DESTINY TO TELL YOU WHAT I KNOW! BUT YOU'RE NOT OBLIGATED TO BELIEVE ME...
LET'S JUST SAY I'M INTERESTED TO HEAR WHAT YOU GOTTA SAY...
IT'S ALL IN THERE, MY BOY! AFTER YOU...
END OF CHAPTER

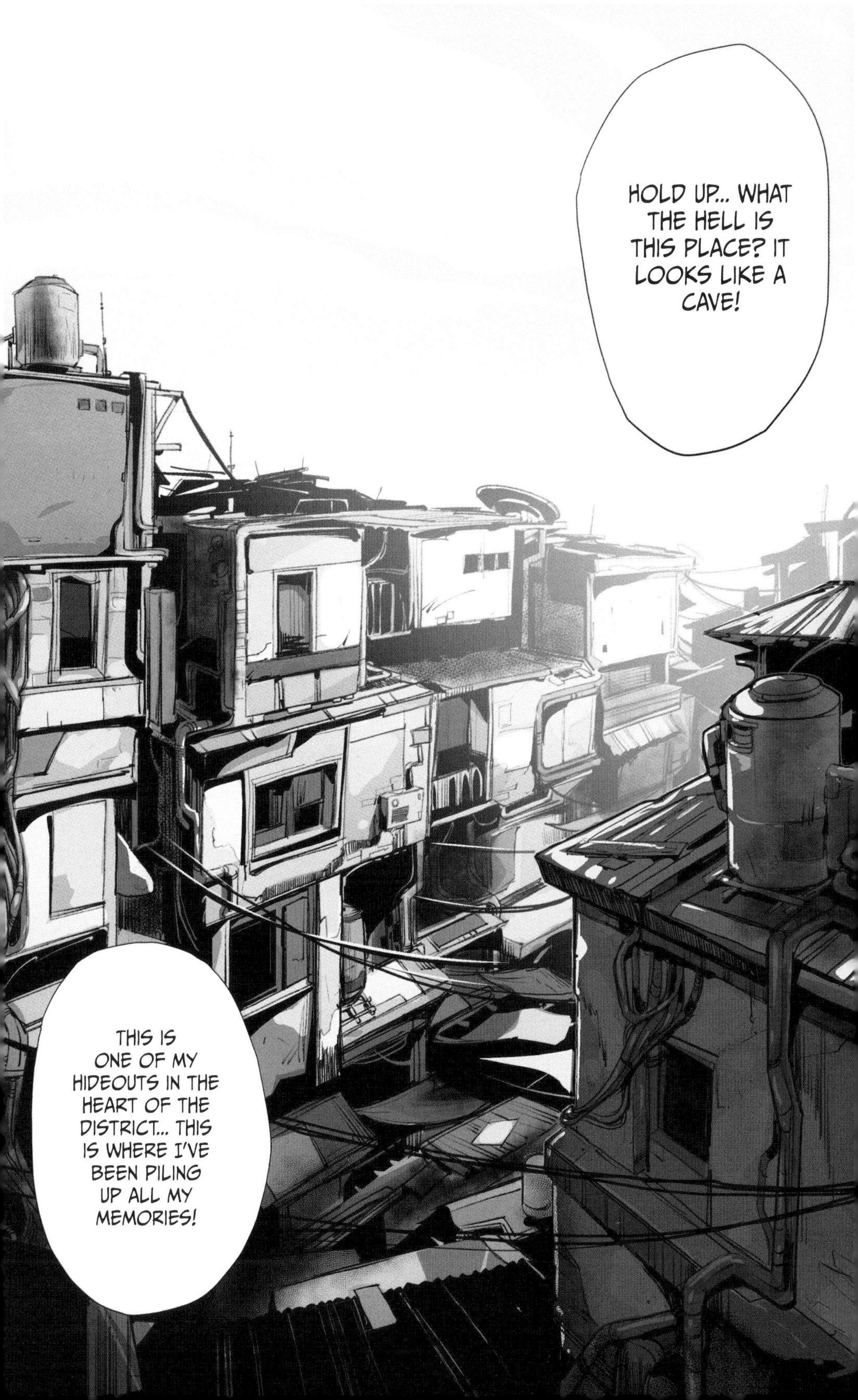
HOLD UP... WHAT THE HELL IS THIS PLACE? IT LOOKS LIKE A CAVE!
THIS IS ONE OF MY HIDEOUTS IN THE HEART OF THE DISTRICT... THIS IS WHERE I'VE BEEN PILING UP ALL MY MEMORIES!

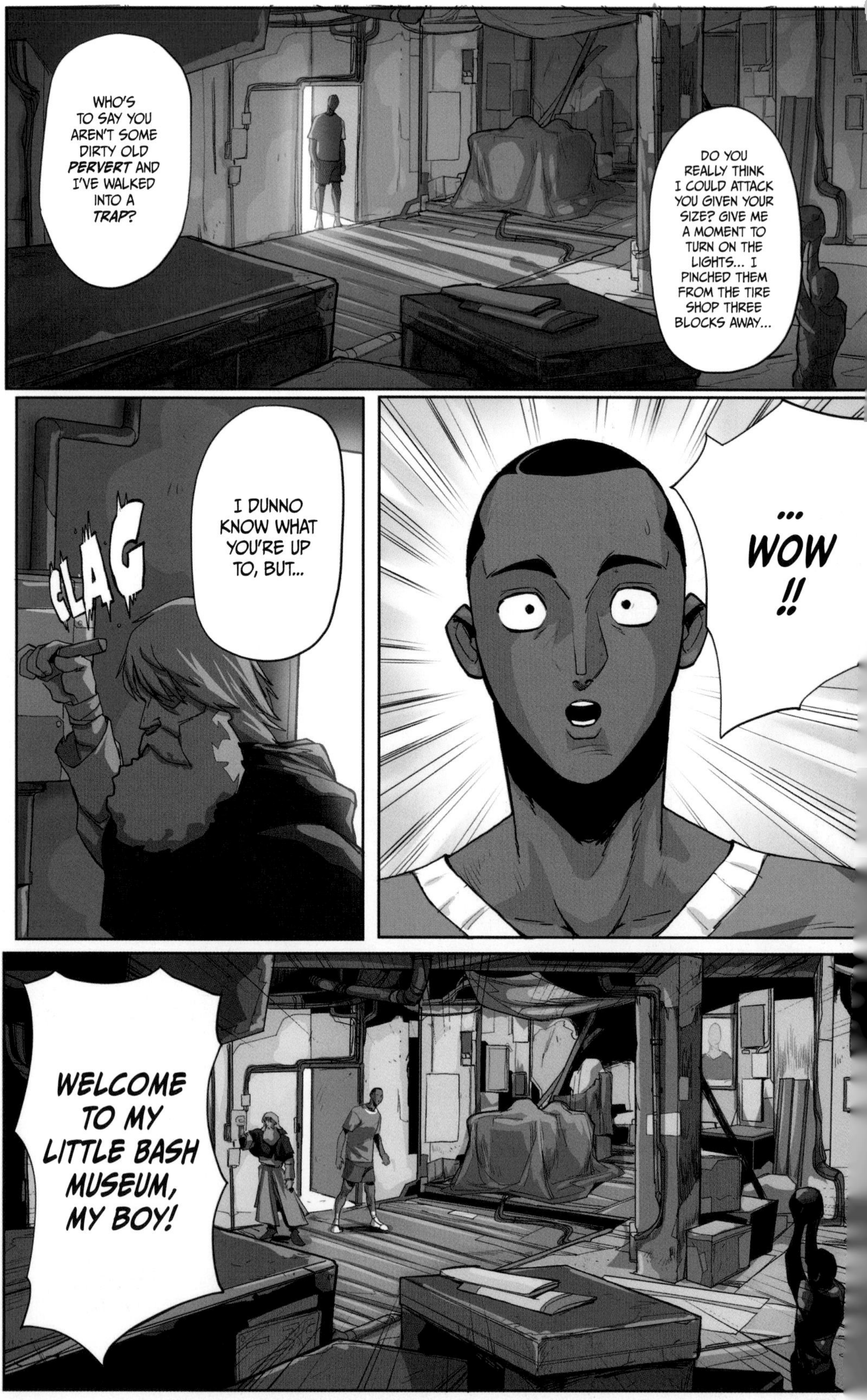
WHO'S TO SAY YOU AREN'T SOME DIRTY OLD PERVERT AND I'VE WALKED INTO A TRAP?
DO YOU REALLY THINK I COULD ATTACK YOU GIVEN YOUR SIZE? GIVE ME A MOMENT TO TURN ON THE LIGHTS... I PINCHED THEM FROM THE TIRE SHOP THREE BLOCKS AWAY...
CLAG
I DUNNO KNOW WHAT YOU'RE UP TO, BUT...
... WOW !!
WELCOME TO MY LITTLE BASH MUSEUM, MY BOY!

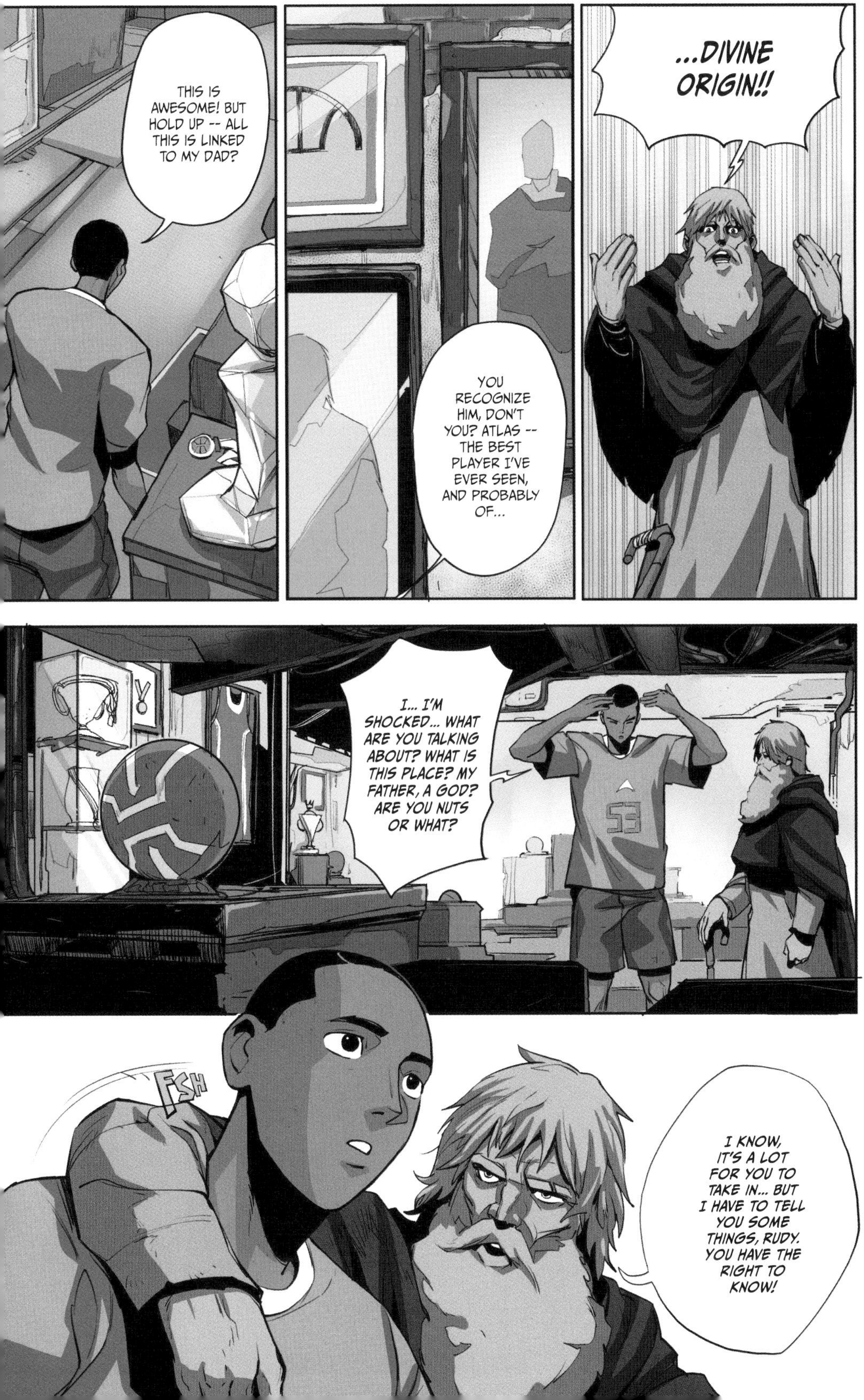
THIS IS AWESOME! BUT HOLD UP -- ALL THIS IS LINKED TO MY DAD?
YOU RECOGNIZE HIM, DON'T YOU? ATLAS -- THE BEST PLAYER I'VE EVER SEEN, AND PROBABLY OF...
...DIVINE ORIGIN!!
I... I'M SHOCKED... WHAT ARE YOU TALKING ABOUT? WHAT IS THIS PLACE? MY FATHER, A GOD? ARE YOU NUTS OR WHAT?
FSH
I KNOW, IT'S A LOT FOR YOU TO TAKE IN... BUT I HAVE TO TELL YOU SOME THINGS, RUDY. YOU HAVE THE RIGHT TO KNOW!

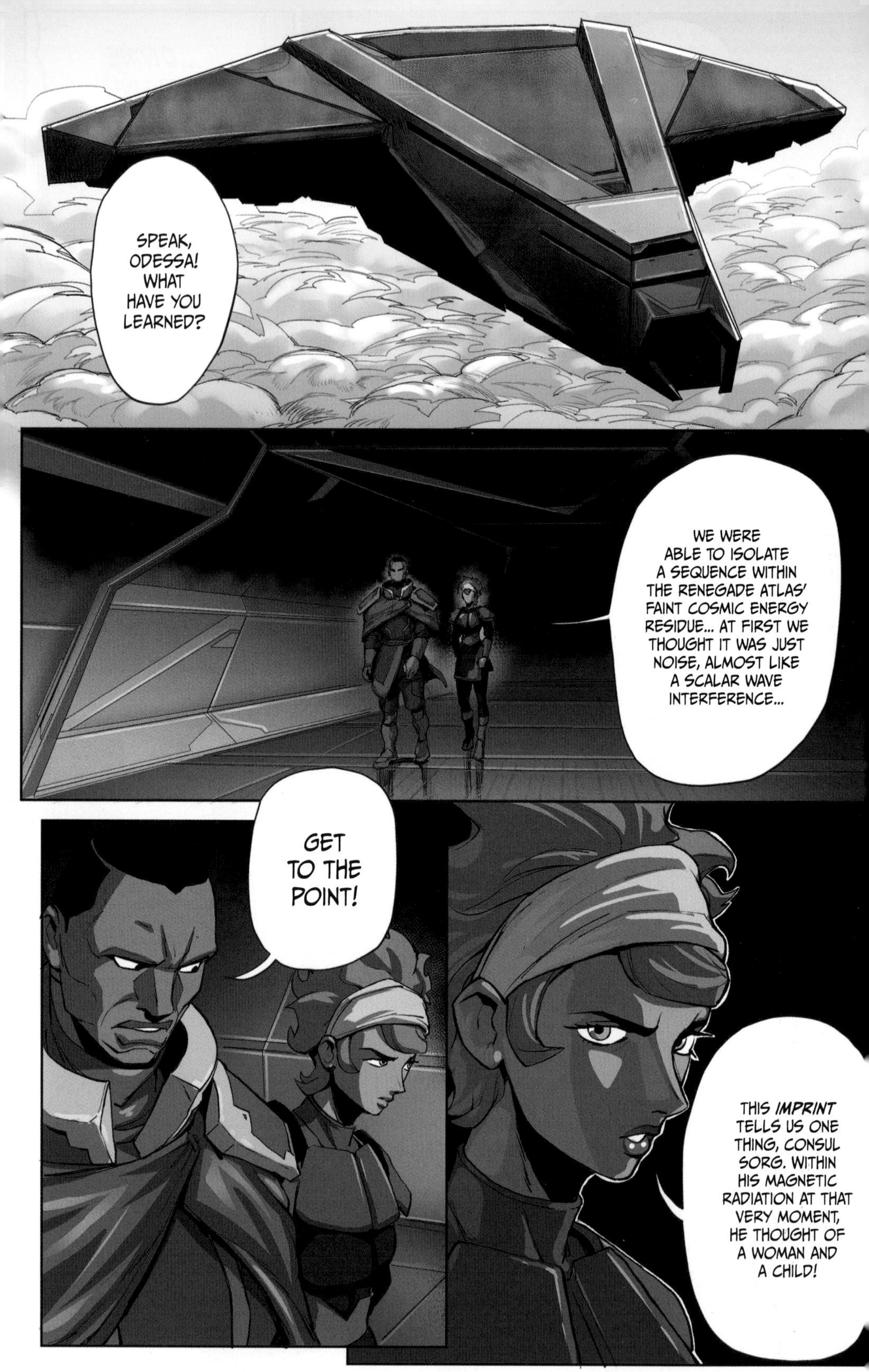
SPEAK, ODESSA! WHAT HAVE YOU LEARNED?
WE WERE ABLE TO ISOLATE A SEQUENCE WITHIN THE RENEGADE ATLAS' FAINT COSMIC ENERGY RESIDUE... AT FIRST WE THOUGHT IT WAS JUST NOISE, ALMOST LIKE A SCALAR WAVE INTERFERENCE...
GET TO THE POINT!
THIS *IMPRINT* TELLS US ONE THING, CONSUL SORG. WITHIN HIS MAGNETIC RADIATION AT THAT VERY MOMENT, HE THOUGHT OF A WOMAN AND A CHILD!

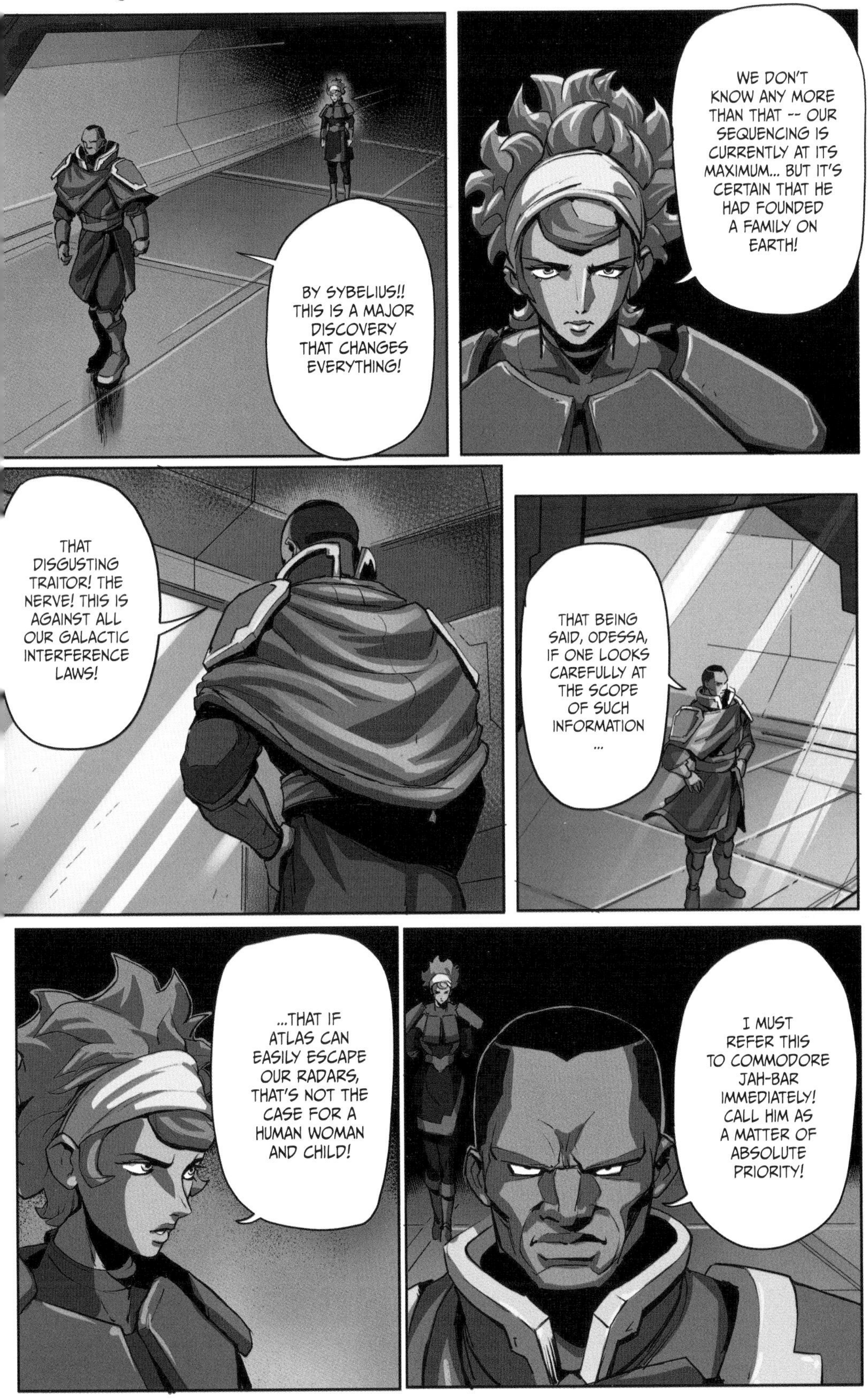
BY SYBELIUS!! THIS IS A MAJOR DISCOVERY THAT CHANGES EVERYTHING!
WE DON'T KNOW ANY MORE THAN THAT -- OUR SEQUENCING IS CURRENTLY AT ITS MAXIMUM... BUT IT'S CERTAIN THAT HE HAD FOUNDED A FAMILY ON EARTH!
THAT DISGUSTING TRAITOR! THE NERVE! THIS IS AGAINST ALL OUR GALACTIC INTERFERENCE LAWS!
THAT BEING SAID, ODESSA, IF ONE LOOKS CAREFULLY AT THE SCOPE OF SUCH INFORMATION ...
...THAT IF ATLAS CAN EASILY ESCAPE OUR RADARS, THAT'S NOT THE CASE FOR A HUMAN WOMAN AND CHILD!
I MUST REFER THIS TO COMMODORE JAH-BAR IMMEDIATELY! CALL HIM AS A MATTER OF ABSOLUTE PRIORITY!

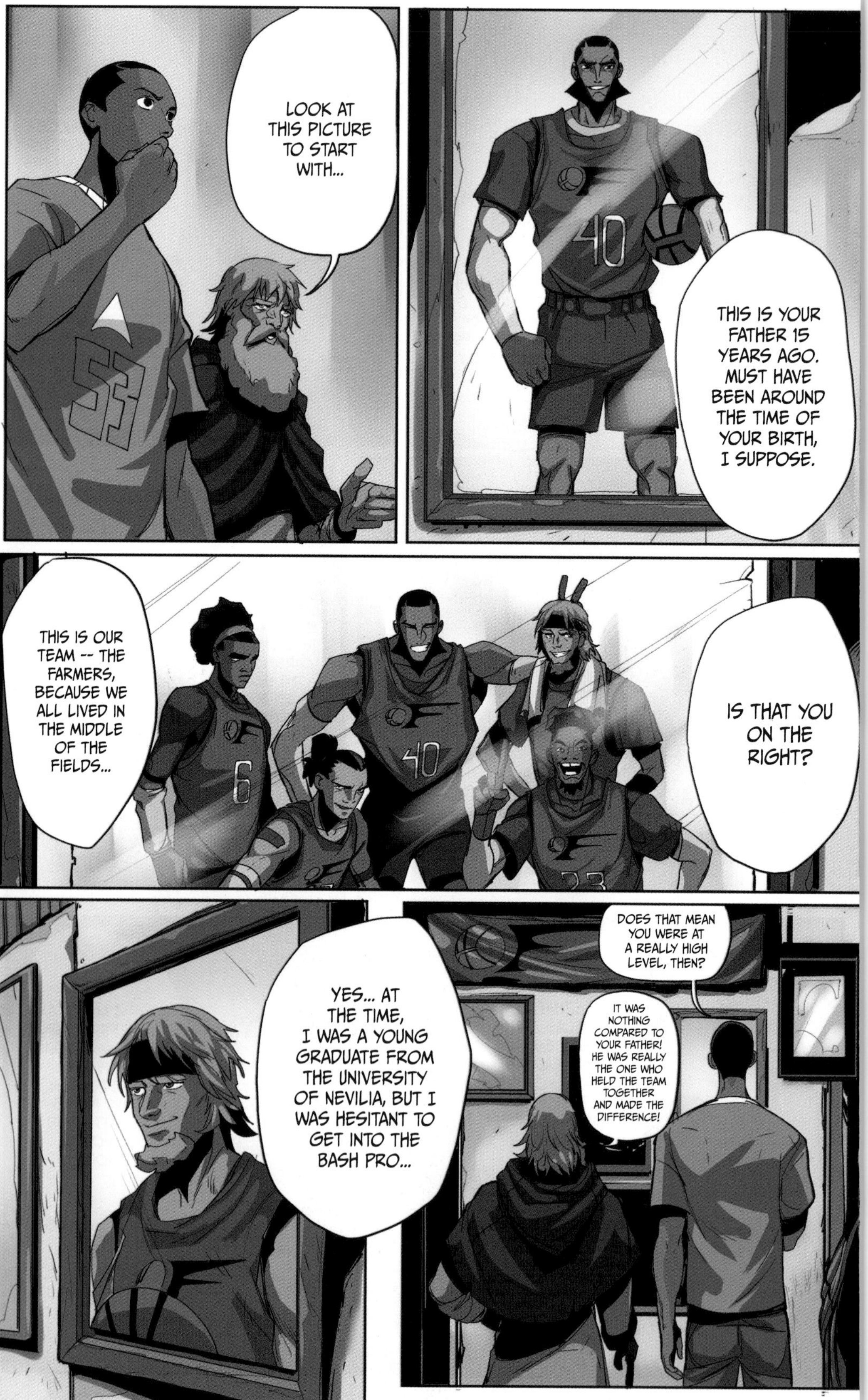
LOOK AT THIS PICTURE TO START WITH...
THIS IS YOUR FATHER 15 YEARS AGO. MUST HAVE BEEN AROUND THE TIME OF YOUR BIRTH, I SUPPOSE.
THIS IS OUR TEAM -- THE FARMERS, BECAUSE WE ALL LIVED IN THE MIDDLE OF THE FIELDS...
IS THAT YOU ON THE RIGHT?
YES... AT THE TIME, I WAS A YOUNG GRADUATE FROM THE UNIVERSITY OF NEVILIA, BUT I WAS HESITANT TO GET INTO THE BASH PRO...
DOES THAT MEAN YOU WERE AT A REALLY HIGH LEVEL, THEN?
IT WAS NOTHING COMPARED TO YOUR FATHER! HE WAS REALLY THE ONE WHO HELD THE TEAM TOGETHER AND MADE THE DIFFERENCE!

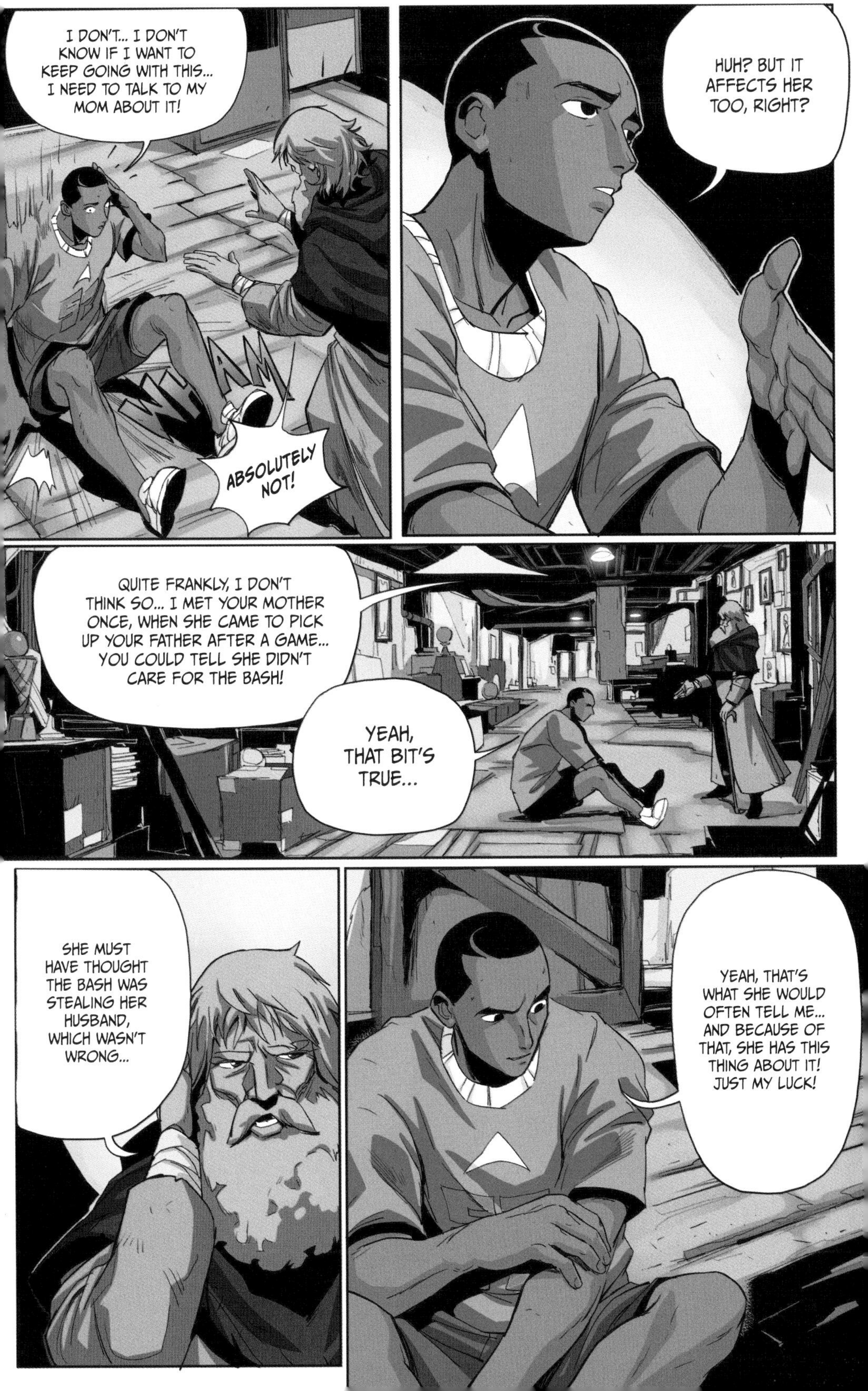
I DON'T... I DON'T KNOW IF I WANT TO KEEP GOING WITH THIS... I NEED TO TALK TO MY MOM ABOUT IT!
WHAM
ABSOLUTELY NOT!
HUH? BUT IT AFFECTS HER TOO, RIGHT?
QUITE FRANKLY, I DON'T THINK SO... I MET YOUR MOTHER ONCE, WHEN SHE CAME TO PICK UP YOUR FATHER AFTER A GAME... YOU COULD TELL SHE DIDN'T CARE FOR THE BASH!
YEAH, THAT BIT'S TRUE...
SHE MUST HAVE THOUGHT THE BASH WAS STEALING HER HUSBAND, WHICH WASN'T WRONG...
YEAH, THAT'S WHAT SHE WOULD OFTEN TELL ME... AND BECAUSE OF THAT, SHE HAS THIS THING ABOUT IT! JUST MY LUCK!

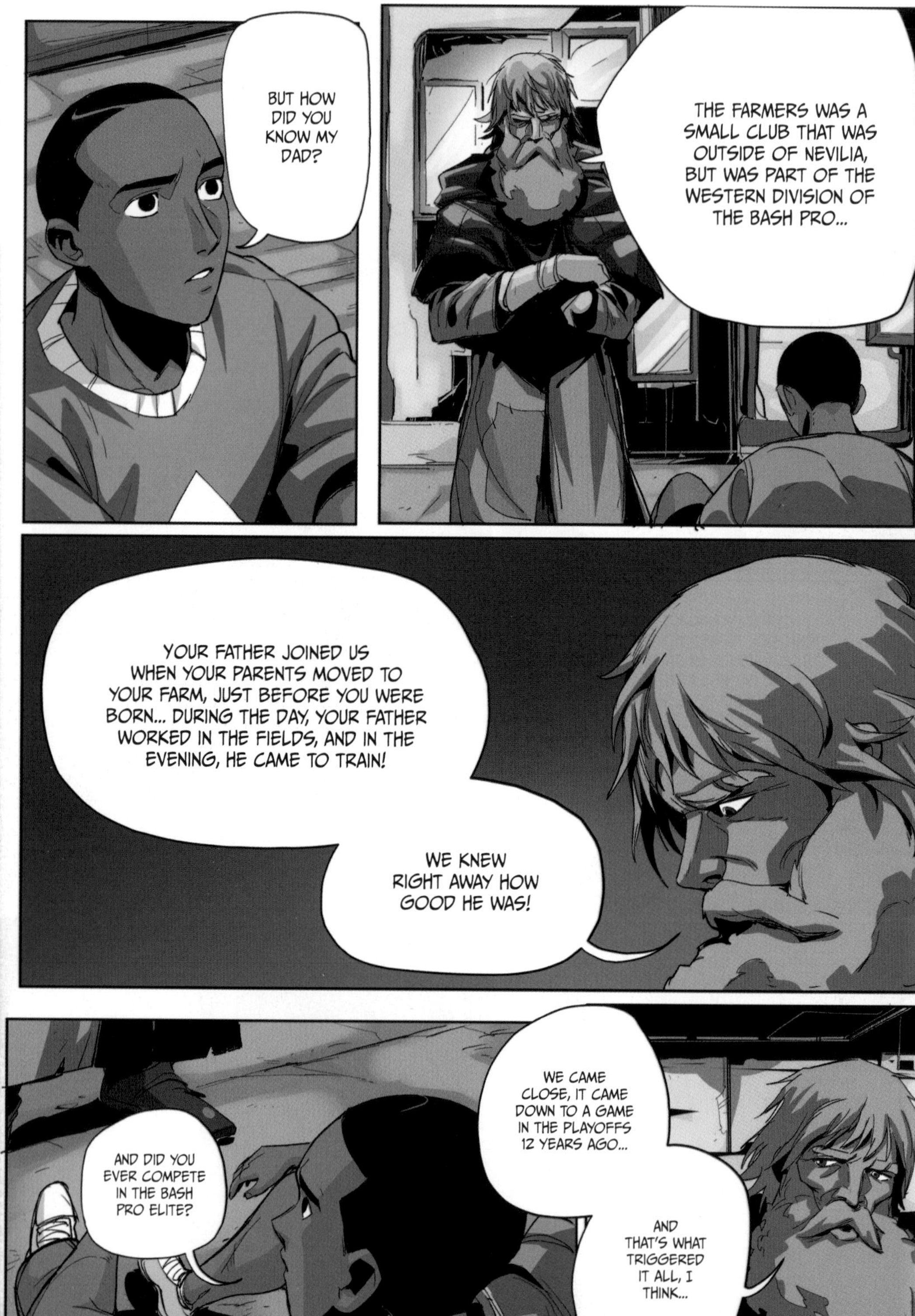
BUT HOW DID YOU KNOW MY DAD?
THE FARMERS WAS A SMALL CLUB THAT WAS OUTSIDE OF NEVILIA, BUT WAS PART OF THE WESTERN DIVISION OF THE BASH PRO...
YOUR FATHER JOINED US WHEN YOUR PARENTS MOVED TO YOUR FARM, JUST BEFORE YOU WERE BORN... DURING THE DAY, YOUR FATHER WORKED IN THE FIELDS, AND IN THE EVENING, HE CAME TO TRAIN!
WE KNEW RIGHT AWAY HOW GOOD HE WAS!
AND DID YOU EVER COMPETE IN THE BASH PRO ELITE?
WE CAME CLOSE, IT CAME DOWN TO A GAME IN THE PLAYOFFS 12 YEARS AGO...
AND THAT'S WHAT TRIGGERED IT ALL, I THINK...

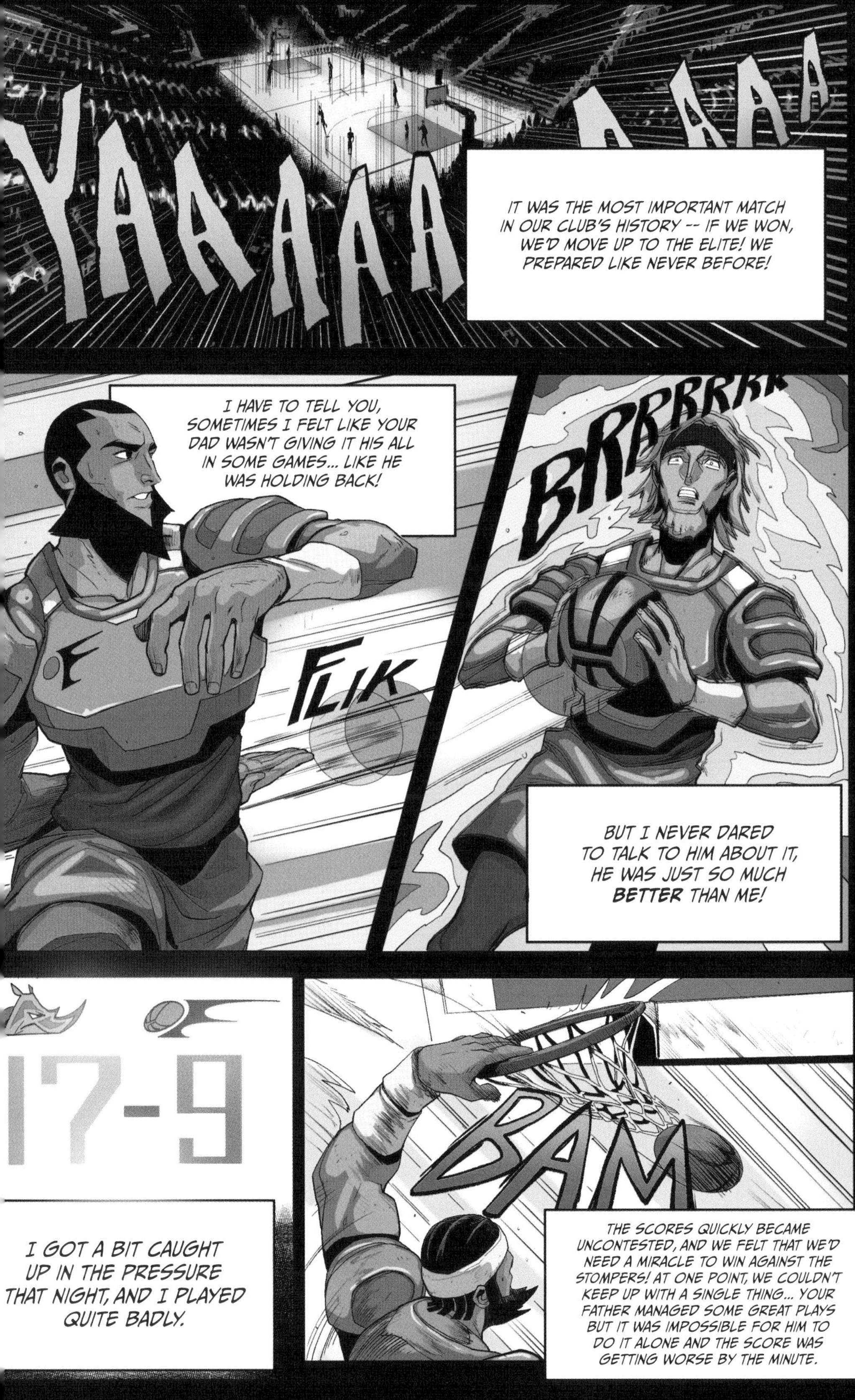
YAAAAAAAAAA
IT WAS THE MOST IMPORTANT MATCH IN OUR CLUB'S HISTORY -- IF WE WON, WE'D MOVE UP TO THE ELITE! WE PREPARED LIKE NEVER BEFORE!
I HAVE TO TELL YOU, SOMETIMES I FELT LIKE YOUR DAD WASN'T GIVING IT HIS ALL IN SOME GAMES... LIKE HE WAS HOLDING BACK!
FLIK
BRRRRRRR
BUT I NEVER DARED TO TALK TO HIM ABOUT IT, HE WAS JUST SO MUCH **BETTER** THAN ME!
17-9
I GOT A BIT CAUGHT UP IN THE PRESSURE THAT NIGHT, AND I PLAYED QUITE BADLY.
BAM
THE SCORES QUICKLY BECAME UNCONTESTED, AND WE FELT THAT WE'D NEED A MIRACLE TO WIN AGAINST THE STOMPERS! AT ONE POINT, WE COULDN'T KEEP UP WITH A SINGLE THING... YOUR FATHER MANAGED SOME GREAT PLAYS BUT IT WAS IMPOSSIBLE FOR HIM TO DO IT ALONE AND THE SCORE WAS GETTING WORSE BY THE MINUTE.

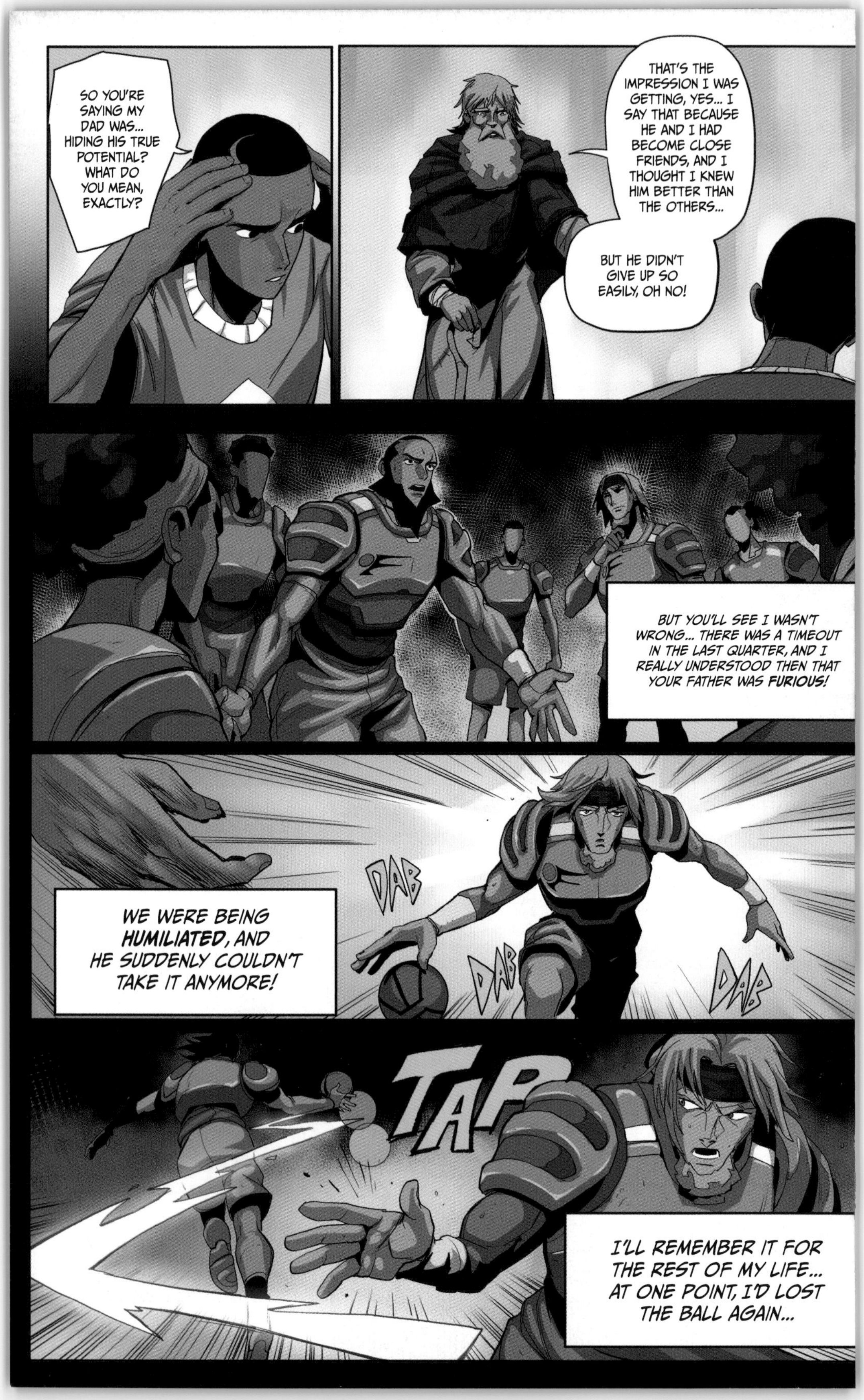
SO YOU'RE SAYING MY DAD WAS... HIDING HIS TRUE POTENTIAL? WHAT DO YOU MEAN, EXACTLY?
THAT'S THE IMPRESSION I WAS GETTING, YES... I SAY THAT BECAUSE HE AND I HAD BECOME CLOSE FRIENDS, AND I THOUGHT I KNEW HIM BETTER THAN THE OTHERS...
BUT HE DIDN'T GIVE UP SO EASILY, OH NO!
BUT YOU'LL SEE I WASN'T WRONG... THERE WAS A TIMEOUT IN THE LAST QUARTER, AND I REALLY UNDERSTOOD THEN THAT YOUR FATHER WAS FURIOUS!
WE WERE BEING HUMILIATED, AND HE SUDDENLY COULDN'T TAKE IT ANYMORE!
DAB
DAB
DAB
TAP
I'LL REMEMBER IT FOR THE REST OF MY LIFE... AT ONE POINT, I'D LOST THE BALL AGAIN...

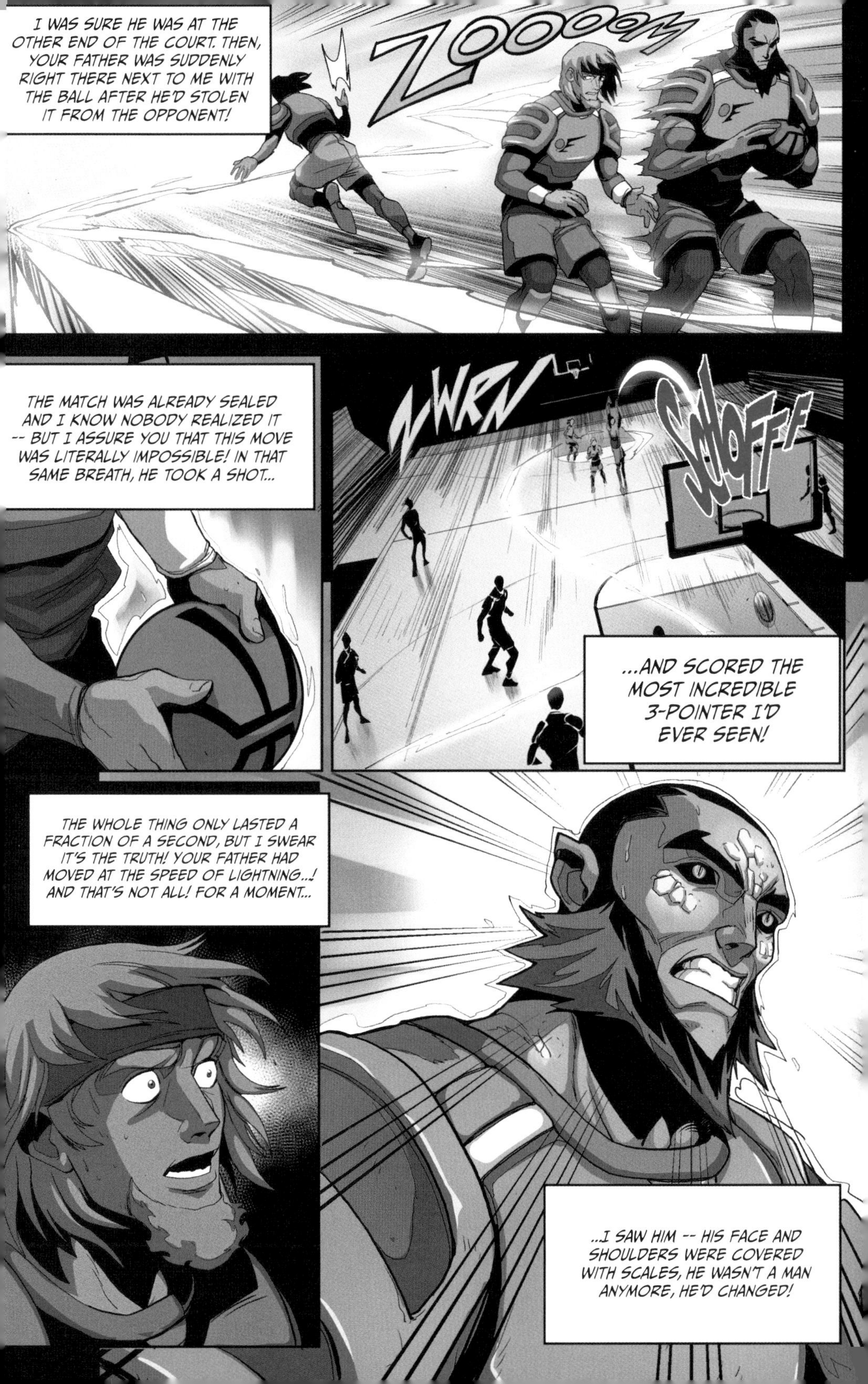
I WAS SURE HE WAS AT THE OTHER END OF THE COURT. THEN, YOUR FATHER WAS SUDDENLY RIGHT THERE NEXT TO ME WITH THE BALL AFTER HE'D STOLEN IT FROM THE OPPONENT!
ZOOOOM
THE MATCH WAS ALREADY SEALED AND I KNOW NOBODY REALIZED IT -- BUT I ASSURE YOU THAT THIS MOVE WAS LITERALLY IMPOSSIBLE! IN THAT SAME BREATH, HE TOOK A SHOT...
ZWRN
SCHOFFF
...AND SCORED THE MOST INCREDIBLE 3-POINTER I'D EVER SEEN!
THE WHOLE THING ONLY LASTED A FRACTION OF A SECOND, BUT I SWEAR IT'S THE TRUTH! YOUR FATHER HAD MOVED AT THE SPEED OF LIGHTNING...! AND THAT'S NOT ALL! FOR A MOMENT...
...I SAW HIM -- HIS FACE AND SHOULDERS WERE COVERED WITH SCALES, HE WASN'T A MAN ANYMORE, HE'D CHANGED!

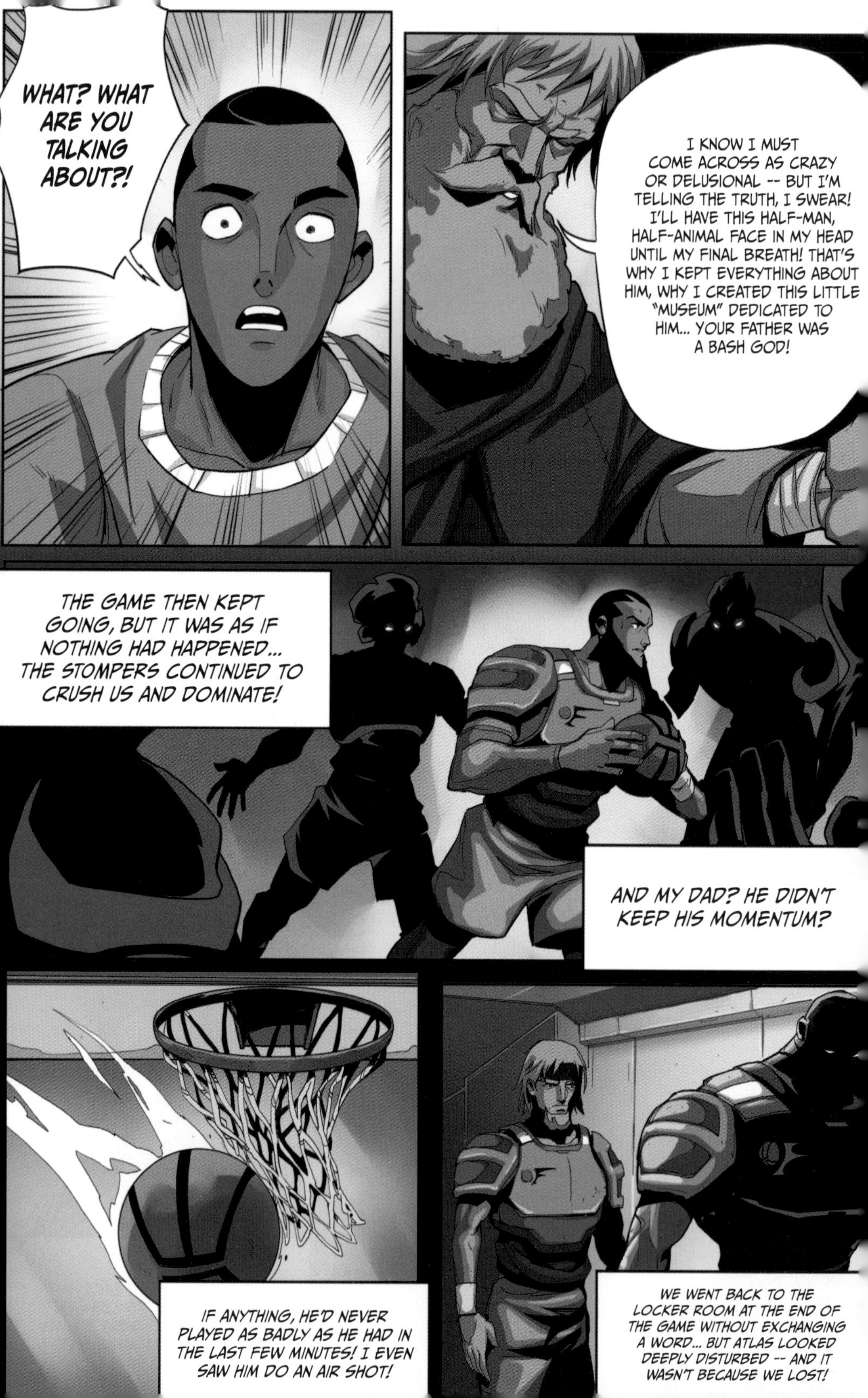
WHAT? WHAT ARE YOU TALKING ABOUT?!
I KNOW I MUST COME ACROSS AS CRAZY OR DELUSIONAL -- BUT I'M TELLING THE TRUTH, I SWEAR! I'LL HAVE THIS HALF-MAN, HALF-ANIMAL FACE IN MY HEAD UNTIL MY FINAL BREATH! THAT'S WHY I KEPT EVERYTHING ABOUT HIM, WHY I CREATED THIS LITTLE "MUSEUM" DEDICATED TO HIM... YOUR FATHER WAS A BASH GOD!
THE GAME THEN KEPT GOING, BUT IT WAS AS IF NOTHING HAD HAPPENED... THE STOMPERS CONTINUED TO CRUSH US AND DOMINATE!
AND MY DAD? HE DIDN'T KEEP HIS MOMENTUM?
IF ANYTHING, HE'D NEVER PLAYED AS BADLY AS HE HAD IN THE LAST FEW MINUTES! I EVEN SAW HIM DO AN AIR SHOT!
WE WENT BACK TO THE LOCKER ROOM AT THE END OF THE GAME WITHOUT EXCHANGING A WORD... BUT ATLAS LOOKED DEEPLY DISTURBED -- AND IT WASN'T BECAUSE WE LOST!

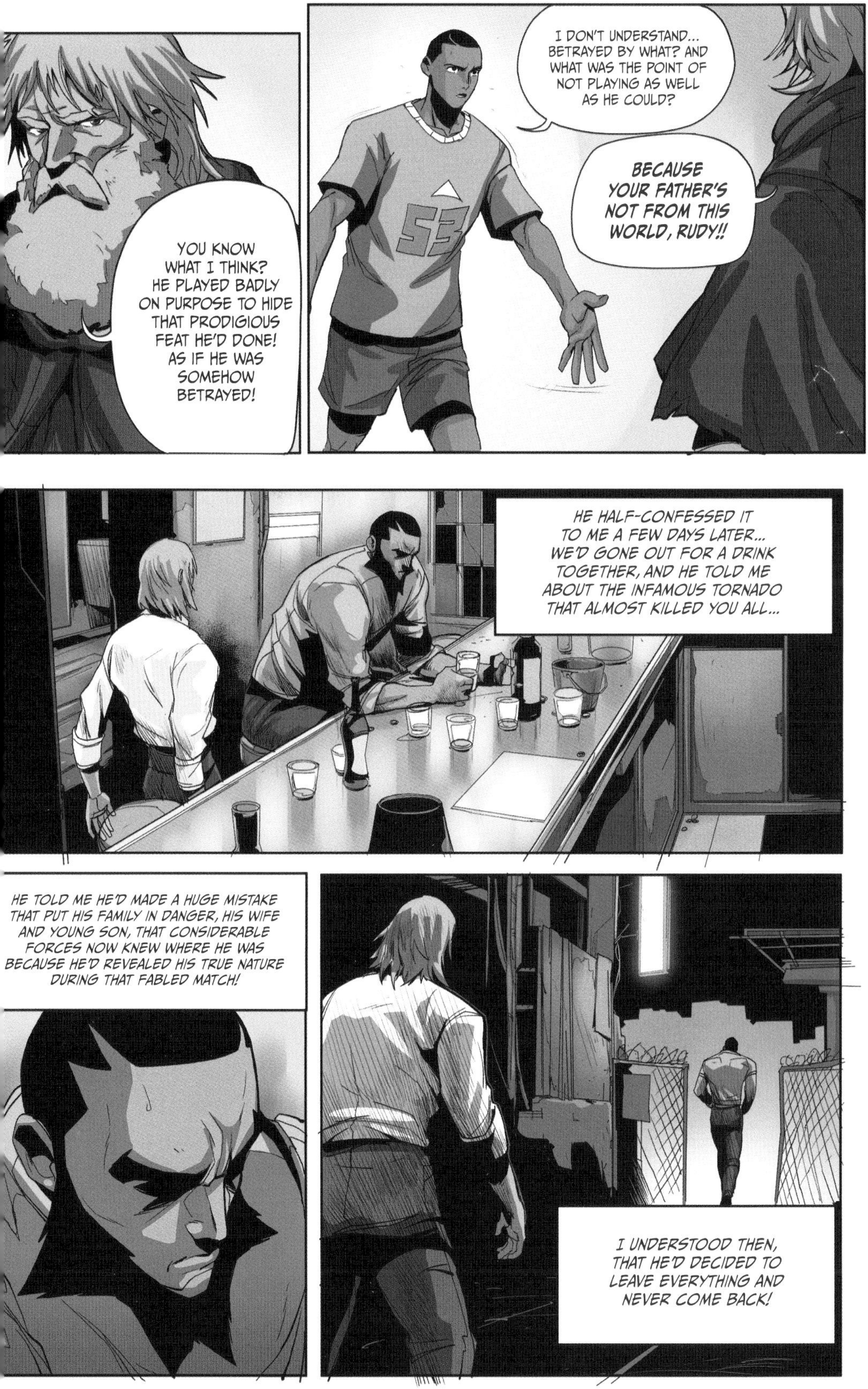
YOU KNOW WHAT I THINK? HE PLAYED BADLY ON PURPOSE TO HIDE THAT PRODIGIOUS FEAT HE'D DONE! AS IF HE WAS SOMEHOW BETRAYED!
I DON'T UNDERSTAND... BETRAYED BY WHAT? AND WHAT WAS THE POINT OF NOT PLAYING AS WELL AS HE COULD?
BECAUSE YOUR FATHER'S NOT FROM THIS WORLD, RUDY!!
HE HALF-CONFESSED IT TO ME A FEW DAYS LATER... WE'D GONE OUT FOR A DRINK TOGETHER, AND HE TOLD ME ABOUT THE INFAMOUS TORNADO THAT ALMOST KILLED YOU ALL...
HE TOLD ME HE'D MADE A HUGE MISTAKE THAT PUT HIS FAMILY IN DANGER, HIS WIFE AND YOUNG SON, THAT CONSIDERABLE FORCES NOW KNEW WHERE HE WAS BECAUSE HE'D REVEALED HIS TRUE NATURE DURING THAT FABLED MATCH!
I UNDERSTOOD THEN, THAT HE'D DECIDED TO LEAVE EVERYTHING AND NEVER COME BACK!

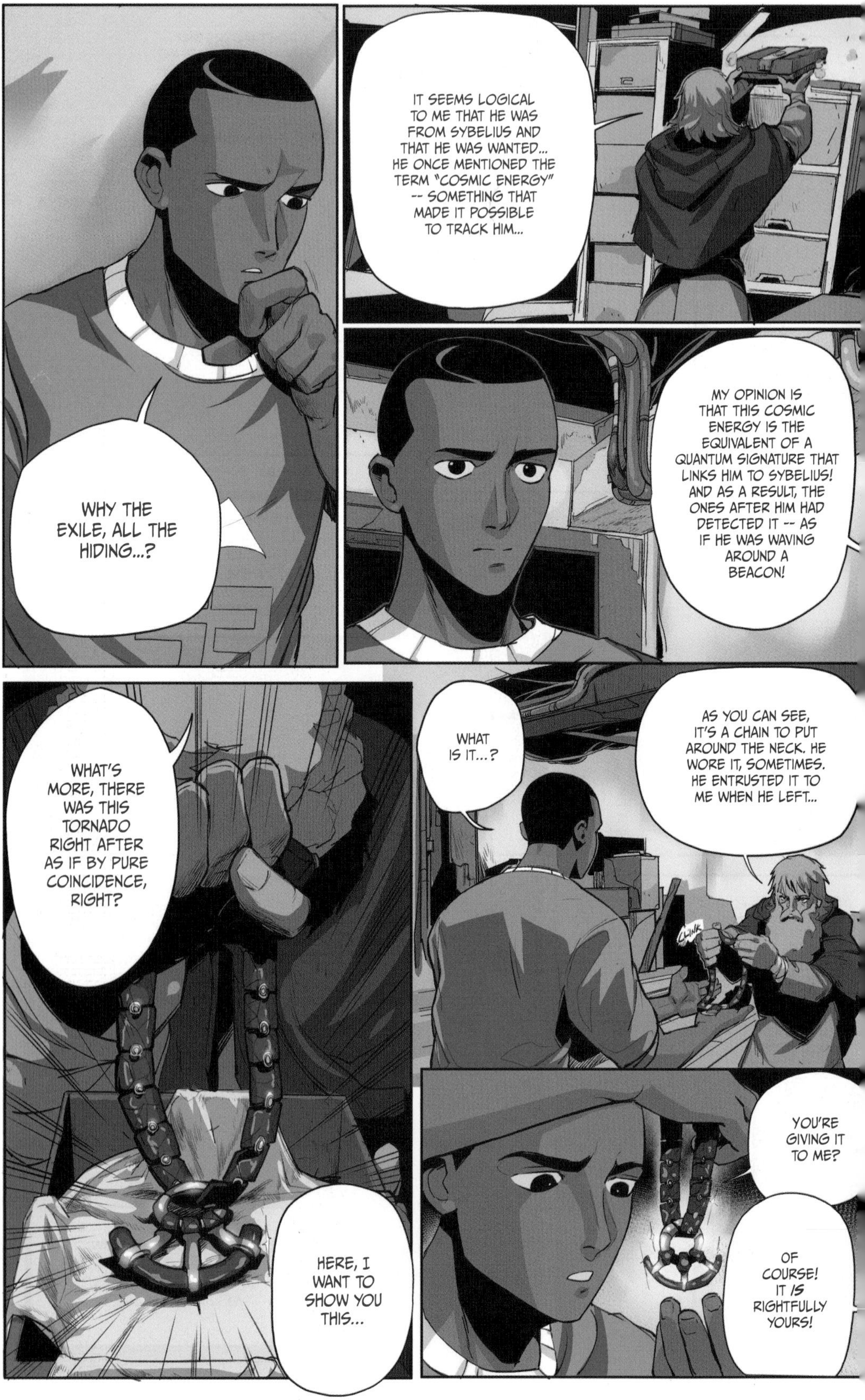
IT SEEMS LOGICAL TO ME THAT HE WAS FROM SYBELIUS AND THAT HE WAS WANTED... HE ONCE MENTIONED THE TERM "COSMIC ENERGY" -- SOMETHING THAT MADE IT POSSIBLE TO TRACK HIM...
WHY THE EXILE, ALL THE HIDING...?
MY OPINION IS THAT THIS COSMIC ENERGY IS THE EQUIVALENT OF A QUANTUM SIGNATURE THAT LINKS HIM TO SYBELIUS! AND AS A RESULT, THE ONES AFTER HIM HAD DETECTED IT -- AS IF HE WAS WAVING AROUND A BEACON!
WHAT'S MORE, THERE WAS THIS TORNADO RIGHT AFTER AS IF BY PURE COINCIDENCE, RIGHT?
HERE, I WANT TO SHOW YOU THIS...
WHAT IS IT...?
AS YOU CAN SEE, IT'S A CHAIN TO PUT AROUND THE NECK. HE WORE IT, SOMETIMES. HE ENTRUSTED IT TO ME WHEN HE LEFT...
CLINK
YOU'RE GIVING IT TO ME?
OF COURSE! IT *IS* RIGHTFULLY YOURS!

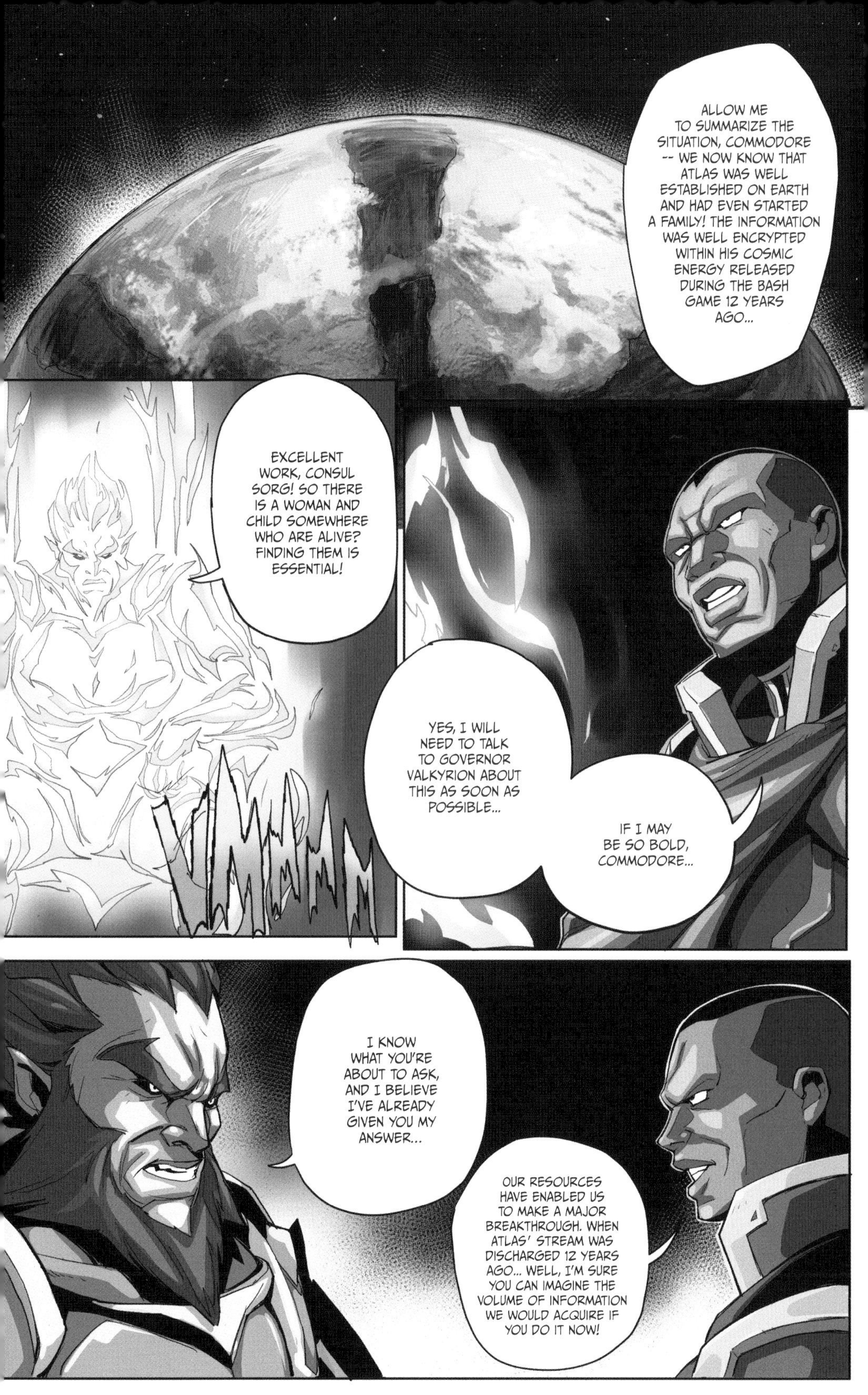
ALLOW ME TO SUMMARIZE THE SITUATION, COMMODORE -- WE NOW KNOW THAT ATLAS WAS WELL ESTABLISHED ON EARTH AND HAD EVEN STARTED A FAMILY! THE INFORMATION WAS WELL ENCRYPTED WITHIN HIS COSMIC ENERGY RELEASED DURING THE BASH GAME 12 YEARS AGO...
EXCELLENT WORK, CONSUL SORG! SO THERE IS A WOMAN AND CHILD SOMEWHERE WHO ARE ALIVE? FINDING THEM IS ESSENTIAL!
VMMMM
YES, I WILL NEED TO TALK TO GOVERNOR VALKYRION ABOUT THIS AS SOON AS POSSIBLE...
IF I MAY BE SO BOLD, COMMODORE...
I KNOW WHAT YOU'RE ABOUT TO ASK, AND I BELIEVE I'VE ALREADY GIVEN YOU MY ANSWER...
OUR RESOURCES HAVE ENABLED US TO MAKE A MAJOR BREAKTHROUGH. WHEN ATLAS' STREAM WAS DISCHARGED 12 YEARS AGO... WELL, I'M SURE YOU CAN IMAGINE THE VOLUME OF INFORMATION WE WOULD ACQUIRE IF YOU DO IT NOW!

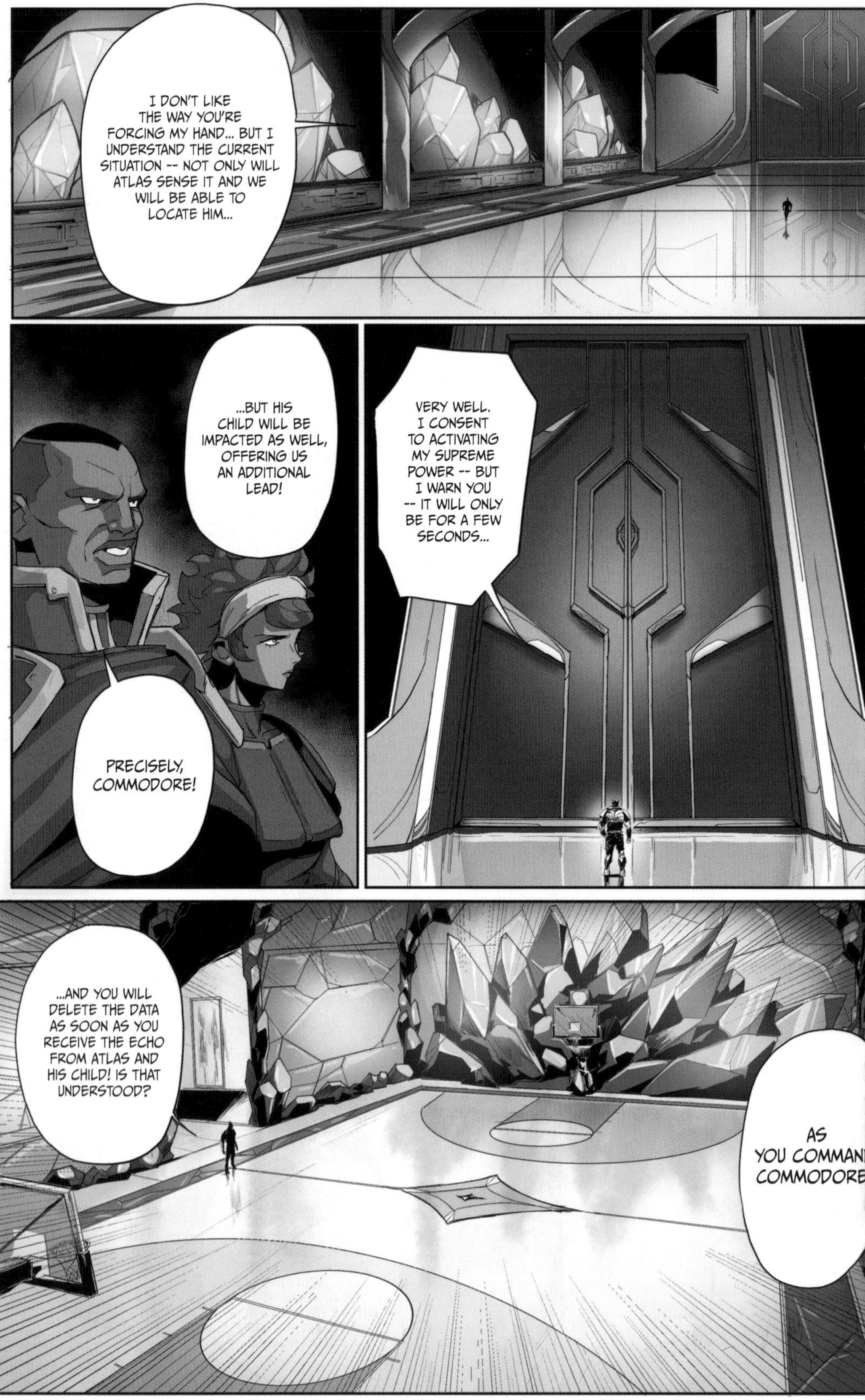
I DON'T LIKE THE WAY YOU'RE FORCING MY HAND... BUT I UNDERSTAND THE CURRENT SITUATION -- NOT ONLY WILL ATLAS SENSE IT AND WE WILL BE ABLE TO LOCATE HIM...
...BUT HIS CHILD WILL BE IMPACTED AS WELL, OFFERING US AN ADDITIONAL LEAD!
PRECISELY, COMMODORE!
VERY WELL. I CONSENT TO ACTIVATING MY SUPREME POWER -- BUT I WARN YOU -- IT WILL ONLY BE FOR A FEW SECONDS...
...AND YOU WILL DELETE THE DATA AS SOON AS YOU RECEIVE THE ECHO FROM ATLAS AND HIS CHILD! IS THAT UNDERSTOOD?

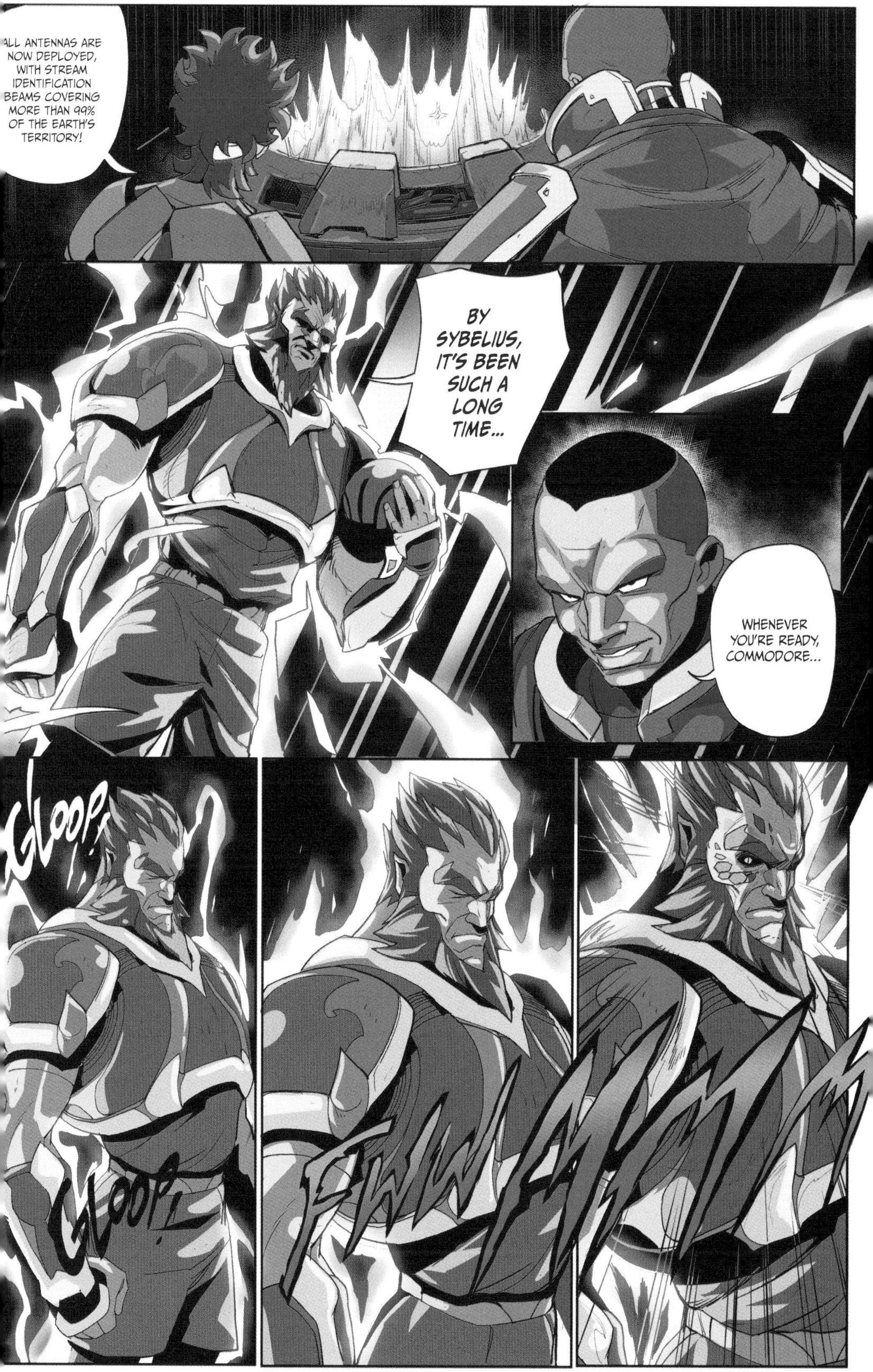
ALL ANTENNAS ARE NOW DEPLOYED, WITH STREAM IDENTIFICATION BEAMS COVERING MORE THAN 99% OF THE EARTH'S TERRITORY!
BY SYBELIUS, IT'S BEEN SUCH A LONG TIME...
WHENEVER YOU'RE READY, COMMODORE...
GLOOP!
GLOOP!
FWAAAM

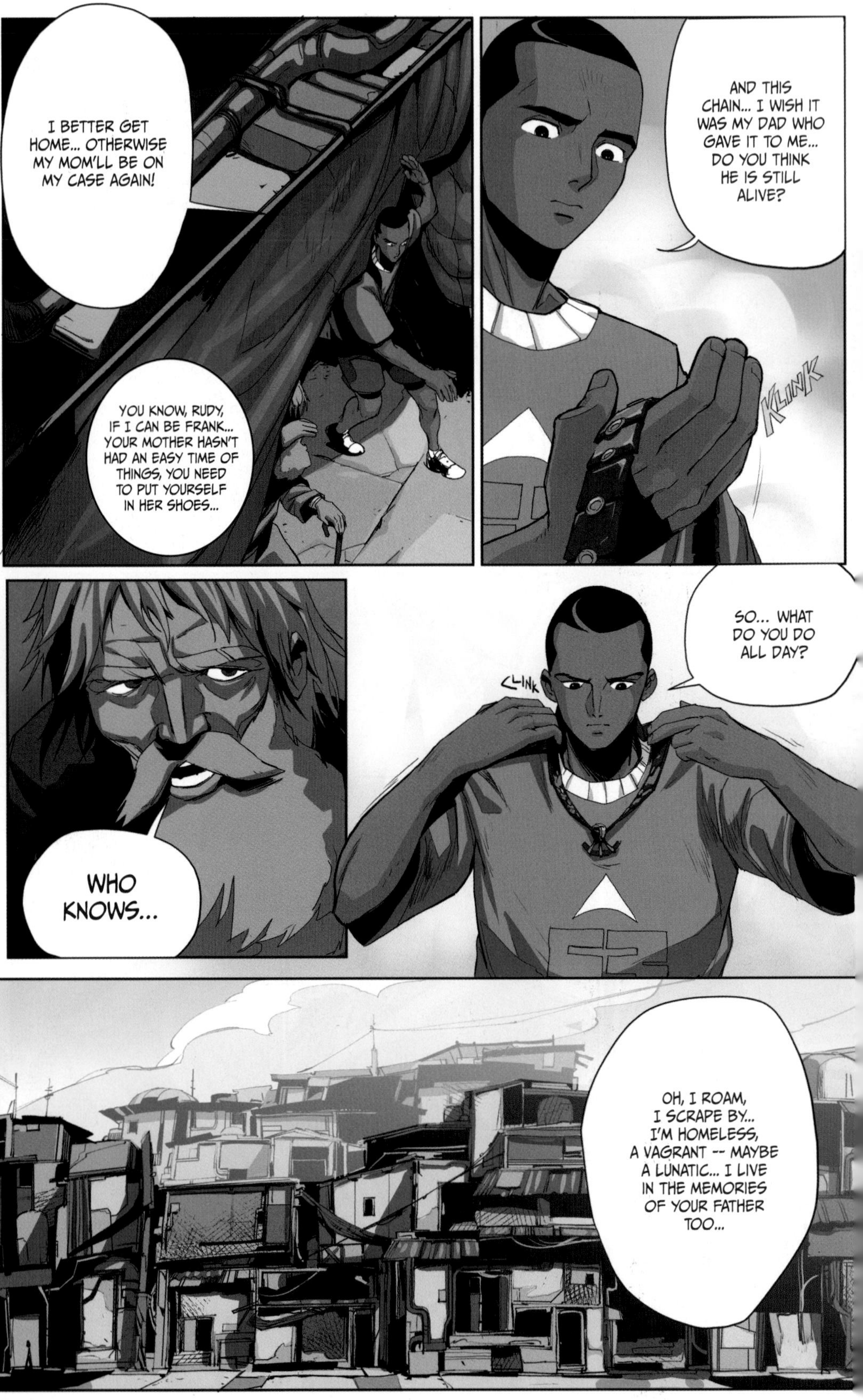
I BETTER GET HOME... OTHERWISE MY MOM'LL BE ON MY CASE AGAIN!
YOU KNOW, RUDY, IF I CAN BE FRANK... YOUR MOTHER HASN'T HAD AN EASY TIME OF THINGS, YOU NEED TO PUT YOURSELF IN HER SHOES...
AND THIS CHAIN... I WISH IT WAS MY DAD WHO GAVE IT TO ME... DO YOU THINK HE IS STILL ALIVE?
KLINK
WHO KNOWS...
CLINK
SO... WHAT DO YOU DO ALL DAY?
OH, I ROAM, I SCRAPE BY... I'M HOMELESS, A VAGRANT -- MAYBE A LUNATIC... I LIVE IN THE MEMORIES OF YOUR FATHER TOO...

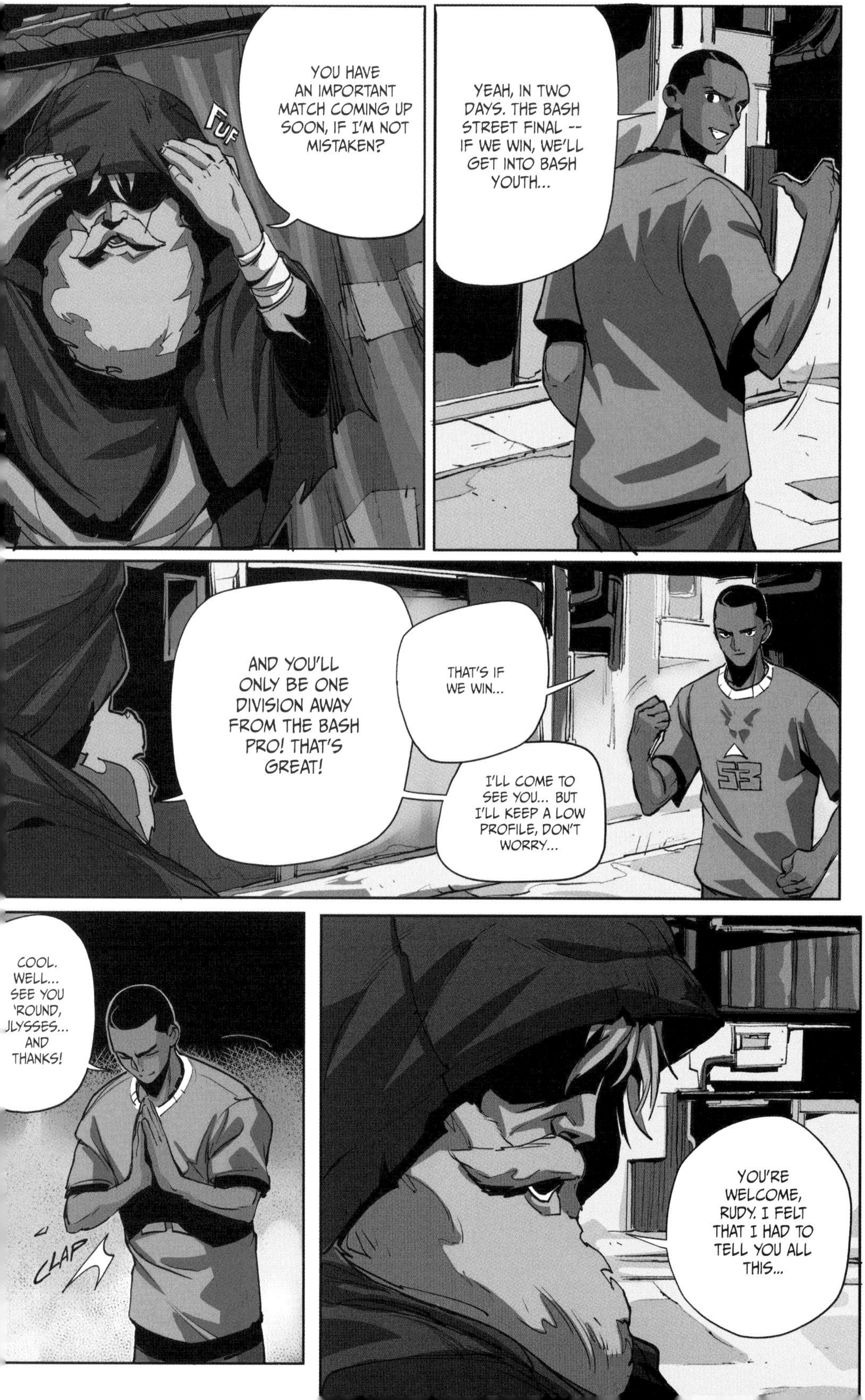
FUF
YOU HAVE AN IMPORTANT MATCH COMING UP SOON, IF I'M NOT MISTAKEN?
YEAH, IN TWO DAYS. THE BASH STREET FINAL -- IF WE WIN, WE'LL GET INTO BASH YOUTH...
AND YOU'LL ONLY BE ONE DIVISION AWAY FROM THE BASH PRO! THAT'S GREAT!
THAT'S IF WE WIN...
I'LL COME TO SEE YOU... BUT I'LL KEEP A LOW PROFILE, DON'T WORRY...
COOL. WELL... SEE YOU 'ROUND, JLYSSES... AND THANKS!
CLAP
YOU'RE WELCOME, RUDY. I FELT THAT I HAD TO TELL YOU ALL THIS...

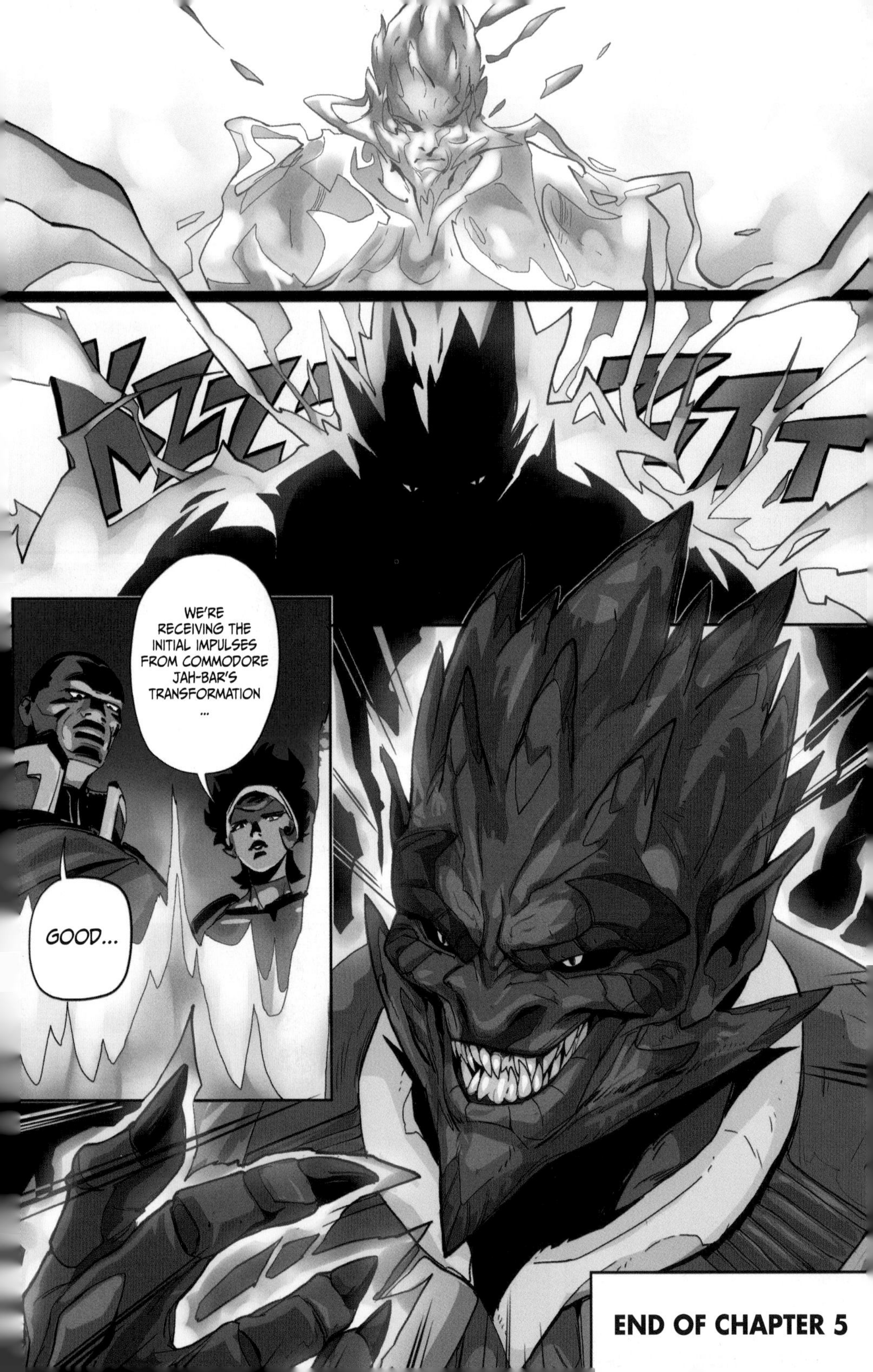
KZZZZT
WE'RE RECEIVING THE INITIAL IMPULSES FROM COMMODORE JAH-BAR'S TRANSFORMATION ...
GOOD...
END OF CHAPTER 5

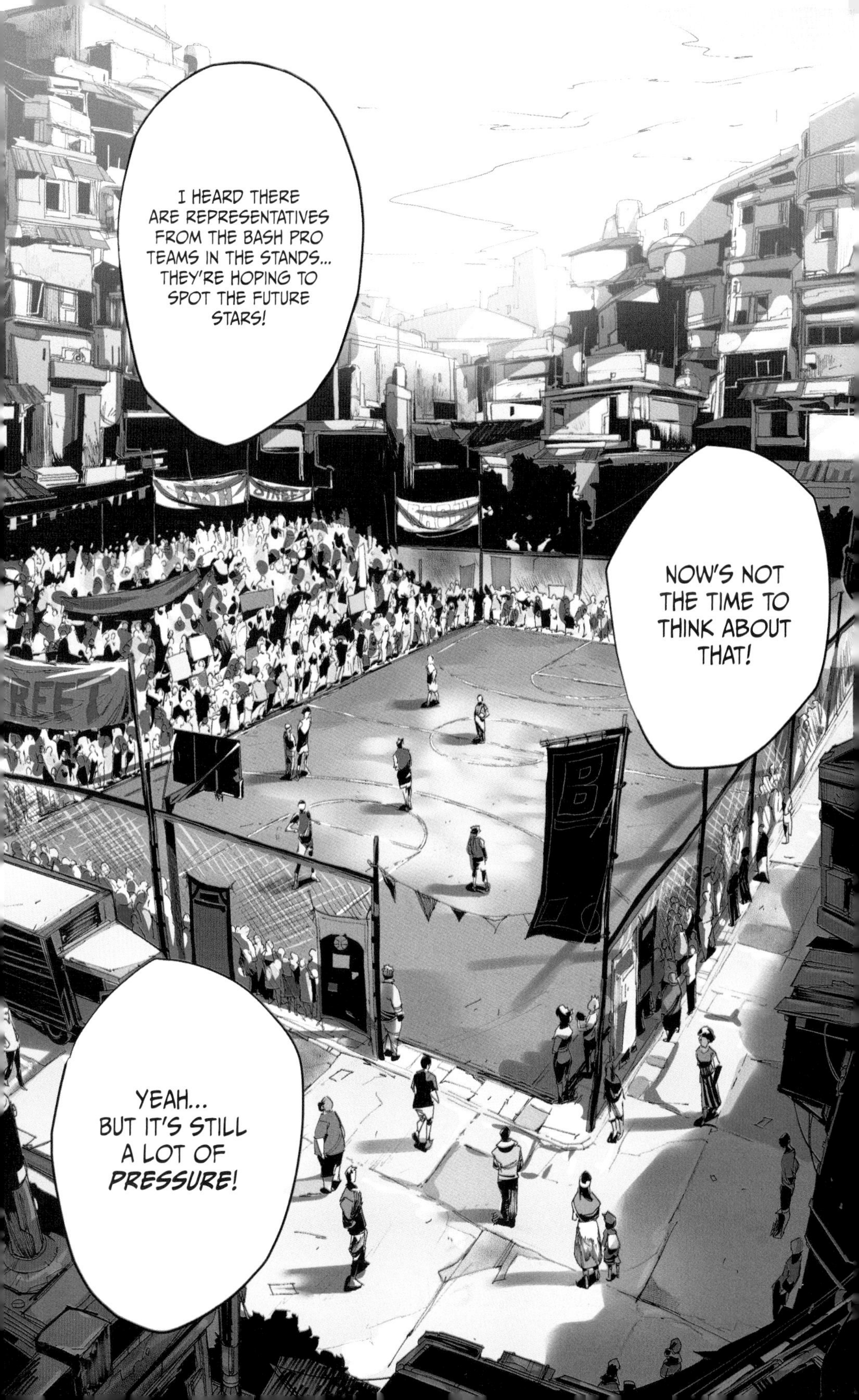
I HEARD THERE ARE REPRESENTATIVES FROM THE BASH PRO TEAMS IN THE STANDS... THEY'RE HOPING TO SPOT THE FUTURE STARS!
NOW'S NOT THE TIME TO THINK ABOUT THAT!
YEAH... BUT IT'S STILL A LOT OF *PRESSURE!*

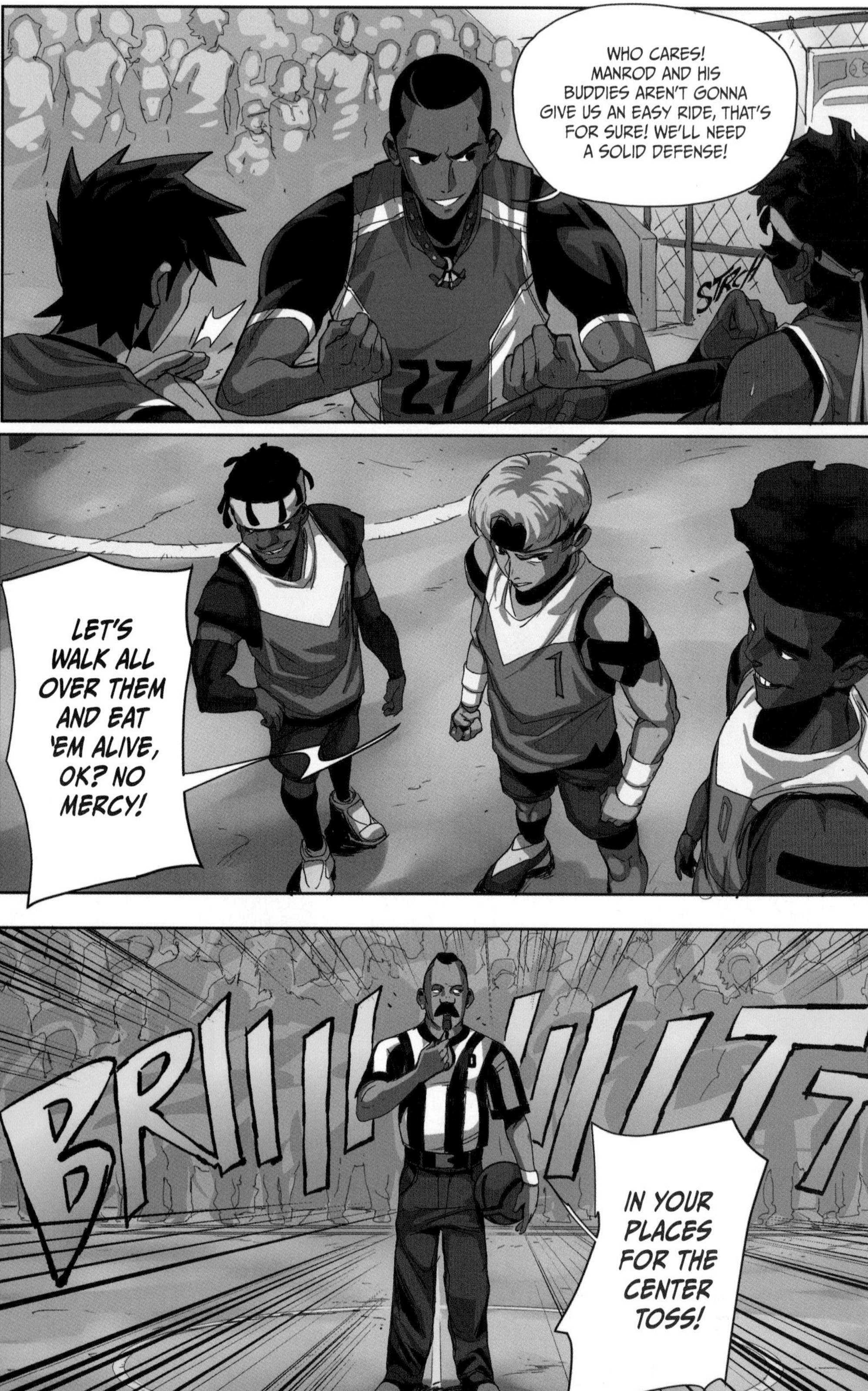
WHO CARES! MANROD AND HIS BUDDIES AREN'T GONNA GIVE US AN EASY RIDE, THAT'S FOR SURE! WE'LL NEED A SOLID DEFENSE!
STRCH
LET'S WALK ALL OVER THEM AND EAT 'EM ALIVE, OK? NO MERCY!
IN YOUR PLACES FOR THE CENTER TOSS!

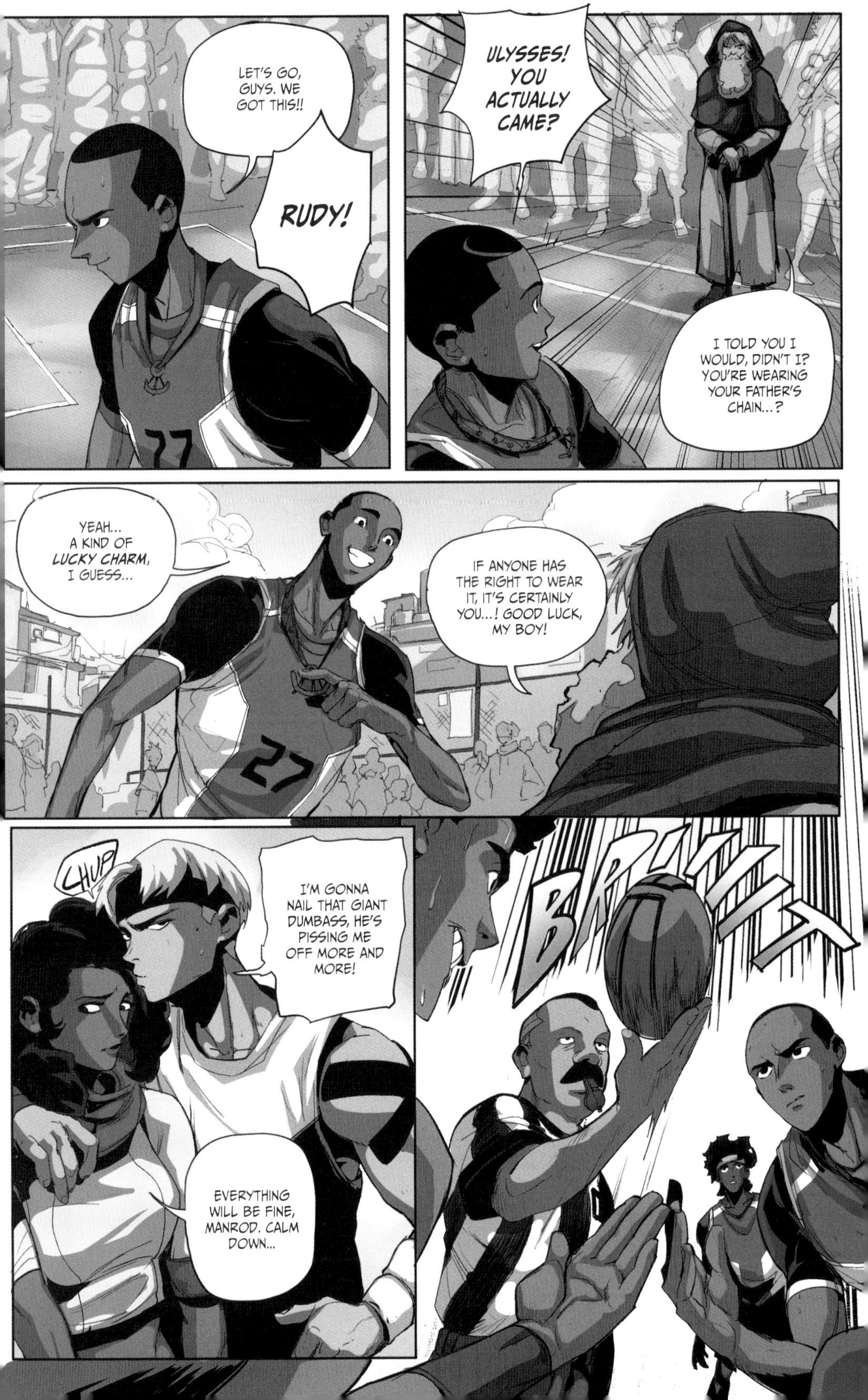
LET'S GO, GUYS. WE GOT THIS!!
RUDY!
ULYSSES! YOU ACTUALLY CAME?
I TOLD YOU I WOULD, DIDN'T I? YOU'RE WEARING YOUR FATHER'S CHAIN...?
YEAH... A KIND OF LUCKY CHARM, I GUESS...
IF ANYONE HAS THE RIGHT TO WEAR IT, IT'S CERTAINLY YOU...! GOOD LUCK, MY BOY!
CHUP
I'M GONNA NAIL THAT GIANT DUMBASS, HE'S PISSING ME OFF MORE AND MORE!
EVERYTHING WILL BE FINE, MANROD. CALM DOWN...

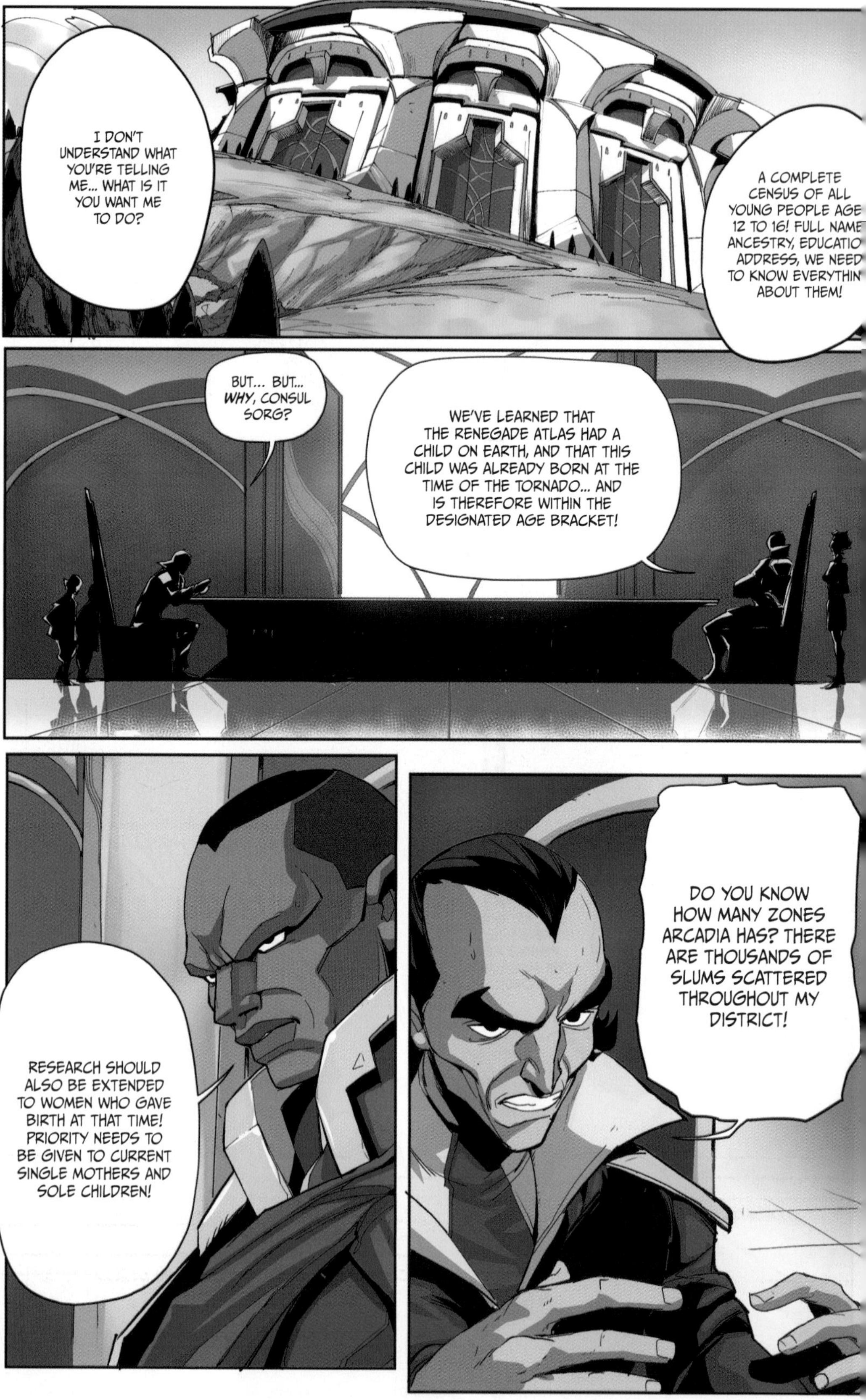

I DON'T UNDERSTAND WHAT YOU'RE TELLING ME... WHAT IS IT YOU WANT ME TO DO?
A COMPLETE CENSUS OF ALL YOUNG PEOPLE AGE 12 TO 16! FULL NAME ANCESTRY, EDUCATIO ADDRESS, WE NEED TO KNOW EVERYTHIN ABOUT THEM!
BUT... BUT... WHY, CONSUL SORG?
WE'VE LEARNED THAT THE RENEGADE ATLAS HAD A CHILD ON EARTH, AND THAT THIS CHILD WAS ALREADY BORN AT THE TIME OF THE TORNADO... AND IS THEREFORE WITHIN THE DESIGNATED AGE BRACKET!
RESEARCH SHOULD ALSO BE EXTENDED TO WOMEN WHO GAVE BIRTH AT THAT TIME! PRIORITY NEEDS TO BE GIVEN TO CURRENT SINGLE MOTHERS AND SOLE CHILDREN!
DO YOU KNOW HOW MANY ZONES ARCADIA HAS? THERE ARE THOUSANDS OF SLUMS SCATTERED THROUGHOUT MY DISTRICT!

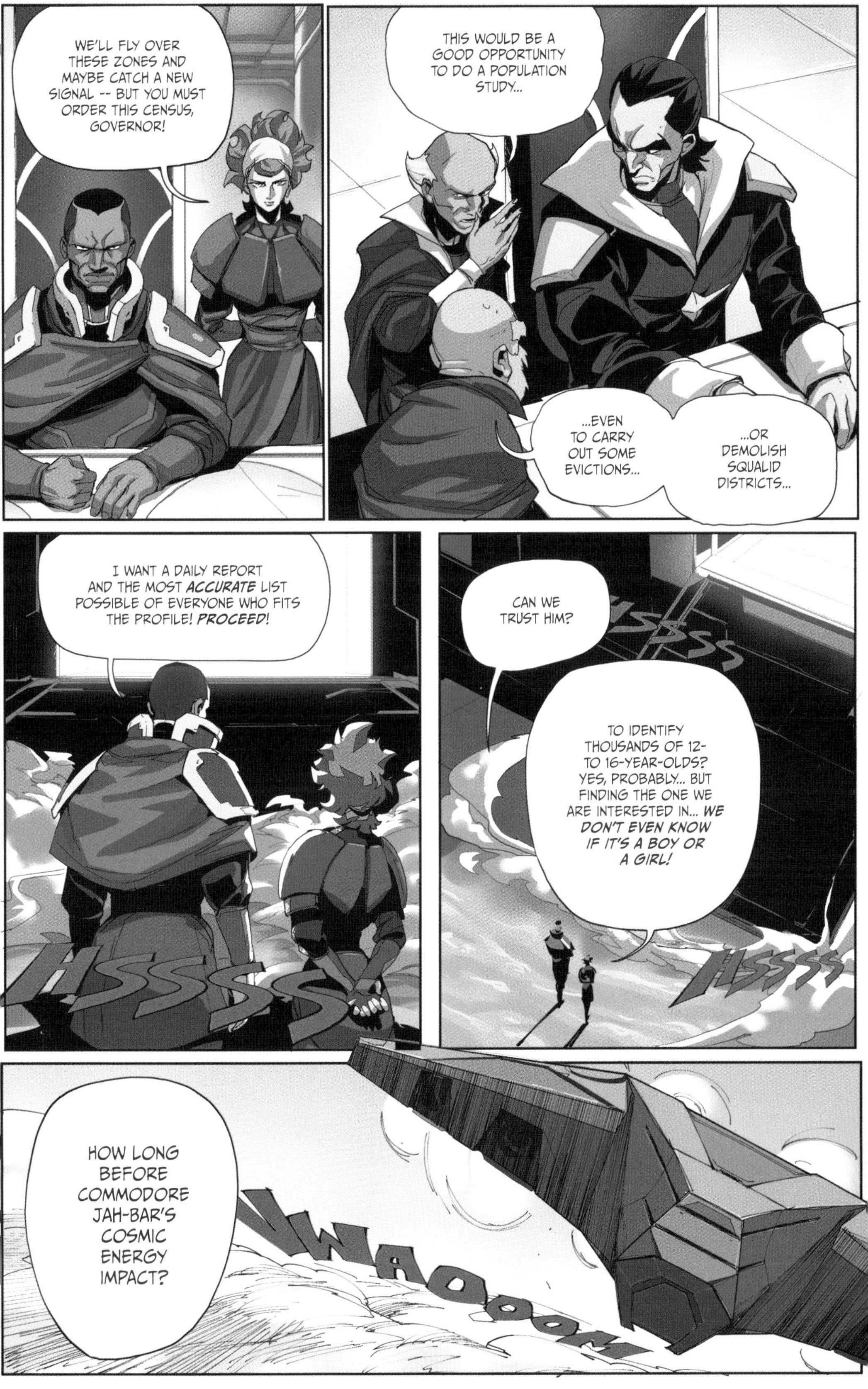
WE'LL FLY OVER THESE ZONES AND MAYBE CATCH A NEW SIGNAL -- BUT YOU MUST ORDER THIS CENSUS, GOVERNOR!
THIS WOULD BE A GOOD OPPORTUNITY TO DO A POPULATION STUDY...
...EVEN TO CARRY OUT SOME EVICTIONS...
...OR DEMOLISH SQUALID DISTRICTS...
I WANT A DAILY REPORT AND THE MOST ACCURATE LIST POSSIBLE OF EVERYONE WHO FITS THE PROFILE! PROCEED!
HSSSSS
CAN WE TRUST HIM?
HSSSS
TO IDENTIFY THOUSANDS OF 12- TO 16-YEAR-OLDS? YES, PROBABLY... BUT FINDING THE ONE WE ARE INTERESTED IN... WE DON'T EVEN KNOW IF IT'S A BOY OR A GIRL!
HSSSSS
HOW LONG BEFORE COMMODORE JAH-BAR'S COSMIC ENERGY IMPACT?
WAAOOOOM

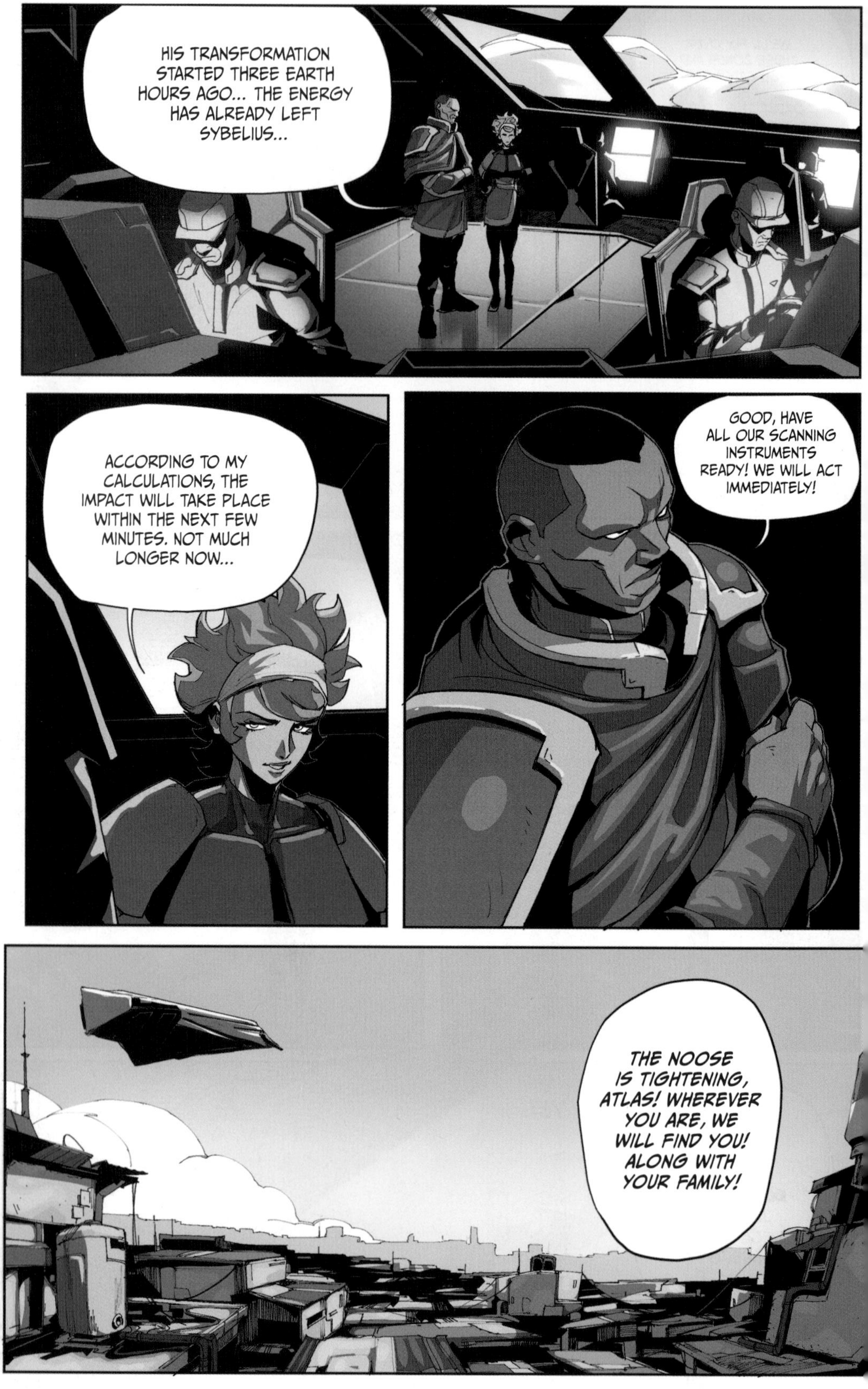
HIS TRANSFORMATION STARTED THREE EARTH HOURS AGO... THE ENERGY HAS ALREADY LEFT SYBELIUS...
ACCORDING TO MY CALCULATIONS, THE IMPACT WILL TAKE PLACE WITHIN THE NEXT FEW MINUTES. NOT MUCH LONGER NOW...
GOOD, HAVE ALL OUR SCANNING INSTRUMENTS READY! WE WILL ACT IMMEDIATELY!
THE NOOSE IS TIGHTENING, ATLAS! WHEREVER YOU ARE, WE WILL FIND YOU! ALONG WITH YOUR FAMILY!

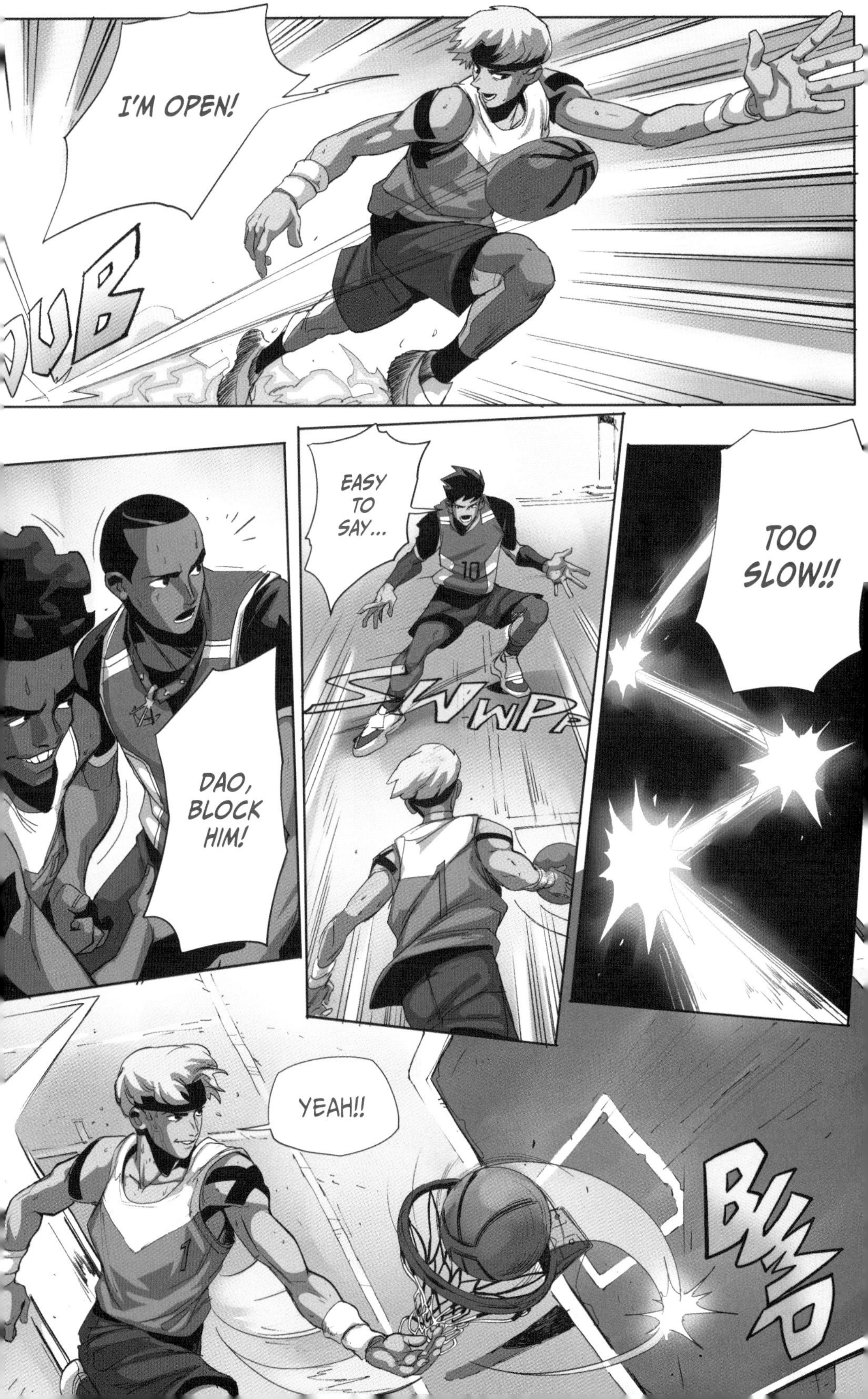
I'M OPEN!
DUB
DAO, BLOCK HIM!
EASY TO SAY...
SWWPP
TOO SLOW!!
YEAH!!
BUMP

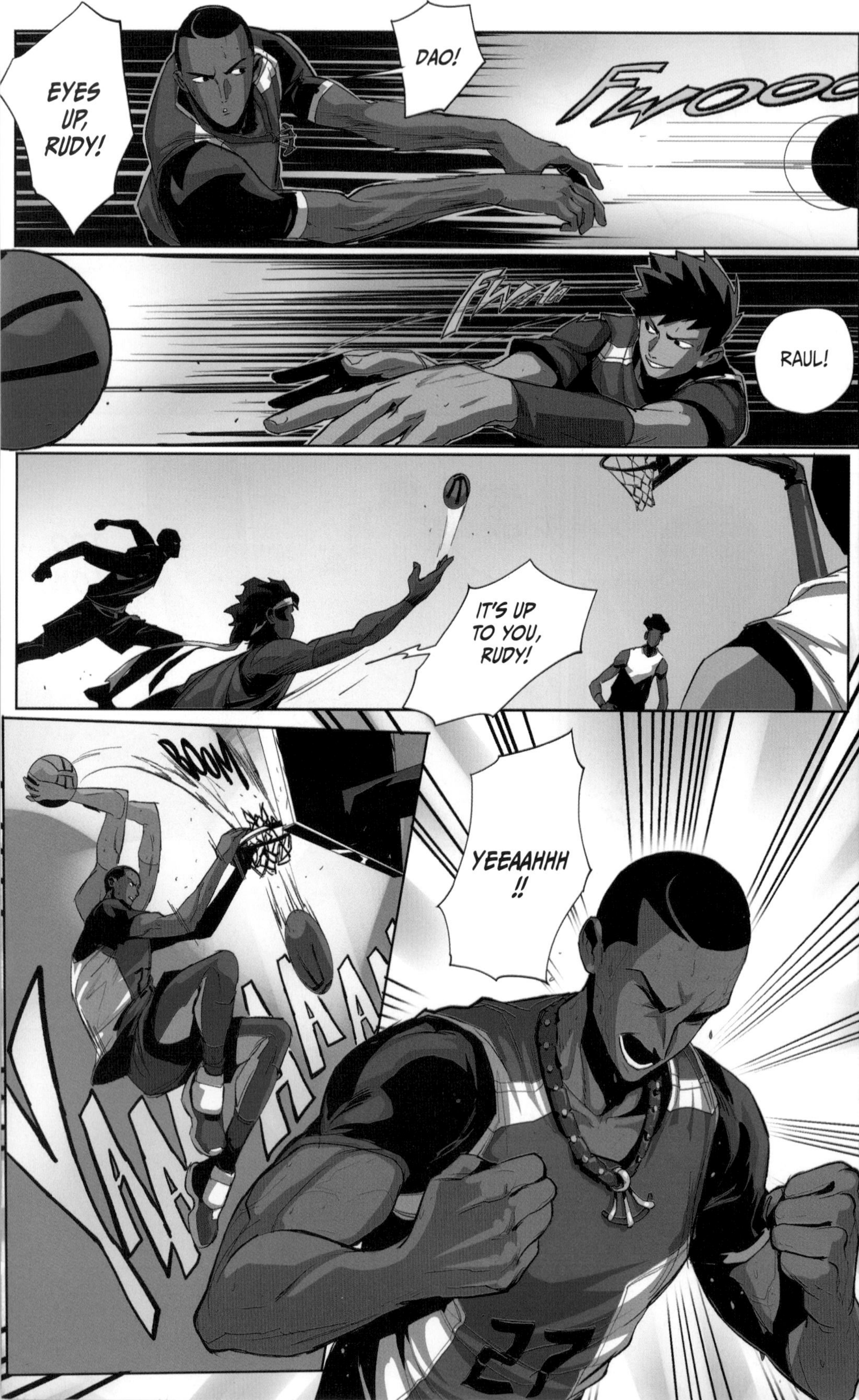
EYES UP, RUDY!
DAO!
FWOOO
FWAA
RAUL!
IT'S UP TO YOU, RUDY!
BOOM
YEEAAHHH!!
HAAHAA

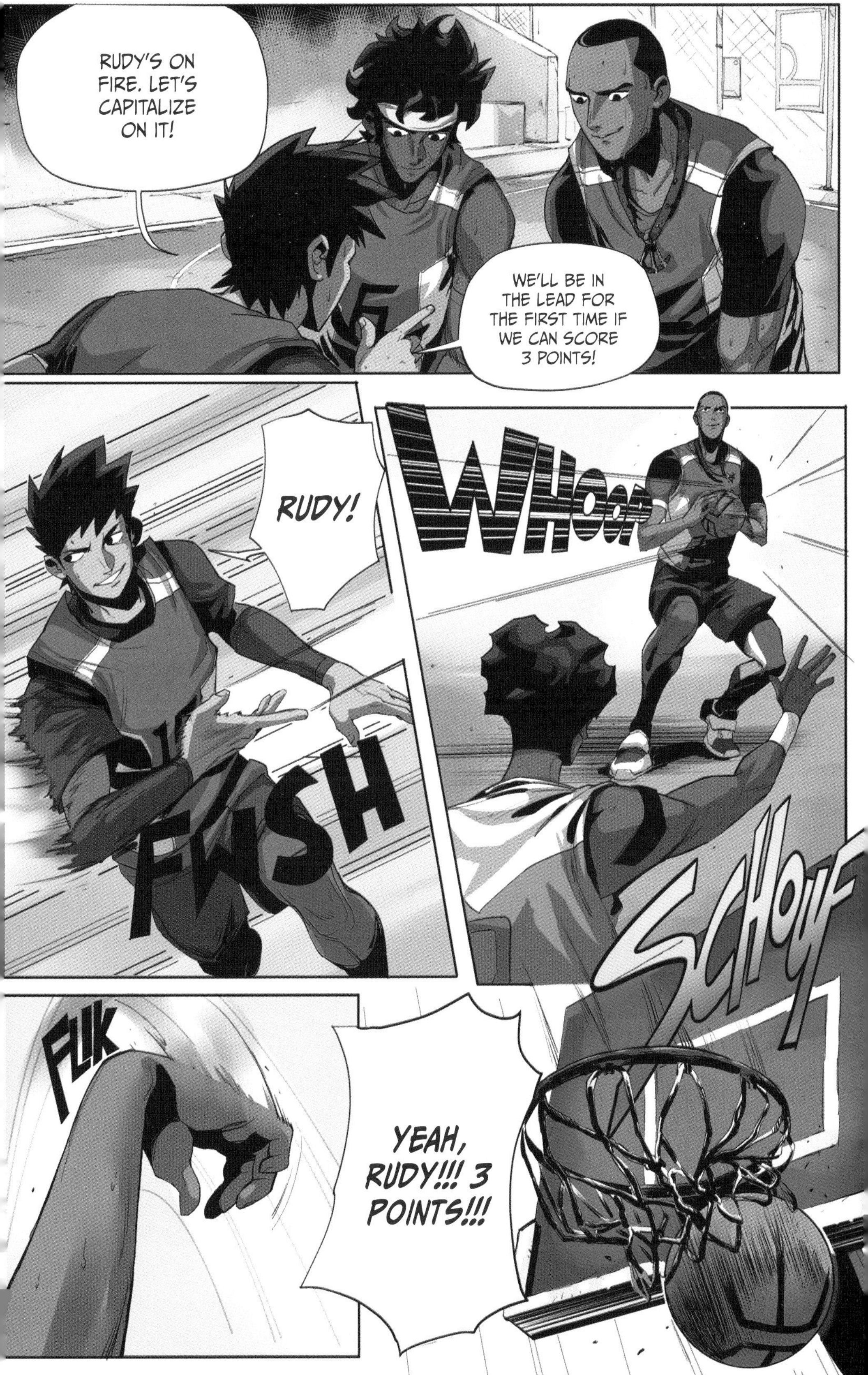
RUDY'S ON FIRE. LET'S CAPITALIZE ON IT!
WE'LL BE IN THE LEAD FOR THE FIRST TIME IF WE CAN SCORE 3 POINTS!
RUDY!
FWISH
WHOOP
SCHOUF
FLIK
YEAH, RUDY!!! 3 POINTS!!!

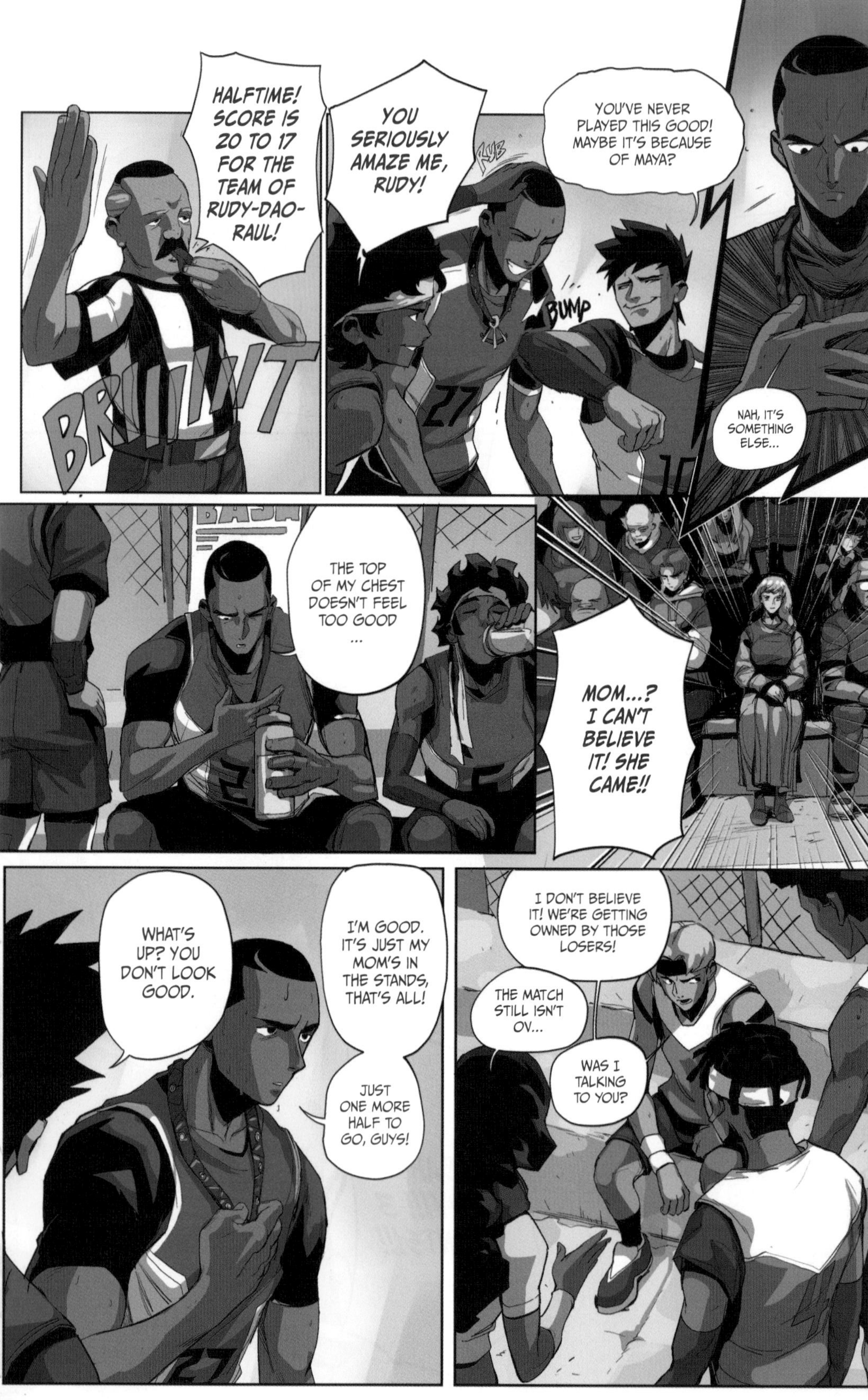
HALFTIME! SCORE IS 20 TO 17 FOR THE TEAM OF RUDY-DAO-RAUL!
BRIIIIIT
YOU SERIOUSLY AMAZE ME, RUDY!
RUB
YOU'VE NEVER PLAYED THIS GOOD! MAYBE IT'S BECAUSE OF MAYA?
BUMP
NAH, IT'S SOMETHING ELSE...
THE TOP OF MY CHEST DOESN'T FEEL TOO GOOD ...
MOM...? I CAN'T BELIEVE IT! SHE CAME!!
WHAT'S UP? YOU DON'T LOOK GOOD.
I'M GOOD. IT'S JUST MY MOM'S IN THE STANDS, THAT'S ALL!
JUST ONE MORE HALF TO GO, GUYS!
I DON'T BELIEVE IT! WE'RE GETTING OWNED BY THOSE LOSERS!
THE MATCH STILL ISN'T OV...
WAS I TALKING TO YOU?

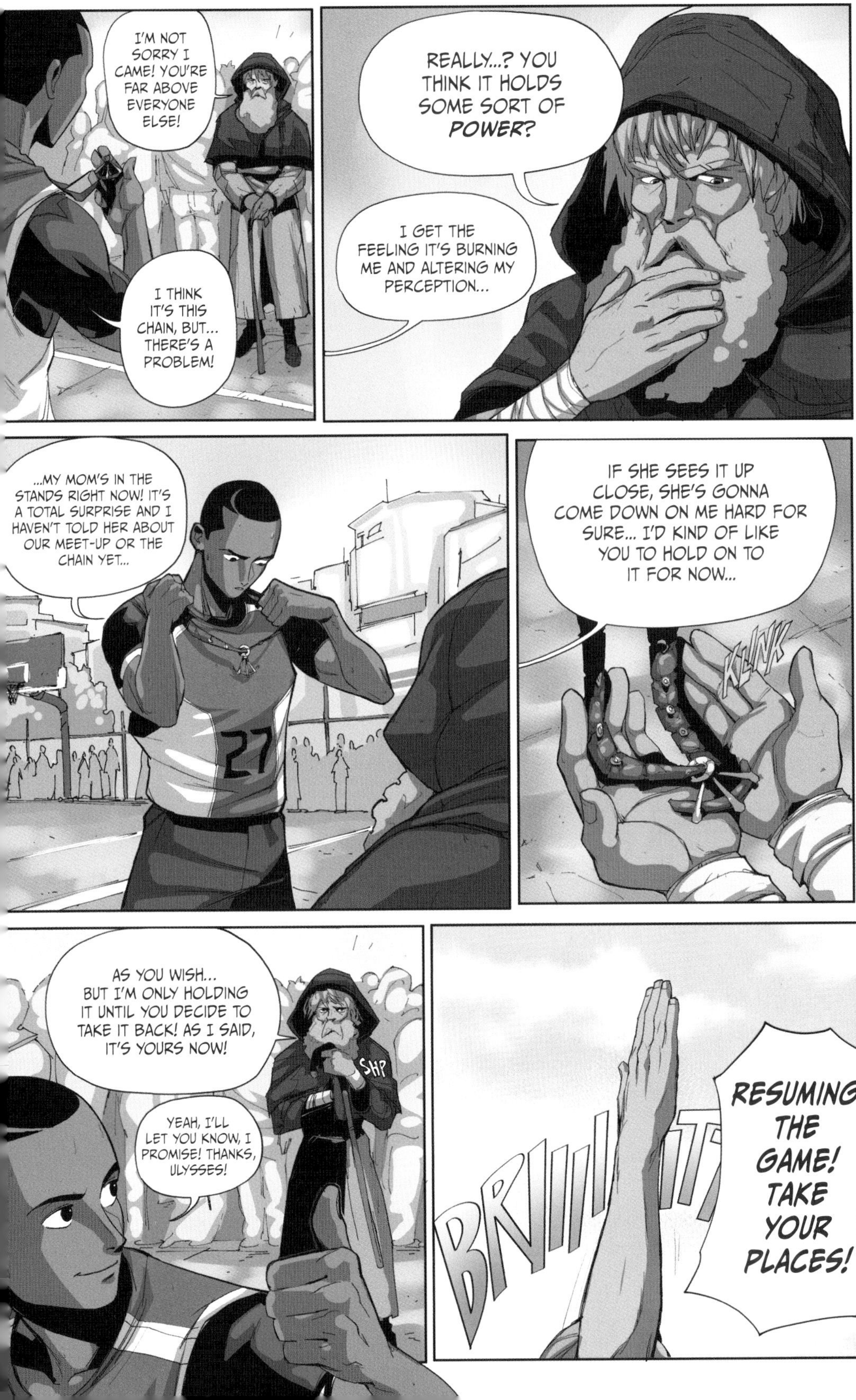

I'M NOT SORRY I CAME! YOU'RE FAR ABOVE EVERYONE ELSE!
I THINK IT'S THIS CHAIN, BUT... THERE'S A PROBLEM!
REALLY...? YOU THINK IT HOLDS SOME SORT OF POWER?
I GET THE FEELING IT'S BURNING ME AND ALTERING MY PERCEPTION...
...MY MOM'S IN THE STANDS RIGHT NOW! IT'S A TOTAL SURPRISE AND I HAVEN'T TOLD HER ABOUT OUR MEET-UP OR THE CHAIN YET...
27
IF SHE SEES IT UP CLOSE, SHE'S GONNA COME DOWN ON ME HARD FOR SURE... I'D KIND OF LIKE YOU TO HOLD ON TO IT FOR NOW...
KLINK
AS YOU WISH... BUT I'M ONLY HOLDING IT UNTIL YOU DECIDE TO TAKE IT BACK! AS I SAID, IT'S YOURS NOW!
SHP
YEAH, I'LL LET YOU KNOW, I PROMISE! THANKS, ULYSSES!
RESUMING THE GAME! TAKE YOUR PLACES!

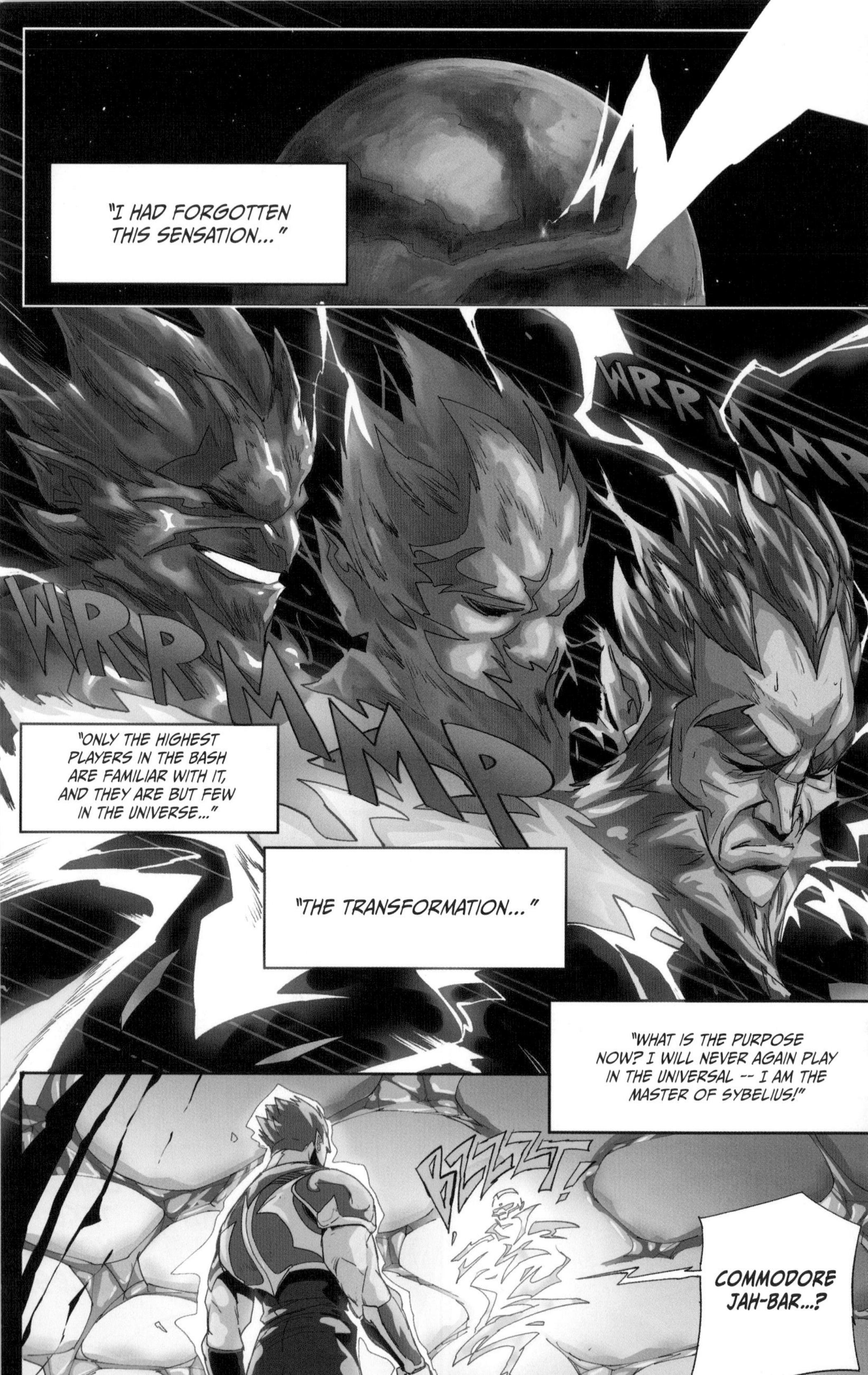
"I HAD FORGOTTEN THIS SENSATION..."
WRRMMP
WRRMMP
"ONLY THE HIGHEST PLAYERS IN THE BASH ARE FAMILIAR WITH IT, AND THEY ARE BUT FEW IN THE UNIVERSE..."
"THE TRANSFORMATION..."
"WHAT IS THE PURPOSE NOW? I WILL NEVER AGAIN PLAY IN THE UNIVERSAL -- I AM THE MASTER OF SYBELIUS!"
BZZZT!
COMMODORE JAH-BAR...?

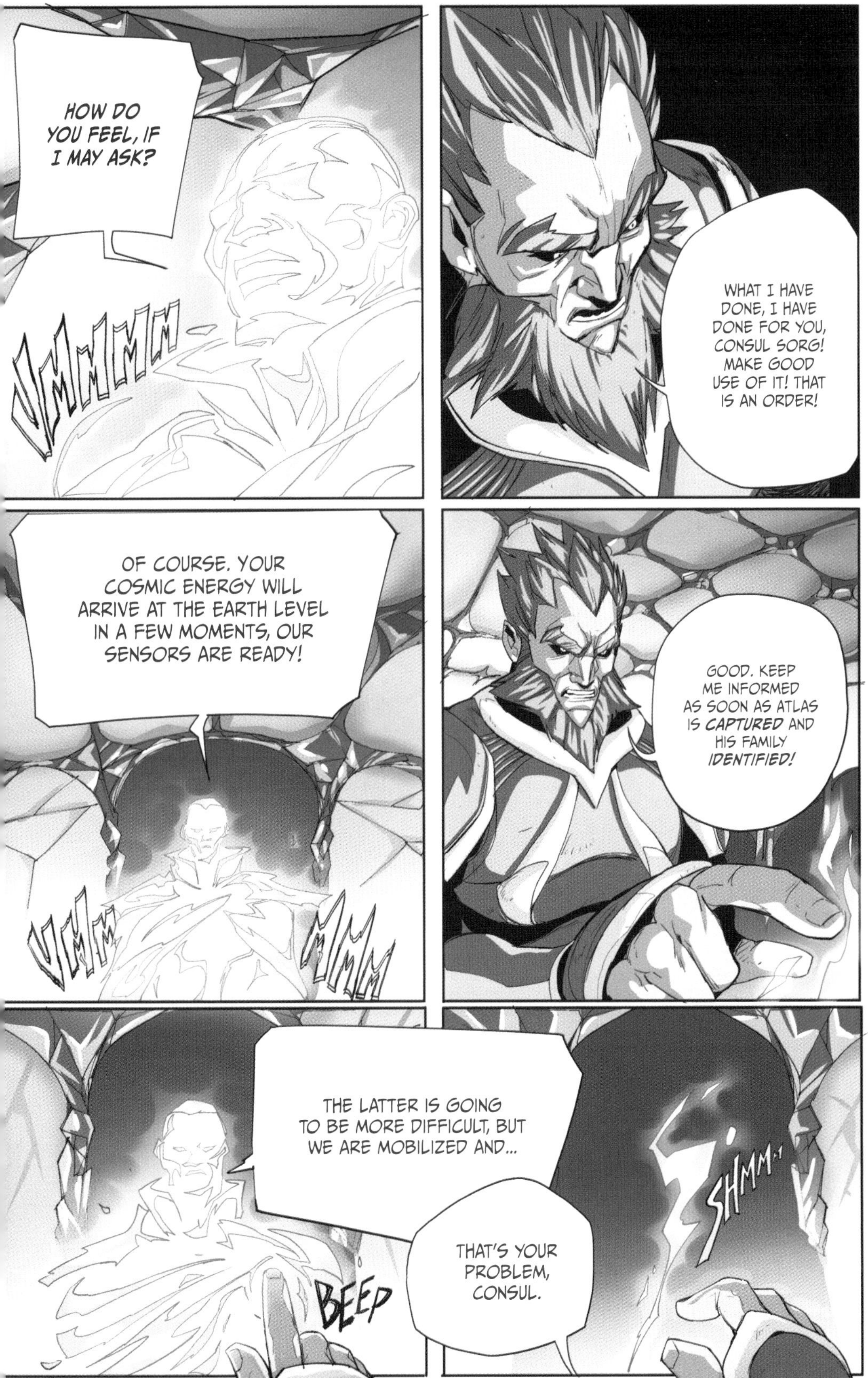
HOW DO YOU FEEL, IF I MAY ASK?
VMMMMM
WHAT I HAVE DONE, I HAVE DONE FOR YOU, CONSUL SORG! MAKE GOOD USE OF IT! THAT IS AN ORDER!
OF COURSE. YOUR COSMIC ENERGY WILL ARRIVE AT THE EARTH LEVEL IN A FEW MOMENTS, OUR SENSORS ARE READY!
VMMM
MMMM
GOOD. KEEP ME INFORMED AS SOON AS ATLAS IS *CAPTURED* AND HIS FAMILY *IDENTIFIED!*
THE LATTER IS GOING TO BE MORE DIFFICULT, BUT WE ARE MOBILIZED AND...
BEEP
SHMM
THAT'S YOUR PROBLEM, CONSUL.

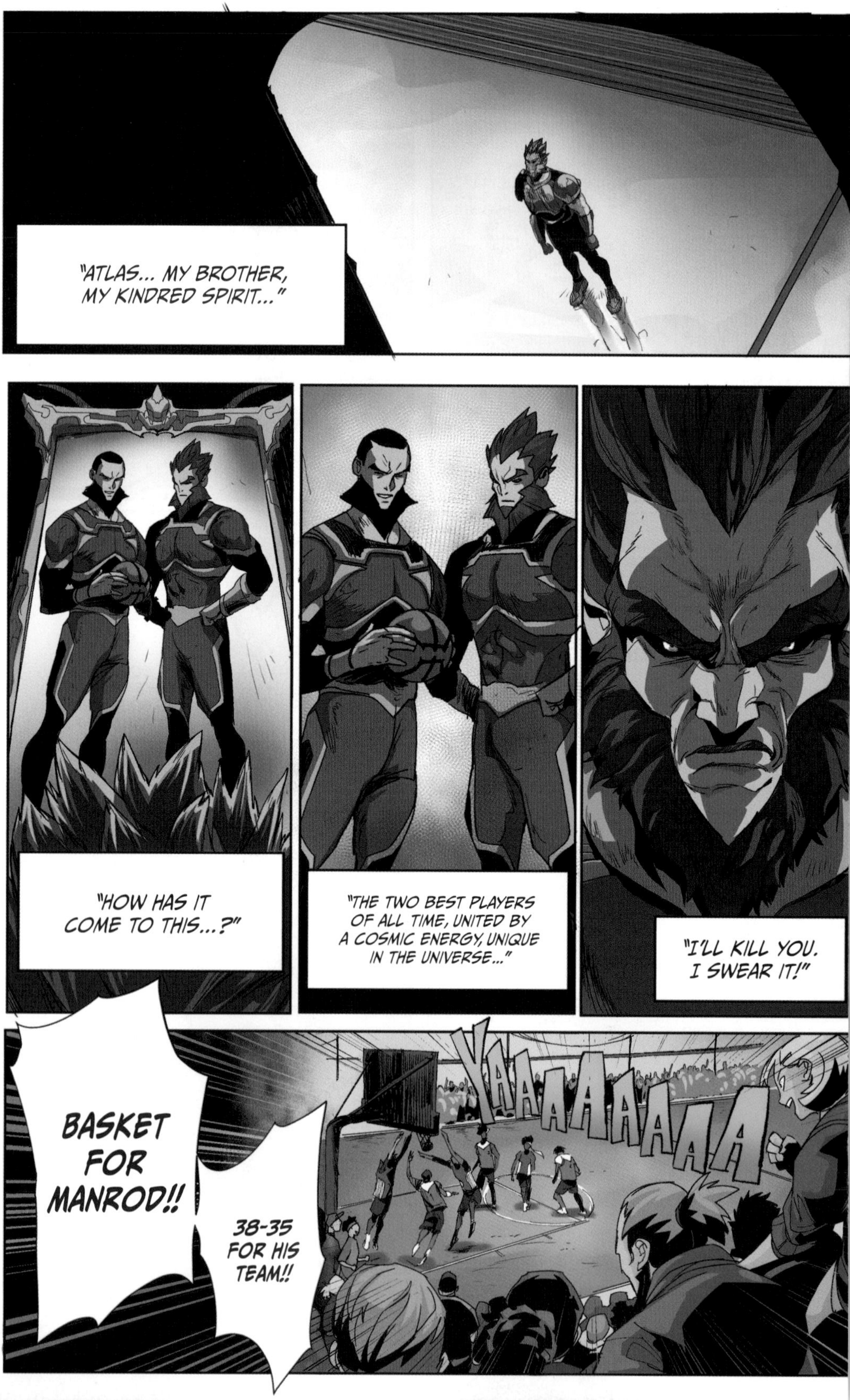
"ATLAS... MY BROTHER, MY KINDRED SPIRIT..."
"HOW HAS IT COME TO THIS...?"
"THE TWO BEST PLAYERS OF ALL TIME, UNITED BY A COSMIC ENERGY, UNIQUE IN THE UNIVERSE..."
"I'LL KILL YOU. I SWEAR IT!"
BASKET FOR MANROD!!
38-35 FOR HIS TEAM!!
YAAAAAAAAAA

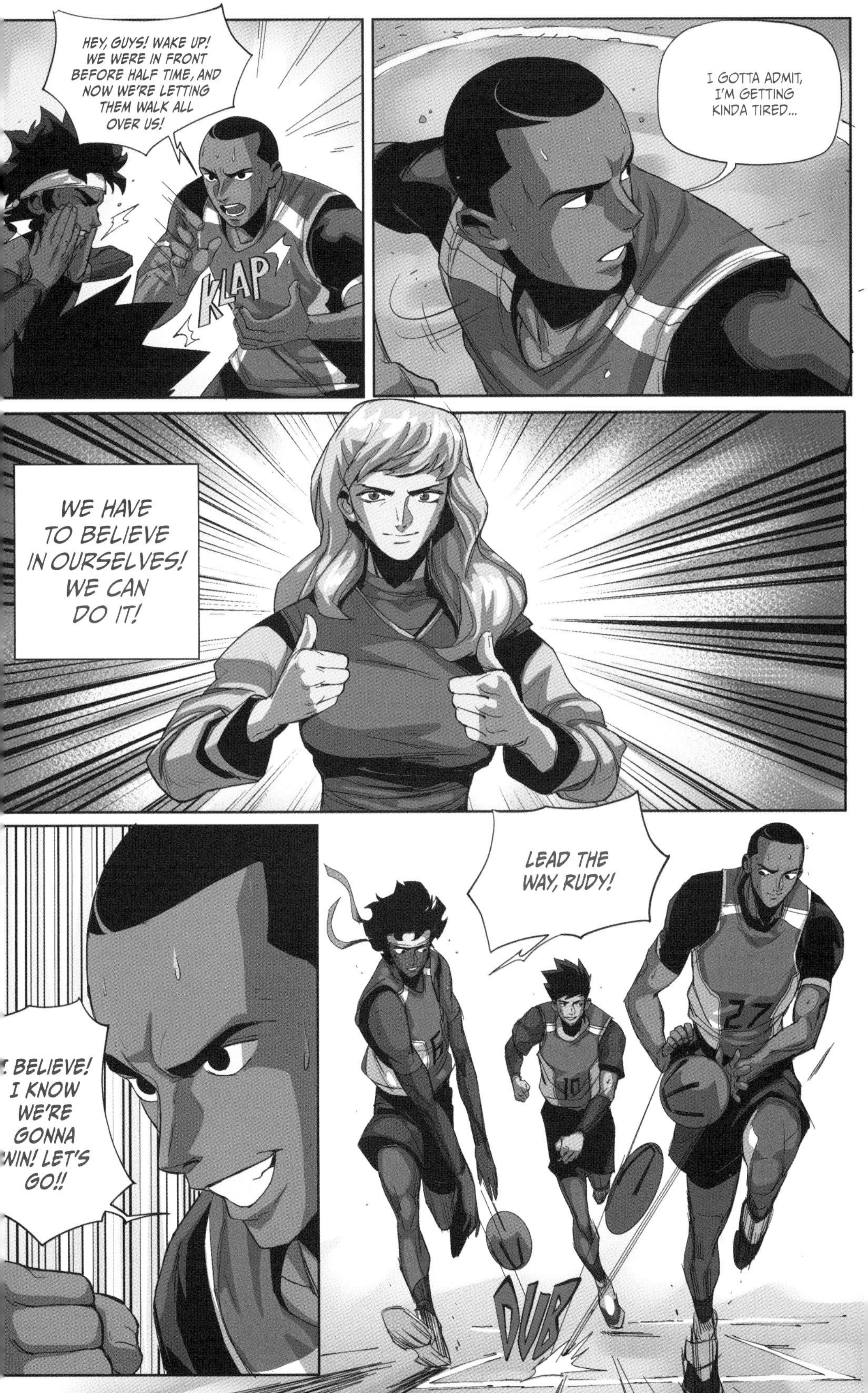
HEY, GUYS! WAKE UP! WE WERE IN FRONT BEFORE HALF TIME, AND NOW WE'RE LETTING THEM WALK ALL OVER US!
KLAP
I GOTTA ADMIT, I'M GETTING KINDA TIRED...
WE HAVE TO BELIEVE IN OURSELVES! WE CAN DO IT!
BELIEVE! I KNOW WE'RE GONNA WIN! LET'S GO!!
LEAD THE WAY, RUDY!
DUB

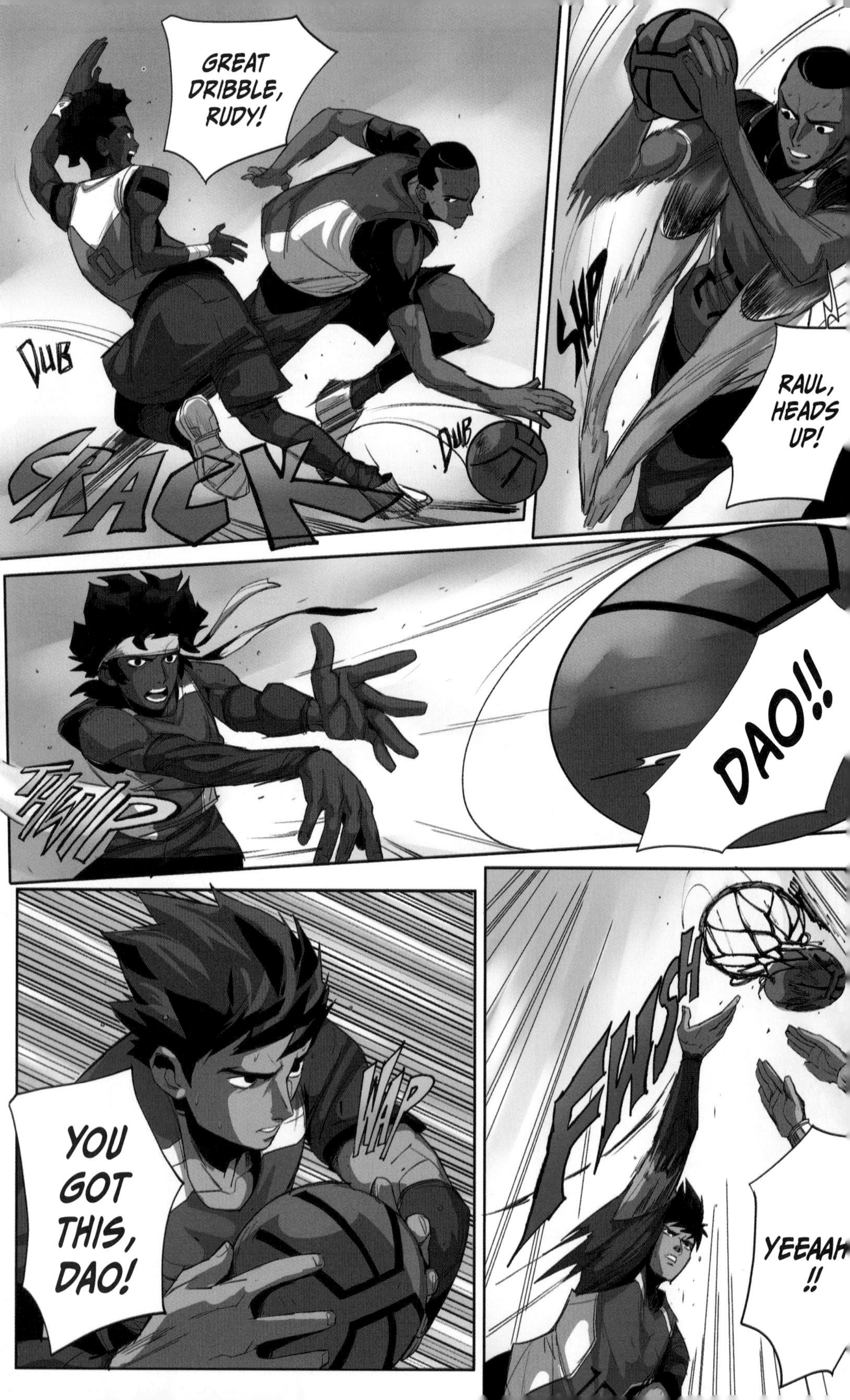
GREAT DRIBBLE, RUDY!
DUB
DUB
CRACK
SHP
RAUL, HEADS UP!
THWIP
DAO!!
YOU GOT THIS, DAO!
WAP
FWISH
YEEAAH !!

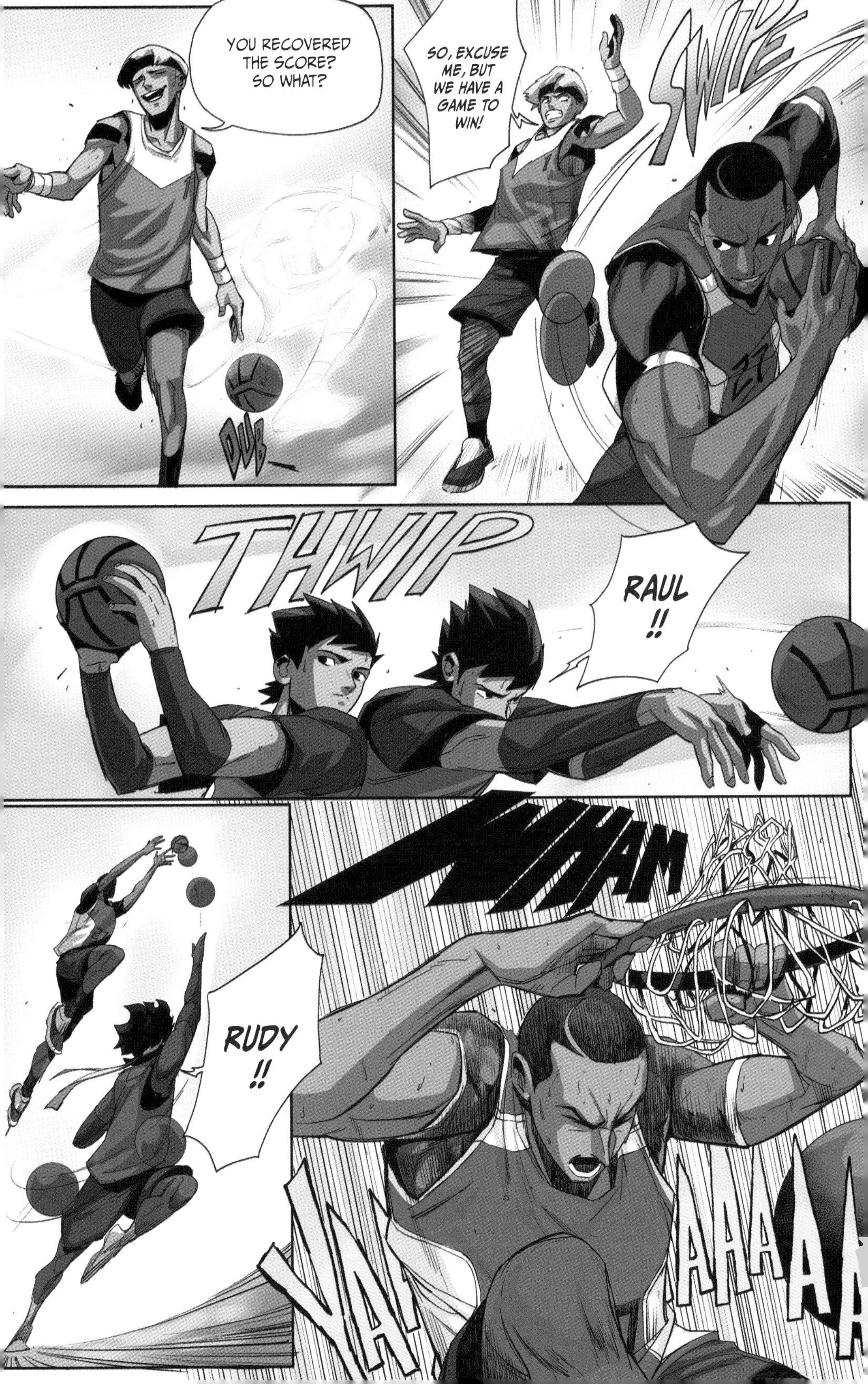
YOU RECOVERED THE SCORE? SO WHAT?
DUB
SO, EXCUSE ME, BUT WE HAVE A GAME TO WIN!
SWIPE
THWIP
RAUL !!
WHAM
RUDY !!
YAAAAAA

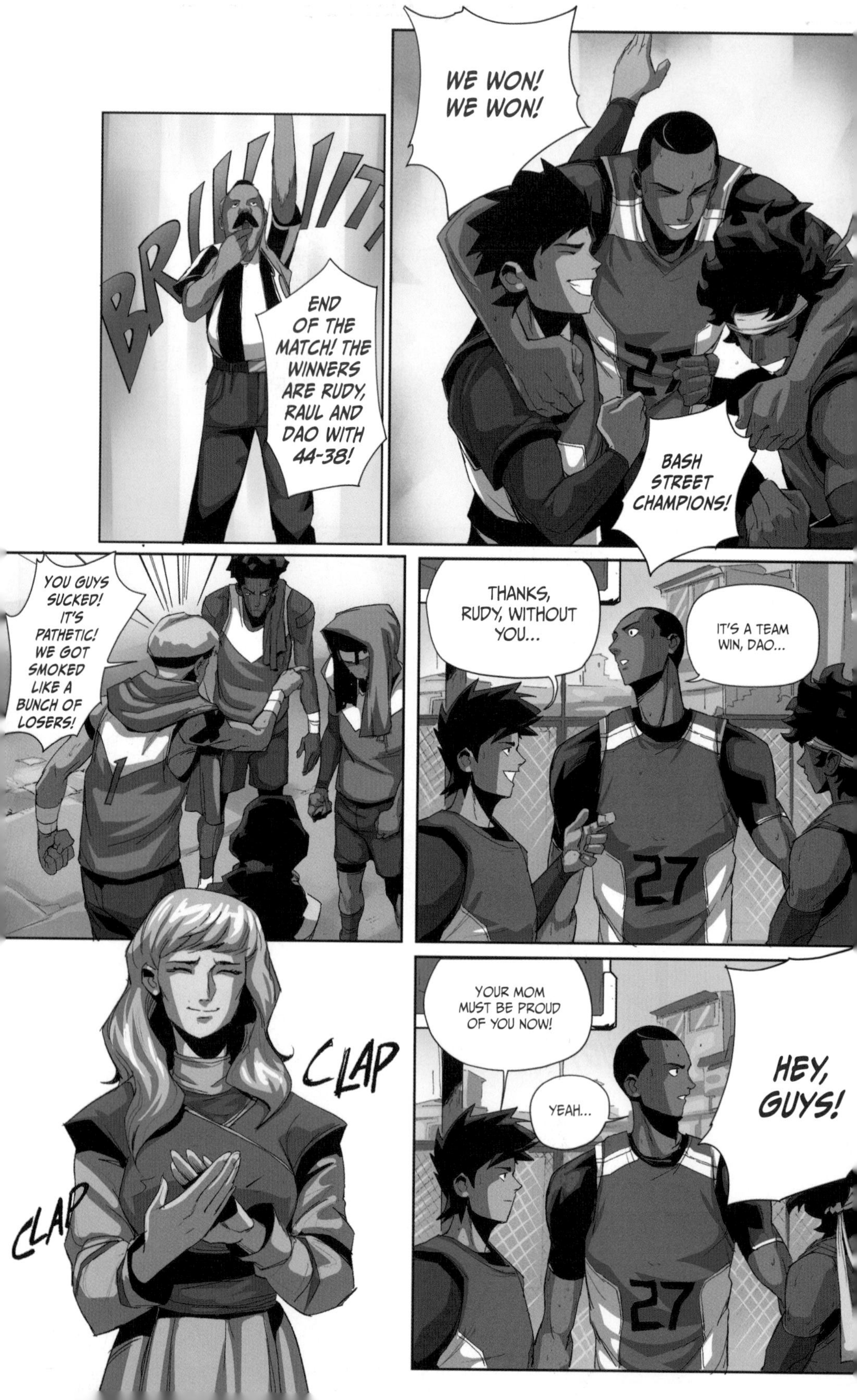
BRIIIIIT
END OF THE MATCH! THE WINNERS ARE RUDY, RAUL AND DAO WITH 44-38!
WE WON! WE WON!
BASH STREET CHAMPIONS!
YOU GUYS SUCKED! IT'S PATHETIC! WE GOT SMOKED LIKE A BUNCH OF LOSERS!
THANKS, RUDY, WITHOUT YOU...
IT'S A TEAM WIN, DAO...
CLAP
CLAP
YOUR MOM MUST BE PROUD OF YOU NOW!
YEAH...
HEY, GUYS!

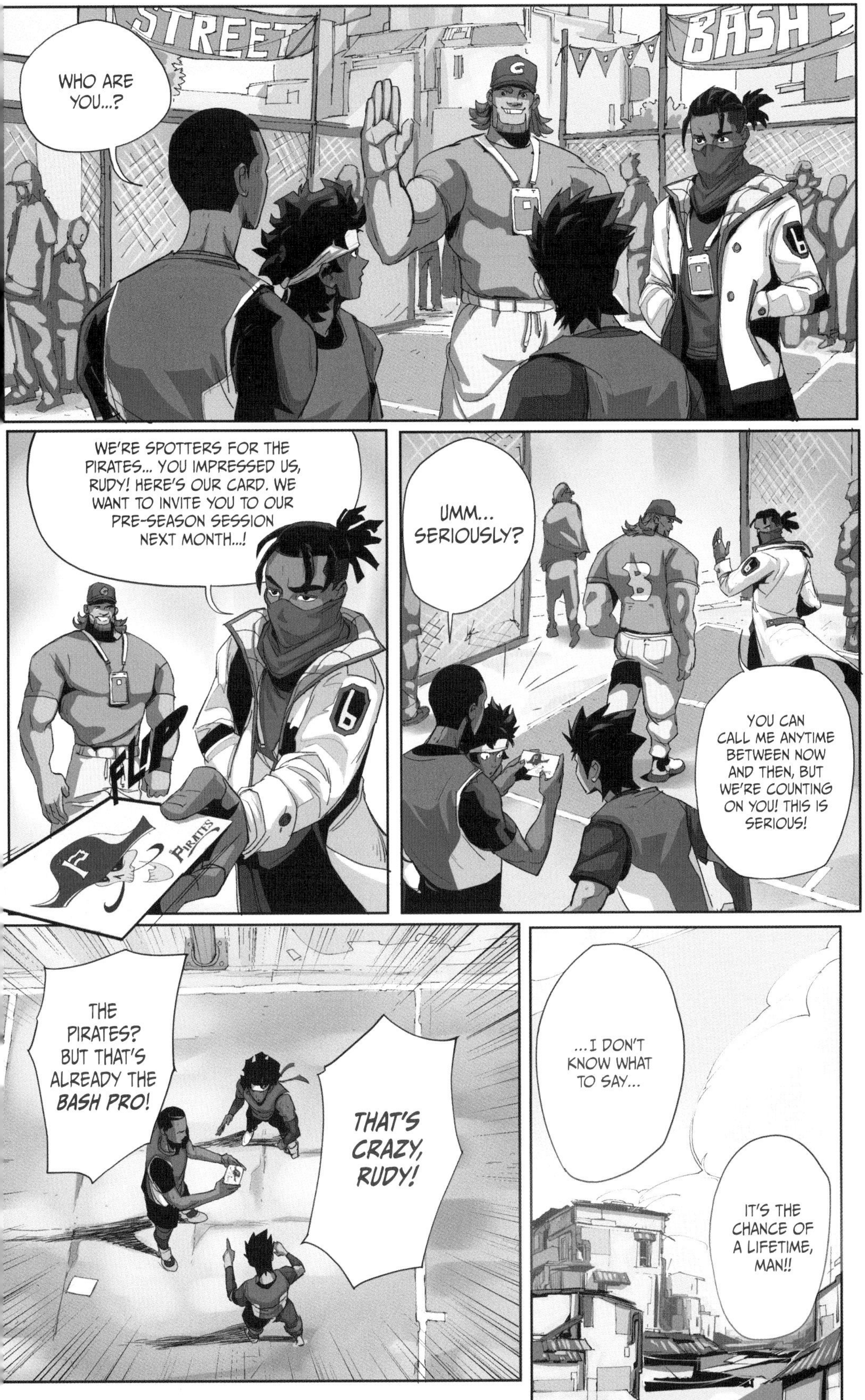
STREET
BASH
WHO ARE YOU...?
WE'RE SPOTTERS FOR THE PIRATES... YOU IMPRESSED US, RUDY! HERE'S OUR CARD. WE WANT TO INVITE YOU TO OUR PRE-SEASON SESSION NEXT MONTH...!
FLIP
PIRATES
UMM... SERIOUSLY?
YOU CAN CALL ME ANYTIME BETWEEN NOW AND THEN, BUT WE'RE COUNTING ON YOU! THIS IS SERIOUS!
THE PIRATES? BUT THAT'S ALREADY THE *BASH PRO*!
THAT'S CRAZY, RUDY!
...I DON'T KNOW WHAT TO SAY...
IT'S THE CHANCE OF A LIFETIME, MAN!!

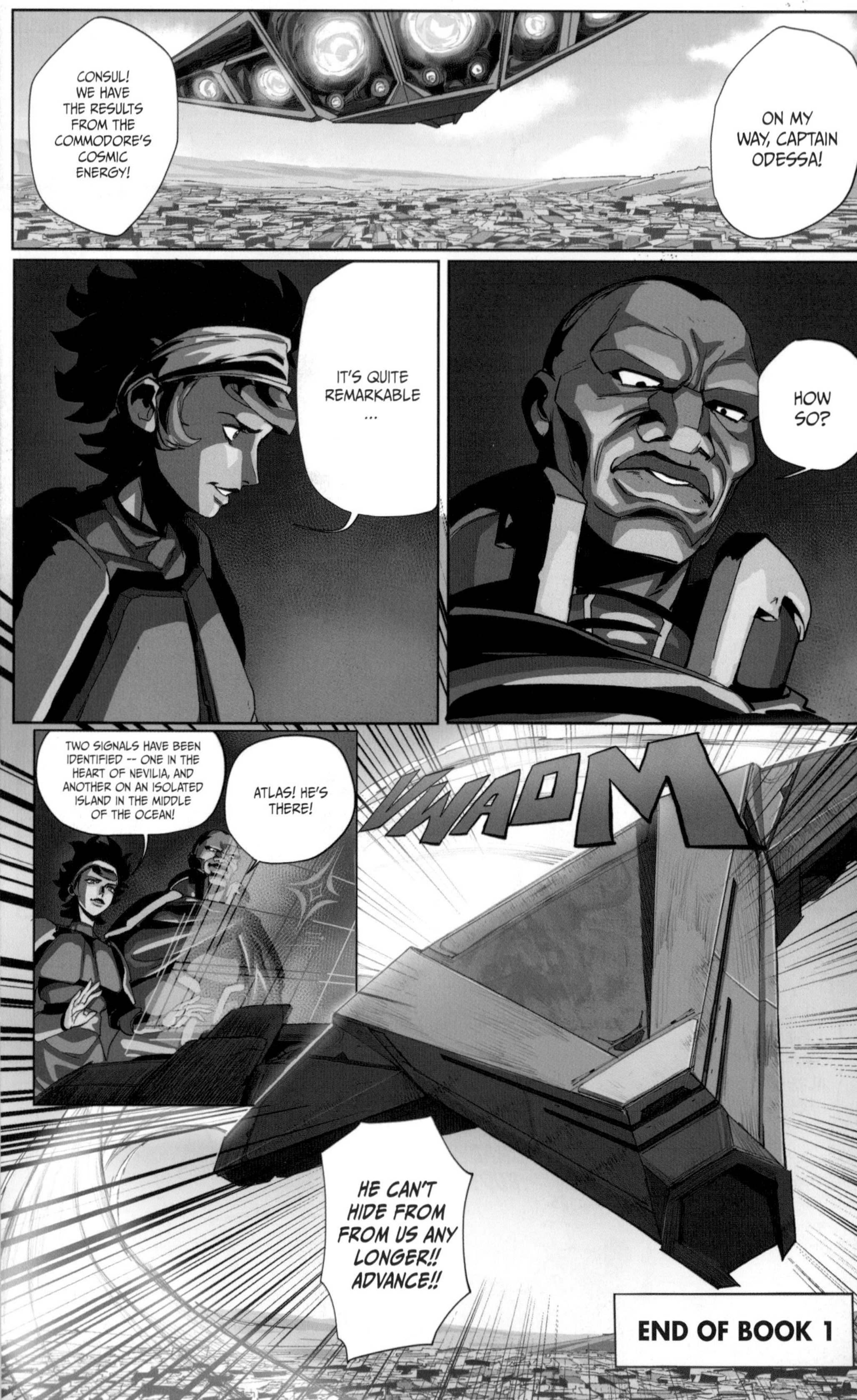
CONSUL! WE HAVE THE RESULTS FROM THE COMMODORE'S COSMIC ENERGY!
ON MY WAY, CAPTAIN ODESSA!
IT'S QUITE REMARKABLE ...
HOW SO?
TWO SIGNALS HAVE BEEN IDENTIFIED -- ONE IN THE HEART OF NEVILIA, AND ANOTHER ON AN ISOLATED ISLAND IN THE MIDDLE OF THE OCEAN!
ATLAS! HE'S THERE!
VWAOM
HE CAN'T HIDE FROM FROM US ANY LONGER!! ADVANCE!!
END OF BOOK 1

PAGE 13

PAGE 38

30
30

BASH!

BONUS

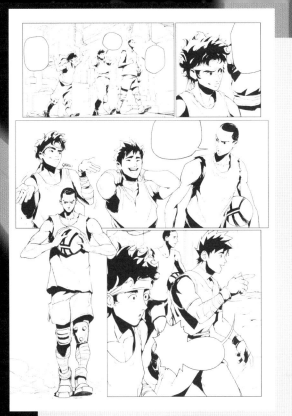

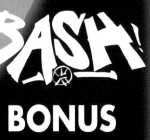

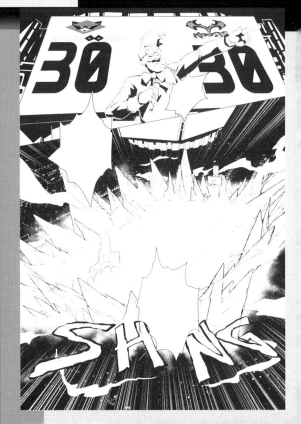

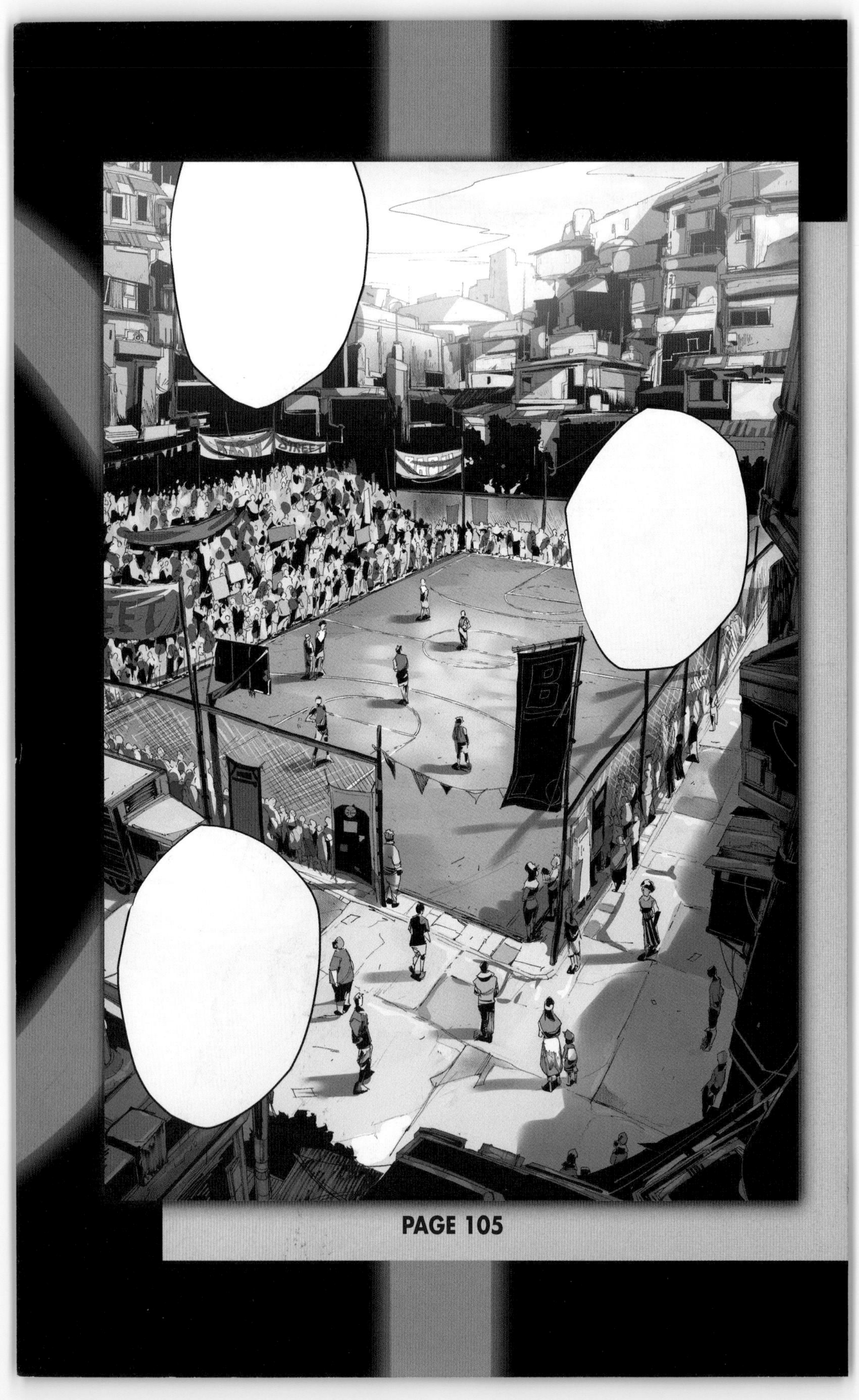
STREET
B

PAGE 105

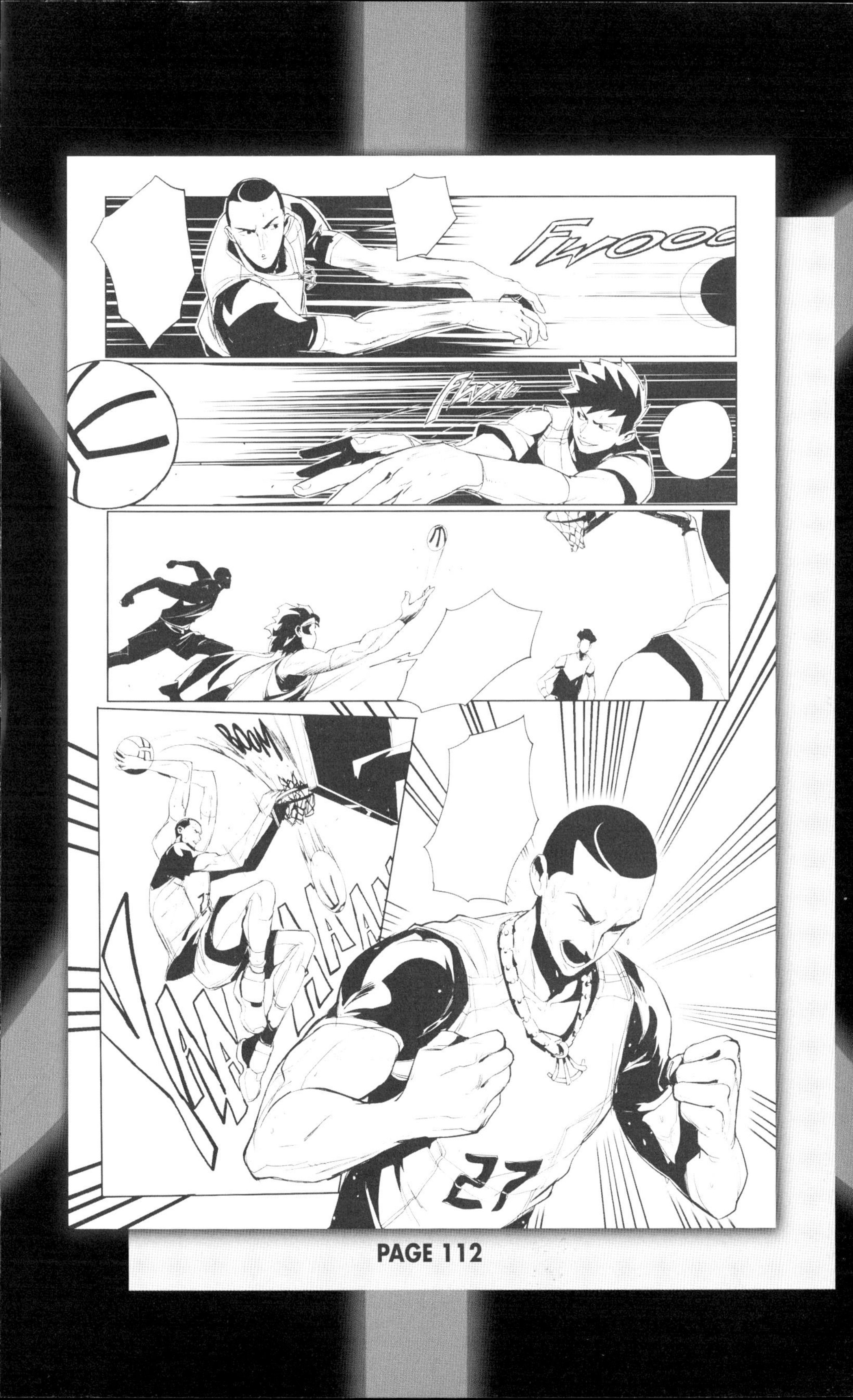
FWOO
FWAH
BOOM

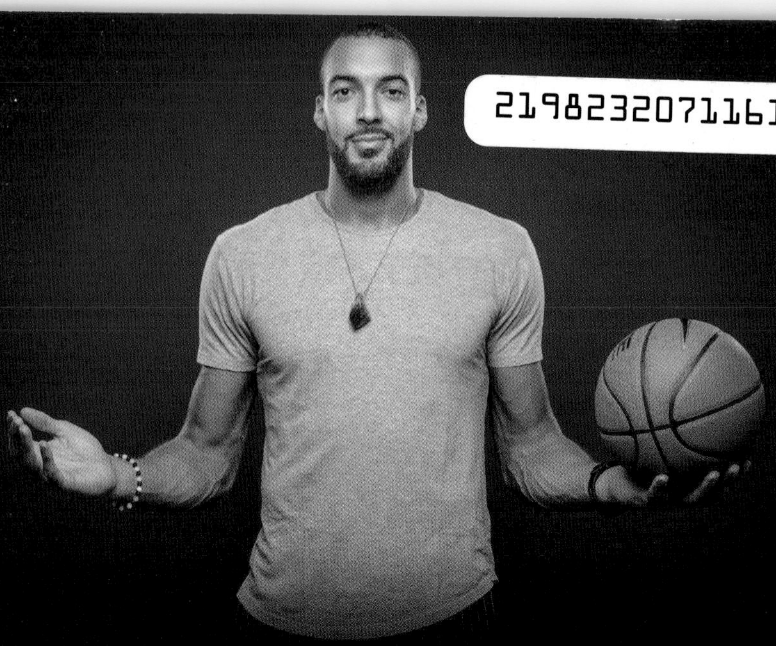

RUDY GOBERT

A Saint-Quentin native who trained at the Cholet basketball club, Rudy Gobert has established himself as one of the major players of the Utah Jazz, where he has played since his arrival in the NBA in 2013. At the end of the 2017-2018 season, he was voted best defensive player of the year. A feat that he since repeated twice in addition to being called on to play among the All-Stars, as well being a cornerstone of the French team. He participated in the 2014 and 2019 World Cups as well as the 2015 European Championship where France obtained third place in all three competitions. He won the silver medal at the Tokyo Olympic Games in 2021.

Bash is the first comic book he has co-written, with a desire to promote the values of courage and selflessness that are so important to him.

VINCE SERRANO

Filipino artist Vince Serrano is passionate about basketball. He has collaborated on promotional campaigns for Adidas and the Sacramento Kings, and created the album artwork for rapper Young Nudy's Rich Shooter before turning to the world of video games. Bash is his first comic.

HELLEF BAY

Lover of both sport and comics, Hellef Bay is a seasoned comics writer and former sports journalist. He co-wrote Bash, which has finally allowed him to join his two passions.